"Is everything to your satisfaction?"

"Wh-what?" Deidra stammered, distracted at last from her incredulous staring.

Casually, Hawkwind gestured to himself. "Do you like what you see?"

"A-aye," she said, struggling to regain her composure. She shot him a heated look. "You appear . . . adequate . . . for the task."

"Adequate?" Hawkwind threw back his head and gave a shout of laughter. "I'm more than adequate, I can assure you, lass." He grabbed for her and pulled her down atop his hard-muscled body. He grinned as she stiffened at the intimate contact with him. "What say you now? Am I just 'adequate'?"

"You seem quite magnificent at closer inspection," Deidra admitted with mock gravity. "But what exactly can it *do*?"

He grasped her about her waist and rolled her over onto the bed. Bearing most of his weight on his arms, Hawkwind smiled down at her. "What can it do, you ask? Most anything you ask of it. But first," he muttered, his voice going hoarse, "you need a bit more gentling . . ."

"Kathleen Morgan shows true genius in this enchanting adult fairy tale that dazzles the audience with its air of fantasy romance _ _ _ llhinding magic." —*The Talisman*

Fire Queen

Kathleen Morgan

SMP

ST. MARTIN'S PAPERBACKS

FIRE QUEEN

Copyright © 1994 by Kathleen Morgan.

All rights reserved. No part of this book may be used or reproduced in any manner whatsoever without written permission except in the case of brief quotations embodied in critical articles or reviews. For information address St. Martin's Press, 175 Fifth Avenue, New York, N.Y. 10010.

ISBN: 0-312-95268-6

Printed in the United States of America

St. Martin's Paperbacks edition/May 1994

10 9 8 7 6 5 4 3 2 1

To my agent-extraordinaire, Natasha Kern. You're a joy to work with—not only as mentor and advocate, but as a friend.

Prologue

I don't like it. We shouldn't be out without yer guard, m'lord."

At the tersely muttered statement Lord Nicholas, newest liege of Todmorden Castle upon the recent and untimely death of his father, swung around in his saddle. He arched a dark brow at his elderly falconer.

"Truly, Hugo, but you worry overmuch." Nicholas chuckled and gestured to the gray turrets topped with hawk emblazoned flags rising from an imposing fortress. "We are still within sight of the castle. And with the king and his son in residence, who would dare raise a hand against me?"

"Treachery can come from within as easily as from without," the old man prophesied darkly. "Yer two younger brothers were far from happy over yer rightful passage to Todmorden lands and rule. Ye saw as well as I their grudging fealty paid ye last eve. 'Tis but a warning o' things to come."

Nicholas shrugged. "And am I not man enough to deal with my brothers? I may have come to my inheritance early, but I'm not without some ability." He lifted his leather gauntleted left hand and arm, where sat a splendid gyrfalcon. "Now, what say you, Hugo? Is Chanson ready for her first free flight?"

Hugo reined in his horse and glanced over at his master. He eyed him solemnly for a long moment. Then, realizing the subject had been pointedly changed, his raggedly cropped gray hair bobbed with the enthusiastic movement of his head. "Aye, m'lord. Yer lady falcon is ready. Just yesterday I tried Chanson again on the creance. She sprang eagerly from the fist to the lure without a moment's hesitation or notice o' her leash, and returned immediately when called."

Nicholas nodded his approval. "You've done well by her. I vow I could hardly wait for dawn, after what you told me of Chanson's rapid progress these past few days."

"And I'd have thought ye would have preferred to stay abed, after last eve's revelry." Black eyes gleamed in an attempt at humor, caught in the vise of wrinkled skin and high cheekbones that met in a halfhearted grin. "Like the king and his son who, if ye'll fergive my saying so, imbibed a significant share o' the wine served and are most likely paying for it this morn."

"The king and Prince William are most welcome to both the wine and today's headaches." Nicholas smiled, a conspiratorial glint in his jade green eyes. "'Twas my plan all along to slip out this morn and try Chanson with only you as companion. 'Tis the only free moment I'll have to myself, I'd wager, until the royal party decides 'tis time to return to Court."

Hugo gave a snort of grudging agreement. "Shall we dismount and tether the horses then? Yer falcon has yet to learn to hunt from horseback."

Nicholas swung down from the gentle gelding he'd chosen to ride this morning. His falconer's unquestioning and wholehearted devotion filled him with gratitude. In such unsettled times, when lords vied for land as the prime source of wealth and even rulers such as the king had difficulty reining in his powerful vassals, Nicholas had sought to seal his inheritance as quickly as possible. Too many coveted Todmorden, for its rich lands as well as strategically placed fortress. Too many, he thought grimly, even when one temporarily set aside the nagging issue of his brothers.

But those issues—and many others now weighing heavily on him at two and twenty—could be dealt with later. As he dropped his horse's reins to the ground beside Hugo's, Nicholas glanced about him. 'Twas a beautiful winter's day, the sun bright in a calm, cloudless sky, the fresh snow sparkling like newly cut diamonds, and he meant to fly his priceless and painstakingly trained gyrfalcon for the first time.

They walked a distance away so as not to distract the bird with the horses. Open countryside, shrouded in white, spread before them. Skeletal trees, stark, black contrasts to the untouched purity, scattered across the land in small, disorganized clumps. As the two men trudged on through snow rising almost to their knee-high boot tops, then crested a hill and dropped down the other side, the castle towers disappeared gradually from view behind them.

Finally, Hugo halted. Nicholas lifted his left fist and, with teeth and right hand, opened the leather braces securing the falcon's hood. Deftly, he removed it and tossed the covering to Hugo before freeing the creance line attached to the bird's leg jesses. Then Nicholas turned his attention back to Chanson.

Large dark eyes, full of a piercing intelligence, glinted up at him, following his every movement. Smooth black feathers, tipped with white, gleamed with health. The gyrfalcon shifted restlessly, her tapering wings lifting, then settling snugly once more against a superbly fit body.

Fierce pride swelled in Nicholas. Chanson was truly a royal prize, the largest and most graceful of all falcons, the hunting bird of kings. A prize he would never have been privileged to possess if not for the favor granted him by the king after his rescue of the crown prince from a boar's attack. 'Twas that act that had not only gained him the gift of a gyrfalcon but also sealed his uneventful ascendancy to Todmorden.

"She is ready, m'lord," Hugo said, intruding on his thoughts. "Methinks she senses something's different about today."

"Aye, that she does," Nicholas agreed. Once more he was back in the present with his beloved falcon, where he fervently wished he could always be. "I can sense her excitement as if 'twere my own."

And he could. From the first time his father had permitted him to enter the mews, Nicholas had felt a strange affinity for the birds of prey housed there. The time not required for his studies or in the acquisition of the more physical skills of a knight, he spent with Hugo, learning all there was to know about falconry. If he'd been other than of noble birth, Nicholas would have been content to live out his life as a simple falconer.

Hugo walked a short distance away and swung the lure in a circular fashion, then dropped it to the ground. With a great leap forward and burst of rapid wing beats, Chanson sprang from Nicholas's fist and into the air. Briefly, she circled low overhead and then flew down to the lure. Just as the gyrfalcon was about to land, Hugo pulled the lure up and away.

Chanson banked left, then around, heading back toward Nicholas. Again Hugo tossed out the lure, this time allowing the falcon to take it on the ground. Nicholas strode over, raised his fist toward the bird, and whistled. She flew up to him.

As he fed her a bit of raw meat for reward, he grinned over at Hugo. "Well-done, wouldn't you say? She truly is the queen of all birds." He cocked his head at his falconer. "Shall we try her one more time at the lure?"

Hugo eyed the gyrfalcon. "Nay. 'Twas her first lesson and one well learned. The morrow is soon enough to push her along." He looked around. "Besides, we've wandered farther afield than I intended. Even the sentries walking the castle parapets cannot see us from here. 'Twould be wise to get back to the horses and—"

An arrow, seemingly from out of nowhere, plunged into the old man's chest. With a startled cry, Hugo staggered backward, then fell. Nicholas wheeled around. There, on a distant hillock separating him from sight of the castle, was a party of ten armed and mounted men. They had come upon them silently, their approach muffled by the thick layer of snow.

Nicholas backed up until he stood beside the fallen falconer. Never taking his eyes from the band of men, he squatted and touched the old man. "Hugo, can you move? The horses are only a short distance away. If we can get to them—"

A gurgle and harsh exhalation of air answered him. Nicholas glanced down. The old man's eyes rolled back in his head and his mouth fell open in slack lifelessness.

"Bloody hell!"

He rose and withdrew the short sword he'd brought along only at the falconer's insistence, silently blessing his old servant for that bit of foresight. The band of men urged their mounts forward. Nicholas turned and raced toward his own horse, Chanson still perched on his hand.

The snow was deep in spots, blanketing dips and rises in the uneven ground. Nicholas stumbled once, sinking to his knees. The gyrfalcon lurched forward on his fist, flapped her wings, then regained her balance.

He staggered up and ran on, even as he heard the clink of metal and squeak of leather, the snorts of excited horses, drawing ever near. Yet, among all the other sounds, his attackers never uttered a word. Swift and silent, they seemingly had only one intent. His death.

Somehow, Nicholas managed to reach his horse before he was overtaken. He paused but a moment to glance at Chanson. There was no chance to fight with the bird in hand. With a shout, he flung the falcon into the air and swung up onto his horse. Chanson gave a harsh cry, circled overhead to await the call of her master's gloved fist, but Nicholas dared not spare her another instant's concern.

The men were upon him, swords raised, surrounding him in a dense mass of dark bodies and heaving mounts. "Yield!" the leader of the band cried. "Yield and we'll make your death swift and merciful!"

Nicholas recognized him. It was John Betson, second in command to the captain of Todmorden's guard. An ambitious, unscrupulous, greedy man easily bribed to any task, good or bad.

Wheeling his horse around, Nicholas faced him boldly, cursing his carelessness in not bringing guards of his own, in not riding his big war-horse. Cursing his trust that no one seriously wished him harm. "Who?" he demanded, his voice raw, harsh, dreading the answer. "Who has sent you on such a foul and treacherous mission?"

John laughed, the sound a mocking travesty of any warmer emotions. "Why, m'lord, who else but the crown prince and your own two brothers? Surely you didn't imagine they'd permit you to rule for long? 'Twas a simple enough task for Prince William to woo them to his cause."

"The king," Nicholas rasped, eyeing the movement of men closing in for the kill. "He'll know. He'll guess."

"The king?" White teeth glittered in a feral smile. "He is already dead, murdered by men 'twill be said you most foully set upon him. Only the crown prince survived. Thanks to a cleverly laid plan between William and your brothers, the land will soon have a new king, and Todmorden a new lord."

A pitying light flared in his dead black eyes. "We thought you had escaped us, when I found your bedchamber empty. Fortunately the chamberlain confessed, just before we slit his throat, that he'd seen you leave the castle earlier with Hugo and your falcon. Unfortunately, however, you resisted our efforts to bring you back for trial and were accidentally killed in the ensuing battle."

With that, Betson signaled his men. Nicholas was set

upon on all sides. He fought them with a ferocious desperation, the long hours spent in warrior's training serving him well. There was no time to mourn the king, a good and kind man, or rail against the cruel fate that had joined his brothers with an evil princeling. There was no time for anything save the battle for survival.

Slashing and parrying, Nicholas cut down three attackers before a vicious thrust from behind took him unawares. The sword plunged deep into his shoulder, skewering him into near immobility even as he attempted to defend his front from further blows. The pain lanced through him, excruciating, breath-grabbing, setting a heavy, gray mist to swirl before his eyes. He forced it aside with a superhuman effort, but that momentary lapse was all the advantage his opponents needed.

A sword tip sliced open the right side of Nicholas's face. Another, barely deflected from its fatal course, cut through his heavy woolen cloak and tunic to lay open a transverse expanse of flesh across his chest. Then a mace smashed into his sword arm, bouncing down to shred muscle and sinew before embedding in the long, strong expanse of his clenched fingers.

Nicholas's face contorted in agony. A spasm wrenched his hand open. The sword tumbled from his grip, disappearing between the surging mass of bodies.

He grabbed for the dagger sheathed at his side, the grip of his powerful thighs the only thing keeping him on his horse as the blows fell in relentless, merciless strokes. He pulled his dagger free, lifted it to defend himself, when another mace slammed into the back of his head.

Nicholas swayed, stunned, unbalanced by the power of the blow. Blackness rushed in to engulf him. He felt himself grow light, the agony of repeated sword thrusts subside. Felt himself falling.

Falling, to strike soft, yielding snow. Snow that stained a deep crimson with each beat of his pounding heart.

Anger, and an impotent frustration, flooded him. Then, nothing mattered. Overhead, just before all consciousness faded, Nicholas heard Chanson, her low, harsh cry a bittersweet song that pierced the pristine winter's day.

Chapter 1

Eight Years Later

He attacked her with all the ferocity of a man held in the throes of a battle crazed bloodlust. To and fro he swung his sword, hacking at her in relentless blows that drove her back, step by agonizing step. The force of blade meeting blade sent jarring vibrations up her arms, until she barely felt the fingers she could only *will* to grip about her sword hilt.

She'd never be equal in strength, Deidra thought in rising frustration, though she practiced for the rest of her days. She could never outmuscle him, as old and crippled as he was. Bardrick was too crafty, too battle hardened, too big. Lean though he was, his body bulged with power. He was tall, solid. Solid as an oak.

But even an oak could be felled if one possessed sufficient skill. And her skill would always lie in her agility, in the swiftness a small, quick body possessed in far greater measure than strength. She backed away even farther, faster, luring the aged warrior to hasten his steps, to hurry into movements his greater bulk had difficulty controlling. She parried, feinted, and waited.

At last the opportunity came. Bardrick lunged forward for the killing blow, momentarily leaving his torso unprotected. Deidra sidestepped, ducked under his outthrust arm, and drove her blade home—a hairsbreadth from her opponent's heart.

Bardrick froze. Ever so slowly, his gaze dropped to the wooden sword pressed to his chest. His own weapon lowered. He touched his blade to his forehead in a congratulatory salute.

"Well done, lass. Ye're an apt student, and no mistake. For all yer feminine form and ways, there's only one other who has yer decided knack with the fancy footwork. Of course," he added with a wry grin, "he also possesses the tremendous strength and stamina required of a true warrior. Strength and stamina that, quite honestly, ye'll always lack."

"So you'd not recommend me seeking this man out in battle then?" Deidra inquired dryly as she tossed aside her wooden sword and flung herself down against the trunk of the nearest tree.

"Nay, lass, I wouldn't. Strength or no, ye'll never be a warrior. Ye haven't the killing instinct." Bardrick chuckled. "But then, ye'd not be alone in fearing to go against Hawkwind. Few men dare such a feat—at least knowingly —and live."

Deidra tossed her long, red-gold braid over her shoulder, swiped the moisture beading her brow with the back of her tunic sleeve, and motioned for her companion to take a seat beside her. "Aye, that I know. He's the greatest warrior alive. How I long someday to meet him!"

At the tone of rapt admiration in his mistress's voice, Bardrick frowned. He knew he mayhap waxed a bit too eloquent in reveling her with tales of his former days as a mercenary soldier and his exploits fighting at the side of the famed Hawkwind, but Deidra was always such an avid audience and she seemed to love the tales so. Loved them as much as she loved their clandestine lessons in the forest outside Rothgarn Castle.

He knew he went a bit too far in that as well, in teach-

ing the Lord of Rothgarn's daughter the art of swordplay.
But what harm could it really do, save bring a bit of excitement into the life of a girl he'd been tasked with serving as
bodyguard, a girl whose eventual destiny lay in the far
more traditional role of lady and eventual prize to some
ambitious nobleman?

He shook his head and smiled wryly. "Yer father
wouldn't be pleased to hear that. Ye're rebellious enough as
'tis. From the first moment I arrived at Rothgarn, I'd heard
such tales of ye, that ye were a headstrong, defiant little
sprite with yer snapping eyes and unruly head of curls."
With a bemused shake of his head, Bardrick lowered himself to sit beside her, his battle-worn joints creaking and
crunching in their usual protest. "And ye haven't changed a
wit since then."

Deidra couldn't help a small giggle, recalling the day
she'd first met her old bodyguard. "The tale of my facing
down the stable master has grown greatly in the ensuing
years, wouldn't you say? 'Twasn't as gallant a feat as all
that."

At the memory of Deidra, that time she'd refused to
back down to a former stable master who'd been beating
one of his servants, a lad hardly older than she at twelve,
Bardrick's expression softened. The man had turned purple
in the effort to contain his rage and, when he thought no
one was looking, had threatened Deidra with all sorts of
lurid punishments.

She'd stood there, her legs planted firmly in the dirt, her
little arms akimbo, and never backed down. Even then,
she'd been a fighter. The stable master had finally been
forced to admit defeat. She was the lord's daughter, after
all.

" 'Twas gallant enough for one of yer age," he replied,
suddenly overcome with a surge of nostalgia.

As kindhearted and courageous as all her efforts were,
Deidra's time of freedom was soon to be over. Her father
doted on her and had given his only child her way in most

everything she desired, but Deidra had finally grown up. She was a wealthy and very desirable young woman. As the sole heir of Rothgarn and its lands, many noblemen now vied for her hand.

Though she'd managed so far to find one reason after another not to accept the offers of the various lords who approached her father, he had finally grown weary of his daughter's recalcitrance when it came to marriage. Deidra was seventeen. Whether she wished it or not, 'twas time for her to wed.

"Do you think 'tis possible?" her sweet voice intruded on his troubled thoughts. "Do you think there might be *some* way to meet Hawkwind? I'd willingly venture forth to find him if 'twere a possibility."

Bardrick shot her a stunned look, only now beginning to fathom the extent and potential consequences of the ideas he'd stirred in her. "What? Are ye daft, lass? What would ever possess ye to think about, much less even want to do that? Hawkwind's a mercenary. He sells his services to the highest bidder, then wages war with no more qualm or thought than he'd give to selling a horse or a fat hen at market."

"Hawkwind has his honor, his own code of justice!" Deidra hotly defended him. She plucked a blade of grass and popped its fat, juicy end into her mouth. "You told me of the respect all the lords hold him in. That they know, when he commits his army to fight for them, he'll honor that promise no matter the cost or consequence. 'Tis why he's so feared yet valued throughout the realm. Any lord Hawkwind brings his army to has never failed to prevail against his enemies."

"Aye, 'tis true enough, lass," Bardrick agreed, "but he's also no sort of man for a lady of yer breeding to frequent with. Ye don't move in the same levels of society. For all his battle skills and warrior's honor, Hawkwind's a hard, bitter man with little respect for the nobility. Or a noble lady." He pressed on, determined to set her straight on some of the more brutal aspects of the man who he had apparently, yet inadvertently, led her to idolize. "He'd have no more use for ye than he'd have for any woman."

"And that use would be . . . ?" Deidra demanded with a challenging lift of an auburn brow. She pulled the blade of grass from her lips and fixed him with an unwavering stare.

Bardrick smiled and shook his head. She'd not be diverted, even by implications of crudity. "Lass, how do ye think a man as rough and battle hardened as Hawkwind has become would use a woman? For warming his bed!"

A rose flush washed up the ivory-hued skin of her neck and face. "I can't believe he views all women that way. A man of honor—"

"A *man* can choose where and when he wishes to be honorable," he interrupted her, motioning aside her protests with a disparaging wave of his hand. "Especially a man who has naught to lose. Times are bad and threaten to become even worse. Survival and the attainment of one's basic needs are all that many can hope for. Thank yer most fortunate of fates ye live within the strong walls of Rothgarn. Ye have plenty of food while others starve, fine clothes on yer back when ye choose it," he said, his glance skimming her simple but finely woven tunic and breeches and pair of shiny leather boots, "and ye still have yer maidenhood.

"Aye," Bardrick persisted relentlessly, despite the deepening of her flush, "'tis a reality of these times, lass. Times that are far too harsh and dangerous for a delicately bred lady such as yerself to be roaming about."

A mutinous, stubborn look tightened Deidra's mouth and narrowed her eyes. "You said yourself only Hawkwind possessed my knack with the fancy footwork when it came to swordplay. I think I'm well able to defend myself if I chose to set out to find him."

"Ye've never fought with a real sword, felt a steel blade taste flesh. 'Tis a far different weapon than ye're used to. And why *would* ye wish to find him?" Bardrick's brow furrowed in puzzlement. "Ye never spoke of such things before."

"I was never before being forced to wed, either," his mistress muttered. She shot him an anguished look. "I don't want to marry the Lord D'Mondeville, Bardrick! I've met him before, two years ago at Court. He's a slimy, manipulative, avaricious man. And even then he looked at me like . . . like I was some prize mare he wished to breed with!"

Bardrick clamped down on a smile at Deidra's accurate assessment of the situation. Lord Basil D'Mondeville did indeed want Deidra in his bed and her lands under his control. But that was to be expected. 'Twas the way of the nobility. What his young charge failed to realize was any man, be he noble or peasant, who cast even one glance at her would wish the same. For all her intelligence and piercing insight when it came to people, Deidra had yet to realize the effect she had upon men. But soon, very soon . . .

He sighed. "Ye've grown into a beautiful woman, lass. Ye've yet to discover yer feminine wiles, but when ye do I pity the man ye choose to ply them upon. The poor bastard won't stand a chance. But, be that as it may, ye're of age to wed and must. 'Tis yer destiny."

"Destiny!" Deidra cried. "Ah, how I've come to hate that word! I've always found it singularly strange how easily that word gets bandied about when someone wants something of you."

" 'Tis still time, lass," he offered gently. Though he loved her like the daughter he'd never have, Bardrick saw clearly the woman his little mistress would very soon become. She'd need a strong man to handle her and Basil D'Mondeville, for all his rough ways, was just the man. "Ye couldn't hope to remain unwed forever. And Lord Basil, though mayhap not of yer choice, is powerful and wealthy. The eventual merger of yer lands will make yer heirs a force to be reckoned with. Yer father has chosen well in accepting Basil's offer for ye."

"Has he now?" Deidra climbed to her feet and tossed her

long, thick braid over her shoulder. Her hands fisted on her hips as she glared down at Bardrick but, though her stance was defiant, tears hovered on the edge of spilling over and burned the back of her throat. "And aren't you so like every other man, to think only of wealth and power! As if 'tis enough for a woman, at any rate. What about freedom, respect—love?"

"A woman is meant to obey her man. In return, he gives her the respect owed her as his lady and mother of his children. And, as far as love goes, 'tis a surer thing ye'll find it with yer own kind, than out in the world chasing after some foolish dream ye've concocted of a mercenary's life and a man ye haven't any hope ever of understanding!"

"I see and understand more than you think, Bardrick."

Thunder rumbled in the distance. For the first time, Deidra noticed the heavy feel to the air, the dampness heralding impending rain. Well, at least some good might come of this day, she consoled herself. Though the drought of the past few years was beginning to wane, they still needed rain badly. And mayhap, if she were *very* lucky, a torrential downpour might preclude the Lord D'Mondeville from even arriving this eve. She was certainly due for a little luck when it came to the issue of their upcoming union.

She eyed Bardrick a moment longer, her gaze warming once more to the sight of him. He sat there, sprawled beneath the tree, an endearingly shaggy haired and grizzled old man, his tunic, breeches, and boots in want of a woman's touch, but his masculine aura proud and imposing nonetheless. He had been her bodyguard ever since his arrival at Rothgarn five years ago, a man broken in spirit and despondent that his many battle wounds had finally forced him to retire from the mercenary life he so loved.

Deidra had taken to him from the first moment she'd met him, and he to her. 'Twas as if they both needed something from the other—Bardrick a healing of body and soul, Deidra, the nourishment of hopes and dreams so long stifled in the close confines of a castle carefully isolated from the horrors of a world gone mad. He was her friend and mentor, servant only in the minds of others, but never in hers.

She gestured toward the distant castle peeking through the leafy forest foliage, its strong walls pierced at measured intervals by rounded towers. " 'Tis past time we were getting back. As much as I loath to think of it, I've a potential husband to prepare for this eve and, if I find continued favor in his eyes, a betrothal ceremony to attend on the morrow."

Her old bodyguard climbed stiffly to his feet. "Aye, that ye do, lass. And mark my words. In a month's time after ye're wed, ye'll see the wisdom of what yer father does in giving ye to the Lord Basil. He's the man for ye. Just give it time."

Once again anger, freshened by Bardrick's well-meant but ill-timed words, surged through her. Deidra turned sharply on her heel and headed back toward the castle. He didn't understand, she thought, filled with an impotent rage and bitter frustration. No one—no man—could. They were all the same, good-intentioned or not.

A woman's fate was to acquiesce to the males set over her, with no recourse, no voice in anything that was decided. Her life, her dreams, her desires were never hers to control. Though *they* had total freedom, she never would.

Her long, strong strides carried her swiftly out of the forest and across fields sparsely covered with spindly stands of golden wheat. The autumn harvest would be meager this year, Deidra knew, but would still be a decided improvement over the past. And, mayhap in time, the crops would once again flourish and no more serfs starve.

Since the wars King William had begun in the attempt to bring his rebel lords under control, shortly after the strange death of his father eight years ago, chaos and famine had ravaged the land. Peasants, barely able to sustain their hungry families, had been forced to forsake their farms and take to a wayfaring life. And the lords, many becoming as desperate as their serfs, turned more and more greedy and treacherous.

Once again thunder rumbled, closer now. Deidra glanced up at the lowering sky hanging like some forboding god over the town sprawled at the base of the castle. High overhead a hawk soared on the air currents.

A curious pain twisted within her. At least the hawk was free. At least his choice of existence was his own, whatever the consequences.

That was precisely what attracted her to the mercenary life, the opportunity to discard all propriety, to turn her back on society and its stifling strictures. 'Twas all Deidra had ever desired. What did she care if she lived and acted differently than others? The bleak, hopeless, helpless fate of a noblewoman seemed far, far worse.

She craved freedom, power, choices. If that demanded the sacrifice of a safe, predictable, comfortable existence, so be it! Though she loved her father, her people and land, her destiny called her to something more. She *knew* that, felt it to the depths of her soul. That much had never been starry-eyed dreaming.

"L-lass, wait!" Bardrick cried from far down the path leading to the town and castle. "Yer father will be livid if ye leave me behind."

He spoke true, Deidra well knew. The land, picked clean by roving bands of brigands and starving peasants, was a dangerous place nowadays. Her pace slowed, allowing her aging bodyguard to catch up with her. When he drew to her side, she shot him a grim-lipped smile.

Bardrick managed a tentative smile of his own. "I'm sorry if I offended ye back there. I meant no harm. Ye know that. I meant only to help ye see the way of things."

Deidra shook her head. "It matters naught, Bardrick. What must be, must be."

And 'twill be, she finished in silent determination. *No man will dictate the limits of my life. Not now—or ever!*

* * *

Deidra paused at the top of the two flights of stone stairs leading from the family bedchambers down to the Great Hall. Nervously, she rubbed palms gone suddenly damp down the close-cut cloth of her kirtle's bodice, momentarily distracted from the revelry below by the storm raging outside.

Her glance lifted high overhead to the soaring, peaked ceiling of arched wooden trusses. Torrents of rain pounded on the lead sheets covering the wooden planks that formed the hall's roof, a staccato cacophony interspersed with rolls of thunder. A terrible storm, promising days of mud and untenable travel which, unfortunately, would most likely delay Lord D'Mondeville's departure.

Deidra sighed and made her way down the stairs. If only the rain had come sooner, *before* he'd arrived.

But there was naught to be done about it. She paused at the next landing. Her searching gaze found Basil D'Mondeville, seated beside her father at the white cloth-covered head table. Around them, save for the empty seat awaiting her between the two men, sat the Rothgarn knights. All good lads, brave and true, she thought fleetingly as she watched her suitor lift his cup in toast, then down its contents in one gulp.

Even from the distance of the first flight of stairs, Deidra saw the wine trickle from the sides of his mouth and dribble down his chin. In a careless gesture, Lord D'Mondeville wiped his lips on the back of a tunic sleeve of scarlet wool, then threw back his head of pale blond, stylishly curled hair and laughed.

Inexplicably, something in the action turned Deidra's stomach. He was too sure, too arrogant, too calculating in every action he made. It struck her suddenly that Basil D'Mondeville never did anything without forethought, or potential advantage to him. He needed no subterfuge in his motives for wedding her, though. 'Twas expected he'd want her for the lands she'd eventually bring him as the Roth-garn heiress, and the children she'd bear.

Chattel. A brood mare. Bitterness welled in Deidra. That was all she'd ever be to him. No matter what Bardrick said, Basil D'Mondeville would *never* be the man for her.

But there was naught to be done but face him. Face him and this night, and see what came of it. There was always hope he'd find her somehow lacking. That he'd back out of the agreement.

As she gathered the full skirts of her pale green silk gown and headed down the stairs and across the Hall, Deidra's mouth twisted in a wry grimace. Hope she always had. 'Twas the dreamer in her, so like her beloved mother, her father frequently said. Her gay, beautiful mother, dead now these past sixteen years. But to hope her newest suitor would willingly grant her what no man yet had ever given was as foolish as her dream of running away and joining—

"Something must be done, and soon, about the merce-nary armies roaming our land!" her father was vehemently stating as she drew near the dining table.

Basil D'Mondeville shrugged in a languid, negligent manner. "Indeed. They pose a great threat to the stability of the ruling class. But our wise and gracious king has so far deigned to turn a blind eye to the problem."

"Is that mayhap because he and his lords use the merce-naries to their own advantage?" Lord Rothgarn muttered. "As long as the king keeps the opposition battling among themselves, and the realm teetering constantly on the brink of outright war, he can only continue to enhance his own position. Though I owe William much, his actions of late disturb me greatly. I sometimes wonder if he hasn't secretly hired the mercenaries at his own call, bidding them to wreak havoc and destruction."

"Have a care, m'lord," D'Mondeville murmured, leaning over to clasp his arm. "As your future son-in-law, I must warn you your words border perilously close to treason."

Crimson stained Rothgarn's cheeks. "And I'll tell you now that I care not a fig for—"

Deidra hurriedly stepped forward. "I beg pardon, m'lords, in being so tardy to table. I hope I've not kept you and the others waiting overlong?"

The Lord D'Mondeville slid back his chair and climbed to his feet. "Lady Deidra, 'tis my greatest pleasure to meet you again. It has been two years past, has it not, since I last saw you? And, if you'll forgive my boldness," he said, his brown-black eyes sweeping her slender figure before pausing to linger on the rounded fullness of her breasts, "I thought you lovely then, but you're even more breathtaking now."

He reached out and took her hand, lifting it to full, sensuously curved lips in a brief parody of a kiss. "You, m'lady, will suit me well."

Carnal desire, which he made no attempt to hide, glittered in D'Mondeville's eyes as he glanced back up at her. Deidra jerked her hand from his clasp, controlling the urge to wipe it off on her kirtle with only the greatest of efforts. She met his heated gaze with a cool, disdainful one of her own.

"Indeed, Lord D'Mondeville? Then the only question still remaining is if *you'll* suit *me*."

His eyes narrowed, then he lazily smiled. "I assure you, m'lady, I'll direct all my considerable prowess to that most pleasurable of pursuits. You're a prize well worth having."

Deidra opened her mouth to snap back some appropriately cutting remark, then, as her glance met her father's, thought better of it. The man was a guest, no matter how vile and arrogant he was. He had sadly underestimated her and her determination to thwart him, however, if he imagined she was the least bit cowed.

She swept her skirts to one side and quickly claimed the chair between him and her father. "Well, at this moment, Lord D'Mondeville, the only pleasurable pursuit *I* desire is that of taking supper."

With that, Deidra turned to her father. "You spoke most harshly of the mercenary armies a few moments ago. Surely you weren't including the army of the famous Hawkwind? From what I've heard, he's nothing like the rest. He is brave, resourceful, and honorable."

"Honorable?" The Lord of Rothgarn's mouth gaped for a fleeting moment, then snapped shut. "The terms *mercenary* and *honorable* are in direct contradiction. Methinks you've had your head turned by Bardrick's tales one time too many."

D'Mondeville's eyes gleamed with interest. "And who, may I ask, is this Bardrick?"

Rothgarn turned. "He is Deidra's bodyguard, an aged, crippled, former warrior."

"A strange choice for a young woman of breeding," D'Mondeville observed. "Especially one of such over-wrought imagination. The mercenary Hawkwind honorable?" He chuckled. "Well, in a sense he is, if one considers the high store he places on money. Whatever honor he may possess can certainly be bought if one has sufficient coin."

"You speak of him as if you've had cause to 'buy' his honor yourself," Deidra challenged with a brittle hauteur, warming to the verbal battle, her hope her defiance might discourage D'Mondeville's continued suit flaring anew. "But I ask you, m'lord, which man's honor is greater?—the one bought or the buyer? Hawkwind can only carry out what task his employer wishes done. If the task is evil, is he the evildoer, or the man who hires him?"

As if suddenly realizing where she was headed, and her motive for the act, her father cleared his throat. "Deidra, this isn't the proper time or topic for a lady to be discussing. You have just met the Lord D'Mondeville. 'Tisn't hos-pitable to engage him in an argument over such a pointless matter." He shook his head in disgust. "By the saints. The honor of a mercenary!"

Lord Rothgarn signaled to the servants to begin serving

the first course. "Now, no more of it, Daughter. 'Tisn't fitting to begin your betrothal on such a disagreeable note." He nodded in answer to her silent look of horror, a warning light in his eyes. "Besides, 'tis a subject best left to men, at any rate."

Servants arrived at that moment, bearing a huge silver tureen of rich bean soup garnished with garden ripe tomatoes and parsley. As the servants moved down the table, ladling out steaming spoonfuls to each of the diners, Rothgarn and D'Mondeville turned hungrily to their meal. Everyone soon followed suit. The huge, half-timbered, and whitewashed hall fell silent, save for the rustling movements of servants across the flower- and rushes-strewn floor.

Watching them, Deidra clamped her lips shut against the now familiar surge of rebellion and frustration, this time tinged with the pain of her father's betrayal. She had seen the slight smile of triumph on D'Mondeville's lips. Even before her arrival to supper this evening, her father had superseded her desires and given her to him. D'Mondeville thought she was already his.

He thought wrong.

The last vestiges of hesitation, of upbringing and duty, vanished in the realization of what lay ahead. Her father had placed her in an untenable position. Tonight was a turning point in her life. She stood at a crossroads, confronted with the one and only opportunity she might ever have to make a choice as to what path to take. And, though one choice was hard, dangerous, and fraught with uncertainty, 'twas also the only one offering her any hope.

"M'lady?" D'Mondeville's smooth, cultured voice intruded. "Forgive my oversight. Do you desire a cup of wine?"

Deidra bit back the impulse to tell him what he could do with his cup of wine and nodded instead. A moment later, she sorely regretted it. He leaned close, his cloying scent of musk engulfing her. Deidra pulled back slightly.

"You mustn't be so shy with me, m'lady," D'Mondeville soothed as if noting her withdrawal, his voice pitched low for her ears only. "Save for the official ceremony, you are now mine." He studied her closely, a speculative gleam in his eyes. " 'Tisn't your mother's shameful past that makes you so defensive, is it? If so, fear not; I am more than willing to overlook it.

"Besides," he added smugly, "I don't believe in witch-craft."

"My mother did naught shameful!" Deidra snapped, struggling past the surge of fear and loathing that mention of the magic coursing in her veins always stimulated. "She merely lost control of her powers, powers I definitely don't possess at any rate. And you presume too much and falsely, Lord D'Mondeville, to think I find her—"

"Basil. Call me Basil," he smoothly cut in. "You speak true in implying I presume to a knowledge I may not fully possess. Fortunately, for the both of us, I plan to accept your father's most generous offer of lodging for the next several days. Ample time for us to get to know each other, beginning tonight when you assist me in my bath." His glance slyly met hers. "You *will* assist me, won't you? As lady of the keep, not to mention my betrothed, I'd expect that traditional hospitality."

Knowing full well 'twould be an insult to refuse if D'Mondeville wished it, Deidra demurred in the only way she could. 'Twouldn't matter at any rate. She'd be long gone before then. Her lashes dipped to cover the anger she knew must burn in her eyes. "If my father requires it of me, I must."

Smug triumph thickened D'Mondeville's voice. "Oh, be assured, lady, he will. He will indeed."

Deidra's eyes lifted. He saw, with a start of surprise, she wasn't cowed by maidenly obeisance after all. Nay, far from it.

D'Mondeville's fingers clenched knuckle-white about the wine ewer. The challenge of her, of subduing her defiant nature, of crushing her will as he crushed her delectably voluptuous body beneath his, surged through him, exciting him, stirring his blood. He would have her, have her lands, have it all. She didn't know it yet, but she didn't stand a chance. No one did, not when Basil D'Mondeville wanted something.

As if the heavens wept out their long pent-up anguish over the cruel vagaries of mankind, rain poured from the blackened skies. The wind blew, gusting sheets of water to slam against castle walls and buildings. Fruit trees, laden with ripening apples and pears, groaned as they swung to and fro, whipped mercilessly by the storm. No one, not even the soldiers sent to walk the parapets, ventured outside.

No one, that was, but Deidra. She slunk along the inner bailey, keeping to the shadows, ducking low beneath the windows of the kitchen and buttery, garbed in dark tunic, breeches, and boots, a black, hooded cloak flung about her, a heavy pack slung over her shoulder, a short sword appropriated from the armorer's worktable strapped about her waist. Her first destination was the stables. Whether or not she was able to ride far tonight, she needed a mount.

The wind whipped at her cloak, twisting it about her legs then flinging it up to blow over her head. Deidra cursed the vicious weather, yet knew it also afforded her the necessary cover to escape Rothgarn undetected. Few castles were as well constructed or defended as her home. Under normal circumstances, Deidra would never have been able to leave without Bardrick or her father's permission.

But this act was nothing either would have permitted and she was thankful neither would know she was gone until 'twas too late. Though Deidra loved them both, each in their own way, she could no longer bow to their desires. One intended, and the other concurred, to give her away to a man she could never love or respect. 'Twas her desires that mattered now. Hers, and no one else's.

The stable was closed and bolted shut. Deidra strained for long minutes before she was able to shove the heavy bolt aside and open the main door. The interior was dark, save for a small oil lamp hung on a post well away from the stalls, and smelled of sweet hay and horse. Deidra slipped in, pulled shut the door and hurried down to where the tack was stored.

From memory and touch, she quickly found Belfry's saddle and bridle. In a matter of minutes, the tall, piebald gelding with the wild eyes was ready, her pack, laden with food and supplies, tied to the saddle. Though many thought the horse dangerously crazy, Deidra trusted the animal with her life. High-strung, skittish, and a bit unpredictable, Belfry, nonetheless, was fiercely devoted to his mistress. And Deidra was just as devoted to him.

He gave a snort of surprise and reared back as she opened the stable door and a blast of rain poured in. Deidra quickly soothed the animal, then led him outside. Scanning the walled enclosure, she heaved a sigh of relief. No one had noticed her sojourn in the stables.

Now, to get to the small door leading to the walkway and boat pier jutting into the moat. She'd briefly considered attempting to fool the guards at the gatehouse and outer barbican by claiming she was one of the midwives called out for a delivery. Belfry's unique coloring, however, was too well-known to contemplate that solution for long. Nay, the castle's boat pier and a swim across the moat was the best of choices.

Wind howled, rain poured, drenching her and her nervous mount as they made their way across the castle yard. The boat pier door was locked, but unguarded, though Deidra saw a light flickering in a nearby guardhouse. She shot the bolt and quickly led Belfry through, then paused to close the door firmly behind them.

The piebald's shod hooves made hollow, clip-clopping sounds on the stone pier, but the storm's incessant wail swallowed up the noise. Finally Deidra drew to the edge of the pier. The water of the moat churned wildly, deep and black as the pits of hell. She didn't savor the thought of leaping down into the murky, malodorous mess, but there was no other choice.

Yet, for a moment more Deidra hesitated. Once undertaken, the die was cast. Was it truly what she wanted?

Lightning flashed. Thunder followed, exploding around her, drowning Deidra in a cavern of unearthly sights and sounds. Everything slowed, stilled . . . and, suddenly, Deidra saw it all.

Her life, as it now was. Her future, as D'Mondeville's wife. And yet another choice, bound to a tall, dark-haired man with haunted, bitter eyes.

She blinked, startled by the vision. Another man? But she wanted no man, no matter how different, how strangely compelling. In the end, they were all the same. Nay, she wanted only freedom. That, and naught more.

Swinging up onto Belfry, Deidra urged the horse down into the moat. There was a momentary gasp as chill water engulfed them, a wild grab at mane to steady her seat. Then they were swimming toward the shore. Swimming toward freedom. Freedom, and the one man who could ensure that for her.

Hawkwind.

Chapter 2

"And aren't ye the resourceful warrior, to be caught sleeping as the enemy approaches!" To emphasize his point, Bardrick gave his still drowsy mistress a sharp nudge in the ribs with his booted foot.

Deidra groaned, rolled over onto her back and blinked. Bright sunlight streamed into her eyes, momentarily blinding her. Then, full awareness returned. She jerked upright, nearly banging her head on the low ceiling of the rocky little cave she'd sought shelter in last night, and grabbed for her sword. It was weighted to the ground by another booted foot.

Swiftly, she changed tack. Her hand slipped to where she'd tucked her dagger beneath the saddle she'd used for a pillow.

"Don't bother yerself about yer little knife, either," her bodyguard growled. "That was the first thing I took from ye."

She scooted out of the cave on hands and knees and glared up at him. "How did you find me?"

Bardrick squatted beside her. " 'Twasn't so hard. Ye left many a clue. And yer father wasn't at all happy when he found ye gone late last night. It took all my considerable skills to convince him to let me set out for ye first. There'll be others soon, though, if I don't bring ye back."

"I can evade them if only you let me go." She glanced up at him hopefully. "You will, won't you, Bardrick?"

He shrugged. "Mayhap. But first I'd like to know what possessed ye to leave Rothgarn, in the midst of a raging storm no less. Was D'Mondeville that offensive to ye? Did he touch ye in some untoward way, or insult ye? If so, I'll personally see to his education when we return."

"Nay. He didn't touch or insult me, at least not with hands or words. But I saw it in his eyes, nonetheless." Deidra inhaled a shuddering breath. "He revolts me. I-I can't bring myself to wed him, Bardrick. I just can't!"

"Then come back to Rothgarn and tell this to yer father. If ye feel this strongly about the man, he'll understand." He held out a hand, a gentle smile on his lips. "Come, lass. 'Tisn't safe out here for ye. I'm only one man and can't defend ye if we're set upon by a large band of outlaws."

She eyed his proffered hand for a long, considering moment, then shook her head. "Nay. I won't come back, at least not willingly. You'll have to force me, and I'll fight you every step of the way."

Puzzlement furrowed the old man's brow. "But what else is there for ye, lass? Surely ye weren't bent on trying to find Hawkwind? Surely ye weren't serious about what we talked about yesterday?"

Deidra's chin lifted. "Aye, that I was. I go to join Hawkwind's army."

Incredulity widened Bardrick's eyes and lent him a slack-jawed appearance. "Join Hawkwind? Are ye daft, lass? He'd take one look at ye and laugh ye all the way back to Rothgarn! *If* ye even got past his men to talk with him," he added darkly. "Ye're quite a fetching morsel, ye know, and not all of Hawkwind's men are as 'honorable' as he."

"Then come with me," she urged, her excitement at the plan threading her voice. "They know you. They'll let me pass unmolested if you're at my side. And two warriors on the road are far safer than one. Come with me, Bardrick. Please."

The old warrior hesitated. Deidra's desperation and sweet entreaty plucked at his heart. Yet the danger—and Lord Rothgarn's rage if he failed to bring back his daughter —was a potent motivator as well. On the other hand, if Deidra didn't relinquish her foolish dreams, there'd still be hell to pay once they returned. He knew her well enough to realize she'd continue on her stubborn course and fight the acceptance of any man her father offered.

Mayhap a short side trip to Hawkwind's army *would* be the best thing. He regretted not regaling her in the past with the more sordid details of war camp life, of the hardships, suffering, and pain, but 'twas too late to convince her now. There was only one sure way to do that—let Deidra see it for herself.

He stroked his grizzled jaw. "I've heard rumors Hawkwind's army is but two days' journey from here, on a campaign for the Lord of Wendover. I could take ye there, but only on one condition." He hurried to silence her eager assent. "One condition, and ye must vow to follow it diligently."

"Aye." Deidra bobbed her agreement. "Anything you wish. I swear it."

Bardrick rolled his eyes. "Ye swear too easily, lass. Have a care, or yer eagerness will be yer undoing. My request is simple. Ye will stay by my side at all times, and not speak to Hawkwind without my leave."

Deidra frowned. " 'Tis the same thing all over again. You want to control me!"

"Nay, lass. I want to assure yer safety. These are dangerous, hardened men used to taking whatever strikes their fancy—and expecting no protest in the bargain. Until I've a chance to reach Hawkwind and renew old acquaintances, we'll both be in a precarious position. 'Tis not only yer life at stake here. 'Tis mine as well."

Something in the seriousness of his tone of voice and expression gave Deidra pause. Though she had freely made the decision to risk her life in this undertaking, she'd not thought to consider Bardrick's. And if anything should happen to him because of her . . .

"You have my word. I'll stay plastered to you like flour paste to a kitchen worktable, and I'll not utter one word to Hawkwind without your leave."

Somehow, Deidra's ready acceptance of his terms did little to ease Bardrick's concerns. He'd almost hoped she'd refuse so he'd feel justified in slinging her over his shoulder and marching back to Rothgarn. Her determination was strong, very strong, to crave freedom so avidly she'd pay for it with such ready subservience to his rigid demands. But he'd made the offer and she'd accepted. There was naught to be done but see it through.

Bardrick motioned to where his horse was tethered beside Belfry. "The morn draws on and the roads are little more than quagmires. The way will be slow and tedious as 'tis. Let's be off."

Deidra gathered her cloak and saddle where she'd spread them last night and sprang to her feet. Sunlight glinted on the tousled, slightly damp mass of her wavy auburn hair, highlighting strands of deep amber and rich red. Nut brown eyes, flecked with gold, gazed up at him in gratitude. "Thank you, Bardrick. You won't regret this. I promise!"

He grimaced, leaned over to pick up her sword, then straightened awkwardly. "Lass, the only thing I regret is ever telling ye of Hawkwind. If ye'd never known, ye wouldn't now be harking off on this hair-brained quest that will surely be the death of us both."

A grim determination flared in her eyes. "I'd have just found some other way. My destiny has never been to submit to a fate chosen for me by others. I tell you, Bardrick, I *know* that. I can feel it to the marrow of my bones!"

Her conviction stirred something in him. 'Twas strong and pure, he realized, and would drive her far past normal limits. But to accept the fact she thought her fate lay with some mercenary army . . .

True, he'd loved the life, its exhilarating independence, unbelievable opportunities for mind-boggling wealth and heart-stopping adventure. But he'd had few other choices. And even those choices had gradually faded, hacked to pieces by an aging body and battle wounds that hampered his ability to defend himself and increasingly threatened his life. If not for Hawkwind's swift intervention in the last battle he'd fought, now over five years past, he'd never have lived to see this day.

Nay, the mercenary life wasn't for him anymore, and certainly not ever for Deidra. Yet she felt the certainty to the marrow of her bones! By the saints, what an innocent!

He sighed and shook his head, signaling for her to lead the way. "Come along then. We've an army to find."

She grinned and stepped out. "Aye, that we do," Deidra happily shot over her shoulder. "An army, an adventure, and a new life!"

Though the rain-soaked, rutted roads slowed their progress significantly, it totally bogged down the merchants' caravan en route to the huge, yearly town fair in distant Carmarthen. An entourage of over twenty wagons, their colorful canvas coverings brilliant flags in the forest's dark green expanse, were mired halfway up their wooden wheels in thick, foot-sucking mud. Even the powerful oxen pulling the majority of the wagons could make little headway.

Bardrick and Deidra came upon the merchant train early that evening, just as the decision was finally made to make camp and wait until the road dried out. A few of Deidra's carefully secreted coins slipped into the right hands assured her a spot in one of the wagons for the night, while Bardrick insisted on making his pallet on the ground just outside.

Though she protested that his bones would appreciate the soft, dry bed in the wagon more, he firmly refused. She was his lady and, though he'd agreed to accompany her on this foolhardy quest, he'd not see her suffer unnecessarily.

Deidra knew him to be as stubborn as she in the right circumstances—as this most obviously was—and finally gave up and went to bed.

Sometime past midnight, in the darkest hours before dawn, a strangled cry woke her. She jerked up in bed, grasping for her sword. Another scream rent the air, and another. Then came the pounding of hooves and the sound of sword and ax.

She scrambled from her bed and stuck her head out of the wagon. "Bardrick? What's amiss?"

He slipped out of the darkness, his sword drawn. "The caravan is being attacked. Dress quickly, then await me here."

"Wait a moment," Deidra said. "I want to—"

"Nay, 'tis too dark," he cut her off, guessing her intent to accompany him. "We might become separated in the confusion. Stay here. 'Tis the easiest way to find ye again."

His words had merit, Deidra admitted, albeit reluctantly. She nodded her acquiescence. "Go, do what you must, but hurry back."

She saw a flash of teeth as Bardrick smothered a grin, then watched him mount up and ride off toward the front of the caravan where the brunt of the attack was evidently being directed. As Deidra dressed, the sounds of battle worsened. The seconds passed with nerve-wracking slowness.

The conflict moved down through the caravan. Merchants ran by, terror in their eyes, clutching what little goods they could carry in their arms. Horses stampeded past, spooked by the noise and flaming torches that suddenly appeared, carried by the outlaws who had begun looting the wagons.

Deidra's heart began to pound in her chest. Her breath quickened and the sword she held grew damp in her hand. Where, by all the saints, was Bardrick? What if something had happened to him? What if he'd been set upon by a horde of outlaws and overcome?

That last consideration made up her mind. As a precaution, Deidra withdrew her dagger from its sheath and slipped it into her boot, pulling her breeches down to hide it. *'Twas never a bad idea to have an extra and unexpected weapon,* she told herself, *in case one later needed it.*

To disguise the fact she was a woman, she flung her cloak about her and pulled the hood forward to hide her face and hair. Then, jumping down from the wagon, Deidra swung up onto Belfry and urged him in the direction she'd seen Bardrick head, straight for the thickest pockets of fighting.

The exodus from the battle grew. Panicked merchants shoved and jostled past to run off into the darkness. Several outlaws rode by Deidra, laughing and shouting encouragement at the frightened men to hurry on. A wagon, evidently emptied of its wares, was overturned and set afire. Oxen bawled loudly, milling about to add to the general melee. Belfry shied at every shadow looming out of the night.

Fighting both her horse and the unsettling chaos around them, Deidra doggedly searched for sign of Bardrick. His tall form, usually so easy to pick out in a crowd, was nowhere to be seen. Apprehension sang through her veins.

"Bardrick?" she cried. "Bardrick, answer me!"

A man on a horse drew up. He leaned over, grasped Deidra by her hood, and flung it back. "What have we here?" he roared. "A lass, by her voice and hair. And prize enough for me this night!"

He made a move to grasp her about the waist and pull her onto his horse. The cold steel of her sword met him instead. "Back away while you still have a throat to speak through," Deidra warned, lowering her voice to a hard, ominous tone. "I've more important matters to concern me than the likes of you."

The man's eyes widened in surprise. "Ah, as ye wish, lass. I meant no harm." He lurched back into his saddle. For a long moment he stared over at her, then grinned. "But beware, my flame-haired wench. The night is still young. I may yet return to risk a prick of yer sword and have another go at ye."

With that, the outlaw reined his horse around and directed it to the nearest wagon being ransacked. Deidra's gaze followed until she was certain he didn't plan to return, then nudged Belfry back in her original direction. But, though she carefully checked each wagon she passed, Bardrick wasn't in or around any of them.

Her attention moved to the head of the caravan, where the outlaws battled with some of the more determined merchants. Smoke billowed around them, the flickering light of red-gold flames licking at several nearby wagons, alternately illuminating, then shadowing the combatants. It was there, far ahead, his broad-shouldered form towering above the rest, that Deidra at last found Bardrick—fighting desperately for his life.

He was on foot, five men battling against him. Five strong, young, well-armed men. And Bardrick was weakening rapidly.

Deidra signaled Belfry forward, urging him into a dead run. Blood hammered through her heart, pounded through her veins. Battle—her first real battle—awaited, and she didn't know how she'd react, or even if her skills were truly sufficient to protect her, much less rescue Bardrick. The thought of turning away, of fleeing into the forest like so many of the merchants, flitted through her mind.

With an angry mental shrug, Deidra tossed the cowardly consideration aside. Honor demanded she face this impending confrontation, even if, in the doing, she died without ever reaching Hawkwind's army. The realization and the freedom of the choice filled her with a fierce elation. 'Twas her decision, no matter the outcome, and that was all she'd ever wanted.

Bardrick moved sluggishly now. Deidra could see that even through the smoke, wavering light, and the bodies of the men crowded around him. He parried, dodged, but suddenly it was no longer enough. A spike studded mace sailed through the air, striking him on the side of his head. Bardrick staggered, lost his balance and toppled over.

"Bardrick!" Deidra screamed. Flinging back her hood, she lifted her sword, an anguished rage surging through her. As she did, hoofbeats intruded into her battle-heightened consciousness. Hoofbeats, drawing near . . . then right behind her.

Something slammed into Belfry—another horse, an attacker. The piebald reared, iron shod hooves pawing the air. Deidra was flung backward, unbalanced, fighting to regain control. An arm snaked about her waist. Before she could turn to face him, her assailant had lifted her up before him and wrenched the sword from her hand.

"Nay!" Deidra screamed, twisting in his grip to claw at his face.

A fist flashed out of the darkness. Pain exploded in her jaw. A kaleidoscope of colorful lights glittered briefly before her. Then everything—sight, sound, feeling—extinguished. Blackness closed in, engulfing her in a deep maw of insensibility.

Hawkwind awaited D'Mondeville in his tent. The day had gone damp and gray again, and he wondered if yet another deluge awaited in the clouds lowering overhead. In an almost reflexive motion, he massaged his right shoulder. Already it had begun to ache and further rain was sure to send it into agonizing throbbing. Then there was the back of his head . . .

He rose from his chair and strode over to the small brass table holding the flagon of dark ale and two cups. Though the brew had been brought in to serve to his guest, Hawkwind decided a preliminary cup or two might ward off the worst of the pain. 'Twas all he had and a man with his responsibilities and commitments couldn't afford to allow his body's failings to overcome him. The injuries would be with him the rest of his life. The ale, if permitted sufficient time, usually worked wonders.

The dark amber liquid spilled from the flagon into his cup in a mesmerizing flow. Its rich, full-bodied scent wafted to his nostrils. Hawkwind quickly gulped down one cup and proceeded to pour himself another. It was then the guard announced his visitor.

Hawkwind swung around, his big, hard-muscled body going quiet, tense. 'Twas always like this at the onset of new negotiations. This lord wanted something of him—they always did. The only question was what and for how much. 'Twas the "how much" Hawkwind was girding himself to go to battle over, especially now, in a realm virtually picked clean of food and shelter by the famine and repeated rape of the land and its people.

Aye, he thought grimly as the tent flap lifted and his visitor strode in, the "how much" had become all that truly mattered.

D'Mondeville strode over to stand before him, a rich wool cloak the color of fire-bright topaz flung over a long tunic of deep, hunter green. Ever so thoroughly, his brown-black eyes took Hawkwind's measure. Something flickered there, some acknowledgment his opponent wasn't a man to be trifled with or discounted, and then he smiled. "You've an impressive army. I'd heard talk all these years, but never imagined . . ."

He paused to gesture about him, at the thick, intricately woven rugs covering the hard dirt floor, at the open chests heaped with coins and silver and gold plate booty, at the large, burl wood bed strewn with pillows and a deep carmine, satin-covered comforter. "Suffice it to say, you've done quite well for yourself," D'Mondeville finished in undisguised admiration.

"As have my men," Hawkwind offered pointedly. " 'Tis why we don't come cheaply. My army shares in my success."

The lord's mouth twisted in a small moue of distaste.

'Twas the bluntness of his demand for money, Hawkwind knew. The nobility always prided themselves on their talent for subtlety, whether they spoke truth or lies. Not that it mattered to him what the nobles liked, one way or another.

He was quite aware his employers viewed his army as a necessary but unsavory evil, little better in standing than the serfs who worked their fields and potentially a lot more dangerous. And Hawkwind knew, as well, how quickly the same men who were willing to pay such exorbitant sums could turn on him, if and when the opportunity arose. Treachery was also their way. 'Twould always be.

"Aye, your services come high," D'Mondeville admitted. His glance encompassed the tall black boots, finely tanned leather breeches, and long, laced vest atop a sable-colored fine linen shirt of the man standing before him. He noted with particular interest the hammered bronze arm gauntlets Hawkwind wore about his wrists and forearms, and the oddly designed gold medallion that glittered at the deep V where tunic met muscular chest.

D'Mondeville smiled ingratiatingly. "But then a quality job costs more than one done poorly. I am willing to pay for it."

Hawkwind arched a dark brow. "Mayhap you will. But I have first to hear the terms. Who will we go up against?"

"Does it matter? I heard you fight for the highest bidder, no matter the cause."

"In most cases, 'tis true." Hawkwind paused to pour out the second cup of ale and hand it to him. "There are a few I'll not fight for, though, King William in particular."

D'Mondeville smirked. "So, you side with the rebels, do you? A most unpopular stance nowadays. William grows rapidly in power."

Hawkwind shrugged. "I care naught for his power or what's popular or unpopular. And I don't side with the rebels any more than I do with any other faction. I just don't support the king."

D'Mondeville sipped his ale, savoring its mellow warmth. He lifted his cup in salute. "A fine brew, and not as bitter as most. You'll have to share the name of your ale maker."

"Indeed?" Hawkwind's jaw tightened. "And why would I wish to do that? You'd only force him into your service and I'd lose my good ale. Find your own, D'Mondeville, just as I did."

Anger flared in the other man's eyes, then was quickly smothered. "As you say, then. In the meanwhile, 'tis best we get back to business. It seems the only topic we find congenial agreement upon."

"Aye," Hawkwind growled, deciding there was something he didn't like about the man. Not that that would preclude a coming to terms. Any lord who hired him would think twice about treachery. 'Twasn't a wise move against an army better armed and trained than any most nobleman could possibly own.

" 'Tis as you said," he continued, forcing his attention back to the matter at hand. "We're not here to make social talk. 'Tisn't realistic to think it possible between two of our disparate standing, is it?"

A grim agreement gleamed in D'Mondeville's eyes. "I suppose not." He downed the contents of his cup, then wiped his mouth with the back of his hand. "I want Rothgarn Castle for my own. I want you to lay siege and take it."

Hawkwind's head snapped up. His green eyes narrowed. "Rothgarn? He's a friend of King William, is he not?"

D'Mondeville shrugged. "As much a friend as any man of conscience can be. Rothgarn has just come later than most to that conscience."

"The gift of another's land and castle does much to ease that in most men," Hawkwind muttered darkly, his fingers tightening about his cup. He paused a moment longer to eye his cup of ale, then swallowed its contents. "Aye, I'll take Rothgarn for you. I've a few weeks more owed to Wendover before I can come to your service, though."

"Your army won't be needed immediately. If things go as planned, mayhap I won't need you at all. I wish merely to keep you at the ready." He untied a bag bulging with coin from his belt and tossed it over to Hawkwind. "There's two thousand gold crowns in the pouch, and another eighteen thousand waiting outside on the packhorses. Half of what I intend to pay you for your services."

Hawkwind's strong white teeth flashed in a lazy grin. " 'Twill cost you that half just to keep us at the ready. Money that won't be refunded if you later change your mind. And, instead of another twenty thousand crowns, I might take the rest of the payment in some other form." He shrugged. "I haven't quite decided yet."

"*You* haven't decided . . . ?" At the piercing look Hawkwind sent him, D'Mondeville's voice faded. "Have it your way. You're a hard man. I should have expected it. Besides, I like knowing exactly where I stand."

"As do I." Hawkwind arched a questioning brow. "Is there more? If not, I've work to do."

A dark, angry look flashed in D'Mondeville's eyes, then was quickly shuttered. "Nay, no more, save the delivery of your money." He gestured toward the flagon of ale. "But first, another cup to seal our bargain. Since you refuse to share your ale maker, I must enjoy it while I can."

And later, when all has been seen to, he added grimly, *I'll extract your man's name before I personally cut out that arrogant tongue of yours. King William won't be thwarted in subjugating Rothgarn and his lands, and you've pushed too far in daring to demand even a part of what has been promised to me.*

D'Mondeville accepted the cup of ale Hawkwind handed to him. *Aye, my greedy mercenary,* he thought, his dark intent rising to encompass him in a swirling, violent mist. *You've pushed one time too many and will at last pay the price for it—to the very loss of your life.*

* * *

Deidra woke to the sensation of hanging upside down, of something shaking her. She groaned, opened her eyes and, momentarily, saw only blackness. Then the ground swayed beneath her, a horse snorted, and full awareness returned.

Someone—her attacker most likely—had her slung across his horse. Her hands were tied, her cloak's hood partially covered her eyes, and a bold hand on her buttocks firmly anchored her in place. Deidra squirmed to throw off his offending touch. For her efforts, she gained a chuckle and lavish caress of her bottom.

"Awake at last, are ye, lass? If I'd realized ye had such a delicate jaw, I'd have taken greater care. I'd not like to mar a wench as lovely as ye."

She recognized the voice. 'Twas the outlaw whom she'd run off last night. He must have quickly tired of looting wagons and returned for her as she went to Bardrick's aid.

Bardrick. The memory of him falling beneath the mace's blow filled her with frustration and fear. Curse the outlaw! Now, she might never know what became of her old body- guard.

Doubts, questions, assailed her. What if he lay back there, wounded and helpless? Or, worse still, what if he were dead?

Anger, at the current plight preventing her from re- turning for him, filled Deidra. This was not how 'twas meant to be, Bardrick mayhap dead, her in some outlaw's clutches, going god-knows-where and to god-knows-what fate.

What *would* the outlaw do with her? A myriad of pos- sibilities flooded Deidra's mind. Sold into slavery or, worse still, given to some man as his leman. Bardrick had warned her of the danger. Now it seemed she had managed to blunder into it within just a day of leaving Rothgarn.

And Bardrick. Was his fate any less dire than hers now seemed to be? Good, loyal Bardrick who had only wished to take her back home, to keep her safe, and who had reluctantly agreed to her foolish quest because she'd begged him and he cared enough to try and please her.

Hot tears filled Deidra's eyes. She'd been a stupid, selfish child, demanding her own way. Now Bardrick might well be dead because of it. Her own fate, unpleasant as it now seemed, she deserved. Though she'd fight with all the strength within her to change it, 'twas still the result of her own free choice. But poor Bardrick . . .

A plan. She must have a plan. Once they reached the outlaw camp, she must be ready to defend herself, to out-wit her captor. But how?

The dagger still sat snugly within her boot, its steel blade cold and hard against her leg. If she could just find some way to get her hands free, she might be able to use it to regain her freedom. But how? How?

After nearly another whole day and night of jostling across the hard withers of a horse, with the last, short rest stop at midnight, the solution to that question took a most natural of courses. By the time they drew near what sounded and smelled like a large encampment, Deidra's need to relieve herself was overwhelming. At last, her cap-tor reined in his horse and swung down.

"What have ye there, Simon? Have ye found yerself yet another wench?"

Hands grasped Deidra about the waist and dragged her off the horse. "Aye, that I have," Simon shouted his reply, "and she's the finest piece of womanhood ye'll ever hope to find."

"Is she now? Bring her over then and let's have a good look-see."

"Please," Deidra gasped when the man called Simon set-tled her on her feet and shoved back her hood. "Please, a moment first to attend to my personal needs."

In the dim light of yet another dawn, shaggy brown hair topping a smoke-blackened face was the first thing that caught Deidra's eye. He hadn't changed much from the previous night, save for the new hardness about his mouth and glitter in his cold blue eyes. She'd get few boons from him, Deidra realized with a sinking sensation in the pit of her stomach. She needed to make the most of whatever she could get and be quick about it.

"Need to relieve yourself, do ye?" he demanded bluntly. He gave her a rough shove forward. "The bushes over there will do ye nicely."

Deidra lurched forward, then caught herself. Her glance skittered from the outlaw to the thick clump of bushes growing about thirty feet away. "I'll need use of my hands," she said, swinging back to him.

"Will ye now?" He grinned suggestively, exposing several rotted teeth. "And wouldn't ye accept my aid?"

She inhaled a steadying breath. "Mayhap later, when we're alone. But, for now, I'd like my privacy."

Simon shrugged. "As ye wish. But later . . ."

"Aye, later," Deidra muttered, turning to offer her hands to him. Cold metal slid beneath her bonds, then her hands fell free. She paused a moment to massage the feeling back into them.

"Off with ye, now," her captor ordered gruffly. "I've a mind to show ye to the others before I take my pleasure with ye, so don't keep me waiting."

Deidra hurried to comply and, as she squatted hidden in the bushes, withdrew her dagger. After fastening her breeches closed, she slid the blade beneath her waistband, pulled her tunic down to hide it, and stood. Stepping out, Deidra made her way back to Simon.

She graced him with her most brilliant smile. "You said you wanted to introduce me to some of your friends. Shall we be on our way?"

A wary puzzlement knitted his brow. "Ye speak most strangely for a peasant lass." With a rough motion, he grabbed her by the arm and shoved her forward. "And ye presume too much to order me about, wench! I decide when and why we do what we do. Not ye. 'Tis yer first lesson about me, and one quickly learned, if ye wish to avoid a beating."

Deidra shot him a mutinous glare over her shoulder, but wisely withheld comment. He'd find out soon enough who he was dealing with, and *his* first lesson would be at knife point.

She scanned the encampment, searching for signs of Bardrick, hoping against hope someone had brought him along. As they drew farther into the camp, they left behind the ragtag element of sleeping vagabonds, brigands, and camp followers and moved onto a core of heavily armed foot soldiers. Piles of weapons, shields, bows and quivers bristling with arrows, spears, axes, and clubs were stacked together at measured intervals. Though most of the soldiers' features and dress marked them as peasants, seasoned warriors could be seen sleeping among the less experienced. All looked well-fed and clothed and many possessed mounts, from the looks of the large strings of horses tethered at the outskirts of camp.

Excitement vibrated through Deidra. She was in an army encampment. But whose?

She turned to Simon. "These men. Are they some lord's, preparing to wage war, or a mercenary army?"

The man threw back his head and gave a huge laugh. "Ah, 'tis a lord's all right. When one pays Hawkwind to do battle, 'tis the lord's army until Hawkwind deems otherwise."

"Hawkwind?" Deidra could barely force the word past a throat gone suddenly dry. "This is Hawkwind's army?"

He shot her a quizzical look. "Aye? What of it?"

She dug in her heels, forcing Simon to jerk to a halt. "I must meet him, speak with him! Can you take me to your leader?"

Simon's eyes narrowed. "And why would I want to do that? Ye're a bit too fine a wench and he's sure to take a liking to ye." He shook his head. "Nay, ye'll not see

Hawkwind, now or ever. Ye're my woman, and mine ye'll stay!"

Deidra's hand slipped to the dagger sheathed at her waist. A moment later its sharp point was pressed to Simon's neck. "And I say you *will* take me to him, or I'll finish what I threatened last night."

The man's throat leaped convulsively. He froze. "And what would ye accomplish, murdering me in the midst of this camp? Ye'd be cut down before ye took another step. Or, better still," he managed a cruel smile, "the whole army would turn on ye and have their way with ye."

"But you'll be dead, one way or another, won't you?" Deidra whispered in his ear, choking back the surge of nausea his crude words evoked. She grabbed the collar of his tunic and pulled his head down to her, pressing the dagger tip a little deeper until it pricked his skin. A thin trickle of blood coursed down his neck. "Well, what will it be?"

Simon hesitated, as if considering his options, then shrugged. "Ye're more trouble than ye're worth. I'll lead ye to Hawkwind. If he takes a liking to ye, I'll sell ye to him and use the money to buy a more gentle lass. Ye're too hard for my tastes, at any rate."

"Good. I didn't care much for you, either." Deidra nudged him along, taking pains to keep the dagger pressed to his throat. "Lead on."

They made their awkward way through camp, stepping carefully where men sprawled across pathways, evidently having decided to sleep where they had fallen. Sonorous snores rumbled from everywhere, smoke from dying campfires tainted the air with its acrid tang, and a few stray dogs picked among the food-laden plates and overturned cups.

There'd been a celebration last night, Deidra realized. She recalled Bardrick's mention of Hawkwind's campaign for the Lord of Wendover. Mayhap 'twas successfully completed. 'Twould account for the stuporous soldiers and general lack of the usual military orderliness.

In the light of a rose-washed sunrise, a large military tent topped by a red pennant emblazoned with a black hawk came into view. Deidra's pulse quickened. Surely 'twas the tent of the great mercenary leader, Hawkwind. Fate had indeed smiled on her, though the method of achieving her goal had altered significantly.

Her plan, upon meeting him, was twofold but simple. She would stand before him, offer her services as the newest of his warriors, and, once accepted, would enlist his aid in returning to the merchant caravan to look for Bardrick. Though after five years many of the mercenaries might not know of Bardrick and his brave service, Hawkwind would. Bardrick had told her time and again of their close friendship, and how Bardrick had once saved Hawkwind's life.

A big man and a slender, blond woman, both garbed in warrior's clothing, were seated outside the hawk-emblazoned tent. They spoke in low voices, but even from the distance still separating them Deidra could hear the ring of authority in their words.

Anticipation pounded through her. The big man up ahead was exceedingly tall, well-muscled, and possessed the bearing of a leader. At last she'd meet the famous Hawkwind!

Suddenly, Simon halted and refused to go a step farther. Deidra's grip about his neck tightened. "Is there some problem?" she inquired silkily.

"I've taken ye to his tent. My job is done. I'll wait for ye here."

"But you've yet to introduce us." She nudged him along.

"Then take the dagger from my throat. I can't be meeting my leader with a wench ordering me about. I've got my pride, ye know!"

Briefly, Deidra considered reminding him he was the one who had brought matters to such a head with his abduction and arrogant handling of her, then thought better of it. Once she'd joined the army Simon would be her comrade. Though she despised him, for now 'twas the wiser course to show mercy.

She lowered the dagger. "Fine. 'Twill be as you ask. Only do me the courtesy of at least introducing me to Hawkwind."

He nodded sullenly. "As ye wish."

Hawkwind and the woman stood as they approached.

"And what have you here, Simon?" the big warrior asked. On closer inspection, Deidra saw his long, black hair was lightly shot with gray and his face was craggy from many years of wind and sun. A man of imposing stature and authority, well-tempered by experience. Exactly how she'd always imagined Hawkwind to be.

"A wench, no more," Simon muttered, apparently changing his mind about introducing her. "And a troublesome one at that."

Deidra quashed the impulse to press her dagger back against his throat. Instead, she smiled shyly up at Hawkwind, hiding her eagerness with great difficulty. Then, recalling her mission, she forced herself to step forward. "My lord Hawkwind. For many years, I've dreamed of the day we'd finally meet." She bowed low. "My name is Deidra and I've come to join your army."

A stunned silence greeted her. After awaiting his leave to rise for an interminable length of time, Deidra slowly straightened. Two pairs of eyes gazed down at her in amusement. Two sets of lips twitched with barely contained laughter.

Deidra frowned. "Is there aught amiss, m'lord?"

The big man shook his head. "Oh, naught, lass, save for two minor details."

"And those are?" Deidra demanded, squaring her shoulders and reaching for all the height and authority she could muster.

"Well, for one, we've yet to be so desperate for soldiers that we accept children into our army. And, two," he said, chuckling, glancing over at the blond woman, "I'm not Hawkwind."

Hot color flooded Deidra's cheeks. She quickly tamped down her embarrassment. How was she to know she'd picked the wrong man? He met all the requirements, and he sat before what must surely be Hawkwind's tent.

She forced herself to forge on. "Your leader, then. Where *is* he to be found?"

The warrior cocked a speculative brow. "At this hour? After a night of drinking and wenching? Where would you imagine him to be?" He turned and gestured toward the tent. "In there, of course."

"Then pray, announce me," Deidra said. "I've a matter of utmost importance to discuss with him."

Once again the man and woman exchanged glances.

" 'Twill take a bigger man than me to waken Hawkwind this morn," the warrior replied, shaking his head in refusal. "Go brave the lion in his den if you must, but be forewarned. He is quite grouchy when woken before he's ready."

"Fine." Deidra resheathed her dagger in her boot. "I'll do just that."

As she resolutely strode up, lifted the tent flap, and ducked inside, the blond woman laughed softly and turned to her compatriot. "Grouchy, is he, Renard? That's a mild term for Hawkwind's temper after one of his drinking bouts, and well you know it."

"Well, mayhap 'twas," the big warrior admitted. "But then, if anyone can soothe Hawkwind's foul mood this morn, I'd wager that flame-haired wench can."

"But he already has a woman with him."

Renard shrugged. "Aye, and what of it? Hawkwind's man enough to handle the two of them, if he's a mind to. 'Twon't be the first time—*nor* the last."

Chapter 3

The interior of the tent was dark. The air smelled faintly of woodsmoke from the dying coals in the tall, bronze braziers situated about the room and the damp mustiness emanating from the tent's closely woven hemp cloth. Deidra took a few steps forward. Her booted toe snagged on the edge of something thick and heavy lying on the floor. Tentatively, she lifted her foot and felt around, discovering a rug.

She arched a brow in surprise. Hawkwind, whoever he was, apparently liked his comforts. Though the realization clashed with her image of him as a hardened warrior, she shrugged it off as inconsequential. In the end, what counted was his prowess in battle, not how he chose to live his personal life.

Her gaze narrowed, searching through the darkness for sign of where he slept. 'Twas supremely forward of her, she well knew, to presume to enter his tent unannounced and then waken him. But his two compatriots waiting outside seemed to think 'twas acceptable, and Bardrick desperately needed help, if he were even still alive. Surely Hawkwind, once he heard her out, would understand.

The bulky form of what appeared to be a big, wooden bed took gradual shape as her eyes adapted to the dim light. Someone stirred within it, mumbled an incoherent word, then stilled. Deidra inhaled a steadying breath and strode out across the tent's considerable expanse. A few steps later, she slammed into a stool and tumbled headfirst over it.

"Bloody hell!" a deep masculine voice snarled from the bed. The familiar metallic rasp of a sword being unsheathed filled the air. A woman's soft gasp quickly followed.

"What is it, Hawkwind? What's wrong?"

"Quiet, Bella," the man hushed her. "And stay here."

Bedcovers rustled. Deidra unwound herself from the stool and shoved to her knees. An instant later, a sword tip pressed to her throat. She froze. Her gaze lifted.

A big, powerful form stood over her, a form quite evidently naked from the tautly sculpted outline of muscle and sinew looming out of the shadows. Deidra's throat went dry. Her eyes dropped to scan his body, and saw nothing but the slightest gradations of light and dark. She looked back up to where she imagined his face to be.

"What the hell are you doing in my tent?" Hawkwind emphasized his demand with a smack of the flat of his sword beneath her chin. "Wench though you be, I'll have my answer—and have it now—or you'll pay for this like any man who dares sneak up on me."

"I-I wasn't sneaking," Deidra stammered, forcing her words past a tightly constricted throat. "Your man . . . outside . . . gave me leave."

"Renard? Renard gave you leave?"

The incredulity and rising anger in his voice didn't bode well, Deidra decided. She must find some way, and quickly, to ease his suspicions. "I don't know what his name was, but he was big and dark, and a yellow-haired woman was—"

"'Twas Renard," he cut her off, an undertone of rising irritation tingeing his voice. "What do you want?"

Deidra hesitated. 'Twas the moment she'd dreamed of, had risked her and Bardrick's life for. She licked her lips.

"My visit is twofold. I wish to join your army as well as enlist your aid in finding my old bodyguard—" She quickly corrected herself, deeming her heritage not the wisest thing to share at this moment. "Er, I mean, my friend."

A heavy silence greeted her words. For a moment, Deidra thought he must not have heard. Then, with a growl, Hawkwind once more pressed his sword to her throat. "Pull out that dagger from your boot and hand it to me hilt first."

"How did you know? . . . How could you have seen anything in this light?" Deidra asked, momentarily unsettled by his surprising knowledge. She leaned forward to ease the removal of her dagger, then carefully offered it up to him.

A large, warm, callused hand closed over hers, then withdrew, her dagger commandeered.

"I didn't," Hawkwind replied. "I just suspected such underhanded actions from a person who'd dare sneak into my tent. And if you think me so stupid as to believe you came here solely to join my army, you've—"

"I am *not* underhanded!" Deidra hotly protested. "I walked in here in good faith, with honorable intentions. And, though I never imagined you'd believe *me* stupid, *your* ridiculous suspicions certainly border on it. Yours and that . . . that Renard outside who evidently wished to make me appear the fool!"

"Stupid, am I? Pray, tell me more of your most flattering opinion of me," Hawkwind prodded in a soft, menacing voice as he tossed his sword aside and leaned toward her. Strong fingers grasped Deidra by the arms, dug into the soft flesh, then jerked her up to him.

Suddenly, her face was on a level with his, her body pressed against the full length of his hard, heaving, and most disturbingly nude body. Dark eyes, smoldering with a burning intensity, captured hers. A faint whiff of ale tainted his breath, then was overcome by a much stronger, but surprisingly not distasteful, scent of man-sweat and leather.

Deidra's heart skipped a beat, then commenced a wild pounding. Only the barest of restraint, she instinctively knew, kept his temper in check. She cursed her unruly tongue, realizing it had finally gotten her into some very serious trouble.

"I-I beg pardon," she hurried to apologize. "I meant no offense. You are certainly not a stupid man. No one as famous and successful as you could ever be deemed stu—"

Hawkwind gave her a hard shake. "Cease your mindless chattering!" He ran his hands up her arms in a more gentle but definitely considering manner. "You're a soft one, aren't you? Hardly the stuff of a warrior, but mayhap nicely suited to warm a man's bed. Are you as easy on the eyes as you are to the feel of my hands?"

Indignation surged through Deidra. She twisted in his grasp, which immediately tightened, intent on breaking free. "Is that all you care about? My body? My physical appearance?" Her hands fisted and she managed to strike him on his bare, smooth-skinned chest. "You insult me by your implications! I came here to join your army, not become a camp follower! Unhand me, I say!"

Hawkwind pulled her back up against him. "And I say, you are in my camp now and under my command. I'll do with you exactly as I see fit."

"And is that all you see women good for, then? As whores for your men?"

His broad shoulders lifted briefly in the dim light. "Most times, aye."

Deidra flung back her head and glared up at him with all the defiance she possessed. "The woman outside. She hardly looked the whore to me."

"Alena?" Hawkwind chuckled. "No man, myself included, would be fool enough ever to call her that. But she's the exception. You, on the other hand, are definitely bed-warming material."

The first tendrils of apprehension wafted through Deidra. "Grant me the chance to prove you wrong."

He ran his hand down her back, pulling her yet closer, his touch assessing, appreciative. "Most assuredly," Hawkwind murmured, his voice dropping to a low, throaty, and very suggestive whisper, "if the proving commences in my bed."

As he spoke, something swelled, hardened against Deidra's belly.

She jerked back at the unfamiliar sensation of an aroused male body, a sensation she'd never experienced but had heard quite enough about. "N-nay! Never in your bed! I ask for the chance to demonstrate my skill at sword, to prove my fitness to join you as a warrior. Like . . . like Alena has."

"Hawkwind?" A petulant voice intruded from the bed. "She is a silly child. Send her away and come back to me. I'll prove anything you like."

"Soon, Bella," he tossed his reply over his shoulder, a tolerant amusement tingeing his voice. "But a few moments more and I'll gladly rejoin you. In the meanwhile, I've a young spitfire to tame."

He turned Deidra around and proceeded to shove her in the direction of the bed, until they reached a chair. Hawkwind pressed Deidra down into it. "Stay there while I dress."

She grasped the chair arms, her fingers gouging into the roughly hewn wood. An impulse, to jump up and run from the tent, rose within her. Only the greatest willpower kept Deidra in the chair. Bardrick. If for naught else, she must endure this most humiliating and disappointing of moments for him.

Her old bodyguard had been sadly mistaken or mayhap viewed his former leader with jaded, masculine eyes. But he'd been so very, very wrong about Hawkwind. He was no man of honor. He was like all the rest, governed by power and greed and by his loins when the proper occasion presented itself—which it seemed frequently to do. She'd been a fool to have imagined 'twould be otherwise.

Bardrick. Was there even a twinge of loyalty or affection in Hawkwind's heart for the old man? If there was no hope left for her, she prayed there was yet for her bodyguard.

The rustling of clothes being donned ceased. The bed creaked slightly as Hawkwind sat to pull on his boots, then creaked again as he stood. The thud of hard soles, as he moved back across the tent to her, was muted by the thick carpets, but Deidra still heard—or did she just sense?—his approach.

A hand clasped once more around her arm and tugged slightly. "Up with you now," he ordered in a flat, authoritative voice evidently used to brooking no protest. "Time to return you to Renard and get to the bottom of this little game."

" 'Tis no game," Deidra muttered through clenched teeth. "And I'm not Renard's. I came with Simon."

"Simon, is it now?" Hawkwind gave a snort of disbelief. "Your story grows stranger by the moment. And where did he find you? In the merchants' caravan he and his men raided two night's ago?"

"Aye, 'tis exactly how it happened." Deidra dug in her heels a few feet from the tent doorway. "Bardrick and I were on our way to join you when we decided to take shelter for the night with the merchants, and then—"

"Bardrick? Old Bardrick of Moresham?"

At the incredulity in Hawkwind's voice, Deidra felt a grim satisfaction. At last she had won his attention. "Aye. When he retired from your army, he came to Roth—" She caught herself before she gave away her home. 'Twouldn't do to reveal that. Mercenaries were well-known for holding people hostage for ransoms as a sideline avocation. "He came to my village and we grew into fast friends. 'Twas he who taught me my swordsman's skills.

"The same ones," she added dryly, "you refuse to believe I possess."

"And where is Bardrick now?"

"Back at the merchants' caravan for all I know, mayhap wounded if not dead."

"And when were you going to tell me about this?"

As he spoke, Hawkwind's grip tightened about Deidra's arm until she nearly gasped out loud from the pain. Her hand moved to cover his, and she began to pry at his fingers. "Stop it. You're hurting me!"

"Am I now?" he asked, his voice vibrating with cold fury. "Mayhap you deserve it. I don't like being made a fool of, or manipulated to another's whim."

"I didn't manipulate you!" She dug her nails into his hand in a desperate effort to free herself. "If you'd use that big, thick-skulled head of yours for a moment, you'd realize that. You never allowed me the chance to tell you about Bardrick!"

His grip loosened slightly. "Well, I'm giving you the chance now."

Deidra considered his offer. "I'd like it better if we continued our talk outside. I don't care to stand in the dark with a man."

"Strange, but I'd have thought you'd have preferred it that way. So much is revealed in a person's eyes. Like whether one is telling the truth or not."

"And what will the light of day reveal about you?" Deidra snapped. "That you care not a wit for an old friend and would rather spend your time leching after every woman who crosses your path?"

Hawkwind flipped back the tent flap. "Aye, mayhap. A lot depends on what kind of woman you prove to—" His next words died in his throat.

The light of the rising sun caught Deidra's countenance, illuminating it and casting her in a soft pink glow. Big, doelike brown eyes, framed by long, lush, red-brown lashes, gazed up from a delicately carved face. Her mouth was full, her cheekbones high and exotic, and a faint, musk-rose flush brushed her ivory-complected skin. Auburn hair curled about face and shoulders where several wavy strands had worked free of her long braid.

The slender, but very feminine body accentuated by firmly jutting breasts, a narrow waist, and well-curved hips, combined to convince Hawkwind the girl was the most beautiful piece of woman-flesh he'd ever seen. The sex that had risen so eagerly at the merest brush of her body against his in the darkness of the tent thickened once again. In spite of Simon's possession through right of booty and Bardrick's supposed friendship, Hawkwind knew he must find some way to make the girl his own. Bella, as voluptuous and enthusiastic a lover as she was, paled before this glorious, ethereal—

"Er, were you two coming out or merely wishing a romantic moment together gazing at the sunrise?" Renard asked, his deep voice piercing Hawkwind's heated thoughts. "If Alena and I are intruding on a tender moment, we can easily depart."

Hawkwind jerked his fascinated gaze from the girl's mesmerizing beauty. "What? Nay, both of you, stay. We were just coming to talk with you." He jerked Deidra out of the tent and let the flap fall back. "Weren't we, wench?"

"My name's not wench!" she cried. "And until you choose to call me by my proper name, I'll not utter one more word to you!"

"Won't you now?" Hawkwind all but dragged her over to stand before Renard and Alena. "Then pray, *sweet lady*, grace us with the honor of knowing your name."

Deidra's lips tightened in a mutinous line. She'd be damned if she would answer him as long as he continued on like that. Her shoulders squared, her head tilted a defiant notch, and a fire as resolute as his sprang to life in her eyes.

He gave her another shake, a dark, menacing look tautening his expression and every powerfully muscled line of his body. He'd be quite handsome, Deidra thought dispassionately, with his long, dark brown hair hanging well below his shoulders and his striking jade green eyes, his straight nose, finely chiseled mouth, and rock-solid jaw. Aye, quite handsome, if not for his ugly scowl and the long scar winding down the right side of his face before disappearing in the thick, but close-cropped expanse of his dark beard. If not for his bloodshot eyes, unfriendly glare, and totally boorish behavior.

He stood there, awesome in form and countenance, dressed in tall black boots, finely tanned leather breeches, a gold, hawk-emblazoned medallion hanging around his thick-muscled neck, and a dark linen shirt hastily tucked in. So much the man of legend . . . and yet, not. Despair filled Deidra. Bardrick had been so very, very wrong but, for his sake, for his life, she must swallow her pride.

"Deidra. My name is Deidra," she answered softly. "Are you satisfied now? Can we set out to find Bardrick?"

"Not so fast, *wench*." Hawkwind smiled, the action little more than a wolfish curl of lips away from teeth. "Tell me first about Bardrick. Where do you know him from? And I'd advise you to tell the truth, for I know where I sent him."

She eyed him, then shot his two compatriots a quick glance. They waited, a studied blankness to their expressions while a gleam of curiosity brightened their eyes. They were enjoying this unpleasant scene with Hawkwind immensely. What a strange, twisted lot they all were!

"I told you before, I met Bardrick when he came to my village, a few leagues from Rothgarn Castle," Deidra reiterated patiently, deciding that revelation should be close enough to the truth to satisfy.

"And what exactly was supposed to have happened to him?" Hawkwind pressed on with more interest, satisfied the girl at least was correct about Rothgarn.

"Bardrick was struck down the night before last by men from your army, intent on looting a defenseless merchants' caravan. Bardrick tried to protect them, but was set upon by too many men. I saw him fall just before Simon caught me up on his horse and knocked me unconscious. 'Twas the last thing I remember, until I woke the next day, slung across Simon's horse."

Hawkwind glanced around and caught sight of the man Deidra named. He stood several yards away, leaning against a tree. Hawkwind motioned him over. "Well, Simon?" he demanded when the other man drew up before him. "Are the wench's words true?"

"Aye, m'lord, or at least the part about me taking her." Simon's eyes flickered nervously. "As to the man she speaks of, I know naught of him." He paused. "Have a care, m'lord. Her tale could well be a trap."

"Aye, that it could," Hawkwind agreed gravely. "But she'll rue the day if 'tis." He paused, cocking his head in consideration. "What is the wench to you, Simon?"

"Why, she's my woman, m'lord," the other man eagerly replied, scenting the long-awaited opportunity for profit. "She's a fine wench, is she not? Once she's tamed, I'd wager she'll give me a fine tumble."

"How much do you want for her?"

Simon feigned puzzlement. "How much? Why, a wench as fine as she could never be for sale. There's no amount of money—"

"Five hundred gold crowns. I'll give you five hundred gold crowns."

"How dare you?" Deidra demanded, wheeling about to confront Hawkwind. "I'm not some piece of horseflesh to be bartered for and sold—!"

He jerked her back against him, captured her snugly in the crook of his arm, and planted a large hand over her mouth. "Well, Simon, what's it to be?"

Simon appeared to consider the offer. "Five hundred is quite generous for any wench, but this one is finer than most. I was hoping for a thousand."

"Were you now?" Hawkwind silkily inquired. "And will seven hundred and fifty gold crowns pose a suitable compromise?"

Simon knew when to accept defeat. Though his leader

was a fair man, there was only so far one dared press him. To push any further would lose him not only the girl, but the money as well. He grinned. "Done, m'lord. The wench is yers for seven hundred and fifty crowns."

"Good." Hawkwind made a dismissing motion. "I'll have the money sent to you by midday."

The other man bowed low, then backed away. "As ye wish, m'lord. 'Twill be soon enough." His gaze lifted and he eyed Deidra with a smirk. "She's a hot one, ye know. Have a care or she'll claw yer eyes out."

"Will she now?" Hawkwind drawled. He looked down at Deidra. "Is that the truth of it? Have I bought myself a little wildcat then?" He lowered his hand from her mouth.

"Aye, you swill-sucking, son-of-a swineherd!" Deidra spat. "I'm no man's property to be passed back and forth. I'll soon give you a taste—"

Hawkwind clamped his hand back over her mouth. He sighed and rolled his eyes at his two friends. "Money poorly spent, I can well see. But that is my problem. In the meanwhile, we've plans to make. Though I may live to regret it, I'm inclined to believe the wench's tale about Bardrick. Renard, gather a force of fifty men and prepare to leave in an hour's time. I will lead them.

"And Alena," he added with a rueful chuckle, "I task you with the duty of seeing that my most costly little prize is properly cleansed, garbed, and kept safe until my return. A task," Hawkwind added dryly, as he shoved Deidra toward her, "only another woman could have any hope of easily managing."

"A moment," Renard hastened to interject. "But a moment more of your time."

Hawkwind arched a dark brow. "Aye, and what is it?"

"Simon's words were true. A return to the merchants' caravan could well spell disaster. Allow me to lead the force instead."

"Nay." Hawkwind shook his head. "Though Bardrick was good friend and true to the both of us, 'tis *my* life he saved those many years ago. I owe him the same, at the very least." His piercing gaze sought out and held Deidra's. "Besides, I doubt there is any trap inherent in the wench's tale. To ensure even such an unlikely possibility, however, she'll be held hostage until my return."

"And if you don't? Return, I mean?" Renard prodded.

Broad, linen-clad shoulders lifted in supreme indifference. "Then put her to death. 'Twill be a poor purchase price for my own life, but a debt of a sort paid, nonetheless."

Alena watched the soldier deposit the last steaming bucket of water in the bathing tub and depart, then let the tent flap fall back into place. She shot the auburn-haired girl standing across the room a mocking smile, and gestured toward the copper clad tub. "Your bath is ready, m'lady."

Immediately, Deidra bristled. "Don't call me that! I don't wish to be your lady, only a compatriot."

The blond woman shook her head. "Well, I hate to disappoint you, but Hawkwind has other plans."

Frustration welled in Deidra. Alena was quite obviously a respected warrior who stood high in the level of command to be so well regarded by the mercenary leader. If she could begin by winning the other woman's allegiance . . .

She eyed Alena. A slim woman of medium height, the female warrior was quite feminine in build with small, firm breasts and graceful curves, but the same, sleek muscles were also quite taut and hard. There wasn't an ounce of unnecessary fat on Alena's spare frame. And the wary, intelligent eyes and stance that appeared poised to attack at any moment bespoke a person always ready for the unexpected.

Aye, Deidra thought wearily, always ready and highly suspicious of everything she had and was about to say. Be that as it may, she had naught to lose by attempting to win Alena over. "You don't strike me as a woman who suffers men to make untoward advances," Deidra carefully began.

"Surely you can understand how I feel about being passed from one man to another, my only value what coin and performance in bed will buy."

Once more, Alena gestured toward the tub. "Your water grows cold. And, hot or cold, you will bathe. Hawkwind abhors filthy women."

"Aye, I can well see that," Deidra agreed, realizing her first tack had failed. Well, there were always others. Her glance scanned the interior of the tent. "He certainly likes his luxuries, doesn't he?" As she spoke, she sat down on the nearest chair and began to tug off her boots.

"Why not?" the other woman replied. "Hawkwind deserves this and more, for all he's done and suffered. If you only knew . . ." Alena paused. "But then, 'tisn't any of your business and never will be. Hawkwind will use you as he has every other woman, then toss you aside when he tires of you."

"He has no special lover, then?" Deidra inquired, her voice momentarily muffled as she pulled her tunic over her head. "There's no woman who has ever claimed his heart, his love?"

Alena scowled. "None of us has the leisure for such frivolities. We are warriors, not foppish noblemen with time on their useless hands."

"Well," Deidra remarked as she slipped out of her breeches and strode over to the tub and stepped in, " 'tis a sad thing, to never know love. No wonder Hawkwind is so bitter, so hard, so unkind."

"Indeed?" Alena walked over and handed her a bar of an exotically scented soap. "Well, mayhap he'll fall in love with you, fine lady that you are, and all. You'd like that, wouldn't you?"

Deidra accepted the soap, then shook her head fiercely. "Nay. I want naught of such a life, where a woman is subservient to a man."

"And you think Hawkwind would make a woman of his subservient?"

"Aye, most definitely." Deidra slid beneath the water until all but her head and shoulders were submerged. " 'Twas quite evident, his opinion of women."

"Yet he treats me as equal to any of his men."

Deidra glanced up quickly, in the act of soaping her arm. "Aye, that I have noticed. Can you help me, Alena, to gain the same regard?"

The blond woman gave a snort of disdain. "You? Help you become a warrior? Why, 'tis an impossibility! I've never seen a more pampered body, or softer skin!" Her blue eyes narrowed. "If I hadn't noted the state in which you arrived and the ragged clothes you wore, I'd swear you were some noblewoman, out playing the little peasant lass."

"But you did see how I arrived," Deidra answered sweetly, hastily moving on to distract Alena from further speculations in that realm. "If you give me but a short time to bathe and dress, I'd be delighted to demonstrate my swordsman's skills as well."

"You err if you imagine yourself better than me," Alena growled.

Deidra shrugged. "Mayhap, but I do possess some ability. Though Hawkwind might have doubted my words, Bardrick and I *have* crossed swords many a time."

"Have you now?" Alena grinned, her anger subsiding. "Well, mayhap you'll someday have opportunity to prove it to me. In the meanwhile, however, Hawkwind bade me keep you safe. And safety entails confining you to this tent until his return."

"Safety?" Deidra laughed. "Confinement will keep me from escaping, but the true safety, it seems, is rather in putting as much distance between me and Hawkwind's lustful advances!"

"Mayhap," Alena admitted, "but if I were you, I'd prefer the bed of the commander, than being shared with half the army. Which is exactly what will happen to you," she finished with a grim light gleaming in her eyes, "if you dare try to leave this tent."

A shiver of revulsion rippled down Deidra's spine, but she masked it with a resolute lift of her small chin. "Indeed?"

Alena smiled thinly. "Indeed."

Chapter 4

The search party headed by Hawkwind returned shortly after noon two days later. Deidra, sound asleep on Hawkwind's huge wooden bed and with little else to do cooped up in the well-guarded tent, was awakened to the sound of voices and horses drawing up outside. Excitement and, conversely, a feeling of dread, rippled through her. Would she find Bardrick among the search party or not? If he were there, would he be alive or dead?

She rolled off the thick, feather tick mattress, straightened her mussed clothes, and shoved a hand through her unbound, freshly washed hair. Alena had insisted she take a daily bath in case Hawkwind should unexpectedly arrive. Deidra grimaced at the memory of the blond woman's blunt statement that, though she felt like the mistress of a whorehouse, making certain Hawkwind's newest leman was constantly ready for him, she still preferred that to disappointing him in any way.

In any other case, Deidra would have admired such loyalty and devotion, but not for a man who viewed her only as a piece of feminine flesh to be used solely as a bed partner. Though Alena represented what she aspired to be, a female warrior well respected and in a position of power, doubts had begun to thread their way into Deidra's mind.

Hawkwind, the famed warrior chief, was naught but a

big, lecherous, hard-hearted lunkhead. Alena appeared little more than his slavish underling. Simon seemed an unfortunately typical representation of the common soldier, and Bardrick was mayhap dead. 'Twould seem she had always been sadly in error, and must now pay for it in the most shameful of ways.

As she pulled on her boots and rose to stride across the tent, her mouth tightened into a grim line. Well, one thing at a time. First, she must discover what had become of her old bodyguard. Then, there was the issue of Hawkwind's intent for her. An intent, she fiercely vowed, he'd quickly change or pay the price for.

Bright afternoon sunshine streamed into Deidra's eyes as she lifted the heavy tent flap and stepped out. Her forward progress was immediately halted by the downward swing and joining of two stout spears. She glanced to either side of her and noted the stubborn set of chin and jaw of both of the guards. Her own desires to the contrary, she would go no farther without someone's leave.

Dust settled about the scene of huge war-horses milling around, men dismounting, and dogs running among the returning warriors, barking in gleeful welcome. In the midst of the clamorous melee stood Hawkwind, bent over a litter slung between two horses. Deidra strained to discern who lay in the litter, but Hawkwind's powerful form blocked her view. There was, however, someone there.

She looked about, searching for Alena. The warrior woman was nowhere to be seen. "Please," Deidra pleaded, her gaze swinging from one guard to the other. "Please, let me go to Hawkwind. He mayhap has returned with my friend and I must speak with him."

"Ye'll go nowhere without Hawkwind or Alena's leave," Bruno, the stocky, ruddy-faced, red-haired, older guard snapped. "Ye know the rules. Now, get back into the tent!"

Anger, fanned by a day and a half of utter boredom and mounting frustration, exploded in Deidra. In a swift motion, she elbowed Bruno sharply in the ribs, then swung to kick Hubert, the other guard, in the shin. With an outraged cry of pain, both men dropped their spears and simultaneously grabbed for her. Deidra ducked low, leaped forward, and the two men slammed into each other.

She didn't spare them a backward glance. She was already pounding across the clearing, straight through the erratically milling horses toward the litter. At the two guards' shouts of warning, Hawkwind half turned. Deidra, trying to skirt him with a sudden dodge to the left, never had a chance.

Hawkwind's reflexes, honed to blinding speed by years of battle, reacted far faster than she. A heavily muscled arm snaked out, caught her by the waist, and jerked her to him. Her soft flesh collided with a rock-hard body. The air escaped from her lungs in a strangled whoosh. Her head smacked against his chest and, for a fleeting instant, stars danced before her eyes.

"I'm truly flattered by your eagerness to greet me," Hawkwind's deep voice rumbled against her ear, "but next time try and temper it with some consideration for my guards." He grasped both her arms in his large hands and shoved her back from him. A ruthless light gleamed in his jade green eyes. "Henceforth, I expect your 'devotion' to me to include obeying my every command."

· Deidra tossed the wild tangle of hair from her face and glared up at him. "I have no eagerness whatsoever to welcome you," she snapped. "And I don't feel any devotion or need to obey you, either! I came only to see if you'd found Bardrick."

He arched a dark brow and subjected her to an amused scrutiny, the long scar on the right side of his face puckering with the movement. "Your concern for him is rather disconcerting. A lesser man might find offense, even jealousy, in your interest."

"But not you, I'm sure," she replied with biting sarcasm. Deidra attempted to twist free of his iron clasp and lean around to inspect behind him. "Did you find him? Is he all right?"

With an exasperated shake of his head, Hawkwind released her. "Aye, we found Bardrick. But he is sorely wounded and may not live."

Even as he spoke the final words, Deidra was already at the old warrior's side, kneeling to examine him more closely. Bardrick lay there, unconscious, pale of face, breathing erratically. A makeshift bandage wound about his head, blood staining the cloth at the base of his skull and the rolled up blanket beneath that served as a pillow.

She stripped back the shabby quilt covering him, searching for sign of other injury. Bloodstains from a few superficial sword wounds reddened his tunic, but Deidra knew they weren't the source of Bardrick's grave condition. 'Twas the mace blow to the back of his head. She stroked his face with a gentle, tender hand, then glanced up at Hawkwind.

He'd been watching her intently, a strange light gleaming in his eyes that was quickly shuttered when her gaze met his. "I fear there's not much that can be done for him," he stated bluntly. "The blow to his head near to shattered the base of his skull."

"Nay." Deidra shook her head in stubborn denial, blinking back a hot swell of tears. "I won't believe that until I've had a chance more fully to examine him. And a physician." She looked wildly around her. "Where is your physician?"

"We have no physician, lass," Hawkwind softly informed her, moved by her quite evident and sincere affection for the old warrior. He took her by the arm. "Come. My men will carry Bardrick to my tent. He can at least die in some peace and comfort there."

She dug in her heels as he attempted to pull her along. "He needs a physician! If you've none of your own, send for the Lord of Wendover's. He owes you that much, at the very least, for your service to him."

Hawkwind's jaw tightened. "I ask no favors from one of his kind. We take care of our own." He jerked her forward.

"Now, come along. I'll not have you make a scene out here. 'Twon't do Bardrick any good at any rate."

"Nay!" Deidra wailed. "If you're too proud to go to the Lord of Wendover, I will. He'll listen to me. I won't let Bardrick die because of you!"

"Not another word from you!" he snarled, his patience at an end. He should have known the wench wouldn't remain reasonable for long. With a swift motion, Hawkwind leaned down, grasped Deidra about the hips, and swung her over his shoulder.

For an instant she hung head down, stunned, her bottom disconcertingly high in the air thanks to his great height, the breath once more squeezed from her lungs. Then, with an enraged cry, Deidra began to squirm and pound on Hawkwind's back. "Let me down, curse you! You have no right to treat me this way. Let me down, I say!"

"Seven hundred and fifty gold crowns says I *do* have the right," he muttered as he strode back up the hill to his tent. "And if you don't immediately cease your squalling, I'll relieve myself of even that loss by selling you to the next available man!"

He emphasized the seriousness of his intent with a swat to her backside. Though red-faced, humiliated, and so angry she could have clawed his eyes out if she could only have reached them, Deidra fought past her rage, knowing this wasn't the time to press her argument. Later, though, she'd make certain he regretted his treatment of her. Later, but not while Bardrick's life was still at stake.

"Fine," she gasped as each jolting stride again and again forced the air from her. "I'll . . . be quiet. But I beg of you, send for . . . someone more skilled to help Bardrick. He said . . . you were his friend. A friend wouldn't let him die . . . without trying everything."

"I don't need you telling me how to treat my friends," Hawkwind growled. "But if 'twill ease that sharp tongue of yours in the knowing, I've already sent for our healer."

"Healer?" she squeaked in relief. "Then you do . . . have a physician?"

"Nay. A *healer.* A woman skilled in herbs and incantations. She travels with the army."

"Herbs? Incantations?" Deidra shifted her weight to take the pressure of Hawkwind's shoulder off her stomach. "But Bardrick has need of more than that! He needs to be bled, mayhap purged—"

"And have it hasten his death as well," Hawkwind added grimly. "You talk more and more like some pampered, ignorant noblewoman, to give such credence to the useless skills of a physician. We prefer to use the services of Maud. She has surprising powers, some of which we don't care to know or dare ask about, but most effective powers, nonetheless."

He halted, grasped Deidra with what she felt was a most intimate touch below her hips, and swung her down. As her feet touched ground, she shrugged out of his grasp and shot him a disdainful look. The effort, however, was distinctly muted by the tousled fall of hair in her face. With an exasperated motion, Deidra flipped her hair back, then turned with as much dignity as she could muster and stalked into the tent.

The litter bearing Bardrick soon followed. Hawkwind motioned the men to carry the old warrior to his bed. After quickly laying several cloths over the pillow to protect it from bloodstains and pulling off Bardrick's muddy boots and cutting away his torn tunic, they laid him on the bed. He groaned, muttered a few incoherent words, then quieted once more.

Deidra pulled the satin comforter up around him. "Has he regained consciousness or spoken at all?" she asked, finally turning to Hawkwind.

"Only once. And then, when he recognized me, he grabbed me in a most powerful grip and uttered the strangest words." His eyes narrowed. "Bardrick bade me take care of you and return you safely home."

Deidra's mouth went dry. "And did he say where my home was?"

Hawkwind shook his head. "Nay. He lost consciousness before he could answer me that. But 'twas no secret at any rate. You already told me you're from Rothgarn lands."

Relief flooded her. "Ah, aye, so I did."

He eyed her closely. "He cares for you deeply. Truly, what are you to him?"

"Naught but good and true friends." Deidra forced herself to meet his gaze, praying her dissembling of the actual facts wouldn't betray her. "I told you that before."

"And I don't believe that's all of it," Hawkwind replied, studying her intently. "There's more here than you care to reveal, isn't there?"

As he spoke, he gently captured Deidra's chin in the callused clasp of his hand and lifted her gaze to his. There was something about the piercing quality of his glance that drew her, something that transcended the heated animosity between them, the anger and frustration. Suddenly, Deidra caught a fleeting glimpse of the man she'd always imagined him to be—good, honorable, with a certain fineness and nobility of spirit that took her breath away. For the first time, she saw the man hidden beneath the harsh exterior, beneath the rough words and actions, the bitterness.

The answer she knew he desired rose to her lips. There was naught to fear in him. Though Hawkwind was a man to be reckoned with, he was also a man to be loved and respected.

In a rush of insight, she saw him as Alena and Renard must see him, as most of his army must see him as well— proud, courageous, resolute. He was also, Deidra belatedly reminded herself, noting the desire that gradually flared in his striking eyes as he continued to gaze down at her, a man of strong physical appetites, capable of a passion that could easily color what he considered right and wrong.

The realization stunned her, for she couldn't perceive from whence this strange new knowledge arose. She had little experience in understanding that darker side of males, of fathoming the smoldering fires that constantly burned so close to the surface of all their actions, impacting on every facet of their relationships with women. Yet, in some primal, feminine way, Deidra saw and knew it nonetheless. And the knowing stirred an answering response within her.

She wrenched her face away, suddenly afraid to delve deeper. "There's naught more," she insisted firmly, no longer able to meet his gaze. "I've already told you all you needed to know. Besides, what does it matter from whence I come?" Deidra gestured toward Bardrick, lying motionless on the bed. "He is what matters—at least to me."

"And to me, as well," Hawkwind softly replied, looking toward the old warrior. "He saved my life many years ago. Can what he's done for you compare?"

"Nay," Deidra admitted, "but 'tis a hard thing to put a price on friendship, on a man who gave me hope, who stirred my dreams and accepted me as more than just a woman and piece of chattel. In one sense, he gave *me* a new life, as well."

The tent flap lifted behind them, a brief glare of sun, before the interior was once again bathed in muted light. Deidra and Hawkwind turned. A woman, of middle age and dressed in a long, green, hooded robe, bustled over. Her thin lips twitched in annoyance as she glared up at Hawkwind. Then, when her glance swung briefly to Deidra, her eyes narrowed, sharpening to an intent, slightly surprised appraisal.

"Why have ye summoned me here today?" she demanded as she seemed to recover herself and round on the big man standing before her. "Ye haven't been to battle of late, so where are yer wounded? Ye know I stay up till near dawn each night, picking and preparing my herbs, so why have ye dragged me so early from my bed? Have ye no consideration for a working woman?"

"Aye, that I do." Hawkwind smilingly tried to soothe her. "But I do have need of your healing services." He stepped aside so she could see his bed. " 'Tis Bardrick, Maud. He is sorely wounded and desperately needs you."

Maud's gray eyes widened in dismay. She hurried over to the bed. "Ah, Bardrick, ye old wolfhound. What have ye gone and done now?" She leaned over, slid her hand beneath his head, and gently probed. "Ah, by the Mother, his scalp is naught but a mass of raw meat!"

The healer withdrew her bloodied fingers and wiped them on her apron. "Quick, fetch me a pot of boiling water," she shot over her shoulder at Hawkwind. "And you, girl," Maud added, eyeing Deidra, "bring over my box of tools and healing potions and powders."

Deidra hurried to do her bidding and by the time Hawkwind returned with a small iron pot of steaming water, the two women had Bardrick on his stomach and much of his shaggy hair cut away more fully to expose his head wound. The injury was indeed serious, the flesh macerated, crusted with blood and already beginning to swell and redden with infection. Through the mangled skin, bits of broken bone could be seen, sharp little harbingers of the damage the mace had done to Bardrick's skull.

"Does he have a chance?" Deidra's big eyes lifted to the healer in silent entreaty. "I wouldn't have Bardrick die because of my foolish desires that led him to this."

"And what exactly did you ask of him?" Hawkwind demanded, drawing up directly behind her. " 'Tis past time you tell me all."

Maud wrapped a cloth about the pot he held and placed it on the small chest standing beside the bed. "And I say, away with ye now, unless ye care to help in this. Yer personal squabbles have no place at a sickbed." She turned back to Hawkwind. "Do I make myself clear?"

He eyed her with a frown and raised brow. For the space of an inhaled breath, Deidra thought he might order the healer from the tent.

Then Hawkwind nodded. "Aye, as always, Maud, you've made yourself clear enough. What the wench and I have between us can wait a time more." He shot Deidra a piercing look. "But not too much longer."

She repaid his glance with a disdainful toss of her head, then turned her attention back to Maud. There was not much for either her or Hawkwind to do, as Maud's nimble fingers flew across Bardrick's wound, trimming dead flesh, removing the pieces of shattered bone, then flushing the cavity with warm water. Finally, she packed the gaping hole full of crushed yarrow leaves, covered it all with a clean bandage and wrapped it snugly in place.

She glanced up at Deidra and Hawkwind. "I've done all I can for the time being. Give him a spoonful of this willow bark tea every four or five hours," she instructed, handing Deidra a small, covered pottery cup. " 'Twill promote his sweating and ease the fever that is sure to come." Maud replaced her tools in her box, closed the lid and rose.

"I'd hoped you'd stay with him," Hawkwind began. "I've little knowledge of such things and she," he graced Deidra with a disparaging look, "shows no apparent talent for healing, either."

Deidra bristled at the insult. "And what could you possibly know about me, you big lumbering lunkhead? All you care about is finding new women to ease your loins with, one of which," she added fiercely, "certainly won't ever be me!"

A thunderous expression darkened Hawkwind's face. " 'Twill if I deem it so, wench. But that's not the issue here right now. Do you or don't you know anything about healing? I'll not leave Bardrick in your hands if you're incapable—"

"I know enough, if Maud will stay a short while more to answer a few questions," Deidra cut him off. "You may go, if you've more important matters to attend to."

"More important?" Hawkwind's bearded jaw tautened with rage. "I have an entire army to see to. As much as I care for Bardrick, I cannot limit myself to the welfare of one man. Some of us don't have the luxury of concerning ourselves with just a few people. Or with just our own, petty desires," he finished acidly, gracing her with a frigid glare.

"My, my," Maud intruded, chuckling in amusement. "Aren't ye two a pair of equally matched hotheads? Well, I won't have such bickering going on around my patient. Get on with ye now," she said, making a shooing motion of her hands toward Hawkwind. "I'll stay with the girl until she knows what she must to care for Bardrick."

Hawkwind shot Deidra one last, skeptical look, then shrugged. "As you wish, Maud. I'll be sure and check back on Bardrick's condition as often as I can."

"As will I," the healer soothed. "But my time now is better spent in enlisting the aid of the Earth Goddess. Only through the enhancement of my natural powers will I be able truly to make the difference between life and death for Bardrick."

Deidra's brown eyes went huge. "What powers are you speaking of? If you mean magic, I don't want you touching Bardrick with those foul skills. He is helpless and cannot defend himself. I'll not let you steal his—"

"There is no evil in what I do, girl." Maud silenced her with a gentle smile. "Though I call upon the ancient arts, the Crafts of the Wise, I am only a simple spell caster. Besides," she added, giving Bardrick an affectionate glance, "the old wolfhound and I are longtime friends. If he could speak, he would ease your fears."

"She speaks true, lass," Hawkwind said. "They were once *very* good friends indeed."

Maud smiled and Deidra was struck by how the action brightened and softened her features until she seemed almost beautiful. As if for the first time, Deidra noted the soft gray eyes, the ebony sheen of her silver-threaded hair, the faint pink flush to her flawless cheeks and lips. Though Maud was a woman past her prime, the lines lightly etching her face marred not a whit the radiance of a woman who had devoted her life in the selfless service of others.

She relaxed, both strangely drawn and filled with the sudden knowledge there was naught to be feared in Maud's magical powers.

"Are ye more at ease with me now?" the older woman asked. "If ye're truly the good friend of Bardrick's ye claim to be, I'd like for us to be friends as well."

Deidra glanced from Maud to Hawkwind and back again. "Aye, that I am, and I suppose you've eased my doubts for the moment. But only time will tell what will happen later."

The healer nodded. "Aye, time will, I'd wager, and in ways ye've yet even to guess." She turned to Hawkwind. "Ye may go. We women have much to do."

As the big warrior leader departed, both women turned back to Bardrick. Back to a man who they, each in her own way, felt a deep, abiding love for. A long moment passed as the two women stared down at him. Then, with a deep sigh, Maud pulled over the large, intricately carved chair sitting nearby.

She perched the ample swell of a womanly hip on the edge of the bed and gestured toward the chair. "Sit, girl. We have much to talk about, not the least of which is the care of Bardrick."

Deidra took her seat, frowning up at the healer in puzzlement. "I don't know what you mean."

Maud arched a brow. "Don't ye now? Then I will state it simply. Ye have powers of magic far surpassing mine. I sensed it from the first instant I walked into this tent. And I ask ye, as one sorceress to another, why have ye come to Hawkwind's camp?"

Hawkwind didn't return to the tent until late that night, after several quick visits throughout the day to assure himself Deidra was in control of the situation. Bardrick's condition didn't change as the hours passed, neither improving or worsening. Deidra didn't know whether to think that a good sign or not.

She had other matters to occupy her as the hours wore on. Matters like the memory of her outraged response to Maud's shocking pronouncement. Despite Deidra's protests to the contrary, the healer refused to be swayed—and also refused to offer further explanation. When she was ready to listen, Maud had firmly informed her, they would speak again of it. But not before.

Deidra had immediately dropped the unnerving subject, refusing to render it any additional credence by further discussion, and the two women had gone on to speak of Bardrick's care. Though she guessed Maud imagined her curiosity would eventually get the best of her, Deidra knew differently. If the healer truly wanted to be friends, she'd picked a most insulting way to begin. Yet, though she fought to keep Maud's strange words out of her mind, the memory returned again and again in the long, quiet hours at Bardrick's bedside.

Finally, near midnight, Deidra dozed off in the chair she'd set beside the bed. The next thing she recalled were hands, sliding behind her back and beneath her thighs, startling her awake. She stirred, her eyes opening drowsily as she was lifted in the air and pressed to a hard, warm body. It was dark, only the glimmering light from a single brazier illuminating the tent, yet sufficient to identify the man who held her.

"H-Hawkwind," she murmured in surprise. "What are you—?"

"Hush, lass," his deep, rich voice vibrated against her cheek. "I've made a pallet for you to sleep upon. There's no purpose served in you sitting up all night. Maud is here and will take watch the rest of the night."

Deidra's gaze swung about the room, searching until she found the healer. She smiled, her earlier anger at the woman muted by her contented sleepiness. "Thank you, Maud. Are you certain you don't wish to rest yourself? I can watch Bardrick now. I just fell asleep for a short time, but feel quite refreshed."

She made a move to push away from Hawkwind, but his grasp about her only tightened. "Nay, lass. You'll sleep. The night is Maud's time. She'll take care of Bardrick now."

"As you wish," Deidra whispered, already falling back asleep, lulled by the strong, rhythmic thud of Hawkwind's heart. "But call me, if you need . . ."

Hawkwind smiled as her voice faded and slumber once more claimed her. He strode across the tent to where he'd laid several thick furs with pillows and a comforter atop them. Lowering Deidra to the makeshift bed, he gently laid her down.

For a long moment Hawkwind stared at her, his gaze missing nothing from the slightly parted, provocatively full and rosy lips to the soft rise and fall of her young, tender breasts. Hungrily, his eyes followed the undulating curves of her slender body, pausing to admire the rounded swell of her buttocks and long, shapely flare of her calves and thighs.

Something stirred in him, a fire, an ardent desire to take her soft body in his arms, to clasp her to him, to know the ecstasy of her deepest, darkest woman's secrets. And he would, soon enough, he vowed.

She was his, fairly bought and claimed. 'Twas but a matter of time before she accepted that fact and liked, nay, eagerly desired it, as all his women eventually did.

For all her fire and defiance, in the end she would be like all the others. She had to. He dared not permit her to be anything else.

Chapter 5

"By all the saints!" Deidra exclaimed the next morning when she awoke to find Hawkwind sleeping beside her. "How dare you presume . . . ?" She paused to fling a hank of auburn hair out of her face and glare down at the man who had drowsily opened his eyes to stare up at her.

He wore breeches, dark tunic, and the now oddly familiar gold medallion that gleamed dully just below the hollow of his throat. For an instant, Deidra's mesmerized gaze snared on the smooth, tautly muscled expanse of his chest, exposed by the deep V of his tunic. Then she wrenched her gaze back up to his.

"How dare you take advantage of my trust to . . . to . . ." she demanded, forcing the words past a mouth suddenly gone dry.

"To do what?" With a devilish smirk, Hawkwind levered to one elbow to bring himself closer to her. "What exactly have I done, your ladyship, by sleeping next to you? Are you naked, or are even your clothes in disarray from my filthy, pawing hands?"

Deidra leaned back, putting a more comfortable distance between them, then glanced down at herself. Her tunic and breeches were quite intact and, as far as she could tell, her body felt the same as always. "It doesn't matter," she stubbornly persisted. "If . . . if I were a . . . a noblewoman, you'd have ruined my reputation. No decent man would have me now."

"But you *aren't* a noblewoman, are you?" Hawkwind reminded her, reaching out to capture a long lock of her hair. Ever so gently, but insistently, he pulled her to him, until their lips were but a hairsbreadth apart. "And everyone here knows you're already mine, so there's no issue of reputation or decency to worry over. 'Tis a pity, though, wouldn't you say, that your reputation has been ruined without any pleasure on either of our parts?"

Deidra jerked back and was rewarded by a painful tug on her hair for her efforts. "I see naught pleasurable in being forced into something I've no desire for, by a man I despise, in the bargain. Let me go, I say!"

"Despise, do you?" Firm, sensual lips curled back from strong, white teeth set in a wolfish grin. "And how can you speak of that which you know naught of? Every man is different, as is his lovemaking. Are you so certain you'd despise what I might do to you?" He pulled her closer, his lips brushing hers. Ever so slowly he stroked her mouth with his, feather-light caresses that traced the soft fullness of her lips.

"D-don't," Deidra quavered, surprisingly unsettled by his nearness and touch. "I don't want—"

"You don't know what you want, sweet lass," Hawkwind huskily silenced her, "until you know what there *is* to want. Don't be afraid. I mean no harm. All I want is a kiss."

A kiss. 'Twas a simple enough thing to give him if 'twould satisfy that suddenly heated look in his eyes. If 'twould get him to let her go and ease the unnerving closeness of their bodies. 'Twas wiser to cede him this tiny victory than force him into action of a more aggressive nature. She knew enough to realize a struggle might only inflame his lust, not quench it.

And there was no one else in the tent to aid her for the moment, Deidra thought as her frantic gaze scanned the interior. Bardrick still lay unconscious in the bed, and

Maud was nowhere to be seen. The choice, and its consequences, was in her hands.

She exhaled a shuddering breath. "A kiss then, if you vow 'twill be the end of it. Just make it quick."

His expression darkened, going taut, angry. "You overstep yourself in making demands. A kiss mayhap 'twill be the end of it this time, but I'll make no vow as to later. And I won't agree to make it quick; either."

Before Deidra could respond, Hawkwind covered her mouth with his, taking her in a cruel, ravishing kiss. The hand not engaged in holding her hair slid around to clasp her upper back, pressing her into him. She squirmed against the close contact, but it did little but tighten his hold on her. With a soft sigh, Deidra yielded, sensing 'twas the best of all options.

His tongue emerged, rough, rasping, to probe at the entrance to her mouth. He parted her lips, only to meet the resolute barrier of her teeth. With a frustrated curse, Hawkwind pulled back.

"You are singularly miserly in fulfilling your part of the bargain."

She glared over at him. "Miserly? Isn't it enough that you force yourself on me? Must you now insult me as well? You asked for a kiss. I have given it to you!"

His gaze narrowed. "Can you truly be as ignorant as you appear? Surely a lass traveling alone with a merchants' caravan can't still be a maiden." He scowled, the first hint of irritation tightening his mouth. "Play no coy games with me, wench!"

"Curse you," Deidra cried, attempting to twist away despite the painful hold he still had on her hair. "I play no games! And I owe you no explanation for my lack of experience, either!"

Hawkwind jerked her back to him, his muscular thighs moving to straddle hers as he forced her onto her back. "Are you a maiden then? Is that the truth of it?"

" 'Tisn't your concern!"

Ever so slowly, he lowered himself atop her. "Ah, but 'tis, wench. I find virgins extremely tiresome, and certainly not worth seven hundred and fifty crowns. I paid for an experienced woman, not some puling virgin! Damn Simon," Hawkwind snarled, growing angrier by the second. "I'll have my money back, and more, for his deception!"

"And how was Simon to know?" Deidra demanded, suddenly more loath to be given back to the equally lecherous soldier than endure his commander's advances. "He had no chance to discover otherwise, and I certainly didn't share the secret of my maidenhood with him. Besides," she sniffed, "until this moment I hadn't realized my purity was something to be despised. Most men—"

"I'm not most men!" he cut her off furiously. With a disgusted grimace, Hawkwind freed Deidra's hair and rolled away. "Get up. Get away from me before I forget myself and forswear a solemn vow I made long ago not to deflower another virgin!"

"Fine!" Deidra snapped. "And be assured of my continued efforts not to tempt you to such a sacrilegious act. Become a monk, for all I care!"

"Well, well, well," Maud's amused voice intruded from the tent opening. "I see the two of ye have made significant progress in getting to know each other."

Both Hawkwind and Deidra hastily sat up and lifted their gazes to where the healer stood. She smiled benignly back at them, then stepped into the tent, letting the glare of the late morning sun disappear behind the falling flap. A pot of steaming water in her hands, she strode over to the table sitting beside the bed, deposited the pot, then turned to them.

"Bardrick is better. He is still a bit feverish, but his breathing has evened and his wound heals. The Goddess has smiled on him."

Mortified she had forgotten all about the old warrior in her angry preoccupation with Hawkwind, Deidra sprang to her feet and ran to Bardrick's side. He had indeed improved, his color less hectic, the bleeding decreased to a slight oozing on his bandages. A fierce joy swelled within her.

She turned to Maud. " 'Twas your herbs and potions that saved him, not some vile powers. How can I ever thank you?"

Maud smiled. "I demand no thanks. I did it out of love. 'Tis the best reason of all to use magic—and the source of the greatest power."

"As you say," Deidra said, reluctant to discuss the subject further, "but, in the end, all that truly matters is Bardrick's recovery." She glanced down at him, her nose wrinkling as his scent wafted up to her. "He badly needs a bath. Is it too soon to dare wash him?"

"So, ye noticed that, did ye?" The healer gave a rare, tinkling laugh. "Men and cheese do tend to a certain rankness after a few days. But, aye, 'tis soon enough. A cool bath will only ease his fever the quicker."

"Rank, are we?" Hawkwind walked over, shaking his head. "Truly, Maud, how am I ever to woo this most feisty of wenches if you persist in insulting men?"

" 'Twas a hopeless effort from the start," Deidra silkily observed. "And I'm not a wench."

"Indeed?" Hawkwind retorted in the same silky tone of voice. "Mayhap when you stop acting like one, I'll stop calling you one."

"Keep your hands off me, and mayhap I will!"

A hard, glittering look flared in his eyes. "And why would I want to give you what you want? Rather, I'd say you need a bit of taming, and I'm just the man to do it!"

"And I want no more fighting around this sickbed," Maud intruded with a stern glance at both Hawkwind and Deidra. She pointed toward the tent doorway. "Off with ye now," she said, motioning to Hawkwind. "Haven't ye duties elsewhere?"

"Aye, I suppose I do," he admitted grudgingly, "but it grows increasingly disturbing to me of late that I'm being constantly thrown out of my own living quarters. Is there no end to the trouble this red-haired spitfire will cause me?"

"Most likely not," Maud replied, already turning back to the task of removing Bardrick's soiled bandages. "But then, I'd say ye brought it on yerself, so I've little pity for ye."

Her only answer was a disgruntled snort before the tent flap fell back in place.

In another two days' time, Bardrick, though weak and unable to mumble more than a few slurred sounds, was deemed well enough to move to Maud's little makeshift hospital. As Deidra, still confined to Hawkwind's tent, watched them carry Bardrick off on a litter, a sinking sensation settled in the pit of her stomach. Without Bardrick's inhibiting presence in Hawkwind's tent, she greatly feared what the warrior chief might do.

The look he sent her didn't ease her growing concern a whit, either. As she'd turned from watching Bardrick being borne away, her gaze slammed into Hawkwind's, who was standing right behind her. His dark green eyes, glittering like bits of jade, gleamed with a strange new light. A light of possessive appraisal and renewed lust, Deidra quickly decided. Two emotions she didn't care for at all. Not at all . . .

With a defiant toss of her head, she stepped around him and stalked back into the tent. No matter how he looked at her, she wouldn't allow him to intimidate her. And if he thought to force himself upon her now that Bardrick was safely away—

A large hand grasped Deidra's arm and spun her around. Eyes, now dark with anger, glared down at her. Dispassionately, she noted the scar trailing down the right side of his face glinted silver in the tautness of his bearded jaw. And, just as dispassionately, Deidra realized she should be afraid. But she was past fear with him. Somehow, she knew he'd not harm her.

"Don't ever walk away without my leave," Hawkwind rasped, giving her a small shake. "My men have suffered severe punishments for even the slightest disrespect or disobedience. I'll not have them seeing you doing the same without receiving as equally a severe retribution."

"Are you threatening to punish me then?" In spite of herself, she couldn't help but taunt him. If he only knew how far he stepped above himself to speak to her this way. "Do you have to beat your women to make them obey? No wonder you don't keep any for long."

He scowled. "I keep them as long as *I* want them. And," he added half under his breath, "you may well be the one I dispose of quickest."

"A most pleasant consideration to be sure." Deidra smiled sweetly. "Mayhap you *should* allow me to join your army. Then you'd have full power to punish me as you do your men."

"You're not joining my army! There's only one way you'll serve me and that's in my bed." Hawkwind flung her away, his mouth grim, his mind made up. "Tonight, wench. Your service to me begins tonight."

With that he turned on his heel and strode out of the tent. Behind him, Deidra's voice, shrill with anger and defiance, followed him.

"Never, do you hear me?" she screamed. "Not tonight or any night! I won't be your whore. I won't!"

Bruno and Hubert, standing outside guard exchanged amused glances and shook their heads. Renard, who was sitting a short distance away, looked up from the sword he was sharpening and exchanged a conspiratorial grin with the two men.

"Hawkwind has bought himself a hellion this time." Hubert chuckled, as he met Renard's eye.

"Aye," Bruno added, bobbing his head as he warmed to the topic. "It only remains to be seen who will tame who in this lovers' battle. Myself, though, I look forward to it, whatever the outcome. A war camp between battles needs a little excitement. And why should our leader always have the women falling at his feet? Aye, 'tis past time he suffer a few pangs of the heart."

A fleeting sadness flared in Renard's eyes. "Aye, 'tis past time, though Hawkwind would be the last to admit it. One way or another, 'twill only do him good."

As the day faded to twilight and then darkness, the panic, long kept at bay, began to gain ground in Deidra's heart. There seemed no hope of escape. The tent was too well guarded, too stout to claw her way through and she had naught sharp enough to cut the heavy hemp cloth with at any rate. By the time she managed to dig a hole out from beneath, the additional guard who walked the tent's perimeter would have made his rounds and found her. And, even if she'd managed to escape there was still the matter of sneaking through the entire camp without detection.

Most of Hawkwind's men didn't know what the woman he kept so secretly ensconced in his tent looked like. Deidra knew if she were caught by any of them she'd be fair game. The thought chilled her to the marrow of her bones. One way or another, it seemed she was destined to lose her virginity tonight. The only choice left her was to wait passively here or take her chances outside. To accept the unwelcome advances of one man, or many.

In the end, 'twould all be Hawkwind's fault, no matter what happened. *He* was the one forcing her into this, whether 'twas he who took her maidenhood or his men. By the saints, she thought, her hands fisting at her sides, how she hated him!

Time and again Deidra scoured his tent, pillaging his clothes chests for anything that might have inadvertently been missed. A small ornamental dagger, a cloak pin, anything that might be used in her defense. But there was naught. For all the sumptuous comfort of Hawkwind's tent, he kept few trinkets about.

The night drew on and still Hawkwind didn't return.

Deidra began to hope he might have changed his mind, mayhap decided she wasn't worth the time and effort, and found his pleasure with one of the many camp followers. Surely Bella still desired him in her bed. Surely—

The harsh slap of the tent flap lifting interrupted Deidra's heartening thoughts. She swung around. There, standing in the doorway, was Hawkwind.

For a fleeting instant, Deidra thought she'd faint right there on the spot. Was there naught that would go her way? Then she squared her shoulders, tossed back her long flow of hair, and glared over at him.

"I'd thought you'd have found easier entertainment than what you'll get here this night," she said.

His mouth quirked. "Indeed? And what do you know of my tastes in women? Mayhap I like a feisty lass with a bit of fire to her. 'Tis said a battle only sweetens the eventual coupling."

Deidra flushed. "I-I wouldn't know, or care to know." She began to back away as Hawkwind let the tent flap fall and advanced on her. "Surely there are other women more suited to your taste. Bella seemed quite pretty, and—"

"Enough of your silly prattle!" Hawkwind confronted her from the other side of the brass table Deidra had scooted behind. "Your talk and avoidance of me will change naught. I've decided I want you, and have you I will."

" 'Twill be rape then," Deidra whispered. "I'll never willingly submit."

A cold wrath settled over his features. "I don't rape women."

" 'Twill be rape, nonetheless."

"Then I'll sell you back to Simon or, if he no longer wants you, one of my other men." Hawkwind's glance skimmed the length of Deidra's body, then lifted to the rounded swell of her breasts. "You're a comely lass. I'll have no trouble getting my money back."

"Is that all you care about?" Her fingers clenched around the raised bronze braiding of the table edge. "Your precious money? What about me? Haven't you a shred of honor, of compassion left in that shriveled thing beating within you called a heart?"

"Honor serves no one, least of all the one who lives by it. And I gave up that foolish ideal long ago." He gestured about him. "This is all that counts, this, my word, and the welfare of my men. Those are the only forms of honor I still live by."

"Then let me join your men, be a warrior in your army," Deidra pleaded, championing her cause with all the eloquence she possessed. "Then I will matter to you. Then you will see me as someone of value, rather than as just a body to be used, or traded away when the whim strikes you. Give me a chance to prove myself. Please!"

If she only knew how beguiling, how near to irresistible she was standing there, Hawkwind thought, her voice low, husky, her beautiful face and form softly illuminated by the flickering firelight. If only she could see herself, she'd realize her cause was lost even before she opened her mouth. She was too much a woman, too delicate, too fine, to dare risk in battle. Nay, 'twould be the worst kind of travesty. He'd rather give her to another than endanger one hair on her head.

"Make your choice, lass," Hawkwind whispered thickly, "and make it fast. 'Tis either me or one of my men. Is there one in camp who catches your fancy? If so, speak his name, or I'll make the choice myself—and 'twill be for me."

There was no hope of swaying him, Deidra thought in rising misery. Why was he being so obstinate, so cruel? Ah, why had she ever left home?

Yet, would her fate have been any different if she'd remained at Rothgarn? 'Twouldn't, save instead of a courageous, albeit arrogant warrior as her lover, she'd have been forced to take that slimy, treacherous Basil D'Mondeville. But was there no other choice?

Time, Deidra told herself. She must buy more time while

she fashioned some sort of a plan to thwart him, thwart them all.

Her gaze dropped to the intricate scrollwork of the brass table. Distractedly, she traced the inlaid swirls and curls with a slender finger. "If I gave myself to you tonight, would you then reconsider letting me become one of your army?" She lifted her eyes and met his boldly. "More than anything I want to be free, to be a warrior. Almost enough to give my body as trade."

"I'd want you for more than one night, lass," was Hawkwind's husky reply. "And I couldn't promise I'd ever let you join my army. You're not the type. You're meant to please a man, not kill him."

Curse him, Deidra thought. He refuses to give anything away. Well, there were other armies out there to be joined. If she could just find some way to take him unawares, to lull him into a false sense of security and then knock him out.

Or wound him, she thought with a wild surge of hope as her gaze dropped to the dagger still strapped to his waist. Once he was overcome, she could use the weapon to quickly cut her way out of the tent as well as defend herself. A dagger had worked before. It could work again.

But to harm Hawkwind . . .

He had said she wasn't meant to kill a man. Well, he didn't believe she was proficient with a sword, either, and 'twas a foolish thing to underestimate an opponent. Bardrick had taught her that again and again. Hawkwind might soon learn the same lesson. But first, she must get him to lower his guard.

She sighed, her shoulders slumping in defeat. "What would you have me do? I cannot win against a man like you. You and I both know it."

"This needn't be unpleasant, lass." Hawkwind smiled and motioned her to come to him. "I'll be gentle, if that's what you want. My women have never had complaint with my lovemaking."

"How wonderful for them," Deidra muttered under her breath as she made her reluctant way around the table. She halted when she stood before him. "Well, what now?"

Hawkwind grinned. "You truly are a maiden, aren't you?"

Irritation filled her. "Aye. I told you that before. Is it my fault you mean to break that holy vow of yours?"

"Nay," he admitted, his expression going intense, solemn, as he gazed down at her. "'Tis my fault, and one I may well rue, but in your case I find I'm willing to make an exception."

"How very kind."

His hand lifted and cupped the side of her face. "You needn't make this so hard, you know." His fingers threaded through Deidra's hair until they clasped the back of her head. Ever so gently yet inexorably, Hawkwind pulled her to him. "If you'd just relax, you might discover there is much to enjoy."

Aye, relax, Deidra told herself. Let him think you have surrendered. 'Tis the only way to catch him off guard and gain his dagger.

She forced a smile. "Help me. Tell me what you want."

"Nay," he growled, pulling her against the full, hardened length of his body, "rather, let me show you instead."

With that, Hawkwind grasped her jaw in the huge expanse of his other hand and claimed her mouth with his. As before, his kiss wasn't gentle. It was all male, demanding, hard, hungry. And, this time, as his tongue boldly prodded for entry, he squeezed her jaw open. In the space of a startled gasp, Hawkwind had claimed the first of her woman's secrets.

He tasted of ale, strong, heady, yet most pleasantly sense-stirring. He smelled of man and leather, musky, hot, and arousing. He felt so hard, the planes and angles of his big, powerfully muscled body wildly exciting beneath Deidra's frantically repelling, then delightedly exploring hands. Suddenly, he was everything she despised and yet everything she'd ever wanted even before she'd even known what she wanted.

Excitement, desire, pounded through her veins. He encompassed her, drawing her to heights she'd never dreamed of. A wild, hot mist engulfed her. Thunder roared in her ears.

Deidra grasped at Hawkwind's forearms to steady herself, clutching at the bronze arm gauntlets. Her fingers dug into the unrelenting metal, gouging frantically in an effort to maintain a grip on reality. But 'twas for naught.

She was back at Rothgarn, the night of the storm, the night she'd slipped away. A face rose out of the wind and lightning and rain. A face with haunted, bitter eyes. A face she now recognized as Hawkwind's.

With a strangled cry, Deidra wrenched away. "Nay! Ah, by the Mother, please! Don't!" She grabbed at the dagger hanging at his side. Before Hawkwind could react she slashed downward with it. Or striking a glancing slice across his back.

He hissed in pain, lurched away, then grabbed Deidra's arm and twisted it behind her. Fingers tightened about her wrist in a cruel vise, clamping the blood from flowing to her hand. Deidra struggled wildly against him, a woman gone mad in her terror and pain. But 'twas to no avail. Her slender body was no match for his overwhelming strength. Her hand finally opened in a spasm of bloodless fingers. The dagger fell to the carpet with a soft thud.

"Why?" Hawkwind snarled. "Why did you do this? I told you I meant you no harm. There was no need!—"

"My freedom!" Deidra continued to squirm in his clasp, beating and clawing at him with her free hand until Hawkwind was forced to capture it as well. "You meant to take away the freedom to choose who I laid with, the control over my own body! I ran away from that at Rothgarn, risked my life and Bardrick's to join your army in the hope of finally having some choice in my life. And then . . . and then you once more try to take it away from me! You," she choked, the tears filling her eyes and spilling over in her frustration and despair, "you, who I always dreamed of, thought would be different!"

He went still. "Different from what?"

"From every other man," Deidra sobbed. "I thought *you* at least would be good, would be honorable. Bardrick said you were, b-but he was wrong. S-so very, very wrong!"

"There's little honor left in the world," Hawkwind replied gruffly. "Why, in a mercenary's camp, would you think to find it different?"

"B-because I was a fool!" She lifted her tear-filled gaze to his, refusing to be cowed, even now, in her moment of greatest defeat. "Because there was naught else to hope for, and I *knew* there was something better, somewhere."

"I used to think that," he muttered, "but learned the bitter truth of it. There's naught out there but survival, and taking from others before they take from you."

"Then how do you live, how do you go on, knowing that?" Deidra whispered.

Hawkwind shrugged. "What else is there to do?"

The utter futility of her naive little quest engulfed Deidra in one mind- and body-numbing rush. She'd been insane to imagine life could be any different. There was no choice, no freedom in anything. Each was bound by his heritage and upbringing. Far better to accept it and find what good there was in a preordained fate than rail in misery for the rest of one's days. Far better to return to Rothgarn and Basil D'Mondeville, than to stay here and be the whore of a soul-dead man.

Which was exactly what Hawkwind was, whether he knew it or not. Something in his past had seared the heart from him and, great leader that he might be, she couldn't follow a man who lived without hope. She couldn't stay with him, no matter the vision, no matter how, in some twisted way, she felt inexplicably drawn to him.

"Let me go home, back to my father," Deidra begged,

swiping away the last, traitorous tear. "I was wrong to come here. I-I made a terrible mistake. Just l-let me go home!"

"Back to Rothgarn?" Hawkwind eyed her with disbelief. "Allow you to set out alone, on unfriendly roads in a dangerous land? How long do you think your precious maidenhood would last out there alone?"

"I don't care! Out there, at least I'd have some chance. Here, I have none!"

"Who are you really, lass?" His voice lowered, softened. "From the start I've wondered about you, thought you too refined, too cosseted to be a peasant, though there seemed no other plausible explanation for your roaming the land with only Bardrick for companion. But now I begin to think you're higher born than you'd like me to believe."

"Does it matter? Aren't all women the same to you?"

"Aye." He nodded slowly. "In most cases they are. But I confess to a most unsettling curiosity about you. And," he added, "I won't let you go until I know the truth."

Hope flared in her eyes. "But once I tell you, you promise to let me go?"

Hawkwind gave a bitter laugh. "Oh, aye. I need no further trouble from the likes of you."

Deidra searched his face, weighing the decision to reveal her real identity, and found a true sincerity burning in his eyes. "You give me your word then?"

Irritation flashed across his face. "Didn't I just say that? Aye, that I do."

She inhaled a steadying breath. "Then I'll tell you, thought I wonder if you'll believe it even then." She lifted her chin and locked gazes with him. "I am the Lord of Rothgarn's daughter."

For a long moment Hawkwind just stared down at her, his mind racing to comprehend this most startling of revelations. He'd expected her to be some wealthy merchant's daughter, and hoped to ransom her back to her family, but this . . . This was more than he'd ever dared hope for.

Excitement, then a fierce elation, coursed through him.

Though he'd thought to finally win back what was right-fully his in bargain with D'Mondeville, this slender, pretty girl standing proudly before him could well hold the key to a far easier solution. *If* she were truly who she said she was.

"The Lord of Rothgarn's daughter, are you?" He released her and stepped back. "And why should I believe you?"

"Take me back and see," Deidra replied, a wild hope springing in her breast. "My father will gladly claim me."

"Will he now?" Hawkwind cocked his head as he studied her with an intent, calculating look. "And will he also pay handsomely for you?"

Deidra's heart sank. "You'd ask for ransom?"

"Aye. I deserve some recompense for the trouble you've caused me, as well as for returning you to him unharmed." A fierce light gleamed in his eyes. "And untainted."

"But you swore to let me go if I told you who I was!"

A grim smile glimmered on Hawkwind's lips. "And I will. But naught was said about how I planned to go about it, was there?"

Anger filled Deidra, anger and a sense of rising frustra-tion. "Then you mean to ransom me, do you?"

"Aye, lass. That I do."

Chapter 6

"What? You want what?" Hawkwind wheeled around from the war-horse he was grooming.

Alena stood there, refusing to back down from his sudden explosive indignation. She knew him well enough to recognize the difference between his rare, smoldering, dangerous kind of anger and the brief, emotional outbursts. She squared her shoulders and lifted her chin.

"I want you to let Deidra out of your tent."

Hawkwind's eyes narrowed. He cocked his head, his stance taut and wary. "Why this sudden concern for the wench? I never noted before that any fast friendship had sprung up between you two."

Alena shrugged. "She grows on you. Besides, anyone who can withstand your overpowering, intimidating presence and still give as much as she gets has my respect. It has been five days now you've kept her cooped up in that tent. I've never seen you be so cruel to one of your women."

"Ah, so that's how 'tis." Hawkwind turned back to currying his horse. "You women are joining forces against me."

"Joining forces?" Alena gave a disparaging laugh. "We don't need to join forces. Either one of us can handle you alone. You're not as tough as you make yourself out to be, for all your masculine blustering."

Hawkwind ceased his grooming and turned. "You can handle me, can you? And how so, Alena? That little harridan continues to claim she is an excellent swordswoman. Do you, too?"

She grinned. How she enjoyed baiting him! "You know I am, but that wasn't my point. I just meant you're not the kind of man intentionally to be cruel to a woman. So, there must be some other cause for it."

"Indeed?" A dangerous light flickered in his rich green eyes. "And what might that be?"

Alena pretended sudden interest in a loose thread on her tunic. " 'Tisn't apparent? Deidra has stirred something in you that no other has."

He scowled. "Aye, that she has. She's the most acid-tongued, vicious—"

"You like her," Alena interrupted before he could continue. "Very much."

Anger flared in Hawkwind's eyes. "Nay, I don't."

"Then prove it. Treat her as any of your other women. Let her at least have the freedom of the camp. Even the men are beginning to remark on your unusual behavior."

"Are they now?" he asked silkily. "That smacks of men idle for too long. Mayhap I'll have to find additional work to still their wagging tongues." He threw the currying brush into the tack box and grabbed up the stiff hide brush. With sharp flicks of his wrist, he swept the loose dirt from his horse's coat. "Thank the Mother we'll break camp soon for the next campaign. Soldiers with too much time on their hands turn into a gaggle of gossiping women!"

"Aye, that they do," Alena agreed. "But what of Deidra in the meanwhile? Can't she come out for at least a few hours a day? She'd like to visit Bardrick."

Hawkwind's head jerked up. Ever so slowly, he turned. "She told you that? She asked you to talk with me?"

"Deidra?" Alena laughed. "Nay. She's as stubborn as you in this battle of wills. I only surmised that's what she'd want to do. It does seem logical, does it not, considering her evident affection for Bardrick?"

"Aye, I'd imagine so," he admitted grudgingly. "You may bring her out for an hour to visit Bardrick and to walk her about the camp. But only for an hour, and I hold you responsible for her conduct and guarding. She's become a very valuable hostage. I'll not have her escaping. Understood?"

Alena nodded. "Understood. 'Tis a kind thing you do, Hawkwind. The Mother will bless you for it."

"The Mother, indeed," he gritted as he swung back to the brushing of his horse. The only thing the Mother had done was curse him with the most aggravating, unsettling of problems, all rolled up in one little provocative face and figure.

The past two nights, since he'd sent Renard off to ferret out the truth about Deidra's claim, had been sheer misery. To even sleep in the same tent with her, though he was now back in his own bed and she adamantly remained on the floor pallet, required all of Hawkwind's considerable self-restraint. His need, however, to keep her under close guard *and* a maiden until Renard's return had gained even greater import with the possibility of her relationship to the Lord of Rothgarn.

One part of him wanted to believe her, for 'twould solve his most pressing problem in the ransom he'd demand and most surely get for the Rothgarn heiress. There were no other children; Rothgarn's daughter was an only child. Though he'd given his word to D'Mondeville and would still lay siege to Rothgarn on the nobleman's command, he'd already have what he valued most out of the deal. D'Mondeville's payment, on top of it all, would now be sheer profit.

Yet another part of him wished her claim was a lie. 'Twould solve his unsettling, growing hunger for her. Liar, schemer, and aggravating little spitfire that she was, Deidra was also the most beguiling, desirable woman he'd ever met. There was just something about her . . .

A most frustrating of dilemmas, Hawkwind decided. The fulfillment of a long-held dream against the increasingly intense craving for a seductively difficult woman. His loins versus his ambition. He knew what his choice should be. Yet he didn't like it. Didn't like it at all.

"Truly?" Deidra wasn't quite sure she'd heard Alena right. "I can come out of this tent?"

"Aye," the blond woman said. "Hawkwind gave you leave to visit Bardrick and walk about the camp for an hour. 'Tisn't much, I know, but 'tis a start. If all goes well, mayhap I can get him to increase it on the morrow."

Deidra laughed in delight. "Oh, 'twill go quite well. I'll be the soul of decorum and modesty. I'll do anything to be free of this dark, dank tent."

"Even thank Hawkwind for his kindness in allowing you out?"

Automatically, Deidra's mouth opened to provide Alena with her true opinion of the big warrior chief. Yet, when she noted the other woman's watchful, speculative gaze, she immediately thought better of it. Alena was testing her, plumbing her resolve not to cause further trouble. Her brief foray into the outside world might well hinge on her response.

Deidra bit her lip and nodded. "Aye, I'll thank him, if that's what you want."

" 'Twould seem the polite thing to do, would it not?" Alena motioned toward the tent entrance. "Shall we be going?"

For an instant Deidra looked confused, then realized the other woman's intent. "Oh, aye. Please." She strode across the tent and lifted the flap. "After you, Alena."

The blond warrior woman grinned, then walked over and slipped out. She waited for Deidra on the other side, then shot her a friendly glance.

Deidra stood there, blinking in the warm summer sunshine, a big smile on her face. A soft breeze caressed her cheek. The scents of a war camp wafted to her—strong, pungent, and sense-stirring. The sounds, of horses whickering, of men laughing and shouting, of birds chirping in the nearby trees, floated to her ears. She felt as if she'd been freed from prison.

She inhaled a deep breath, threw out her arms, and wheeled around. "By the saints, 'tis good to be back in the world!"

"A far different one than you've been used to, I'd wager," Alena offered dryly.

Deidra halted and shot her an uncertain glance. "What do you mean?"

"You needn't play games with me. Hawkwind told Renard and me who you claim your father is. He finds it useful to share most things with his two war captains."

"You're a war captain?" Deidra breathed in admiration. "Hawkwind would truly allow a woman to rise that far in his army?"

"He's not the ogre you imagine him to be. In his own way, he can be quite reasonable when the situation serves."

Deidra's lips tightened. "Well, I have yet to see anything reasonable about him. He hasn't given me one chance to prove myself."

"Nay, he hasn't," Alena admitted. "It seems you touched him the wrong way from the start. I've never seen him act quite like this before."

"What can I do to change his dislike of me, Alena?" Deidra turned to her, concern furrowing her brow. Impatiently, she flung back an auburn curl the breeze had blown into her face. "I want naught of him, save that he give me a chance to join his army. He's just so . . . so pigheaded and close-minded. Please, Alena. Tell me what to do and I'll strive to do it!"

"Why would a fine lady such as yourself—if you truly are who you say you are—care so much about what

Hawkwind thinks or wants? And your desire to join our army is . . . well, 'tis insane!"

A bittersweet pain flashed in Deidra's eyes. "Aye, it must seem so to you. But you have never known anything but freedom and total control over your life and fate. I, on the other hand, have always lived constrained by others, my life, the ownership of my own body, my fate all predetermined. I am naught more than a pawn in men's hands to further their own goals."

"Yet a soft, safe life, nonetheless. I find it hard to pity you."

"I ask not for yours or anyone's pity!" Deidra cried. "I make no excuse for what I did in leaving Rothgarn. I take full responsibility for what has happened and may happen. 'Tis all I've ever wanted—the ability to make my own choices, and live with the consequences."

"Even to nearly getting Bardrick killed?"

Deidra's face fell. "I regret that deeply. I never wished for him to be harmed. He came after me when I left Rothgarn, intent on bringing me back. I convinced him, instead, to bring me here."

"And you seriously intended to join our army? To become a warrior?"

"I know it seems passing strange," Deidra said with a small smile, "to hear this from a noblewoman. It seems strange to me, when I pause to consider it. But ever since Bardrick came to Rothgarn and my father appointed him my bodyguard, he has told me tales of Hawkwind and his exploits. He taught me to use a sword—and I swear I truly can—and nourished my heart and mind with hope for a better way."

"A better way?" Alena gave a snort of disbelief. "Living as a mercenary? Enduring the filth, the cold, the stink, the pain? Knowing your life won't see its natural span and always wondering if your next battle will be your last? I'd say you're a spoiled, headstrong, stupid girl who doesn't know when she has it good!"

"Mayhap." Deidra shot her a thoughtful look. "Don't you think I haven't considered that, in these past days imprisoned in Hawkwind's tent? It sickens me, every time I think about it. Yet the fire still burns within me to live this life and bear with whatever its consequences. Though I may not as yet truly fathom the difficulties, you also have no concept of what 'tis like to live without freedom." She smiled sadly. "Until you ever do, Alena, you've no cause to judge me so harshly."

The blond woman eyed her. "Aye, 'tis true enough. I've always done what I wished and know no other way. 'Tis just passing hard to consider that one such as you could put such high stock in it. I think you're not at all like the usual noblewoman."

Deidra sighed. "Aye, that much is true, or at least my father and Bardrick constantly tell me so." She glanced around. "Speaking of Bardrick, is it possible we can visit him now? My hour is fast waning."

"Oh, aye." Alena paused, a strange glint in her eyes. "But first, I think it only proper that we pay Hawkwind a short visit."

Deidra frowned. "Why?"

"To thank him, silly one. You did agree to that, didn't you?"

"Aye, that I did," Deidra admitted reluctantly. She squared her shoulders and indicated Alena should lead out. "Let's get it over with, shall we?"

The warrior woman chuckled. "Come along then. And don't make it sound so like you're going to your execution. He is but a man, of flesh and bone as are we."

He was definitely more than just flesh and bone, Deidra thought with a strange, aching pang as they approached him a few minutes later. Hawkwind was bent over one of his war-horse's huge front hooves, picking it clean. He was shirtless, a light sheen of sweat glinting off the broad, golden expanse of his back. The ripple and swell of muscle and sinew as he worked filled her with a breath-grabbing, primal heat.

Deidra had seen men bare chested before, had distantly noted if they were fit or not, but nothing had ever prepared her for Hawkwind. He was in superb condition, not an extra bit of fat on him, his sun bronzed skin stretched taut over bulging muscle. But, on closer inspection, the added aspects of his now exposed and heretofore unseen flesh filled her with a startled, confusing swirl of emotion.

Hawkwind was severely scarred. A multitude of old sword wounds crisscrossed his back in an irregular pattern of puckered, white slashes. One particularly large one in his right upper shoulder had drawn in the flesh so severely it quite obviously hampered the full movement of his arm.

Deidra felt herself go light-headed, her vision cloud. She jerked to a halt, struggling for breath. Then, briefly, her gaze cleared to a scene not at all what she had expected it to be.

The day was shrouded in white, a bright winter sun glinting off the snow like so many diamonds. A band of heavily armed warriors on horseback surged around a single man, their swords lifting and falling as they fell upon him. In a moment suspended in time, Deidra saw it all, the cruel sword thrusts, the mace blow that finally stunned the man, providing the final opportunity his opponents needed.

They attacked him then like a swarm of bees, hacking and cutting, driving their swords deep into his body. The onslaught was too fierce for the man to bear for long. His sword dropped from his hand. He toppled from his horse into the new-fallen snow. And, at long last, Deidra saw his face. 'Twas Hawkwind, years younger, but Hawkwind, nonetheless.

A rough shake of her shoulder jerked Deidra back. She blinked and turned slowly to meet Alena's gaze. The other woman shot her a quizzical look, then, noting her shocked expression as she glanced back at Hawkwind, silently shook her head in warning. Deidra swallowed hard, masked her horror and confusion, and forced herself to stride on.

"I see you lost no time in freeing the wench," Hawkwind threw over his shoulder when they drew up behind him. He never paused or looked back as he lowered his horse's hoof gently to the ground and moved to the rear one. " 'Twill be a wasted effort, I fear. I doubt she'll appreciate it."

In the anger of the moment, all consideration of the unsettling vision fled Deidra. She scowled and opened her mouth to tell him what she thought of his disparaging remark, when a hand firmly clasped about her forearm. She glanced over at Alena, who once more shook her head.

"In that you are mistaken. Deidra deeply appreciates the gesture," the blond woman hurried to offer. "And I didn't realize you'd placed restrictions on when we took the hour."

"I didn't, and you know it," he growled. "Just get on with it."

"Oh, we will," Alena replied sweetly. "But first, Deidra has something to say to you."

Momentarily he paused, then resumed his task. "Does she? Well, what is it, wench?"

"My name is Deidra, *not* wench, and I'd appreciate the courtesy of you facing me when I speak to you."

Hawkwind went still, straightened, then turned. Beside her, Alena expelled a low groan, but Deidra didn't care. The cursedly arrogant, blatantly rude man needed to learn some manners. And if he wished a measure of courtesy from her, he'd damn well render her the same!

"Well, get on with it then, *Deidra*," Hawkwind demanded tightly, a muscle leaping in his bearded jaw. "What is it your queenship desires?"

At his thunderous glower, Deidra swallowed hard. Suddenly, she couldn't quite seem to meet his gaze. Her glance dipped to his chest and upper torso. What she saw there, however, did nothing to restore her rapidly waning composure.

A long white scar transversed his chest from left shoulder to his right lower rib cage. Several smaller scars marred the smooth, broad swell of pectoral muscles and rippling abdomen. And his right forearm bore signs of a horrible mace blow that had torn open his arm.

Once again, the memory of the battlefield vision flooded Deidra. 'Twas where Hawkwind had gained the majority of his now healed wounds, she realized, and certainly the most life-threatening ones. But why? And how had he survived them?

"I await an answer," Hawkwind's deep voice, tinged with barely contained irritation, harshly intruded. "I've no time for a social visit."

Deidra threw aside her disorientation with a fierce shake of her head. "I-I came to thank you for your kindness in allowing me out of the tent." She lifted her gaze to meet his. "'Tis truly appreciated."

Her open, sincere attitude caught Hawkwind by surprise. He'd expected further argument and defiance, but not this. And the sudden softening of her mouth, the glow in her eyes as she lifted her long-lashed gaze to his, sent his heart to pounding and the blood to pool in his groin.

Hawkwind choked back a frustrated groan. Would even the simple sight of her soon rouse him? At the rate he was going, he'd never make it until Renard's return! And neither would Deidra's maidenhood . . .

"Your thanks is accepted," he growled, then paused. When nothing more was forthcoming from Deidra, he arched a dark brow. "Is there more? If not, begone with you. I can't idle the day away in nice talk with noble ladies."

"Why you arrogant, ill-mannered knave!" Deidra exclaimed in outrage. "I'll have you know—"

Before she could enmesh herself further, Alena was dragging her away. "Come along, Deidra," she said. "Your time grows short and you still wanted to visit with Bardrick, didn't you?"

The reminder was enough to put a halt to Deidra's angry diatribe. "Oh, aye, that I do. And I have little time to spare in idle talk, either." To punctuate her point, she shot Hawkwind one final, scathing look before turning on her heel and striding away.

Alena glanced over at Hawkwind, pursed her lips in disgust, and shook her head. "A pair of squabbling crows, you two are. I don't know why I even bother!"

"Neither do I," Hawkwind muttered. "And no one asked you to, either."

Her gaze narrowed for an instant. Then Alena turned and followed Deidra. Hawkwind gazed after the two women for a moment more, then resumed the grooming of his horse. His good mood for the day, however, was permanently ruined.

Deidra hesitated when they drew up outside Maud's tent. Alena shot her a puzzled look. "What's the matter, Deidra?"

"Naught," she lied, knowing quite well 'twas her reluctance to endure the probing eyes and further cryptic words of the healer.

The woman unnerved her, if the truth be told, and the recent, unsettling vision of Hawkwind and how he'd acquired his terrible scars did little to ease Deidra's apprehension. There was something very strange, almost magical, about how the vision had come to her. Just as strange as the vision of Hawkwind that night of the storm . . .

Never before had she had any hint of magical powers about her. Never, until they came to her, unbidden and unwanted, in regards to Hawkwind. What did it all mean? And why were they only about him?

Deidra shivered, the first tendrils of premonition wafting through her. Her fate had always been meant to join with his. Somehow, for some reason, their lives had been destined to entwine. But was this magic, or just destiny? Suddenly, Deidra didn't want to know, no matter the source.

As if they were no longer of consequence, she shrugged her nagging thoughts aside. Plastering a bland smile upon her face, Deidra motioned to Alena. "Please, after you," she said, indicating the tent opening.

Alena nodded, then paused. "I saw your look when you noted Hawkwind's scars. I'll warn you now; he doesn't like mention made of them."

"They pain his heart as well as body, don't they?"

The blond woman gave a small start of surprise. "How did you know? . . . How *would* you know that?"

Deidra realized she'd inadvertently revealed more than was wise. She shook her head. "Isn't it obvious? Most of the scars, especially the most terrible, look about the same age. It doesn't take much imagination to surmise they were all delivered in the same battle—one that must have surely nearly taken his life. That memory would leave lasting scars on anyone's soul."

"Well," Alena began, still eyeing her warily, "I won't comment further on Hawkwind's private matters, save to repeat not to speak to him of it. You have only begun to taste his anger if you dare broach the subject."

"I thank you for the warning," Deidra gravely replied. "I asked you for help in dealing with him, and I deeply appreciate your counsel."

Alena managed a wry grin. "I'll do my best. Hawkwind's been like a brother to me—the only one I'll ever know—all the years of my growing. I'll do anything to spare him harm or pain." Her gaze sharpened. "Be forewarned, as well, that I'll help you and your cause just as long as it doesn't hurt Hawkwind. If it ever does . . ."

Deidra lifted the tent flap. "I understand. He has always been there for you. 'Tis only fitting you render him the first loyalty." She paused, carefully considering her next words. "I'll tell you true, though, Alena. I wish him no harm. He's the most infuriating, arrogant, pigheaded man, but there is still something about him . . ."

Once again, a premonitory shudder wracked her slender frame, but Deidra fought past it and managed a wan smile. "Come, let us enter and visit Bardrick."

"Nay." The warrior woman shook her head. "You go in and see him. I visited the old war-horse earlier. I'll wait for you outside."

The thought of facing Maud without Alena's solid presence beside her didn't set well with Deidra. She opened her mouth to protest, then thought better of it. The issue of Maud was hers to deal with, not Alena's. Deidra nodded. "As you wish."

She stepped through and into the tent, wishing she didn't feel so much like a man going to his doom. Behind her, far in the distance, thunder boomed, heralding another storm. That prospect didn't improve Deidra's glum mood at all.

Rain poured down upon the thick hemp fabric of the tent roof, an incessant, repetitive, mind-numbing staccato that only intensified Deidra's sense of confinement and rising anxiety. It had been eight hours now since she'd completed her visit with Bardrick and returned to her cloth prison. The brief freedom outside had only made her sojourn back in the tent seem even worse.

Bardrick was better, if the disappearance of his fever and continued healing of his wound could be considered an improvement. But he still remained largely unconscious, save for short periods when he awoke, confused, slurred of speech, and restless. 'Twas naught anyone could do but wait, Maud had solemnly informed her. That and give him the best care possible.

Deidra had sat by his bedside until Alena called for her, holding Bardrick's hand and stroking his brow. He seemed to calm when she did that, ceasing his restless tossing and turning, his unintelligible mutterings and anxious, vacant stares. Even Maud had commented on the soothing effect she had on him.

The reassurance would have eased some of Deidra's guilt if she hadn't also noted the speculative gleam in Maud's eye as she mouthed the words. Deidra knew what the healer was thinking—'twas magic that had made the difference. She chose, instead, to ignore the frequent openings the other woman gave her to discuss the topic further, just as intent on avoiding the discussion as Maud was to broach it.

But now, as she restlessly paced the spacious confines of her luxurious prison, Deidra wondered who she dreaded being with most—Maud or Hawkwind. Both, in their own way, reminded her, nay, taunted her, with a mystery she'd never before faced. And Hawkwind, to add even further to her uneasiness, also affected her on a more primal, lust-driven level.

If his overt comments about his desire for her, that night she'd revealed her true parentage, hadn't been enough, the heated looks he frequently sent her each evening since then, before finally ordering her to bed, would have given her sufficient cause to worry. He still wanted her, and she sensed, in some instinctive, feminine way, that his lust would only increase as the days passed. She knew the tension building within her, whenever she thought of him or was near him, certainly was.

As if her thoughts had summoned him, Hawkwind strode into the tent just then, dripping wet though he wore his cloak, and shivering. Deidra jumped up from the chair she'd just forced herself to take a seat in, and whirled around. At the fierce look he sent her, her heart began to thud beneath her breast.

He was pale, the skin pulled taut over the bones of his ruggedly hewn face, and a dark, haunted, agonized look gleamed in his eyes. His long hair, matted damply against his head in sleek, shiny hanks, trickled a thin, continuous stream of water down his face. With a savage curse, Hawkwind flung aside his cloak, shoved his hand through his hair to get it out of his eyes, and strode over to where the flagon of ale sat.

With a shaking, surprisingly unsteady hand, he poured himself a cup of ale, downed it in two gulps, then poured himself another. That, too, was dispatched as quickly as the first. He didn't stop there. Hawkwind filled yet another cup to the brim with ale before he finally turned to confront Deidra.

"What are you looking at?" he demanded in a pain-rasped voice. "Why aren't you already abed?"

"I-I couldn't sleep." Deidra's wide-eyed glance scanned him, noting the harsh, ragged breathing, the shudders that racked his body. She strode over to the chest and pulled out a blanket. "Here," she said, striding back to hand it to Hawkwind. "Strip out of those wet clothes and wrap yourself in this. 'Twill warm you better than that ale."

"I don't drink the ale for warmth, damn you," he growled, all but ripping the blanket from her grasp. "I drink it to ease my pain."

"Your pain?" For an instant, Deidra was confused, then comprehension filled her. "From your battle wounds, that day they set upon you in the snow?"

Hawkwind's cup halted halfway to his mouth. He stared over at her, a thunderous expression building in his eyes. Then, ever so slowly, the cup lowered. "Who told you about that? I vow, if Alena spread tales . . ."

"Nay, 'twasn't Alena," Deidra hastened to say. " 'Twas . . ." Her voice faded. By the saints, why had she spoken so thoughtlessly? 'Twas her compassion at seeing his physical anguish, that she well knew, but now there was no way to hide the truth. *Whatever* that might actually be.

"Then speak," Hawkwind growled. "I haven't patience this night for your games." He lifted the cup and gulped down its contents, then strode over and poured himself yet another, the blanket still clenched in his other hand. "Well?"

"I saw you in a vision," Deidra began, "though I know

not how or why it occurred. That is all I know. You were set upon by a band of men and viciously attacked."

"A vision was it?" He cocked a dark brow. "Are you a sorceress like Maud then?"

Revulsion shivered through her. "Oh, nay. Never that!"

Hawkwind downed his cup of ale, then set it on the table and strode over to her. In a swift movement, he grabbed Deidra by the arm and jerked her to him.

"Then what *are* you?" He gave her a rough shake. "Mayhap not Rothgarn's daughter at all, but a spy then? Sent to undermine me?" He gave her another hard shake, until Deidra's teeth rattled in her head. "Speak, wench. Answer me. Now, before I forget you're a woman and force the truth out of you by any means I can!"

Chapter 7

"I am the Lord of Rothgarn's daughter, and naught more!" Deidra cried. She twisted in his grasp and lifted a fisted hand to strike him hard on his shoulder.

Hawkwind winced at the blow. Capturing her free hand, he forced it to her side. "Curse you!" he gritted. "If you've any sense about you, stop this struggling immediately. I told you before—"

"Aye, I know what you told me," Deidra cut him off. "Mayhap 'twould be better if we discuss this later, when you've a chance to calm."

"Calm? Later?" Hawkwind gave a harsh, disparaging laugh. "I won't calm, sweet lady, until the rain stops and the bulk of the dampness eases. 'Tis *that* which causes my pain."

At the barely contained anguish in his voice, her brow furrowed in sudden concern. She forgot the anger and frustration that had so recently driven her and peered anxiously up at him. "Surely Maud has something to soothe the ache?"

"Nay. Naught she has tried has ever worked."

"Then what of her purported magic? Will she not use it to aid you?"

"Her magic is not for me." He shook his head and released her. "Naught works, save the ale, if consumed in large enough quantities."

"So, you drink yourself into a stupor, do you? Poor man." Deidra's hand lifted to stroke his cheek.

A large hand shot out to capture her wrist. "What do you think you're doing?" he demanded, his voice cracking like a whiplash.

"N-naught," Deidra stammered, startled by his unexpected response. "I thought only to comfort you."

"You thought to *pity* me," Hawkwind growled, "and I want none of it!" He spun her around and escorted her across the tent to the door.

"What are you about?" she cried, digging in her heels and writhing in his grasp. "I meant no harm. I meant only—"

"I don't care what you meant. I don't want it!" Hawkwind swung up the tent flap and called to his guard. The man hurried over.

Rain poured from the skies. The gusts of wind only intensified the chilling blasts of water swirling through the camp. Deidra shrank back, but the solid wall of Hawkwind's body standing behind her prevented her retreat.

"Aye, Chief?" the dripping wet guard asked. "What is it ye wish?"

Hawkwind shoved Deidra into the astonished man's arms. "Here. Take her to Maud until I next send for her."

Before Deidra could turn around to face him, much less utter a protest, the warrior leader stepped back inside and pulled down the tent flap. For an instant, anger flared inside her. Then the rain, pelting down on her head and clothes, beckoned Deidra back to reality. 'Twas better she find shelter elsewhere this night than endure Hawkwind's boorish mood.

Deidra turned to the guard. "If you please, I'd like to get out of this rain."

The man gaped at her momentarily, then nodded. "Aye,

lady. 'Twould seem a wise plan." He took her by the arm and hurried across camp to the healer's tent. Once there, he unceremoniously shoved her inside.

She glanced around, bemused at finding herself in Maud's presence twice now in one day. The interior of the tent was quite spacious, only Hawkwind's private quarters and the command tent being larger. Several cots were lined up along the wall nearest the tent opening, half filled with warriors nursing a variety of ailments. Three large chests stood conveniently nearby.

One was open and neatly sectioned into cubicles and trays filled with dried herbs, jars of salves and potions. Deidra stepped farther inside. Trained as she was in a smattering of healing arts as Lady of Rothgarn Castle, her experienced nose quickly caught the aromatic scents of mint, thyme, chamomile, vervain, and rosemary mingled with the more pungent odors of garlic and onion bulbs.

She smiled. Maud was well-grounded in the use of the medicinal herbs, for all her claims to more mystical powers. The older woman caught the smile as she looked up from her ministrations at Bardrick's bedside, shook her head, and smiled in return.

"He tossed ye out, didn't he?"

"Nay, 'twasn't that way . . ." Deidra drew up beside her, flushing hotly at the knowing gleam in the healer's eyes. She sighed and nodded. "Aye, that he did and I don't understand why. He's tolerated far more dissension in the past and not sent me from him."

Maud indicated the small stool beside her. "Come. Sit, child. 'Twill be a time now before he'll ask for yer return. His old wounds pain him fiercely on nights such as these. He did ye a service in sending ye away. All he'll do is drink himself senseless, but until he does, he can go near mad from the pain."

"Then we must do something for him!" Deidra cried, filled with a sudden mixture of fear and frustration. " 'Tisn't right to let him suffer like that!"

The healer arched a speculative brow. "Ye care that much for Hawkwind, do ye?"

"N-nay," Deidra hastily replied, desperate to avoid such a topic. "I-I just feel the same compassion for him as I would anyone in pain. No one deserves to suffer so terribly."

" 'Tis a pity then," Maud said with a sigh. "I'd hoped ye cared enough to try yer magic on him. 'Tis the only thing that might help him."

"My magic?" Deidra's throat went dry. "I possess no such powers. Why do you persist in claiming I do?"

"Are ye not the flesh and blood of yer mother?" Gray eyes leveled on her. Deidra felt as if they probed to the depths of her soul. "Have ye no knowledge passed on from her?"

Confusion clouded Deidra's eyes. "What are you talking about? My mother died when I was but a babe. I never knew her. And my father never spoke of her passing on any magical powers."

"Yer father wouldn't have. 'Twas his secret shame, that his beloved lady wife was a sorceress. In the end, 'tis why she ran away from him."

"Ran away from him?" Deidra's heart commenced a wild pounding. "What are you saying? That my mother didn't die, killed by her own hand, but instead left my father?"

"Aye, that I am, child." Maud's gaze never wavered. "She loved him, and tried to adapt to the strictures of a noblewoman's life, but never could. Something finally snapped within her after she bore ye. 'Twas the choice she felt she had to make—either renounce her sanity and freedom, or her family."

"A poor choice to my way of thinking," Deidra muttered. "Freedom over the love of her husband and a child who needed her."

"Was not yer decision to leave Rothgarn and join Hawkwind based on that very same need?"

Deidra stared over at the other woman. " 'Tisn't the same

at all. Besides, why should I believe you? How could you have possibly known my mother?"

"She came to me after she left yer father. I gave her sanctuary until the day she died."

Somehow, gazing into Maud's clear, guileless eyes, Deidra knew she spoke true. Still, the logical side of her demanded further proof. "Give me some sign, something that will assure me you truly knew her."

"She had yer coloring and yer look, though never yer strength of mind or body. 'Twas why she sickened and died after only a few years of living in abject poverty." The healer arched a dark brow. "But as far as some sign that would convince ye, I can tell ye she bore a birthmark she said ye carried as well. 'Twas the mark of yer powers."

"Where?" Deidra couldn't help but snap out the question, at once eager to know the truth and fearing it. "Where was this birthmark? What did it look like?"

" 'Twas about where yer left breast would now be. 'Twas a flame-shaped mark." She eyed Deidra closely. "Am I right, or not?"

Deidra's mind whirled. The woman couldn't have possibly seen her birthmark. Even Alena, the only one ever present for her bath, had never had opportunity to note it, placed as 'twas on the underside of her left breast. "Aye, you're right," she finally and most grudgingly admitted. "But it changes naught. My mother still deserted me."

"What good would she have been to ye if she'd gone insane?" Maud asked. " 'Twas better to leave, to disappear from yer life and remain a beautiful memory, than to wither and rot into something neither ye nor yer father could ever have lived with."

'Twas too much to fathom, especially coming from a simple, peasant woman. Deidra fiercely shook her head. "You may have known my mother, but that doesn't explain why I should possess her powers! You fabricate tales to manipulate me to your whims. Whims," she added bitterly, "I cannot fathom the reason for."

" 'Tis indeed strange," the healer agreed, "why I'd care so much to convince ye of yer powers. But 'twould be a greater travesty to let such powers as ye possess go to waste. Hawkwind needs ye too badly."

"Hawkwind?" Deidra gave a shrill laugh. "He needs naught from me than what my ransom will bring. And the warming of his bed, if he dared try, now that he knows me for who I am."

"Ye have the power to ease his pain."

"I? Nay . . ." Deidra's voice faded. She'd been ready again to deny it, to say she didn't care how much he suffered—that he most likely deserved it—but the words died in her throat. She *did* care, especially knowing now how he'd received them. But to admit to, much less use some horrible magic—magic with the potential to control and ruin her life as it had her mother's—to aid him . . .

Her shoulders slumped in defeat. Despite her fears, she couldn't let Hawkwind suffer. "I-I don't know how." She lifted her gaze. "Will you teach me?"

"Teach ye what? The natural way or the magical?"

"Both. I will learn what is necessary to help Hawkwind, but no more. After that, 'twill be the end of it. And you must promise me whatever I do won't harm him."

"All magic isn't meant for evil, child," Maud chided gently. "The Craft of the Wise is the power of nature, of sacred waters, of the flame and the form, of herb, plant, and tree lore. They are of the earth; there is naught to be feared in them."

She smiled then. " 'Tis good, though, that ye care enough about Hawkwind not to wish him evil. The affection ye hold for him will aid yer magic."

Deidra blushed. "I don't feel 'affection' for him. I'd be daft to, after how he's treated me. Nay," she reiterated firmly, " 'tis naught but an honest concern for a fellow human being."

Maud shrugged. "Have it as ye will."

She rose from Bardrick's bedside and walked over to her

wooden storage chest. As she rummaged through it, Deidra turned her attention to her old bodyguard. He slept peacefully, his color almost returned to normal. Deidra smiled. At least he seemed to be recovering.

The movement of Maud, closing her chest and walking over, effectively distracted her attention from Bardrick. Deidra glanced up to find a small vial of some pale yellow unctuous fluid held out to her. She accepted the glass container and lifted it to the light of the oil lamp hanging from the tent frame overhead. The fluid gleamed and glowed in the flickering light, roiling gently in the vial as Deidra tipped it one way then another.

"What is this used for?" A frown of puzzlement furrowed her brow.

"Ye must apply it to Hawkwind's injuries. 'Twill ease their pain."

Deidra lowered the vial, which suddenly felt almost alive in her hand. Even now, she sensed its coiled energy, its potential power, awaiting the right words and touch to loose its miraculous abilities. "If 'twill ease his pain, why haven't you used it on him before?"

"Because the oil requires more than just a soothing touch to awaken its true powers. It requires a special magic to imbue the oil with its famed healing abilities." She smiled sadly. " 'Tis a magic beyond my humble abilities."

"Yet you seem to think 'tisn't beyond mine." Deidra sighed and shook her head. "Truly, Maud, this is all too much for me to comprehend, much less accept."

"Aye, I imagine 'tis so," the healer softly agreed. "But 'twill work, nonetheless, if ye permit it to. Ye possess sufficient magic. All else it needs is a willing heart and mind, and a deep caring for the recipient of the spell. Do ye possess those qualities?"

Deidra considered the question. "I'd like to think so," she honestly replied, "but 'twould be arrogant to say aye. Especially since so much depends on my true abilities."

"Ye can only do the best ye can, child."

"Aye, that I know." Deidra managed a tremulous smile. "But to fail Hawkwind when he needs me so badly . . ."

"He'll appreciate the intent, no matter what happens."

"Will he?" Slowly she shook her head. "I don't know, Maud. He seems so fierce, so oft angry with me. He may well view my efforts as yet another attempt to aggravate him."

A strange, bittersweet smile curved the healer's lips. "Strong emotions, even the most negative of ones, can be but a mask to hide those of the more tender kind. Emotions one oft fears to reveal."

Wonderment filled Deidra's eyes. "Hawkwind? He doesn't appear to me a man who fears aught. And tender emotions? For a woman, no less?" She laughed, the sound harsh and bitter. "Nay, never for a woman!"

"There is always one special woman who can make a special man change for the better. A woman who can inflame his heart and pierce it like no other. Even a heart as hard, as shielded as Hawkwind's."

"Well, 'twon't happen this eve, I'd wager." Deidra looked toward the tent opening. "And a bigger problem just now is how to convince the guard to take me back to Hawkwind's tent. He has orders to keep me here until Hawkwind summons me again."

"He will obey me. 'Tis but a simple matter to bespell him." Maud made a motion toward the tent flap. "Call him in, child."

As Deidra strode across the tent to do as she was bid, the healer lit a small cube of incense sitting in a squat little brass urn. When the guard stepped inside at Deidra's request, Maud walked over, wafting the smoking fumes toward him with the back of her hand.

"Inhale deeply," she intoned, her voice soothing, hypnotic. The man's eyes widened; he swallowed convulsively but did as requested.

The scent spread throughout the tent, strong, sweet, pungent, reminding Deidra of lavender and meadowsweet, and something she couldn't quite discern. Her own head began to spin. She felt light, dizzy. Then, with a clench of her fists, she shook aside the mesmerizing spell.

"Ye will take the lass back to Hawkwind," the healer murmured, smiling as she spoke. "Hawkwind has need of her."

The man swayed unsteadily, righted himself, then nodded. "Aye, that I will." His sluggish glance met Deidra's and he held out his hand. "Come, lass."

Deidra turned to Maud. "Thank you."

The older woman nodded. "Nay, thank *ye*. 'Tis long past time Hawkwind find some peace for his ravaged heart."

At the reminder of the deeper purpose Maud seemed convinced was inherent in her healing of Hawkwind's physical complaints, apprehension flared within Deidra. She said nothing, though, only pursed her lips, nodded her farewell, and turned to follow the guard from the tent.

Immediately, the storm caught her up in a shrieking swirl of sound and rain and blackness. As if the elements conspired to slow her progress, the wind whipped the cloak about her legs and her hair into her eyes, an incessantly blustering, buffeting force. Though the storm only seemed to mirror Deidra's own reluctance to face Hawkwind, there was naught else to do. Naught, if she was ever to ease the anguish of a man she found both frightening and compelling, a man of dark secrets and even darker emotions. Yet a man who suffered, and desperately needed solace.

With that thought to fortify her, Deidra clasped the vial in her hand, lowered her head, and slogged on.

By the Mother, Hawkwind thought in agony, would the night never end? Would the throbbing ache in his shoulder never cease? Would the pounding rush of blood filling his skull, the pulsating behind his eyes that threatened to drive him mad, the nauseating dizziness every time he turned his head, go on until he screamed aloud from the torment?

His fingers dug into the comforter, pulling and twisting the down filled bedding until it lay bunched beneath him. The effort was for naught. Hawkwind tried lying as still as he could, his head turned to one side, loath to even breathe. The pain went on, only slightly abated.

In spite of his clenched teeth and best intentions, a small groan of weary frustration escaped him. How many more times could he endure this? For years now, ever since that brutal mace blow to his head and sword driven deep into his shoulder, he had suffered the most excruciating torments. Every time it rained . . .

An errant breeze wafted by, chilling his sweat-damp skin. He shivered, then went taut, as the ever so slight movement sent his head to throbbing anew. By the Mother, if only he could lose consciousness, but even that small blessing was denied him. There was naught left to him but lie here and bear it, as he always had in the past like some dumb, suffering animal. Bear it, each and every time, until death at last freed him.

Another breeze, stronger this time and laden with moisture, gusted over him. It came from the opening of the tent. Hawkwind inwardly cursed. Who dared intrude? His men knew better than to—

"H-Hawkwind?"

He went rigid. Deidra. How had she managed to return, when he'd given orders for the guard to keep her at Maud's tent? He made a move to lever himself up and turn his head, when a fresh bolt of pain stabbed through his skull. For a blinding instant, all he saw was light. Then the room-whirling dizziness struck him, followed swiftly by the urge to vomit.

Hawkwind fell back on the bed, panting openmouthed to dispel the nausea. Fresh sweat broke out on his brow. Through it all, however, his trained warrior's hearing noted her hesitant approach.

"Why did you come?" he forced himself to ask, hoping

he didn't sound as weak and anguished as he felt. "I told you to stay with Maud!"

"I know." Deidra halted beside his bed. He sensed her presence rather than saw it, for his head was turned away. "But she gave me this oil and bade me use it to ease your pains."

"I don't want it," Hawkwind gritted. "'Twill do no good. Naught does. I *told* you that before!"

"Please, let me try. 'Twon't hurt to try and—"

"Nay!" He choked back a groan at the fresh surge of agony his single shouted word elicited. "Why do you torment me by your stubborn persistence? Do you like watching me suffer? Is that it?"

"'Tis only you who is being stubborn." Deidra moved to sit on the edge of the bed. "And so pain-wracked you can't think straight, either. You don't need to do anything save lie here. And, for once, you're going to do just that."

For an instant, the impulse to swing around and grab her filled Hawkwind. If she would no longer heed his warnings, he'd have to take more forceful measures. Measures, he belatedly realized, he had neither the strength nor inclination to carry out in his current condition. 'Twas best to let her have her way. . . .

He heard her open something, caught a faint whiff of a floral scent, then felt her hands on him, tentative, searching.

"Where does it hurt most?" she asked. "'Tis best if I start there first, don't you think?"

"You told me to lie here and not do anything," Hawkwind snapped. "Why are you asking me?"

"Fine." She sighed in exasperation. "I'll start on your head. 'Tis where most of the problems lie at any rate, within that thick, pigheaded skull of yours."

"And aren't you the tender, ministering angel?"

Deidra didn't bother to reply. She poured a small amount of the special oil into her hand, then rubbed it about on her fingertips. Ever so carefully, she brought her hands around on either side of Hawkwind's forehead. Just as carefully, she began to massage the muscle-taut skin in a gentle, circular motion.

.The oil eased the glide of her fingers, warming to the friction until it once again felt alive beneath her touch. She closed her eyes, forced her own tense body to relax, and breathed slowly, deeply. An image of Hawkwind formed in her mind—proud, virile, and healthy once more. He laughed suddenly, a sight Deidra had heretofore never seen, leaped upon his great charger, then glanced in her direction.

A boyish, disarming smile lifted the corners of his sensual mouth. She smiled in return, tears stinging her eyes. Then, with a toss of his long mane of hair, he wheeled his horse about and rode away. Deidra watched him until he disappeared from view, visually reinforcing the image of his big, powerful, healthy body.

"Ah, that feels good," Hawkwind breathed from beneath her. "What are you doing to me? The pain is already easing."

At the wonderment in his voice, Deidra's eyes snapped open. His own eyes were still closed, but the look of twisted anguish that had tightened the skin of his face had slackened considerably. A wild hope swelled within. Was it possible? Could she truly help him?

" 'Tis as I said before. The oil has special healing properties."

"It smells like a flower garden," he muttered. "I'll be the laughing stock of the army on the morrow."

"You can always bathe before you go out to see them," Deidra offered. " 'Tis a small price to pay, to my way of thinking, for the alleviation of your pain."

"Aye, I suppose so," he agreed. "The thought of you aiding in my bath possesses a certain appeal."

Deidra's ministrations ceased. "That was never part of the bargain."

The faintest glimmer of a smile lifted the corner of his

mouth. "And have you never bathed a man before? I'd thought 'twas part of castle hospitality for the lady of the manor to bathe the male guests."

"You are hardly a guest in your own camp. And I'm most definitely not the lady of the manor!"

He turned his head slightly and opened his eyes. Piercing green eyes locked with hers. Deidra drew back her hands.

"But you are *my* woman until I deem otherwise. And I find I very much like the feel of your hands on my body." His glance moved to her fingers, long, slender, and glistening with oil. "My head feels surprisingly better. Mayhap we should now turn your healing touch to my shoulder."

Deidra stared down at him, mesmerized by the burning intensity lighting his eyes. She swallowed hard. By the saints, if he ever guessed how strongly he affected her!

She wrenched her gaze away, using the vial of oil as an excuse for breaking visual contact. "If you're quite certain your head is better"—she turned back to him, fresh oil glistening in her palm—"then roll over onto your belly and I'll work on your shoulder."

Her refusal to comment on his ownership of her wasn't lost on Hawkwind. He smiled, but did as she bid. Tentatively, Deidra touched him, spreading the soothing, mysterious oil upon his mutilated shoulder and upper back.

Despite the still painfully throbbing shoulder, Hawkwind exhaled a contented sigh as she began gently to massage the muscles and bow-string taut sinews. There was something very strange about this oil and the fact Maud had never offered to use it before, but he'd deal with that mystery on the morrow. Tonight, what was left of it, would be spent in savoring the miraculous relief and the wondrous feel of Deidra's hands.

Almost as rapidly as it had worked on his agonizing headache, the oil's warm essence seeped into his shoulder, penetrating the joint to ease the painful throbbing.

Hawkwind inhaled deeply, savoring the scent of lavender, rose, and jasmine.

It took him away, to another time, to the summer-lush castle garden of his youth. In the background, water cascaded from a pearl gray marble fountain, filling the air with its gay, tinkling sound. A soft breeze caressed his face. A fat, black-and-yellow bumblebee droned nearby in a rosebush and a hummingbird buzzed overhead, pausing but a moment to seek out some succulent flower, then dive toward it.

'Twas all so peaceful, so beautiful, Hawkwind thought as he strolled through the riotous swell of colors and scents. 'Twas heaven, 'twas home. Home at last . . .

"Is it helping?" Deidra's sweet voice intruded. "You seem more relaxed and the tightness in your shoulder has subsided . . ."

"Aye," Hawkwind murmured, his voice a velvet caress as he willingly followed her back to an equally pleasant reality. "I don't know how you've managed it, but the pain is all but gone."

"Shall I stop then?"

"Nay!" He barely caught himself in his uncharacteristic show of eagerness. "A short time more, if you please. Just to make certain 'tis all gone."

Deidra smiled, well aware of his strong desire to continue to enjoy the massage and his failed attempt to hide it. "As you wish. Mayhap, in time, 'twill even beckon you to sleep."

"Aye, that it might." Hawkwind shifted to a more comfortable position. "Will you stay with me tonight?"

Wariness filled her. "But you ordered me to Maud's tent until you called for me."

"Well, you're ordered back."

"I see." Deidra bit her lip, considering how to phrase the next question. "You aren't angry with Maud, are you, for helping me return?"

"Should I be?"

She hesitated, not certain where this turn of conversation was leading. "Well, in my opinion, nay, but knowing your temper I'd guess our disobedience, however well intentioned, most likely did anger you."

"And are you sorry for it?"

Deidra gave a wry laugh. "What do you think?"

He rolled over onto his back. "Why doesn't that surprise me?"

Her eyes narrowed. What game was he playing with her? She feigned a nonchalant shrug. "Mayhap because I've told you time and time again of your pigheadedness, and this was but another case of the same behavior. You should know by now that I—"

"Refuse to obey me when I'm being pigheaded," he finished quietly.

Humor gleamed in his jade green eyes yet, beneath that friendly glint smoldered something else as well. Something hot, sensual, and very disturbing.

Deidra's heart quickened in her breast. She turned away to stopper the vial of oil, when a big hand came down on her wrist. Startled, she turned back to him.

"Stay with me tonight."

She frowned in puzzlement. "But you already said that was the way 'twas to be."

"Stay with me in this bed."

For an instant, Deidra thought she'd heard wrong. Then full comprehension flooded her. Fiercely, she shook her head. "Nay." Warmth flushed her cheeks. "I-I couldn't . . . You said you wouldn't . . ."

"Aye, I know what I said. That you'd remain virgin until I knew the truth about your claims to Rothgarn." Nonetheless, he tugged on her wrist.

She resisted. "Then why? Why now?"

"I don't want to mate with you this night, just sleep beside you. After what I've been through in the past hours, I'd hardly possess sufficient strength to make love to you at any rate." He tugged again, less gently, pulling her down to him. "But the warmth of your body next to mine, the comfort of knowing you're close if the pain should return . . ."

Hawkwind's mouth lifted in a tentative, twisted smile. "Won't you please reconsider? You have a wondrous ability, this magic of yours. It may be selfish, but I want to hold you, savor it for a while longer."

Deidra stared at him, dumbfounded. He had *asked* her, given her a choice for the first time! And he requested such a small thing, just her presence in his bed and naught more. 'Twas indeed so small a thing . . .

"I'll have your word on it, before I agree," she replied, knowing, even as she did the closeness of his body, of lying in his arms, was just as danger-fraught as allowing him to kiss her, or do more. But when he looked up at her with those deep, penetrating eyes, eyes that beguiled her even as they pleaded, she knew she couldn't deny him. Nor even wanted to.

"You have it."

The words were uttered in a low, husky rasp, but gave her the answer she craved. Deidra nodded, then moved to lie on his huge, burl wood bed.

Hawkwind arched a brow at the wide gap still lying between them. His mouth twisted wryly. "I had something more cozy in mind." He grasped her about the waist and dragged her over until their bodies touched.

Deidra's eyes widened. "I've never slept like this before, so . . . so close to a man."

"Well, get used to it," Hawkwind growled, then flipped her over on her side to face away from him. "I might grow to like it this way."

With that, he pulled her snugly into the hard wall of his body, settled his face alongside hers, and promptly fell asleep.

The same repose was long in coming for Deidra. Engulfed in a cloud of flower-fresh scent, a warm, sleeping man pressed intimately against her backside, she lay there for a time, filled with wonderment and a most strange, yet curiously soaring joy.

Hawkwind's words echoed over and over in her mind. *You have a wondrous ability, this magic of yours . . .*

There had been no revulsion, no horror in his voice when he'd said the words. And his gratitude for his healing had been sincere. For the first time, Deidra felt needed, appreciated for something more than her superficial value as a potential brood mare and heiress. The realization filled her with a sense of power and soul-deep satisfaction.

Yet to have found it first in the act of making magic also terrified her. The powers had never brought her mother much happiness. In the end, their relentless demands had driven her from her family and killed her. As seductive as the magic had been, Deidra's own abilities were also a potential source of pain and self-destruction. She must tread very carefully.

Her glance snared on the vial of oil lying on the floor where she'd dropped it, its liquid shimmering and golden in the flickering firelight. Mayhap 'twas all a trick, Deidra mused, instigated by Maud to woo her to a path she'd long ago chosen not to follow. Mayhap Hawkwind's "healing" had actually been the result of the considerable amount of ale he'd imbibed, and the soothing effects of her hands upon him. Mayhap there was naught of enchantment about the oil at all.

Aye, Deidra thought as drowsiness finally filled her, 'twas all too strange, too easy. As wondrous as the experience had been for both Hawkwind and herself, 'twasn't the way things happened. Life, especially in times such as these, just didn't work that way.

Chapter 8

"You can't be serious!" Deidra stood there, openmouthed, as Hawkwind motioned in the first two water bearers for his bath the next morning. "I am *not* bathing you!"

His mouth quirked in amusement, but he said nothing until the soldiers had departed, empty buckets in hand. "Careful, lady, or you'll wound my tender feelings."

"Tender feelings!" Deidra gave a small snort of disbelief. "'Twould take more than a few words to wound you. Mayhap," she muttered disgustedly, "more like a herd of war-horses pounding you into the ground."

Hawkwind gave a negligent shrug. "Most likely." He paused. "Let me phrase it another way. Am I less worthy of your consideration than the noble scum you're used to frequenting with? I'd have thought, considering your eagerness to join my army, such class considerations were beneath you."

"'Tisn't class considerations and you know it!"

"Then what? What unsettles you so?"

At the devilish, predatory glint in his eyes, Deidra quickly realized where this conversation was leading—and wanted none of it. Further discussion of the reason for her discomfort at bathing Hawkwind would only draw her deeper into trouble. How could she possibly admit the thought of touching him again, of running her hands over his powerful, moisture-slick body, of his total nudity shielded only by the thin veil of water, was more than she could deal with?

Last night had been difficult enough, as focused as she had been on Hawkwind's pain and its easing. Even then the animal heat of him, the sensuous feel of his smooth-muscled flesh, the aura of his warrior's magnetism had risen like some warm, mesmerizing cloud to engulf her, draw her to him. Deidra wanted no more of that queer, knee-buckling, aching feeling. She *never* wanted to feel that way about a man.

But she had to give him some answer or reveal the truth. Hawkwind was not a man easily fooled or led astray. Deidra chewed her lip for a brief moment more, then sighed. "'Tis simple, really. You don't like me, nor I, you. I see no reason to force any more closeness than is required."

"Ah, so that's how 'tis?" He smirked and shook his head. "Truly, Deidra, I'm disappointed in you. For all your aggravating quirks, I'd never thought you a coward."

"Coward?" She all but choked on the word and would have swiftly and graphically apprised him of her opinion of his taunt, if not for two more soldiers who entered at that moment with steaming buckets of water. It was all Deidra could do to contain herself while the men took an interminable length of time to complete their task and depart.

"I'll have you know," she then said as she advanced on him, hands fisted at her sides, her slender shoulders squared, "that I'm no coward and have never run from a fight in my life. And I'll certainly not do so because of you!"

"Then face your feelings, your desire for me," Hawkwind challenged, staring calmly down at her, "and deal with it like a woman, not some silly little girl."

"Silly little girl!" Deidra paled, then flushed as she suddenly recalled the precise intent of his words. "And you're an arrogant, rutting boar to think I desire you! You're one of the last men I'd ever choose for a mate!"

"We're both fortunate the choice has never been yours to

make, then, aren't we?" Hawkwind stepped closer, looming over her. "In the meanwhile, you've really no valid excuse to avoid washing me, do you?"

"None," she gritted, "unless utter loathing for you counts as anything."

He cocked his head for a considering moment, then shook his head. "Nay, it doesn't."

The tent flap lifted again. Two more buckets of hot water were carried in. Ten minutes later, the tub was full and sufficiently cooled for comfortable immersion by the addition of two buckets of cold water. Hawkwind walked over to one of his wooden chests and extracted a covered pottery bowl containing a spicy scented soft soap, a thick sponge, and large toweling cloth. He laid them on the bed and began to disrobe.

"Are you just going to stand there and strip in front of me?" Deidra asked in rising horror. "Have you no decency?"

He shot her a quizzical look. "The decency is yours to avert your eyes, if you choose to do so. It matters not to me. I'm not shy about my body."

"Nay, I'd imagine not," Deidra muttered, hastily lowering her gaze to the rug as Hawkwind unfastened his breeches and let them drop. "A man as magnificent as you seem to think you are must enjoy the feminine adulation."

"Most men do, Deidra."

She jumped in surprise. He'd finished undressing and silently strode up behind her. Her head jerked up, but she refused to turn, knowing he stood there completely naked. "F-fine," she gulped. "Please get in the bathing tub. This woman would prefer to 'enjoy' you from there."

A deep, rich chuckle rumbled from behind her. "Well, in your case, I suppose that's more than I dared hope for."

She heard him move, then the splash and slap of water against the beaten copper tub as he climbed in and settled himself. Finally, the sound of agitated water faded.

"I'm decent now, Deidra. 'Tis safe to look."

His tone of amused tolerance sent a surge of anger through her. Deidra clenched her fists and stomped over. She grabbed up the wash sponge, shoved it in the water, then wrung it out over his head.

"I'm not afraid to look at a naked man, curse you!" she stormed as she proceeded to soap up the sponge and apply it to the broad expanse of Hawkwind's scarred back. "I just have no interest whatsoever in seeing *you* naked!"

"How would you know that, until you've seen me?" he asked mildly. "I might be more to your liking than you realize."

"I hardly think so." Deidra moved to his right arm, lathering it from shoulder to fingertips in a few quick, efficient movements.

Hawkwind turned. "Mayhap 'twould be best to test out that certainty. Would you care for it to be now?"

His gaze locked with hers, hard, challenging, gleaming with a fierce, sensual light. Deidra paused, her fingers buried in the pot of butter-soft soap. Her heart commenced a wild pounding.

"You'd like that, wouldn't you?" she whispered, forcing the words past a tightly constricted throat. "But *I* wouldn't, so I must decline your most generous offer."

For the space of a tautly drawn breath he stared up at her, then shrugged. "Well, mayhap some other time."

Relief flooded Deidra. "Aye, mayhap," she hurriedly agreed and went back to the scrubbing of his body.

As she reached his broad chest, her actions slowed, stilled. Once more Deidra's attention was drawn to the curious medallion Hawkwind always wore about his neck. The hawk emblazoned there caught her eye. The more she looked at it, the more familiar it became. She had seen it somewhere before, but where?

She flipped it over in a surreptitious motion as she scrubbed his upper chest. Something was engraved on the back. Out of the corner of her eye, Deidra read it.

"To the wing, to the wind, the hawk rises to fly again," it said.

'Twas a motto . . . a motto of some noble house. Suddenly, a memory filled her mind, a scene of a huge bronze hawk, one outspread claw clutching a branch of oak leaves, hanging above a massive stone fireplace. Below the hawk, on an ornately swirled bronze banner, were the words. Words she'd seen long ago when, but a girl of twelve, her father had taken her with him on a trip to inspect his outlying possessions. Possessions that, thanks to the largess of King William, had included Todmorden Castle.

Deidra's fingers captured the medallion. "Where did you get this?" she demanded, lifting it on its chain to his view. " 'Tisn't some trinket one buys at the summer fair. I'd wager 'tis the family medallion of the Todmordens."

Immediately Hawkwind grasped her hand and pried her tightly clenched fingers away. "Is it now? And what is that to you?"

She jerked her hand back from his clasp. " 'Twas the lord of Todmorden's, I'd wager. Did you steal it?"

His bearded jaw went tight. "I don't have to *steal* anything. How I obtained this medallion is my affair, but be assured, I didn't steal it."

"Then who did you buy it from?" Deidra persisted. "My father is now lord of Todmorden and its lands. No one but he has the right to sell Todmorden goods."

Hawkwind shoved the wash sponge into her hand. "And I, more than anyone else, don't have to account to your father for anything that's Todmorden's! Get on with my bath. This subject is closed—permanently!"

She opened her mouth to dispute his statement, then noted the look of warning glittering in his eyes. 'Twas a small thing, at any rate, Deidra assured herself. 'Twas only a medallion after all, and not even one of special value. Though 'twas of gold, 'twas old and dull, as if its original luster had been worn away over the course of many years.

Nay, 'twasn't worth another argument, not in the strange mood Hawkwind was suddenly in.

Accepting the sponge, Deidra soaped it thoroughly and returned to his bath. Gradually, as she worked, his bowstrung taut body relaxed again. Soon, Hawkwind's arms and upper torso were clean. He leaned back and thrust a hairy, iron-thewed leg from the water. Though not as heavily scarred as his upper body, it, too, had seen its share of wounds.

"By the saints, is there not one place on you that hasn't been injured?" Deidra exclaimed in dismay.

The merest hint of a smile glimmered on Hawkwind's lips. "I can think of a few spots. Would you care to see them?"

"Nay!" Deidra dropped his leg back into the bathing tub and made a move to rise.

He halted her with a hand over hers. "Easy, lass. I was but jesting with you."

Her lips set in a thin line, but Deidra calmed. "I'll take your word for it." Suddenly, she was filled with an overwhelming need to finish the bath. She motioned to his leg. "Lift it back out again so I may wash it."

Hawkwind smiled but said nothing. He raised his leg and propped it on the side of the tub, exposing a disconcerting expanse of flesh halfway up his muscled thigh before the bath water once more covered him. Deidra eyed it, swallowed hard, then began to soap his foot and lower leg. All the while, she could feel Hawkwind's gaze upon her, hot, heavy, and full of a strange anticipation.

She paused at midthigh. "Why are you stopping?" Hawkwind immediately asked.

Deidra's head lifted. She frowned. "Isn't that obvious? I've no intention of washing your male parts."

"Since when is my leg part of my 'male parts'?"

She flushed. "'Tis sufficiently close." She locked gazes with him, daring him to argue the point, then offered him the sponge.

Hawkwind arched a dark brow. "Aye, I suppose you're right." He gestured at the sponge. "Please finish my other leg."

She considered him a moment longer, then moved to add fresh soap to the sponge. "Lift your leg from the bath, then."

With a cascade of water, Hawkwind's other leg appeared to drape on the opposite side of the tub. Deidra hurriedly lathered it and began her scrubbing, anxious to finish before Hawkwind changed his mind about maintaining any decency or sense of honor about this bath. Call it sixth sense but, as the seconds passed, Deidra was engulfed with a feeling of urgency, a premonition of mounting desire, of a hot, thick mist that seemed to surround them in a private world of intense awareness.

It could well be the heat of the bathwater, rising to curl the hair about her face into tight, damp little tendrils and moisten her tunic to her body until it clung like a second skin. Deidra desperately hoped 'twas so. Yet, somehow, she doubted 'twas so simple.

There was just something about Hawkwind, something that had slowly changed in the past few minutes—the sharp, aroused look in his eyes, the aura of musky, masculine sensuality that hadn't been there before. Even his breathing was now ragged and his body taut. 'Twas as if . . . as if he were growing excited. But about what?

She quickly discovered the source of his unsettling agitation. As her hand reached the point where water once more joined with flesh, Hawkwind grasped her wrist. Startled, Deidra lifted her gaze to his.

"You rouse me, lass," he whispered thickly. "Let me show you how much."

Before she could mouth a protest, much less pull back, Hawkwind had drawn her hand into the water and toward him. Coarse body hair brushed along her fingers, then something long, hard, yet surprisingly smooth, grazed the back of her hand. In the next instant, he had guided her fingers around it, covering them with his own strong, unyielding clasp.

Her eyes widened. Her mouth opened. Deidra flushed crimson. She jerked back, hard, violently, but to no avail. Hawkwind's intent and strength was too much for her.

"Do I frighten you with my size?" he throatily demanded. "Have you never held a man's shaft in your hands before?"

"N-nay." Her breath came in erratic gulps. "Let me go. I don't like this. 'Tisn't proper!"

"Mayhap not," he agreed, loosening his grip on her hand only enough to guide it up his hardened length and back down again. "But 'tis what I've wanted and needed since the first time I felt you, and saw you for the beautiful, desirable woman you are. And damn it all," he groaned as he gradually increased the speed and friction of their hands, "whether you be Rothgarn's heir or not, I mean to at least have this much of you!"

As she struggled futilely against him, wild, crazed emotions roiled within Deidra. An admixture of fear and revulsion warred with an equally stimulating and surprisingly pleasurable excitement. What did Hawkwind mean to do?

Her thoughts turned jumbled, irrational. Did he intend on seducing her? Was this but a prelude to a frenzied coupling on the floor with their bodies entwined in a heated, damply passionate embrace? Somehow, the possibility no longer repulsed her.

He forced her languorously to stroke him, from the base of his dense nest of hair and long, thickened sex to the swollen, flaring, velvety smooth head. Gradually, Deidra found her own body responding. Found, as well, the thought of feeling that same organ within her was hotly exciting. He was so big, so strong, so jutting and hard . . .

And he wanted her.

She lifted her gaze from the water, which rippled in unison to the pumping actions beneath it, to meet Hawkwind's. He stared back, a taut, ravaged expression in his eyes. His handsome jaw was clenched tightly, the muscles and tendons in his neck, shoulders, and arms stretched, straining. If she hadn't been told men found the stroking of their organs intensely pleasurable, Deidra would have imagined Hawkwind in pain.

He was like a bowstring pulled so tight he might snap at any moment. A man rigidly controlled who teetered on the brink of a wild release. And 'twas she who held the power, Deidra realized suddenly in a flash of feminine insight. She who possessed the ability to lead him where he dared never allow himself solitarily to go.

She should stop, now, before he lost control. Before he revealed yet another facet of himself she didn't dare risk seeing. Already, Hawkwind called to her heart, prying open the heretofore tightly guarded gate she had vowed no man would ever breach. She didn't dare risk letting him in. He, like all the others—nay, even more so, with his forceful personality and domineering ways—wanted only to subdue her to his will.

Yet the feel of him, long, strong, and thick beneath her fingers, the way she made him breathe so fast, so hard, the hot, smoldering hold of his eyes, all beckoned her on where she'd never wished to venture before. He groaned, the sound low, anguished, and so very male. A fierce joy surged through Deidra. In some instinctive feminine way, she knew to quicken even more the rhythmic strokes that pleasured him.

"A-aye." Hawkwind sighed, throwing back his head and closing his eyes. "That's it, lass." His hand released hers and fell away. "Don't stop. Ah, but you make me feel so good."

His breathing quickened and he moved restlessly now, his loins arching rhythmically with each downward glide of her fingers. His big hands moved from the water to grip the sides of the bathing tub, clenching knuckle-white. "Ah, aye," he breathed. "Faster now. Aye, that's it. Don't stop. Whatever happens, I beg you, don't stop!"

She felt the tension rising in him, felt it building to unbearable heights. The muscles bulged in his forearms and biceps, swelling and bunching in his big pectoral muscles. His chest heaved. His eyes clenched shut. His face contorted.

Then, with a strangled cry, Hawkwind found his release. His body lurched, grew rigid, then shook with the fierce spasms that shuddered through him. All the while as Deidra watched in a mesmerized, heated, triumphant fascination, her hand never ceased in its relentless stroking.

Finally Hawkwind went limp, his harsh pants the only sound in the tent. He gripped Deidra's hand, stilling her movements.

"Enough, lass. I can't take any more!"

He released her then and, still in a daze, Deidra pulled away. She stared down at him, caught up in the sheer masculine beauty of his darkly bearded face, his strong spade of a nose, his firm, sensual lips. Then Hawkwind smiled, and the change it brought to his expression was like sunlight bursting through clouds after a terrible storm.

In that instant, she knew a fleeting sense of union with him. There was nothing she wouldn't do for Hawkwind, even if he demanded she give up her dreams of being a warrior and become his lover. His happiness, so long denied him, mattered more than her own petty whims or desires. Nothing else mattered, nothing. . . .

Deidra inhaled a sharp breath. What was wrong with her, to so easily, so willingly surrender it all for the joy of a man's smile? Had she gone daft? Had her mind turned to a bowl of porridge?

Gazing up at her, Hawkwind saw Deidra's languid, sensual expression gradually transform to one of horror. He saw her lift her hand, stare at it as if transfixed, then turn back to him.

"N-nay . . ." Slowly, she shook her head. And, just as slowly, she drew back from him.

Puzzlement swelled in Hawkwind. He leaned forward to catch her hand. Deidra, with a quick movement and look of revulsion, jerked back. In a lithe flow of slender limbs, she rose.

He cocked his head to look up at her. "What's wrong, lass?"

She fiercely shook her head. "Naught. Naught is wrong. I-I just don't wish to ever do . . . do that again." She shuddered. "What we did was disgusting!"

Her words slashed through him, shattering the new and fragile emotions that had so briefly flared to life. A white-hot anger swelled within. Hawkwind stood in one effort-less, pantherlike motion.

At the sight of his fully exposed body, sleek and shiny with the water coursing from him, Deidra gasped. Her glance dropped, took in the now flaccid but still quite large shaft and hair-roughened sac, then jerked back up to his face. Once again, the heat stole into her face.

"Disgusting, was it?" Hawkwind demanded harshly. "Truly, you're the most irrational and unsettling of wenches! You gave me pleasure, and derived a bit for your-self in the giving, and now you dare look upon me and what we did as disgusting?" He motioned toward the en-trance of the tent. "Get out of here. Get out of my sight. If what we did was so horrible for you, be assured I won't force my loathsome attentions on you again."

Stung by his startling fury, she backed away, her own anger rising. "Do I have your word on that, *mighty* leader?"

"Aye, you most certainly do!"

"Then I'm no longer your woman?" she persisted, driven by a sudden, perverse need to see how far she could push him.

"You never were to begin with. You and I know that." Hawkwind grabbed the toweling cloth and flung it about his lower body. "I'll not tolerate a female around me or in my bed as unstable as you."

"Then there's naught else for me to do but become one of your warriors."

"What?" His head jerked up from tucking in the cloth

about his hips. "Are you daft? In case the fact has suddenly escaped you, you're still being held for ransom!"

Deidra lifted her chin and stood her ground. "So, what of it? You once told me all who followed you must serve in some useful way. I'm weary of sitting about in your tent and since you no longer wish to tolerate my presence near you . . ."

"You could help Maud with the sick and wounded," Hawkwind growled, already regretting his hasty words now that he saw where Deidra had led him. "You do have some talent for healing."

"Not as much as I have with the sword," she countered stoutly. "You owe me the chance to prove it. Like you would any *man* who came to you."

"Fine." In a rush of exasperation, the words fell from Hawkwind's lips. By the Mother, but he was weary of battling with her, of drawing her close and then having the ungrateful, foolish wench pull back in loathing! If she was so set on having her head whacked and her body beaten and bruised, so be it. She'd have her warrior's testing, but 'twould be as hard, as brutal as any man's.

"What did you say?" Deidra asked, not daring to believe he'd said what she thought she'd heard.

"I said fine." Once again, Hawkwind gestured to the tent flap. "Go, fetch Alena. If 'tis a warrior's testing you desire, I'll make certain she gives it to you."

At the flare of joy in her eyes, Hawkwind held up a silencing hand. "But you *will* still be confined to my tent at night, as well as under close guard during the day. Your virginity is too precious now to risk it out there sleeping with my men. And I, at least, am now immune to your 'charms.'"

"Fine," Deidra agreed tersely. "That'll be fine with me."

"Aye," Hawkwind muttered, "I'd imagine so. But I warn you, one way or another you'll soon rue your decision to turn from me to a warrior's life. I vow it, my little fire-haired queen. And you'll learn soon enough, if you haven't already," he said with a brutal smile, "that I always keep my word."

"I . . . hate . . . him!" Deidra gritted between clenched teeth as she fought back yet another of Alena's punishingly brutal assaults. For the past two days she had endured the worst the warrior woman could deliver, and consistently come out the worse for it. Today was no different.

She'd been summoned from a hard, exhausted slumber at the first glimmer of dawn and rolled from her pallet, a bruised and aching mass of overworked muscles and strained sinews. After a five-mile run with the seemingly tireless Alena, Deidra had tended to Hawkwind and his two war chiefs' chargers, feeding and watering, then grooming them to a spotless sheen. Only then had she been allowed a few minutes to gulp down a Spartan breakfast of warm ale and a wedge of cheese.

Then the warrior's training had begun in earnest. From midmorn to sunset, with only one other short break for the midday meal, Alena had put Deidra through the myriad of weapons used in battle. Though the use of sword had consumed a fair amount of the day and physical effort, Deidra had also worked at the long bow, the mace and spear, and an endless slew of battle techniques on horseback. The stiff, aching muscles from the frequent falls as she learned the various methods of fending off attack were a constant reminder of her decided lack of talent and expertise while horsed.

Yet, as awkward and unskilled as she was in other forms of battle, Deidra knew she had already proven to Alena that her claims to a certain expertise with the sword had not been unfounded. Hawkwind, on the other hand, was a different matter.

For the first two days, he had taken what seemed to be unusual care not to linger in the vicinity of Deidra's training with Alena. When she all but crawled into his tent at the end of each exhausting day, grimy and battered, he had hardly spared her a look, and certainly no comment, before she collapsed on her pallet. But today, as Deidra engaged in the final workout before the evening meal, the warrior chief had suddenly appeared, pulled up a camp stool, and commenced avidly to watch her efforts.

Aye, she certainly and most vehemently hated him. How could one *not* hate a man who sat there, a smirk on his lips and a mocking light in his eyes as Alena slowly and very methodically once again beat her to a pulp?

She didn't fault the woman. Nay, Alena had explained the seriousness of her intent from the start. If Deidra was determined to become a warrior, she would help her. 'Twould be hard and painful, but it could be done if Deidra persevered. Deidra had set her indomitable will on that very goal and would die trying rather than fail. Whatever it took to prove Hawkwind wrong, she would do.

But Hawkwind's sudden interest was another matter. He wanted her to fail. He wanted her to admit defeat and come crawling back to him, begging for another chance to be his woman. 'Twas egotistical mayhap to think that, but the way he looked at her, the burning intensity of his gaze that all but seared a hole in her back as she battled her way to and fro across the small training field, only reinforced what her woman's instincts knew to be true.

He wanted her. Despite his words to the contrary, the wild, heated moments she'd spent with him two days ago at his bath had only served to stir the fires of his passion. And stirred her feelings for him as well. Mayhap that was what angered her more than anything—the fact, in spite of it all, she wanted to be with him, to delve deeper into his heart, to pry open, bit by bit, the tightly guarded door shielding his emotions, his innermost dreams and secrets. But that was a foolish, futile wish. Hawkwind wanted naught of closeness or trust—and especially not from a woman.

At the painful admission, renewed anger surged through

Deidra. She intensified her assault against Alena, slashing at her with wooden sword in a rapid succession of thrusts and blows.

The blond woman's eyes widened momentarily, then her lips set in a fierce resolve. She allowed Deidra to drive her back for a time, biding the right moment to take her unawares. Waiting, parrying, retreating, until her greater battle experience sensed the moment was right.

Then, with a quick feint and graceful turn, Alena drew Deidra off balance and thrust low, going straight for her upper torso. Deidra froze, fully aware of the fatal position of the other woman's sword tip, pressed just below her heart. Her own sword lowered in acknowledgment of defeat. As she stood there, chest heaving and face burning, Hawkwind rose and strode over.

"You're far too naive in the ways of battle," he growled, "so foolishly to allow yourself to be drawn into such an untenable position. Fine swordplay or not, you'd never stand a chance against a seasoned warrior. And your battle strength and stamina," he added, casting her trembling, sweating body a disparaging glance, "is far from adequate. You'd last about ten minutes, if that long, against a hardened warrior."

Deidra inhaled a ragged breath. "So I should give it up? Is that what you're saying? That no matter how hard I work at this, I'll never be capable of anything more than the warming of your bed?"

He grinned. "Something like that."

A cold fury swelled within her. "I'd sell my soul to the devil before I'd ever come crawling back to you! I'd rather die from exhaustion or a clean, honorable sword thrust in battle, than lower myself to settle for the sordid, shameful existence you offer."

Hawkwind's mouth tightened. A muscle twitched in his suddenly taut jaw, fleetingly whitening his scar to silver. "Careful, wench. Your unreasoning pride will be your destruction. That, and the refusal to admit to your own woman's desires. Desires you most assuredly have for me," he said, "whether you've the courage to face them or not."

"You lie, you insolent, swaggering, lust-crazed beast!" Deidra took a step toward him, her wooden sword in hand, before she was halted by the fierce warning light that had sprung to his eyes. A light that was part threat and part excitement, and all but begged her to press on.

"A lying beast, am I?" he prodded softly. "Pray, don't hold back so in your true opinion of me. Tell me more."

There was something dangerous lurking in the steel-edged timbre of his voice. Deidra froze, swallowed hard as the realization of his intent engulfed her. He only waited for an excuse to overpower her, to throw her over his shoulder and carry her off to his tent. Somehow, Deidra knew this time he'd not let honor or ransom, and certainly not her pleas, sway him from his predetermined course.

She lowered her sword and dropped her gaze, knowing to continue to taunt him would only make matters worse. Yet how she hated constantly submitting to him! Just once, she'd like to beat Hawkwind, to force him to concede defeat!

Deidra lifted her gaze. "I have said enough," she replied softly. "To say more would only make things worse—for the both of us."

Something flickered in his eyes. "Or settle things between us once and for all." He cocked his head, a knowing smile glimmering on his lips. "But somehow, I'd wager you're not ready for that."

She considered his meaning for a long moment, then nodded. "Nay, I'm not. I thank you for your willingness to go slow with me and," she paused to add emphasis to her next words, "permit me to try my hand at warrior's training."

He frowned then. "You haven't much time, one way or another."

Confusion shadowed her eyes. "How so? You never put a time limit on it."

Hawkwind gave a negligent shrug. "Mayhap I didn't, but my next employer certainly has. We break camp in two days' time. Another battle awaits us in Lord Firston's lands."

Chapter 9

ℌer day totally ruined by Hawkwind's visit and unexpected pronouncement, Deidra grumpily made her way to Maud's tent after the supper meal. She hadn't had much opportunity to visit with Bardrick in the past two days, as busy as Alena had kept her. Tonight, though, she meant to see him and talk with Maud as well.

She had meant what she'd intended when she vowed to become a warrior and this last interaction with Hawkwind had only strengthened her resolve. She would prove him wrong about her no matter the cost. And the healer woman, with her mysterious, magical powers, might well hold the solution as to how to achieve that goal.

The thought of actively seeking out Maud's magic frightened Deidra. All she had ever heard of or seen was the darker side of those strange and unfathomable powers, and what they'd ultimately done to her mother. Though Maud had assured her magic could also be used for good, Deidra wasn't so certain. She had only the surprising results of the strange oil she'd used upon Hawkwind that night for proof of the potentially positive power of magic. And that could have just as easily been the result of her hands upon him than of some enchantment of the oil.

But she would now listen to Maud and consider the possibilities, not only, Deidra admitted reluctantly, in order to best Hawkwind, but because of some of the things the healer woman had said about her—and her mother. Though she'd been loath to admit it at the time, Maud's description of her mother seemed uncannily accurate. Uncannily, because aside from the similar looks and coloring, there was the birthmark and the same, heart-deep longing for freedom.

Maud had struck close to the mark when she'd challenged Deidra to admit she'd made the same decision in leaving her father and people as her mother had done when she'd deserted her husband and child. There indeed *was* little difference. Neither could bear a destiny not of their own choosing, no matter how the bonds of duty tugged.

For the first time in her life, Deidra felt close to her mother, a woman she had never known. And if magic, as much as she still feared it for what it had done to her mother, could draw them yet closer, she was willing to delve into that now as well. She would just be very careful, very judicious with its use. And she would never lose control of it.

A chill wind blew through the camp, setting fires to sputtering and sparks to scattering wildly into the deepening twilight. Men crowded closer to the blazing campfires for warmth, hunkering down, hands extended. Their voices lowered, assumed a more serious tone.

Deidra glanced up at the sky. Dark clouds raced across a sliver of ivory-tinged moon. In the distance black thunderheads loomed on the horizon. Another storm was brewing.

As she hurriedly made her way across camp the wind rose to gusting blasts, rampaging through the camp to topple piles of neatly stacked weapons, tearing at the stout ropes that staked down the tents, whipping away blankets and clothes hung out to dry. Suddenly, the scene was one of pandemonium. Men leaped to their feet to scramble after belongings sailing off on the wind, their enraged shouts swallowed by the rising howl of the storm.

Deidra paused before Maud's tent to survey the camp, smiled wryly and shook her head. Then, with a sweep of her hand, she lifted the tent flap and strode in.

For a change, the healer's makeshift little hospital was empty save for Bardrick lying in his bed. Maud sat beside him, slowly spooning soup into his mouth. Deidra squared her shoulders and walked over.

"How goes it with the soldier's training?" Maud asked without even glancing up. "Are ye ready to concede defeat?"

"To whom? Hawkwind?" Deidra gave a small snort of disgust. "Hardly. That's why I came to you. I'd know more of these powers you claim I possess."

"Would ye now?" Maud put down the spoon and bowl of soup and rose from the stool she'd pulled up to the bed. "Well, mayhap in time, but first, visit a bit with yer old friend. He's been asking about ye."

"He has?" Deidra moved closer, her anxious gaze seeking out the man who lay so quietly in the bed. "Bardrick, 'tis Deidra. Can you speak?"

Maud moved aside and motioned for her to sit. "Aye, he can speak but only a few words, and most of them garbled. Yet ye can tell by the look in his eyes his mental faculties have returned. He grows better with each passing day. If only the strength in his right side would return, and the corner of his mouth wouldn't droop so."

Deidra sat and took his hand in hers. Dark eyes gleamed up at her. The left side of his face crinkled in a smile. She returned his smile and squeezed his hand. He squeezed back.

"You're looking well," she murmured. "Maud is taking good care of you."

"Aaagh," he growled. "Aa-aye."

Deidra shot the healer woman a joyous look. She smiled and nodded.

"Are you eating well for her?" Deidra prodded. "That's

what you need now. Some good food in your belly to give you strength."

"Aaagh." Bardrick awkwardly disengaged his hand from her clasp. In a slow, painstaking movement, he lifted it to Deidra's face and gently stroked her cheek. He half frowned as his fingers traced the rivulets of dried sweat tracking through the grime on her face.

"Whaa . . . what haapp?"

She flushed. She hadn't meant to reveal Hawkwind's bargain with her, nor the terrible exertions she'd had to endure because of it. " 'Tis naught." Deidra caught his hand, brought it to her lips for a swift kiss, then lowered it back to lie upon his chest. "I came here to learn to be a warrior and Hawkwind has granted me leave to do so. 'Tis naught to worry yourself over."

He pulled his hand from hers and clenched it on his chest. "Naah . . . naah." Bardrick paused, inhaled a ragged breath, and tried again. "Na-nay!" He moved restlessly, attempting to lever himself up with his good arm. "Nay. Naa . . . no m-more!"

A hand settled firmly on Deidra's shoulder. " 'Tis enough for one night, child. He upsets very easily as yet. 'Tis mayhap better not to extend yer visit."

Deidra shot Bardrick an anguished look, then glanced back at Maud. "Aye, mayhap 'tis best." She turned to her old bodyguard, leaned down and kissed him lightly on the forehead, then rose. "I'll come for another visit on the morrow. I promise."

Bardrick slumped back in bed, his struggles to rise only weakening him further. "Aaagh . . . aye. Maa-row."

Deidra turned to Maud. "Can we speak together?"

The older woman glanced around at the heaving sides of the wind whipped tent and nodded. "Aye. Outside seems a poor alternative, though. The far side of the tent should afford us some privacy."

She picked up the stool and made her way across the tent where a small pot was suspended over a brazier. The liquid within the pot bubbled merrily, heated by the tiny fire burning beneath. Maud set down her stool and motioned to a narrow wooden table nearby. On it was a cunning pottery teapot gaily painted with violets, a covered bowl, and two cups.

"Would ye care for a cup of borage leaf tea? It does wonders for giving one a 'lift' after a hard day." She paused to shoot Deidra an assessing glance. "I'd planned on a cup myself, but ye look like ye need it far more than I."

"Aye." Deidra sighed as she sank onto the stool. "I can use whatever you offer. It has been a trying day, with more to come, I fear."

"He's been hard on ye, hasn't he?" Maud asked in sympathy. She poured a little of the boiling water into the pottery teapot, swished it around to rinse it, then dumped the water on the ground. Next, she uncovered the little bowl, which held dried borage leaves mixed with pretty blue flowers, and tossed a handful into the teapot.

Deidra watched in fascination until the healer paused and glanced back as if awaiting her reply. "Hard? Oh, aye, that he has been." She sighed again and ran a hand raggedly through her tousled red curls. "He means to see me defeated. To have me beg him to take me back."

"And ye won't, will ye?" Maud filled the teapot with boiling water, then covered it with its lid. "Not in the manner he wishes, at any rate."

"Nay, never like that." Deidra vehemently shook her head. "I left one life, infinitely safer and more comfortable than this, to escape becoming a man's chattel. I refuse to become one now, even for a man such as Hawkwind."

"Yet ye care for him, nonetheless."

Overhead, thunder boomed. A moment later, the delicate, almost tentative patter of rain began. As the seconds passed the rain intensified until it pounded on the tent roof. The wind howled, battering against the woven hemp walls as if trying to force its way inside. And, amidst it all, the two women stared at each other, one calmly awaiting the other's reply.

⋅ With a soft sound muffled by the now torrential downpour, Deidra lowered her head. "What does it matter what I feel for him?" she mumbled. "He wants only to use, then discard me, as he has all his women. And I can't ever let him do that. 'Twould be my undoing."

"His shield about his heart is strong. Ye must never give up. Ye must wear him down until he lowers that shield."

"And *why* must I do it?" An angry frustration swelled in Deidra. She leaned forward and rested her face in her hands. "What good could it possibly do—for either of us?"

Maud shrugged and turned to the pot of tea that had simmered until its fragrant scent permeated the air. She poured out two cups, then handed one to Deidra. "What else but win ye the love ye've always sought, and Hawkwind an end to his soul rotting bitterness and heartsick loneliness." She stared down at Deidra. "He needs ye, child, more than either of ye have yet to realize."

"Well, he certainly has a strange way of showing it," Deidra huffed. " 'Tis part of the reason I came to see you this eve. Hawkwind is convinced I haven't the stamina or strength to succeed as a warrior. I want you to give me something to prove him wrong."

"Indeed?" Maud walked over and took the other stool. She clasped the cup of steaming tea in her hands and inhaled deeply of its soothing aroma. "And I thought ye didn't care much for magic?"

Soft brown eyes considered her for a long moment. Then Deidra sighed. "I don't. I'm not even certain I truly have the powers, but I wish to learn more of them. If my mother thought so highly of her powers, I can do no less than study them for a time. It doesn't mean I'll accept the magic, even if I possess such abilities," she hastened to add, "but I will try and listen if you'll instruct me. I want *that* badly to best Hawkwind, to show him he's wrong about me."

" 'Twon't be easy," Maud softly replied. " 'Twill take time to master the various skills and crafts. The necessary mental faculties and aspects of yer inner being ye must call to task to evoke the magic have been long buried within ye. Are ye willing to persist when it seems naught is happening, when yer unseen forces lie silent and still, just below the surface?"

"Am I patient? Is that what you're asking?" Deidra gave a wry laugh. "Nay, I'm not, but I *am* determined. As determined to best Hawkwind as I am to face whatever destiny lies in store for me."

Maud smiled, then took a sip of her tea. "Ah, the borage has steeped nicely. Drink, child. We've much to discuss and the night draws on. Much I will tell ye requires a time of contemplation and soul-searching, but we will begin."

Deidra raised her cup and tasted of the pungent brew. "And a potion to strengthen me in my warrior's training? Will you give me that as well?"

"Aye, but 'twill cost ye. I may wish a boon from ye someday. Will ye give it then, no matter what the cost to yerself?"

Deidra frowned. "You put a heavy price on a simple potion. What is it you want from me?"

Maud shrugged. "I cannot say as yet. Only time and events still to come will determine if I need even ask it. In the end, 'twill all depend on ye."

"I won't agree ever to wreak evil."

"And I'll never ask it of ye, child."

"Then you have it," Deidra said, "whatever it may be."

"Good." The healer chuckled. " 'Tis past time we get on with yer training then. Didn't I say ye needed to wear Hawkwind down? And what better way to begin than to teach him a little lesson about women?"

A few hours later, Deidra made her sodden way back to Hawkwind's tent, totally overwhelmed by the amount of knowledge Maud had managed to cram into their time together. She had never imagined magic could be so much a part of the natural progression of life and nature. Of long-forgotten talents buried within each and every man. Of inner peace and tranquillity, of new ways of healing and self-awareness.

'Twas strange, Deidra mused as she slogged along, how good and noble Maud made it all seem, how much an innate part of the human nature. Though she was still cautious and skeptical, another part of her was equally heartened and hopeful. If little else came to fruition, Deidra smiled to herself as her fingers clenched about the slim flagon, she now had the potion Maud promised would strengthen her to the hard training days ahead.

The matter of Hawkwind and his old injuries was a different matter. Though Deidra begged the healer for another vial of her magical oil to soothe the big warrior chief's pain, Maud had adamantly refused. 'Twas her abilities, and only her abilities, that had aided him before, she had slyly informed Deidra. The oil had been naught but some simple lamp fuel.

Deidra, however, knew better. The oil had been thick, yet warmed easily to a slick unctuous fluid with the heat of her hand. The fragrant perfume of a flower garden had been unmistakable, wafting up from the strangely alive and stimulating liquid. 'Twas no simple lamp fuel. She was certain of it.

Yet, be that as it may, she had naught else to offer Hawkwind this night. The realization sent a tremor of apprehension through Deidra as she paused before his tent. The two guards barely spared her a glance as they lifted the flap and motioned her in.

Their routine acceptance of her right to be there inexplicably filled Deidra with irritation. Despite her utmost efforts in the past few days and the skills she'd demonstrated with the sword, none of it had meant aught to anyone. She was still viewed as Hawkwind's woman.

Well, 'twould take a time longer than she'd originally

anticipated, Deidra consoled herself as she stepped inside, but she'd yet change their minds.

Her glance scanned the tent's luxurious interior, seeking out the man who was the cause of all her current difficulties. A scathing retort formed on her lips, but 'twas all for naught. Hawkwind wasn't there.

"That man keeps the longest hours," Deidra muttered as she pulled off her rain-soaked cloak and hung it over a nearby chair to dry. He was probably deep in conference with his war captains, planning their next campaign. Alena was most likely with him, Deidra thought with an uncharacteristic twinge of jealousy. *She* was accepted, one of them, her opinions of value. Not like her, relegated to crawling onto her little pallet to await her lord and master.

Suddenly infuriated at the unfairness of it all, Deidra flung herself onto a sturdy oak chest and tugged off her boots, taking a perverse pleasure in noting the muddy footprints she had tracked across Hawkwind's fine carpet. She tossed her boots carelessly aside, then quickly stripped off her sweat-stained, grimy tunic and breeches, which she dropped atop her boots. Hawkwind, a surprisingly tidy man for a warrior, wouldn't take kindly to the mess.

Which suited her immensely.

She stood, opened his chest, and pulled out one of his finely woven linen tunics, knowing he wouldn't like that, either. After quickly washing herself clean in the basin of water always kept at the ready, she slipped the tunic over her head. Striding over to her pallet, where she kept a small bag of personal items, Deidra withdrew her hairbrush. She spent the good part of the next fifteen minutes dragging its bristles through her tangled mane, cursing Hawkwind, his pigheadedness, and plotting new and even more aggravating ways to thwart him.

At long last her hair lay damp but neatly brushed out. With nimble fingers, Deidra wove the auburn strands into a single braid, tied it off, and flipped it over her shoulder. Hawkwind still hadn't returned. Her plan to await him and his reaction to the slovenly mess she'd created gradually lost its appeal. Stifling a huge yawn, Deidra crawled beneath the comforter covering her pallet and promptly fell asleep.

A muffled groan awoke her in the wee hours of the morning. She was suddenly aware the rain had stopped, the braziers had burned down to a dim red glow, and someone was in the tent with her. She shoved to one elbow and blinked in an attempt to adjust to the muted light. As she did, another low groan rose from the vicinity of Hawkwind's huge bed.

He was back—and in pain.

For a fleeting moment Deidra hesitated. If she went to him, he'd expect her to ease his torment. Yet, despite Maud's assurances to the contrary, she wasn't so certain she could without the miraculous oil. Mayhap 'twas better to lie here and feign sleep. Mayhap his old wounds wouldn't pain him so badly this night. Mayhap, now that the rain had ceased . . .

Hawkwind levered himself up and glanced in her direction. "Deidra?"

The whispered plea, so full of a reluctant need and tormented anguish, cut straight to her heart. She sat up. "Aye?"

"My head . . . my shoulder. Can you . . . mayhap . . . ease their throbbing again?"

He was so proud, a strong, indomitable man. Instinctively Deidra knew how hard it had been for him to ask for her assistance, aware of the simmering animosity between them, the chaos of barely leashed emotions and unrequited passion.

A battle raged within her. To go to him now would be to surrender some part of herself. To face the possibility of her magic as well. Yet he needed her, and, as arrogant, as infuriating as he was, she couldn't turn from him.

She rose from her pallet and padded over to him. "I have

no more of Maud's special oil," she whispered, "but if my touch alone would help . . ."

He moved, his hand snaking out to grip her by the arm. His clasp was tight, bruising. A tautly strung tension radiated from him. "Anything!" he gasped. "By the Mother, do what you can before I go mad from the pain!"

All reservations, all hesitation, all doubts as to her abilities to ease his torment fled Deidra. She climbed up onto the bed beside him and reached for his head. Long, slender fingers encircled his forehead and temples. Before she could question her intent, Deidra began her massage.

Something flared to life within her, a force, a determination, a power that had heretofore been a weak and fragile thing. Hawkwind needed her. He suffered and she possessed the skills to ease his suffering. From whence the realization came, Deidra didn't know, didn't care. It just grew, burgeoning to a heated life of its own, then flowed out of her and into him.

"Ah, lass," he breathed. "You have the most wondrous hands. If only you'd the power to cure me of this, once and for all . . ."

To cure him. Maud had spoken of the permanent healing of ills as a potential result of magic. Yet she had also named it a more advanced skill. Was she overstepping herself to attempt such a thing so early in her training?

'Twas worth a try, Deidra decided. If her powers even sufficed to ease his pain this night, 'twould be enough. If it did more, so much the better. She had naught to lose. For Hawkwind, she'd risk it all.

Eyes clenched shut, Deidra summoned every bit of strength within her, gathering it, marshaling the swirling mass of untested, unbridled power into a firm intent. It grew, flared hot and bright, then shot down her arms and into Hawkwind. He gave a strangled cry, went rigid, then limp.

Terror filled Deidra. She jerked her hands away. Hands that glowed brightly in the darkness, fiery and pulsating.

Horror-struck, she stared down at them for long, agonized seconds, watching as the red glow slowly faded and the only light in the tent was once more the fire-lit braziers. Then she turned to Hawkwind. He lay there, unmoving.

Cautiously, Deidra reached out to touch him. He was warm, his heart still beating. A shaky breath escaped her. He lived. She hadn't killed him, only struck him unconscious.

Uttering a soft cry, Deidra crawled over and lay alongside him, pulling his head down to cradle it upon her breast.

Hawkwind awoke slowly, as if pulled gently from a deep, healing sleep. The merry sound of chirping birds teased his ears. The scent of morning cook fires tantalized his nostrils. His bed was warm, soft, and far too inviting to consider leaving.

Something equally warm and soft snuggled against him. He glanced down and smiled. Deidra.

Last night—the memory of the renewed pain of his old injuries and Deidra's healing hands upon him—came back with a rush. The last thing he remembered was a surge of heat entering his body. The next thing was waking this morning.

Hawkwind brushed a stray, auburn lock off Deidra's cheek. She had done something to him, something outside the realm of normal healing. But had the powers been hers, or come from Maud? Somehow, it didn't matter. What she had done for him was good. In his heart, despite the continued friction between them, he knew Deidra could be no other way.

Her tunic—or rather his, he noticed with a twinge of amused chagrin—had pulled up while she slept. It barely covered her now. His glance slid down the sleek expanse of ivory thigh, past an endearingly dimpled knee and curvaceous calf to a dainty little foot. Desire welled in him with a breath-grabbing intensity.

His sex filled, thickened, throbbed in unison to the beat of his heart. A fine sheen of sweat broke out on his brow. Hawkwind swallowed a savage curse. Would he never look upon her without wanting her? And when she was gone, would she still linger in his memory and dreams?

He feared so.

What was it about her? True, she was a most alluring specimen of womanhood. Any man would find her attractive. Aye, *if* they could ever get past her sharp tongue and stubborn, headstrong nature, he added wryly. Yet, in his mind, those very aspects made her even more enticing. That, and the fine breeding of a noblewoman underlying everything she did.

As loath as he was to remember, much less admit it, she was of his kind. Somehow that added bond strengthened everything else he found attractive in her. She had never been and never would be a woman he could use and casually toss aside. Mayhap that was why he was so loath to take her. Mayhap he instinctively knew she would sear her essence into him just as surely as he'd possess her body in the act of their lovemaking. And mayhap he feared that consequence, more than anything he'd ever feared before.

Yet the tantalizing allure of her, of her sweet, white flesh revealed so innocently yet provocatively to his hungry gaze, was more than Hawkwind could resist. Ah, just to have a moment of her, he told himself. To have just one feel of her, one feather-light stroke of a fingertip down the sleek, silky length of her leg, would be enough. He'd make it be enough.

Deidra stirred, mumbled a few incoherent words, then snuggled even closer to him, seeking out the heat radiating from his big body. Hawkwind swallowed hard, gritted his teeth, and touched her thigh.

The act was almost his undoing. She was warm, soft, and

so exquisitely smooth. His fingers splayed, spreading out to encompass as much of her as he could. She felt so good!

He should stop now, Hawkwind told himself. Now, before he totally lost control. But the feel of her!

She moved restlessly, then settled down once more. Her leg shifted, lifting to rest upon his outthrust knee. Hawkwind groaned.

Deidra's slumbering action had exposed her firmly rounded derriere and a seductive view of her dark red woman's thatch. As if drawn by some unknown force, Hawkwind's fingers reached for her, to lightly stroke her buttocks and brush down past the dense curls guarding her most secret parts. Excitement pounded through him. He swelled to his fullest expanse, his glans flaring, agonizingly sensitive. How he wanted to join his flesh with hers! 'Twas an exquisite torment, the need *and* the denial.

Then, with a ragged, tormented breath, Hawkwind drew back his hand. He didn't want Deidra this way, unawares, sleeping. He would either have her awake and responsive, or not at all. She must crave him as desperately, as passionately as he craved her, or he didn't want her. To use Deidra against her will would destroy something special in her— and what little that remained of any decency in him.

He rolled away, one hand clenched at his side, the other fisted, his arm flung across his eyes. Eyes that clamped shut, fighting the unrequited desire burning through him. And, as he fought, shuddering with the ferocity of his battle, his movements were finally enough to awake Deidra.

Her lids lifted. Hawkwind lay beside her, the lower half of his face contorted in some private agony. Apprehension raced through her. Had she harmed him last night in her failed attempt at healing?

The memory of her glowing red hands returned. She shuddered in fear and revulsion. What was she, some monster, some devil, to have summoned such powers?

Deidra forced the unnerving questions from her mind. They could be dealt with later. What mattered now was

Hawkwind. Her glance lowered, trailing down his battle-scarred bare chest and muscled abdomen to where the breeches clothed him. A taut bulge strained the cloth covering his groin.

Startled, Deidra turned her gaze to herself—and saw her nakedness. Renewed horror of a different kind filled her. With a hasty motion, she jerked down the bottom of the tunic to cover herself.

He had seen her, she realized. Seen her and become aroused. And was even now fighting that arousal.

For a fleeting moment, a sick panic welled in her. Had he touched her, done forbidden things to her body? Glancing back at Hawkwind, she doubted it. His erection was ample proof he'd yet to find his release.

The sickening sense of fear faded. Compassion, and a strange satisfaction, filled her. For all his gruffness and attempts to distance himself from her, Hawkwind's physical response just now confirmed what she was already beginning to suspect. He wanted her, yet was torn by other considerations as well.

Was it just the hope of her ransom money and the need to keep her untouched to assure the receipt of it? Or was it something more—mayhap even a real affection growing for her, and the need first to win her heart before he claimed her body?

'Twas a forbidden desire, and too dangerous to assume. Only Hawkwind could tell her which 'twas. But she didn't dare ask—not now, not as physically *and* emotionally vulnerable as she suddenly felt.

She lifted on one elbow and touched him tentatively on the chest. He immediately stiffened.

"Aye?" His voice was thick and husky, strained.

"How do you feel? After last night, I mean?"

"Fine. Gloriously refreshed," he gritted. "Thank you so much for asking, but I presently have greater problems to deal with than my health."

"I can see that." A flush stole into her cheeks but she forged on. "I am sorry if I caused you pain."

His arm swung down from his eyes, eyes burning with the most heartrending yearning Deidra had ever seen. "You could also be the one to end that pain."

Silence hung heavy on the air as their gazes met and locked. The blood pounded through Deidra, hammering in her ears, flooding her body with a sudden surge of heat. She felt light-headed, giddy, and so very confused.

He hadn't said he loved her, or even cared for her. He hadn't made any offers of marriage, nor assured her he would treat her as an equal or allow her her freedom. Nay, all he'd done was ask her to ease his physical torment. 'Twasn't enough. Not even from a man such as he.

She exhaled a deep breath, willing her own excitement at the thought of coupling with him to subside. Aye, she wanted him, mayhap as much as he wanted her, but the wanting in and of itself was too superficial, too fleeting. If she didn't win his heart, his respect in the bargain, 'twould soon be over between them at any rate. He would never grant what she wanted then. He wouldn't need to. And Deidra knew, in her secret heart, she couldn't bear that.

"Your pain is of your own doing," she forced herself finally to respond. "What I did in innocent slumber grants you no right to expect what I've no wish to give."

His green eyes narrowed. "My honest response to you as a man deserves no derision, either."

"I wasn't deriding you," Deidra hotly protested, stung by his unfair assessment of her reply, "just denying you. If you didn't constantly measure everything I do or say from the sorry view of your loins, you'd save yourself a lot of grief!"

"Would I now?" he muttered, a dangerous light flaring in his eyes. "Well, mayhap if we clear up this little 'misunderstanding' between us, once and for all, 'twill also improve my sorry view of things!"

With that, Hawkwind grasped her about the waist and jerked her down to him. Before Deidra could utter protest, his mouth came down on hers, hot, commanding, and brutally passionate.

Chapter 10

A brief moment, no more, of outrage and shock, then Deidra pushed away and hastily sat up. Hawkwind frowned up at her, a look of puzzlement in his passion darkened eyes. Deidra took his hand in hers. "That wasn't wise. You know that as well as I."

"Do I now?" he drawled sarcastically and pulled his hand from her clasp. "I don't recall asking your permission. This time I decided to take what I wanted. What I've had the right to all along."

There he went again, acting the insufferable, arrogant stud, Deidra thought. Her owner and lord and master. By the saints, how could she have so easily forgotten the real man hidden beneath the outrageously handsome and seductive exterior!

"Have you forgotten the value of my maidenhood?" She forced herself to meet his furious gaze. "Is your pleasure suddenly of more import than my ransom?"

"Mayhap," he gritted. "Would it have been such a terrible thing if we'd coupled? Tell me true, Deidra."

She lowered her head. "I-I don't know."

"Then why . . . ?" Hawkwind turned her face back to him. A confused tenderness gleamed in his eyes. "Why, lass, do you continue to refuse the pleasure we both seek? I'm not a crude man. I can be gentle with you."

She tried to jerk her face away, but Hawkwind refused to let her. Gazing down at him, a fierce surge of desire filled her. He was so handsome. She lusted after every inch of him, from his scarred, bearded face, striking green eyes and long, luxurious fall of brown hair, to his firm, sensual lips, strong, stubborn jaw, and magnificent body. But it didn't matter. He wasn't the man for her. Not even in some superficial, carnal way.

"I-I don't know," she finally replied. "Ah, but you confuse me so! One minute I want you and the next . . . the next I know it can never be between us." Tears filled her eyes and, despite her attempts to control them, spilled over onto her cheeks. Furious with her show of weakness, Deidra angrily swiped them away. "Just let it be, Hawkwind. Let it be!"

"And will it change what still burns between us?" he gently prodded, strangely moved by her tears. At every turn she revealed yet another aspect of her complex, intriguing personality. And, instead of pushing him further away, it only drew him closer. 'Twas dangerous, very dangerous. *She* was dangerous. Yet still he was drawn to her.

He released her and shoved a hand through his hair to still its sudden trembling. " 'Twon't be over until 'tis settled between us, lass. Why not make love, and see where 'twill lead?"

"B-because 'twon't be love, and you know it!" she choked, her tears now interspersed with sobs. "You aren't capable of l-loving a woman. Why, you aren't even capable of t-trusting one!"

His features hardened into a mask of cynical incredulity. Ever so slowly, Hawkwind pushed himself to a sitting position. "What has trust got to do with it? Or love, for that matter?"

"N-naught to y-you." She hiccuped. "But everything t-to me."

"By the Mother!" Hawkwind threw back his head, his eyes clenched shut in frustration. "Women!"

"Women?" Deidra scooted over and socked him on the chest. "And what is that supposed to mean?"

He glared down at her fist, then back up at her. "Careful, Deidra," he warned. "You're beginning to act like a wench again."

"Oh, fine," she snapped. "Try and change the subject because I've struck too close to the mark! Talk about being a typical *man!*"

"I'm not afraid to discuss any subject." His gaze narrowed. "But beware. You might not like the answers."

A defiant spark lit her eyes. "Well, you won't know what I like or don't like until you try me."

"Fine. What was the question?"

Deidra rolled her eyes. " 'Twasn't a question, you thick-skulled lout. 'Twas a statement."

"And that statement was . . . ?"

She considered him for a long moment. "That you're not capable of trusting a woman, much less loving one."

Hawkwind gave a snort of disgust. "I'm capable of anything I *choose* to be capable of. And I find the talk of love a bit premature, at any rate."

"So do I, but what of trust? Is that premature as well?"

"Aye. Content yourself with the fact I've shared my tent for over two weeks now with you, slept nearby without worry you'd rise and stab me in my sleep. And I've even allowed you to begin warrior's training—mind you, against my better judgment, but nonetheless, I have."

"And if I succeed, you'll permit me to join your army?"

He scowled. "That subject is a sore one with me and not open to discussion just now."

Again, Deidra rolled her eyes. "Nay, I suppose 'twouldn't be." Her expression went solemn. "Well, at any rate, I was speaking of another form of trust."

"And that is?"

"The trust of intimacy. When one feels secure enough with the other to share private thoughts, hopes, and dreams. And troubles as well."

"What?" Hawkwind stared down at her, openmouthed. By the Mother, would she never cease to amaze him? "Are you daft? My private thoughts are my own, as are my troubles. I share those with no one!"

"Not even Renard and Alena? Not ever with Bardrick?" Deidra shook her head. "Then, truly, what kind of friends are they?"

"They're different. I've known them for years, have suffered alongside them and bared my soul to them."

"And doesn't a man and woman bare something of their souls, as well as bodies, when they couple?"

"You're naive, Deidra. Not to mention hopelessly romantic." He shot her a lopsided grin. "I'd not expected that in such a fiery, independent-minded little lass as you make yourself out to be, but I must admit I like it. It softens you, makes you more feminine."

"A decided compliment, coming from you," Deidra muttered.

He immediately sobered. "You ask for too much, too soon, lass. 'Tis no insult to you if I guard my heart closely. I have my reasons, but good ones they most certainly are."

She exhaled a deep breath. "And mayhap I push too hard, too fast. I've always been an impatient sort. But if we could only begin, even if 'tis slowly. 'Twould give me hope."

"Hope for what?" Hawkwind eyed her suspiciously. "I promised naught—"

"Oh, I know that." She waved his cautiousness away with an imperious motion of her hand. "I only want to know one thing for the present. 'Twill satisfy me."

"And that one thing is?"

"What happened that winter's day you were attacked by those men? Why were they trying to kill you?"

A savage curse rumbled deep within his chest. He had forgotten about the supposed vision she'd said she'd had. The wench must indeed be a witch! 'Twould make sense, if one chose to believe the now old rumors the Lord of Rothgarn had wed a sorceress.

Hawkwind arched a dark brow. "You're the witch," he said mockingly. "You tell me."

"I already told you everything I know. I didn't summon the vision and wouldn't know how to do so again at any rate. I only asked you of it because I care, and would see it as a token of your trust in me."

"Nay," Hawkwind muttered, a dark, thunderous expression forming in his eyes. "'Tis a sad and sordid tale. 'Twould sicken you." *And mayhap drive you even further from me,* he silently added. "Ask aught else, and as long as it doesn't endanger me or my army, I'll tell you. But not that. 'Tis best you forget what you saw. 'Tis none of your concern."

"And why not?" Deidra demanded, his words stirring her frustration and anger anew. "Why do you refuse to view me as an equal? Am I not worthy of your trust and respect? By birth I am already far above you, but have I ever belittled you or made you feel below me? Yet at every turn you try to put me in my place, which is apparently far below you!"

His gaze turned icy. "And how do you know what I truly am—or was? As if the privilege of birth should ever be the true criterion for judging the worth of a man! Some of the foulest, most treacherous and cruel men I've ever known have been of noble birth. Some of the finest have been the most humbly born!"

"I didn't say differently," Deidra hastened to interject. "I only used the difference in our births as an example of my confusion at why you treat me so patronizingly. Just because I'm a woman—"

"Is precisely why I treat you as I do." Hawkwind inhaled a ragged breath. "As man to woman you may not be my equal and I may not care to tell you all about myself, but you *are* special to me. Can't that be enough for now?"

Enough for now? Special to him? A joyous acquiescence rose to Deidra's lips before she caught herself. What had he really offered her, but the consolation of a few words of encouragement? What, indeed, did being "special" to him mean? Mayhap he felt that way about all his women. 'Twould make the most sense, or at least 'twas the safest course of thought to take.

Deidra sighed and shook her head. "Nay, it can't. I cannot lie with a man who doesn't respect and cherish me. Nor trust me." She rolled off the bed and paused beside it.

"Where are you going?" he growled, his face turning dark with annoyance.

"Already it grows late." Deidra met his stare. "I have a full day of training ahead and mustn't keep Alena waiting." She smiled grimly. "Otherwise, I'm certain my tardiness would be construed as a lack of proper enthusiasm and reported to you. Have I your leave to go?"

"Go, with my blessing," Hawkwind snapped. "Have no fear I'll question your enthusiasm for your warrior's training. The only thing you lack is the enthusiasm and courage to be a real woman!"

Maud's potion worked wonders. Deidra was suffused with an exhilarating surge of energy that, though it couldn't make up for her lack of battle prowess against the more experienced Alena, certainly provided the warrior woman with a significant challenge. As Deidra fought her that morning, the energizing sense of power and enhanced stamina finally drove away the lingering memories, with their frustration and anger, of Hawkwind. He could just be damned for all she cared, Deidra thought as she slashed to and fro against Alena, as pigheaded as he was in continuing to deny her his trust.

Relentlessly, methodically, she drove the other woman back, giving no quarter or opportunity for Alena to regain her balance or the offensive. A wild, fierce exultation thrummed through Deidra's veins, fueling her relentless assault. Yet, when she'd finally backed the blond warrior woman up against a tree with nowhere to go, the battle lust drained from Deidra in one debilitating rush.

'Twas Hawkwind she had fought, at least in her heart and mind. There was no glory, no honor in humiliating Alena because of it. With a shuddering sigh, Deidra lowered her wooden sword and stepped back. She glanced up at the sun, even then reaching its blazing zenith.

" 'Tis time for a break, wouldn't you say?" she asked spiritlessly. "I'm famished."

As she wiped the sweat from her brow, Alena shot her a quizzical look, then nodded. "Aye, that 'tis. You did well this morn. Mayhap we'll advance to a real sword this afternoon, if you think you're up to it."

Excitement flared briefly in Deidra's eyes. "Aye, I'm up to it." Her face fell. "But will Hawkwind permit it? You know as well as I he but humors me in this training. He has no intention of ever allowing me to join his army or go to battle."

"You can't know that for sure, Deidra." Alena tossed her wooden sword aside. "He's a reasonable man. He'll concede his error in time."

"Not in my case," she muttered glumly.

"Well, mayhap, but mayhap not," the other woman said. "Go, eat your midday meal, then take an extra half hour break. You've more than earned it. Besides, I've some business of Hawkwind's to see to. Meet me back here in an hour's time."

Deidra managed a wan smile, then did as she was bidden. After a quick lunch of leftover roast quail, a slice of crusty brown bread, and a pear, washed down by a leather flask of barley water, she decided to take a short walk about the camp.

Though the tents were still up, most of the soldiers were busy packing for the long journey to the next battle campaign on the morrow. Several paused, however, to hail her as she passed by.

"Greetings, mistress," Bruno, her ruddy-skinned, red-haired former guard called out to her. She waved, then ambled over.

He was engaged in the attempt to stuff all of his worldly possessions into a small, threadbare rucksack. The toes of an extra pair of boots poked through one rather large hole, the handle of a tarnished and bent spoon protruded from another. And still Bruno couldn't quite seem to get the entire sack laced closed. Deidra smiled down at the unwieldy mess, then squatted beside the aggravated soldier.

"Need a bit of help there, do you?" she asked smilingly.

He glanced up, his face beet red and sweat sheened, and nodded vehemently. "Aye, mistress, if ye could find some way to help me, I'd be much in yer debt." He shook his head in bemusement. " 'Tis a strange thing, is it not, I can hack off arms and heads with the best o' them, but when it comes to a simple packing of my belongings, I'm as helpless as a newborn babe."

Bruno cocked his head as he glanced over at her, all sincerity and befuddlement. "Why do ye think that's so, mistress?"

"I think we all have our special talents," Deidra replied as she took the rucksack and dumped its contents out on the ground. "Instead of bemoaning what we don't do well, we should celebrate what we do."

The soldier squinted in thought. "Aye, ye're most likely right, mistress. Jest like ye should find yer contentment in loving the chief, rather than fighting so hard to be a warrior, which ye can never hope to be good enough at."

Deidra froze in her nimble and efficient efforts at repacking Bruno's rucksack. She lifted her gaze to him. "Who bid you tell me that? The 'chief' himself?"

The soldier stared at her for a long moment, struggling to comprehend the meaning of her words. Then his eyes widened and he vehemently shook his head. "Oh, nay, mistress. I've never spoken to Hawkwind about ye. 'Twouldn't be proper and all. I jest watch when ye practice and, as fine as ye are in swordplay, ye haven't the killer's instinct.

" 'Tisn't meant as an insult," he hastened to add as Deidra scowled and commenced angrily to stuff the rest of his belongings into his pack. "Yer talents, jest as ye said mine did, lie in other things."

Despite the haphazard packing job, Deidra still managed to contain it all in a much more orderly fashion. She laced the rucksack closed and handed it back to Bruno. "My thanks for your thoughtful observations on how I should live my life, but no matter what you and the others—Hawkwind included—see as my proper place in life, I refuse to view it thusly. In this case, I'd prefer being a mediocre soldier than the most brilliant of mistresses!"

She rose in one fluid motion and stomped off, Bruno's mumble of apology following her. "Beg pardon, mistress. I meant no offense. Truly I didn't. What did I say to offend . . ."

The day, Deidra decided, despite her success in her earlier sword lessons, suddenly threatened to become a total failure. Not only had naught been accomplished with Hawkwind, save to stir the fires of their mutual passion yet hotter, but Bruno had voiced what apparently was a popular opinion around camp as to her proper role. And then there was the deceit she'd used in leading Alena to think her swordsman's stamina was a normal evolution of her training. For all her fine dreams and efforts, all she'd managed to accomplish were lies and mediocrity. Mayhap her greatest talents *did* lie in bed, as sorry a consideration as 'twas.

Immersed in her morose thoughts, Deidra failed to note the crowd gathered around a tree, nor the harsh cry of a large bird, until she was almost upon them. Her curiosity piqued, she pushed through the gathering of men to get a better look. As she did, Simon's voice rose on the air.

"Kill it," he cried. "Kill the bird! The ungrateful animal bit me when I tried to catch it." Simon held up a grimy finger. A tiny drop of blood glistened on its tip. "The falcon is crazed. 'Tis no use to anyone. Kill it!"

To emphasize his point, he grabbed a large stone and lifted it over his head. As if sensing its peril, the falcon glanced up, its once bright eyes dull and glazed, yet it didn't move or attempt to fly away. 'Twas sick, Deidra realized, and had bitten Simon in a feeble attempt to protect itself. Compassion for the bird welled in her.

"Halt, Simon!" she cried, raising the husky timbre of her voice above the din of rough male voices urging the soldier on. "The bird is ill, not crazed. You'd have done better to hood it before trying to catch it. Any falcon, tame or wild, would've bitten a stranger attempting to handle it."

Simon wheeled around. For an instant, surprise flickered in his eyes. The stone dropped from his hands. Then, a mocking grin twisted his mouth. "And what have we here? Tired so soon of yer new avocation as warrior-in-training, have ye? Well, I'd say better that ye hie yerself back to Hawkwind's tent and make amends. If ye're fortunate, he may take ye back." He made a shooing motion with his hands. "Hurry now. Don't linger where ye're not wanted."

Heat flushed Deidra's face and she had to inhale a few slow, deep breaths to contain her anger. Simon had never forgiven her for her humiliation of him that morn she'd forced him to take her to Hawkwind. Nor would he ever, it now seemed.

Her glance scanned the gathering. Some men appeared as angry as she over the slight paid to her as Hawkwind's woman, others averted their gazes, and still others nodded as if in agreement with Simon.

Well, what had she expected? Deidra asked herself. Save for her appearances outside in her walks with Alena and, more recently, her warrior's training sessions, she meant little to Hawkwind's men save for whatever value she possessed for him. Be that as it may, it changed naught. She'd be damned if she'd let Simon harm a sick and weakened bird.

Squaring her shoulders, Deidra shoved through into the small circle formed by the men. She strode over to confront her former abductor. "I have no dagger this time," she calmly stated, "but that makes me no less determined.

Leave the bird, Simon. What honor is there in killing the falcon? Save your energies, instead, for the battles to come."

"And what will ye do with it then?" he snarled. "Take it to Hawkwind's tent? 'Twon't do ye any good. He hates the hunting birds even worse than I. Mark my words. He won't let ye keep it."

Startled by the revelation, Deidra stood there, momentarily speechless. Hawkwind hated birds? Somehow, she couldn't envision him hating or harming anything smaller than himself, and certainly not an animal of any kind. She shrugged off Simon's dire prediction.

"Nonetheless, I want the falcon." Deidra forced herself to meet the man's sullenly hostile gaze. "What I arrange with Hawkwind is my problem, not yours. Will you let me have it?"

The approach to winning Simon's agreement was markedly less assertive than the stubborn assault upon the stable master five years ago. If Deidra had learned aught in those past few years, 'twas that diplomacy won more allies than confrontation. Save in a few special cases, like Hawkwind's, it usually worked.

"Aye," he grudgingly conceded. "Have the cursed bird if ye wish. But don't come wailing to me if it bites yer hand as well." With that, Simon made an impatient motion to clear a way for himself back through the crowd.

Deidra watched until the men dispersed, then turned to the falcon. 'Twas a peregrine falcon, she realized, now that she had the leisure to examine it more closely, and a tame one at that, noting the tattered leather jesses and tiny bells hanging from its legs. It looked thin, huddling there on the ground, feathers ruffled, wings hanging limp at its side, and eyes half-lidded and dull. Its breathing appeared ragged, with mouth open. Occasionally, it twitched. She needed to get the bird into some safe place and examined, but first she must subdue it long enough to capture it.

A hood. Though the bird was apparently someone's

hunting falcon gone astray, she still needed a hood. Deidra glanced up, her mind racing. Her gaze met Alena's.

"Simon was right, you know," the blond warrior said. "Hawkwind won't take kindly to you bringing a falcon into his tent."

"He truly hates them then?"

Alena shook her head. "Nay, but that, in itself, is a long story. Suffice it to say, 'twould be best if you found someone else to take the bird."

Deidra's brow wrinkled in thought. "But who? Maud?"

"Mayhap. 'Tis worth a try, at any rate." Alena eyed the peregrine with a jaded look. "I've no experience with such birds. Is there some way to safely capture it?"

"Oh, aye." Relief filled Deidra. "All we need is something to cover its eyes. Once it's hooded, the bird will be quite docile."

Alena cocked a dark blond brow. "Is the falcon wild or tamed?" She dug one of her leather gloves out from beneath her belt and tossed it to Deidra. "Will this work as a makeshift hood?"

Deidra deftly caught it and rolled up the glove halfway. "'Tis tame." She pointed to the leather thongs fastened about the bird's feet. "See, the falcon wears jesses." She grinned over at the other woman. "And your glove will do quite nicely, if only the falcon is willing to trust me a bit more than it did Simon."

"Do you know what you're doing?"

Though a goodly portion was sheer bravado, Deidra had indeed had a bit of experience with falcons. She'd handled several over the past years when she and her father had gone falconing with various visiting nobles. Whether she could soothe a sick, frightened, and strange bird, however, was another matter.

Deidra walked over to the peregrine and sank to her knees. The bird flapped its feathers and cried out in warning, but even that required too much effort for it to sustain for long. It quieted and crouched low on the ground.

"There's naught to fear, brave bird," Deidra crooned as she drew near. She knew she'd have to capture the falcon's head in one hand and slip the glove on with the other. That necessitated two hands coming at the peregrine at once, something sure to make the bird uneasy. And, though apparently very ill, it had already struck out and drawn blood once.

'Twas a very small thing, Deidra reassured herself, even if the falcon did manage to bite her. A warrior expected to suffer far greater wounds in battle. And this battle bore the potential of hopefully saving a life, not taking it.

"Naught to fear," she murmured over and over, lowering her voice until it was hypnotic and soothing. The peregrine eyed her suspiciously, hopped a few steps away as her hands reached out toward it, then stilled, its gaze fixed on Deidra's approach. At last, with one strangled cry, it allowed itself to be caught.

An instant later, Deidra had the hood over the bird's head and tied loosely in place with a small strip of cloth she'd torn from her tunic hem. She glanced up at Alena, a smile of triumph on her lips. "See, 'twasn't such a hard thing after all. The falcon knew I meant it no harm."

Alena gave a snort of disbelief. "Aye, and mayhap Simon had already worn it out for you. At any rate, let's get it to Maud. If the bird is too far gone, 'tis best we know it forthwith. We still have a half day's training to complete."

She shot Deidra a wry grin. "And I've a mind to see if you're as energetic this afternoon as you were this morning."

Chapter 11

Hawkwind strode through camp, exhausted after a wearying day of final plans and arrangements for tomorrow's journey. Though not his usual wont, he planned on a short nap before the supper meal and subsequent hours more of meetings. Deidra should still be out with Alena for another few hours, so the tent would be all his.

He didn't think he could risk facing her right now as 'twas. She was rapidly working her way under his skin, and he didn't like it. Curse her, Hawkwind thought, his fists clenching at his sides as he made his furious way to his tent. He'd decided long ago the tender emotions must be permanently discarded, that there was no place in his life or heart for such distracting and fruitless, not to mention dangerous, yearnings. And, for the past eight years, he'd managed to do that quite admirably.

Renard. Where the hell was Renard? It had been over a week now since he'd sent his second-in-command to spy out the truth about Deidra's claim. He needed the answer, —and damn soon, before he could decide what to do about her.

Time and again he'd been tempted to forget the whole ransom idea, telling himself she lied. Yet, somehow, someway, he knew she didn't. There was too much of breeding, of education and refinement about her, for Deidra not to be some nobleman's daughter. If only she weren't Rothgarn's!

Too much was at stake—his revenge, his stolen inheritance—to risk bedding her until he knew for certain. The ransom money he and his army could live without. D'Mondeville's advance would adequately pay their way through the countryside until they reached the Lord of Firston's lands. But the return of his *own* lands and castle was another matter altogether.

He might well be able to wrangle that concession from D'Mondeville as the second part of his payment, but what if the man changed his mind about attacking Rothgarn? If that happened, there'd be no further payment coming. Nay, 'twas safer to hedge his bets, Hawkwind decided, and Deidra was the solution to the dilemma—and need—that had been eating at him for the past eight years.

Hawkwind reached his tent, heaved a great sigh, and stepped inside. Immediately, a sensation of another's presence assailed him. He glanced around. As his gaze swept over Deidra's pallet, he choked back a tormented groan.

She knelt there, hastily drawing a dark cloth over what looked to be a wooden box. At the nervous, guilty look she shot him, Hawkwind's eyes narrowed. The wench was up to something. 'Twas written all over her face.

He forced himself to approach her. "What have you there in the box?" He motioned toward it. "Collecting all your belongings for the journey tomorrow?"

Deidra rose. "Nay," she began carefully. " 'Tis a sick animal. I found it today and took it to Maud. She refused to keep it in her tent, however, so I thought . . . mayhap you wouldn't . . . mind . . ."

"I have no aversion to you having a pet, as long as 'tisn't potentially lethal." He stepped around her and leaned toward the box. "What did you rescue? A rabbit or a baby bird?"

She caught his hand before he could reach the cloth and

flip it back. "Don't. The bird needs darkness to keep it calm and I just finished feeding it. Let it rest, Hawkwind."

There was something about the alacrity in Deidra's movement that stirred Hawkwind's suspicions. She was hiding something, but what? Did she think him so heartless he'd deny her the freedom to nurse a sick animal?

A squawk and flutter of wings interrupted his thoughts. The wooden box shook with the force of a large body shifting within. Hawkwind's gaze riveted on Deidra, who had gone suddenly pale. "What in the heavens do you have in there? A full-grown chicken?"

"Nay." Deidra swallowed convulsively. " 'Tis a-a falcon."

"What?" Despite his best efforts to contain it, the old, uncontrollable surge of panic struck him. "You've got a falcon in there?"

"Aye." Deidra nodded slowly, her worst fears stirred to life by the stricken look on Hawkwind's suddenly pale face. "I rescued him from Simon, who was intent on flinging a big stone onto him because the falcon had bitten him in self-defense. Then I took the bird to Maud, who pronounced it ill and needful of rest and food, but who refused to keep it in her hospital. So, I had no other place to bring Mystic but here."

"Mystic?"

" 'Tis his name. Mystic. Would you like to take a quick peek at him? He's a hunting bird, from his jesses and bells," Deidra offered, thinking mayhap a look at the magnificent bird would ease Hawkwind's acceptance of him. When he didn't reply, she lifted the cloth and gestured to the huddled mass of brown feathers and black-crowned head. " 'Tis a peregrine falcon."

He shot her a pained look, fighting back the surge of nausea and, conversely, strange attraction the sight of the bird stirred. "I know. But he can't stay here."

At the flat, "brooked no argument" tone to Hawkwind's voice, Deidra's heart sank. 'Twas so unfair, and so unlike Hawkwind to be this way. But then, she reminded herself, what did she truly know of the real man he kept so tightly guarded, and the past life that had caused him to become that way?

"I can't believe you truly hate birds," she said, letting the cloth cover the box and falcon within again. She lifted her gaze to meet his. "It must be something more."

"I don't hate them," Hawkwind replied abruptly. "I just don't like to be around them."

"Why?" Deidra prodded. "Because they remind you of something unpleasant? Then why did you take the name of a hawk and fly it on your standard, if you hate the birds so?"

He shot her a sharp glance. By the Mother, did her witch's powers now include mind reading? "Whatever my reasons, they're mine and no one else's. Don't pry where you're not wanted, Deidra. 'Twill do you no good. I already made that clear this morn."

"Aye, that you did," she agreed grimly. "But 'tis one thing to shut me out. 'Tis quite another to condemn Mystic to death because of some unreasonable fears. 'Tisn't the falcon's fault, whatever may have happened to you. It did naught wrong."

Fury blazed in his eyes. "I never said 'twas the bird's fault!"

Deidra shrugged. "Nay, you didn't, but from your reaction, 'twas still quite evident you thought it. You needn't involve yourself with the falcon. The tent's big. Please, Hawkwind, 'tis only for one night," she pleaded, warming to her cause. "On the morrow, we set out for a good four days' journey. I can easily keep Mystic away from you then. 'Tis just for one night, Hawkwind."

He gazed down into big brown eyes appealingly flecked with gold. Eyes staring up at him with the most alluring and entreating of looks. Hawkwind felt his resolve slipping. 'Twas as she said. 'Twas only for one night, and there was naught about the falcon itself that threatened him. 'Twas only the memories it stirred. Memories he must come to terms with sooner or later.

"I am not an unreasonable man." Hawkwind shoved a hand through his tousled mane of hair and sighed. "Do you know how to care for a bird of prey?"

For an instant, Deidra stared up at him, not quite certain she'd heard what she hoped she'd heard. Then joy flared and she grinned. "Maud showed me how to give Mystic a feeding through a hollow reed until he's able to eat normally again. And she said 'twas best to keep him quiet and warm."

"And what do you plan to feed him?"

Deidra frowned in thought, then shrugged. "Rabbit, finely chopped, until Mystic is stronger? And water?"

He nodded. "'Twill do for the time being, but quail is best. I'll send a few men out to catch some."

She smiled in gratitude. "Thank you, Hawkwind. I knew you weren't the kind of man who'd intentionally be cruel to an animal."

A warning light flared in his eyes. "I didn't say I wanted anything to do with the bird. But there are few here who know anything about falconry."

"Yet, you do." Deidra paused, studying him intently. "How did you come by such knowledge?"

Bitterness twisted his mouth into a tight, grim line. "In a way you'd never begin to imagine." He rose. "Now, no more of it." He cast her a narrow-eyed look. "Why aren't you out training with Alena? The day is still young and I gave no special dispensation for you to work a modified schedule."

Deidra flushed in anger. Why must he always slam down that barrier between them just when they were beginning to draw a little closer? 'Twas his reluctance to reveal his past, she realized, a subject they skirted more and more oft of late. Well, she must content herself with the fact he seemed to trust her a little and that, bit by bit, she was insinuating herself into his life.

His life. Suddenly, the thought struck her, though Renard had yet to return, he must certainly do so soon. Once he did, Hawkwind would be forced to make a choice. Would he still offer her back to her father for ransom or decide, instead, to keep her at his side? The consideration was unsettling enough, but what was far worse was Deidra's uncertainty over which option Hawkwind would choose.

An impulse to ask him that very question rose to her lips. Only the greatest of effort controlled it. 'Twas too soon to demand the decision she hoped he'd make. But in the meanwhile . . .

Deidra rose. "I'm going to find Alena right now. She gave me leave to settle Mystic, then return to my training." She walked over to stand before Hawkwind and, before she lost her nerve, lifted on tiptoe and kissed him on the mouth. Then, ignoring his startled look, Deidra turned and departed the tent.

As she strode through camp and back to the training field, Deidra couldn't help a small grin of triumph. Her quick little kiss had worked as intended. 'Twas all part of her new plan. Keep Hawkwind unsettled, off balance, never certain of what she'd do next. Keep him wanting her until he finally realized she was so firmly entwined about his heart no amount of ransom could ever make him let her go.

After the supper meal, Deidra made a quick trip to check on Mystic and feed him a thin gruel of water and finely ground rabbit. Then, as the warrior's potion the healer had given her had invigorated her and she had no desire yet for sleep, she decided to pay Maud a visit to discuss the disturbing results of her attempts to heal Hawkwind last night.

Though the big warrior chief seemed no worse for the wear for his healing, Deidra was convinced her powers had gotten out of control, had become dangerous. That frightened her. Maud was the only one who could help.

Bardrick was awake and sitting up in bed, awkwardly attempting under Maud's patient supervision to feed himself. Deidra watched until Bardrick finally gave up and motioned for a brief respite from his frustrating and messy undertaking. Then she strode across the tent to his bedside.

Her old bodyguard managed a lopsided grin. Deidra smiled back. "Every day your progress seems greater and greater. I'll soon have you stalking after me, lecturing and threatening, won't I?"

He nodded. "A-aye. That y-ye will."

"And complaining about my cooking, and back rubs and the close confines of this tent as well," Maud added with a chuckle. She tossed Deidra a quick glance over her shoulder. "How goes it with yer falcon?"

"Mystic? Oh, he's fine, though for a time I thought Hawkwind would toss him out of the tent."

"But he didn't?"

"Nay, he didn't."

Maud turned back to Bardrick. "Try again, love. Ye need to get more nourishment into ye if ye wish to be up and about again soon. Deidra and I will take a short walk in the meanwhile. We've a few women's things to discuss."

With that she rose and motioned for Deidra to precede her out of the tent. Deidra arched an auburn brow, then did as indicated. Once outside, though, she turned to the healer. "You don't seem surprised that Hawkwind accepted the falcon. Why is that?"

She shrugged. "Because ye have an effect upon him no other woman has ever had. Ye force him to look back on his life and question his former decisions—and look forward and dare hope for something better."

Deidra frowned in puzzlement. "Better than a mercenary's life? What could that be? Hawkwind's a free man. He can go wherever he chooses, do whatever he wants. No man, not even the king, would dare bid him nay without great consideration. What better life could he wish for save what he already has?"

Maud motioned for Deidra to follow her from the tent and toward the outskirts of camp, where they walked for a time in silence until out of earshot of the soldiers. " 'Tis true Hawkwind has freedom of a sort," she finally began again. "But 'tis only of an outward kind. He's not free in his heart, his soul, nor from the bitterness of his memories. He isn't yet free to love a woman, nor take one to wife, nor to rear a family in safe and contented stability. All he knows anymore is pain, emptiness, and war."

The healer grasped Deidra by the arm and drew her to a halt. "He was bred and reared to a far better life than he now lives."

"Then why—?" Deidra paused, confusion flooding her. "I don't understand, Maud. Who *is* Hawkwind? And what kind of life did he come from?"

"He yet refuses to tell ye, does he?" Maud sighed and shook her head. "Then the truth—and his healing—will mean naught until it comes from him. I can tell ye no more, child."

" 'Tis something terrible, isn't it?" Deidra demanded. "Something that has twisted his body and life, and seared a wound upon his soul that will not heal." She wrapped her arms about her in a protective manner, lowered her head and shivered. "I don't like it, not knowing the answer, yet I fear the knowledge all the same."

"Why, child?" the other woman softly challenged. "What could have ever happened to Hawkwind that could frighten ye so, or drive ye from him? Do ye imagine him evil, or capable of an evil act?"

Deidra's head jerked up. Fire flashed in her eyes. "Nay. Never! Hawkwind, for all his stubborn arrogance, is a good man. He . . . he is brave, kind, and honorable."

"Then why are ye so afeared of knowing the truth?"

"I-I don't know." Deidra shook her head. "Mayhap I fear my own inability to help him, to be the woman he needs. I don't want to fail him. Mayhap, as well," she continued softly, "I fear he'll find me lacking."

" 'Tis a hard thing, to bare one's heart to the uncertainties of love," Maud solemnly agreed. "And sometimes, even when the love is there, 'tisn't enough to overcome the needs and wants of the other."

"Like with my mother?"

"Aye, like with yer mother, and with others."

At the look of ineffable sadness that crossed the healer's face, Deidra inhaled a startled breath. "You loved a man, yet couldn't be with him, didn't you, Maud? And now 'tis over between you."

"Nay." Maud slowly shook her head. "Though 'tis true we can never be together, the love between us will never die. That knowledge is mayhap more painful to bear than never having known I was loved at all." She lifted tormented eyes to Deidra. "The old wolfhound can't accept my powers. My magic sickens him, no matter how hard he fights to overcome it. And I can't give it up, no matter how much he desires it. 'Tis a part of me. I am not who I am without my magic."

"Bardrick?" Deidra breathed. It all made sense now, the healer's fierce protectiveness of him, her faithful attendance at his sickbed, the strange, arcing, aching looks Deidra had caught them occasionally sharing. Maud loved Bardrick, and he, her. Yet he had left her five years ago to find service with Deidra's father and never returned until fate had once more drawn them together.

"I'm so sorry, Maud," she murmured, not knowing what else would be of comfort. " 'Tisn't fair, is it, for a man to hold such unreasonable beliefs? I'd never thought it of Bardrick. I've always known him to be so good, so kind, so gentle."

"And he is," the healer hastened to agree. "He simply couldn't overcome his upbringing. Bardrick is from Moresham, a town in a region fraught with superstition and horrible experiences with sorcerers and witches. Do ye remember tales of the Curse of Moresham Castle?"

"Aye." Deidra couldn't help a small shudder. "The Lord of Moresham refused to pay a sorcerer for services rendered and instead had him burned at the stake. In return for his treachery, the sorcerer laid a curse upon him just before he died. A curse that would carry through the generations of the lord's family, driving them all to insanity by their fortieth year of life.

"A curse that waited for its fulfillment until each bore children to carry on the name. For each to live long enough to know and dread their eventual fate." Maud sighed. "The Lord of Morseham was Bardrick's liege. He saw it all in the years of his youth and young manhood. The curse and its magical origins left an indelible impression upon him, sickening him to all magic."

"He'll not like it any better in me, then," Deidra observed defiantly, "when he discovers my powers."

"Yet can ye turn from the magic calling ye? That smolders deep within, awaiting but the call to flame anew?"

"I-I don't know." Deidra shook her head. "How can anyone ignore the pain of another when one possesses the ability to ease it? 'Tis so wonderful, so seductive, no matter how frightening." She walked over to a towering oak tree and flung herself down beneath its leafy haven. "I never asked for it, yet can no longer deny 'tis a part of me. Though I don't know if I would dare wield my magic again, nor show my powers to others, they are still there, lurking just below the surface."

"What if someday Hawkwind turned from ye because of them? Would ye deny them then?"

Deidra frowned. "I-I don't know. Such an act seemed impossible for my mother. In the end, could I be any different?" She shook her head. "I doubt it. 'Twas the reason I left Rothgarn and the safe, pampered life of a lady. I knew even then my destiny called me elsewhere.

"Aye, elsewhere." She laughed wryly. "But only to an

even more complicated fate. Everything seemed so clear just a short time ago. Freedom was all I desired. Or, at least that was what seemed to call me. Now, I'm no longer certain what 'twas. Mayhap 'twas Hawkwind. Mayhap 'twas the magic."

"And mayhap 'twas both."

Troubled brown eyes lifted. "Aye. I hope so. I couldn't bear to care for him and not have it returned, nor not be able to have a life together. I don't know how you do it, Maud."

"Ye do what ye must, child. Bear what must be borne." Maud walked over and squatted before her. "Now, no more of me and Bardrick. What is between us is our concern." She cocked her head. "Tell me of last night. How went Hawkwind's healing?"

"Fair enough, I suppose." Deidra paused, considering briefly how to phrase her next statement. "I think I lost control of my powers, though. I thought to attempt a cure of his old injuries and called upon my magic with everything within me. The force of them, flowing into him, knocked Hawkwind unconscious. And afterward . . ." Deidra's voice faded and she shuddered at the remembrance. "Afterward, my hands glowed brightly in the darkness, as if—"

"As if they were on fire?" Maud finished quietly. "Is that what ye meant to say?"

"Aye." Hope flared in Deidra. "So, you know of such abilities? Know what they mean and how to utilize them safely?"

"I know of the special fire powers," Maud replied, "but have never experienced them myself." A look of concern wrinkled her brow. "They come rarely, even to those of great skill and education, and are not to be taken lightly. They can be quite dangerous in untutored hands or when used by those less scrupulous or good. Ye must be very careful with the fire powers, child."

"Aye," Deidra agreed slowly, her mind awhirl. "I've no

wish to do harm. How can I learn to control them? You must help me, Maud."

"Ye aren't afraid, then? Ye've no wish to turn from yer gift?"

"They are mine, aren't they? As hard as it has been for me to accept, I was meant to use them." Deidra rose and brushed off the bits of leaves and dirt clinging to her breeches. "And I'd wager untutored powers are far more dangerous than accepting and learning how to properly utilize them."

Maud stood. "There's truth in yer words. But once ye've faced them, there's no turning back. 'Twill irrevocably change ye. Are ye ready for that?"

Deidra paused to consider the healer's question. "Aye. 'Tis my destiny, is it not? How can I turn from it?"

"There are many who lack the courage to face their true destinies. And ye haven't even begun to plumb the depths of what yers will entail, of that ye can be sure."

A small chin lifted resolutely. "I am not afraid."

The healer smiled. "Good." She motioned for Deidra to join her as she stepped out once more. "Now come. We must adjourn to an even more private place if I'm to continue yer lessons. They are fast becoming more complicated than I anticipated. Already, ye possess an amazing talent that far exceeds even yer own mother's. The need for ye to learn to contain and direct it grows more pressing by the day."

A fading moon shed its meager light upon the sleepy land. Twinkling bits of light dotted the black canopy of the heavens, cheerfully reassuring, comforting. Hawkwind heaved a weary sigh as he finally made his way back across camp. Only one task more lay unfinished before he could at last take his rest. Renard.

The final plans for tomorrow's journey had just been completed when a message had arrived from Renard, bidding Hawkwind meet him down by the ancient spring the camp used for its water. As Hawkwind approached, his captain immediately stepped from the leaf shaded gloom of a large oak. The two men grasped arms in a brief greeting, then stepped apart.

"Did you discover what I needed?" Hawkwind demanded.

"Enough, I'd say," his captain replied. "Rothgarn's daughter did indeed disappear about a month ago, Bardrick was sent after her, and naught has been heard of them since."

" 'Twould agree with what we've seen. What did you find of description of the Rothgarn heiress?"

"Brown of eyes and fiery of hair, just like your little hostage."

Hawkwind gave a snort of disgust. "And you took a week to discover that? I could've sent a lad to do your task, and still had him back in half the time."

Renard shrugged, unperturbed by his chief's burst of anger. "Mayhap, but would a lad have been able to discover a secret identifying mark shared only by Rothgarn's wife and daughter?"

"Deidra bears no special mark."

His friend chuckled softly. "So, the lass has kept you at bay all this while, has she? She must be very special indeed, to have resisted your manly charms."

"I tire rapidly of your jests, Renard," came a warning growl. "What do my manly charms, or lack of them where Deidra's concerned, have to do with this special mark?"

"Ah, naught, save the Rothgarn lass bears a small, flame-shaped birthmark beneath her left breast. A breast," Renard added snidely, " 'tis quite evident you have yet to see."

"My time to take a woman is my own," Hawkwind snarled, "and no concern of yours!"

"True enough." Renard laughed and held up his hands in surrender as his leader advanced threateningly on him. "But until you at least bare her breasts, you'll never be certain if she truly is who she claims to be. Or, what you'll do with her."

Hawkwind dragged in an unsteady breath and willed his anger to cool. 'Twasn't Renard's fault, not any of this. He shoved a hand through his hair. "And Rothgarn? Does he seem eager to have his daughter returned?"

His dark-haired captain grinned. "*Extremely* eager."

Hawkwind smiled grimly. He finally had Rothgarn where he wanted him. The only question remaining to be answered was how far the man was willing to go to retrieve his daughter.

Yet, even as the triumph surged through him, it was met and muted by the realization he'd have to give up Deidra. Frustration, then renewed anger, filled him, roiling beneath his breast until he wanted to shout his pain to the heavens.

At last he'd have his vengeance, one way or another. If Rothgarn refused to return his lands, he'd extract so much ransom money in turn he'd beggar the man. Yet, in the process, he must relinquish the woman who was fast becoming so inexplicably bound to him he risked losing whatever pleasure he'd ever gain in the bargain.

The realization startled him. All he'd dreamed of for the past eight years was revenge, against King William—who had stolen not only his birthright and taken part in the destruction of his two brothers—but the Lord of Rothgarn, who had so quickly and greedily accepted his lands as reward for his loyalty to the new king. With an anguished sigh, Hawkwind again lifted his gaze to the heavens. This time, there was no solace to be found even there.

The victory, which now seemed almost within his grasp, had suddenly lost the attraction of possessing any lasting satisfaction. His life, his family, were here with his army. And surprisingly, most disconcertingly, in the arms, as well, of a defiant little spitfire who fought him even as she inexorably drew him to her.

" 'Tis possible the lass isn't who she claims to be," Renard softly said, correctly reading his friend's sudden change of mood. " 'Twill be the loss of a fine opportunity to regain your lands, but there'll be others. And she suits you well."

Hawkwind wrenched his tormented gaze back to Renard. "Does she now? I fear I've long ago lost the ability to know what I need in a woman, or the courage to dare hope for, much less try to find one. I'll have the confirmation I seek tonight, though, in my heart, I already know the answer."

As he turned to go, Renard gripped his arm, halting him. "I've had much to ponder on the journey back here. There *is* yet another solution. One that could solve everything."

Hawkwind's dark eyes locked with his. "And that is?"

"If she is truly Rothgarn's spawn, claim her as yours. Rothgarn might be willing to accept your subsequent marriage once you've had her. Especially," he added pointedly, "when he learns his future son-in-law is of as noble lineage as his own."

Hawkwind gave a harsh, disparaging laugh. "Why would it matter? It bothered him not when he first took my lands."

"There were many then who thought you a traitor, king killer, and brother murderer."

"What has changed in the meantime?" Hawkwind demanded tautly. "Why would he now choose to accept a man stripped of his castle and lands, his life declared forfeit if ever he should reveal his true identity? What would Rothgarn now have to gain, save the king's enmity and the loss of rich holdings if he chose to accept me? You forget he is fiercely loyal to William."

"Loyal?" Renard chuckled. "Not so anymore. Rumor has it the Lord of Rothgarn has grown disenchanted with William's cruelty and greedy manipulations. Rumor has it, as well, the king now seeks Rothgarn's fall."

"What do I care, one way or another? I'll not go crawling to Rothgarn, even for Deidra," Hawkwind snapped. "Let the king and the Lord of Rothgarn destroy each other. 'Twill solve all my problems in one fell swoop."

Renard shrugged. "Have it as you wish, but I'd think you'd prefer a man who, though misled in the past, has finally found his conscience, over a corrupt, father-murdering king. Especially when the peaceful return of your lands would come with a sweetly beguiling lass."

Hawkwind fiercely shook his head. "She'd never have me as husband."

"She seems to like you well enough as a mercenary leader, if Alena's tales are even close to the truth. Surely a bit of blue blood coursing through your veins would only sweeten her taste for you."

"Alena talks too much!"

Renard shrugged. "Mayhap, but I needed some company while I awaited your arrival, and she suited quite nicely. According to her, you and the fire-haired lass seemed to have developed quite an attachment for each other while I was gone."

"She thinks I wish to control her. We barely get along."

" 'Tis a hard thing, deciding on the choice of one's wife," Renard commiserated. "Mayhap, in time, the lass can be tamed. And she *is* a fetching little morsel."

Hawkwind's mouth curved in a considering smile. "Aye, that she is." Then, as if remembering himself, he scowled darkly. "Curse you, Renard! How, by the Mother, did we ever stray onto the topic of marriage? I want no wife, no matter who she is! Deidra is naught to me save a source of ransom, and that is all she'll ever be!"

His mind suddenly made up, Hawkwind turned on his heel and stalked off into the night.

"And where, pray tell, are you headed?" was his captain's amused, parting query.

"Where else?" Hawkwind's defiant reply floated back to him on the night's gentle breeze. "To check on a certain birthmark."

Chapter 12

Dealing with Deidra wouldn't be as simple as his words to Renard had been. Hawkwind knew that more surely with each step he took back to his tent. Proof of her true identity or not, she wouldn't be easily convinced to bare her breasts to his gaze. And he didn't need the added turmoil the sight of them would surely stir, or the resulting battle that would ensue once the issue of her ransom was faced.

By the Mother, Hawkwind silently cursed, the wench had complicated his life from the moment he'd met her—and in ways he'd never imagined! Damn her for being the woman she was, damn her for touching his heart! If he'd only guessed the trouble she'd cause, he'd have sent her away immediately . . . before he'd ever known who she might be or her potential value.

But now 'twas far too late. He must face what must be done this night and the only decision he could make. 'Twasn't just his need for revenge against Rothgarn that drove him. 'Twas his God-given right to regain his land and people.

Yet despite his firm intent not to give Renard's suggestion another thought, the consideration of taking Deidra to wife nagged at him. If she *was* the Rothgarn heiress, he could have her and his lands through the simple expediency of marriage. Not a particularly honorable approach, considering his underhanded plan as to how to go about it, but noblewomen were wed all the time for their wealth.

Why shouldn't it be him to take Deidra to wife, rather than some other lord? She at least cared for him, felt a similar fire whenever they were together. Their coupling would be good—very good—and he knew Deidra felt that certainty as strongly as he. Already they had formed a bond few noble marriages could ever hope to possess.

The more Hawkwind considered it, the more attractive the idea became. In one simple move, he could have it all. Deidra, his lands, the eventual control of even Rothgarn lands upon the demise of her father, and all the money he'd saved over the years. He'd also, in a sense, gain some revenge against the Lord of Rothgarn when he brought Deidra back to him as his wife. There'd be naught her father could do then, naught but accept what Hawkwind had already taken from him.

His white teeth flashed in the darkness as he considered Rothgarn's impotent rage at being forced to take him as son-in-law. 'Twas a small repayment, indeed, for the pain and suffering Rothgarn's greedy takeover of his lands had wrought those many years ago, but 'twas payment of a sort, nonetheless. And once he'd ensconced himself in a position of power, he could finally begin the long and difficult process of clearing his name—a process that would ensure the downfall of King William and mayhap even Rothgarn, as well.

It seemed a foolproof plan, with a much simpler and quicker ascent back to the life he deserved. The only problem remaining was Deidra. Hawkwind truly didn't know if she'd take him as husband. There was still no assurance she'd wish to wed someone she could only possibly view as a mercenary soldier. And he dared not yet reveal his true identity to her.

She may have well heard the tales about him, his betrayal of the old king and subsequent murder of his own brothers. 'Twould seem likely she had. They only seemed to grow more horrible and revolting as the years passed, rather than die away.

Then, there was her loyalty to Rothgarn. Deidra was far from a slow or stupid woman. Once she learned who he truly was, all the pieces would fall into place. Hawkwind didn't know how she'd react or feel about him then.

Nay, 'twas wiser to keep the truth about himself from her for a time longer. Wiser to allow their own relationship to grow and strengthen, until the bonds of husband and wife were stronger than those of filial attachments. Then, if all went well, 'twould be time enough to tell her.

In the meanwhile, he planned to manipulate her, a fact she'd be furious about if she ever suspected. He'd have to hope she never would and court her, find some way to make her love him so deeply, so ardently, until naught else mattered. Naught, not even her father or lands, or his unwilling use of her.

He didn't like treating Deidra this way. Bloody hell, he didn't like treating anyone this way! But especially not Deidra.

Time and again she'd told him how she hated being used, hated being a pawn in the hands of men, and here he now was plotting to use her in the same fashion. Guilt filled Hawkwind, snaking through him until it entwined its cold, clammy tendrils about his heart.

Deidra. Infuriating, stubborn, frequently more trouble than he could bear. Yet so sweet, so tender and beguiling as well. If he hurt her, if she turned from him because of his deception . . .

What kind of man was he becoming, all in the name of vengeance and justice?

He'd make it up to her later, Hawkwind vowed fiercely as he strode through the dark silence of a sleeping army. He'd make her see 'twas all for the best. That, ultimately, she would stand to gain as much as he. That, someday, whatever came of all of this, 'twould be theirs together.

Aye, Hawkwind thought as he drew up before his tent,

for a time longer he must keep Deidra at arm's length and use her without revealing his plans. In the end, though, 'twould all be for the best. One way or another, whether she was Rothgarn's daughter or not, it had to be.

She didn't realize she was no longer alone until Mystic squawked in alarm and stirred restlessly in his box. Deidra wheeled around, the hairbrush she'd been running through her long tresses clenched in her hand. Hawkwind stood over her.

Though the fine carpets had been rolled up and packed on the supply wagons just outside, the furniture, save for the big bed and money chests, removed as well, Hawkwind's approach had been as soundless as before. He gazed down at her, hands on his hips and legs spread, his stance guarded, wary.

Deidra frowned. Was he still nervous about the bird? She twisted slightly and flipped the cloth over to cover Mystic. Then she turned back to Hawkwind. His expression and stance hadn't changed.

Foreboding filled her. "What's amiss? You look like a storm waiting to break."

He offered her a hand instead of an answer. "Come here, Deidra."

Cautiously, she placed her hand in his and allowed him to pull her to her feet. She wore only his tunic as bed clothing, and had to hastily pull down one edge of the shirt to cover a long expanse of bare thigh. Only a flicker betrayed his interest in her action before he locked gazes with her.

"Renard has returned."

The flat pronouncement sent a shiver rippling through Deidra. Her throat went dry. She licked her lips. "And what did he discover?" she forced herself to ask. "Do I fit the description of Rothgarn's daughter?"

"Aye, in all the external ways." His glance dipped to her bosom. "There's yet one last proof I need, though. If you're who you claim to be, you should have a flame-shaped birthmark on the underside of your left breast." Jade green eyes, fierce-burning and bright, lifted back to hers. "Do you, Deidra?"

For an instant, she imagined Maud had revealed her secret, then realized 'twasn't so. The healer had no reason to betray her. Nay, Hawkwind's virile captain had most likely managed to buy, if not charm, the secret from one of her serving maids. And now the moment she'd been dreading was at last upon her.

She cursed the unfortunate circumstances that had brought them to this. If only she'd had more time. If only she'd been able first to win Hawkwind's heart . . .

Why that was suddenly of such import, she didn't know, nor even wished to delve too deeply into the reason. All that mattered was the thought of leaving Hawkwind sent a sharp pain stabbing through her. Mayhap she should have given herself to him when she'd had the chance. Mayhap the act of coupling with him would have bound them. But now 'twas too late.

Or was it?

A plan formed in her mind, fueled by the desperation of a woman who fought not only for the freedom she'd always dreamed of, but for a dark, tormented, stubborn man who had insinuated himself into her heart. Deidra smiled, a slow, provocative curve of lips over dainty white teeth. Though she knew little of the art of seduction, she must ply all the skills she possessed this night.

Ah, if only she'd had Maud teach her how to prepare a love potion! But, as desperate as she now was, Deidra knew she'd never be able to use it on Hawkwind. She wanted his love honestly won and given, not coerced by some drug against his will.

"If you care so much to know, why not look yourself?" As she spoke, Deidra unlaced the front of her tunic until his overlarge shirt fell open to her navel. A tantalizing glimpse of curvaceous breast lay exposed to his gaze. "Unless you're afraid to face the truth?" she added coyly, intent on goading him on.

He arched a dark brow. His hands fell to his sides. "And since when have you dared offer me access to your body? Beware the little game you play, wench. You might lose more than you bargained for."

Deidra shrugged a slender shoulder, causing the tunic to slip sideways. In the process her left breast, firm, plump, and jutting, was exposed. As he stared down at it in rapt attention, her soft, pink nipple seemed to respond to his heated gaze, growing taut and hard. She made no move to cover herself.

Hawkwind inhaled a ragged breath. His heart began a heavy thudding within his chest. By the Mother, what was she about? He had only to reach out to touch her, to feel at last the silky white flesh, the satisfying weight of her in his hand. And lift her breast, as well, to look for the telltale birthmark.

But if he touched her now . . . . He swelled, thickened, grew hard and throbbing at the mere thought of it. Was it possible? Was Deidra unaware what she offered by not covering herself, by offering to let him touch her? One glance into her eyes told him she knew.

Desire and a meltingly deep yearning burned there, setting afire his own long pent-up passion. He'd not intended to take her this night. His plan for a slow, careful wooing hadn't included so quick a coupling. Yet, why should he turn aside what she seemed finally to be offering him? 'Twould only seal their bonding and the fulfillment of his plans all the sooner.

Once again guilt knifed through Hawkwind. What Deidra offered freely, without terms or subterfuge, he would take with full knowledge of his own deceit. Not that even guilt would sway him from taking her. 'Twas too late for that.

His hand lifted, moved to gently cup the straining, swollen breast exposed so freely to him. He raised it, saw the birthmark, then met her glance. "I guessed as much."

The husky timbre of his voice sent a ripple of excitement coursing through Deidra. His response to her had been too strong, too immediate, to be anything more than primal and totally masculine. The emotion he felt was for her as a woman, not for the title and position he was now certain she possessed. Triumph surged through her.

"What will you do?" Deidra's voice was husky with barely repressed anticipation. "Now that you know?"

"What do you wish for me to do?" His hand fell away.

For a fleeting instant she pondered her reply, knowing whatever she said could well determine the future course of her life. A life lived with Hawkwind—or without him. Suddenly, all fear, all hesitation fled in the rush of emotion. Of need . . . of love for him.

"I wish," Deidra began carefully, wondering at the most unexpected revelation, "to stay with you. To be a part of your life no matter the hardship and danger. I wish to be free to live as I desire, and share that freedom and its joys with you. And I wish as well," she added in a hushed whisper, "to have you make love to me this night."

Hawkwind stared down at her, fighting to master the wild excitement pounding through him. His fists clenched at his sides. His breathing went awry.

"Do you know what you ask, lass?" he finally forced himself to say. No matter how desperately he wanted her, he'd not take her without her full knowledge of what she did. "Your father will not like having his daughter sullied by a lowly mercenary, no matter how powerful or wealthy. For that matter, how will *you* feel about it on the morrow? You might well regret this one night's passion."

He subjected her to an intent scrutiny. "Be honest with yourself, Deidra—and with me. Do you only want me because I excite you, because, in any other circumstances, I'd be forbidden to one such as you?"

"Nay." She firmly shook her head. "Though I do want

you because you intrigue and excite me, I want you as well because you're brave, and kind, and honorable." She blushed and lowered her head. "And because I have come to care deeply for you."

"I thank you for the compliment." His solemn voice pierced the fires of her embarrassment. "I have long hoped, nay, dreamed you'd come to me willingly someday. But what if I were to get you with child? 'Twould ruin all your fine aspirations to become a warrior. And I'd not thought you'd wish to bear *my* bastard."

At the crudeness of his statement, Deidra jerked her gaze back to his. "I-I hadn't thought of that. I had only thought of us . . . and the joy the joining of our bodies would bring."

"Well, you are young and inexperienced in such things," Hawkwind offered gently. "I'm sorry if I offended you, but 'tis better you realize the extent of the possibilities. I'd not want you saying I seduced you into this against your will."

"Seduced me?" Deidra gave a disbelieving laugh. "I could have sworn 'twas me doing the seducing a few minutes ago, not you!"

"Nonetheless, the consequences are potentially greater for you than for me, lass. I'd have you know it all. Or at least what there is safe to know just now," he added bitterly, averting his gaze.

"I don't understand," Deidra murmured. "What isn't safe for me to know?"

He swung back to her, his eyes bleak, his jaw hard, the painful swell of feelings for her forcing more truth from him that he'd ever planned on revealing. "Even now, sharing what little I can with you, there is still so much more I cannot tell you, save to say that to align yourself with me may be very dangerous. Yet you must accept that if there's to be any hope for us. I know how important trust is to you. I know you still wish for me to share the truth about my past, but I can't, not yet."

"But someday? Can you at least promise to tell me someday?"

The sweetly hopeful note in her voice plucked at Hawkwind. Self-loathing at his depravity, at his deception of her vibrated through him. Though he dared not yet share his deepest secrets with her, she was willing to trust him enough not to demand what she had every right to know before committing to him. All Deidra hoped for was some small reassurance that *someday* he would tell her.

He wasn't worthy of her and never would be! Yet still he wanted and needed her. And would have her.

"Aye, lass," Hawkwind sighed his agreement. "Someday, if all goes as I hope it will." Anguish twisted his face as he spoke the words he secretly wondered would ever come to pass, but Hawkwind forced himself to say them nonetheless. To do otherwise would drive Deidra from him.

She reached up gently to stroke his bearded jaw. " 'Twill, Hawkwind. Together, we'll make it go well."

The gentle, loving look in her eyes nearly sent him to his knees. He'd never known such a woman! An impulse filled him to tell her all about his past and plans to use her to manipulate her father. Only the most superhuman of efforts stanched the words that surged to his lips. But the fear in the telling, he'd lose Deidra before he had a chance to win her, was suddenly stronger than his sense of honor.

With a groan that was part tormented conscience and part anguished desire, Hawkwind turned his mouth to her palm in a reverent, ardent kiss. He captured her wrist then, to hold it as his lips lowered to the warm, silky flesh there. With the lightest of touches, his mouth brushed across the wildly throbbing pulse.

Her woman's scent, delicate as rain washed lilac blooms, wafted to him. He inhaled deeply, savoring her special fragrance. His tongue emerged to caress, then taste the unique flavor of her. A sound escaped him, half-groan, half-growl, and full of a primal male possession.

Hawkwind's head lifted. For one last time, he gazed into

her eyes, searching, asking. The sweet, yielding look she sent him told him all he needed to know. He pulled Deidra to him, pressing her soft, slender body into his. And, where her belly met his sex, he ground himself into her.

Suddenly, Hawkwind couldn't get enough of her, nor find enough flesh to make contact with. He could feel himself losing control, and the wild little writhing movements Deidra made against him only stoked the fires of his passion. Savagely, he captured her face between his hands and, lowering his mouth, devoured Deidra's. Hard lips slanted over hers. He took her, his tongue hot, probing, insistent.

With a small mew of surprise, Deidra opened to his marauding demands. As he rocked his thick erection against her, Hawkwind plunged his tongue into the warm, honeysweet recesses of her mouth. One hand slipped from Deidra's face to glide down her shoulder and back, then slid up beneath the linen tunic until his fingers closed on a round, naked little buttock. He pressed her even more tightly to him and groaned.

"I need you, lass," he rasped, his voice thick, ragged. "And I fear I can't be gentle with you this first time. I-I'm sorry."

"I don't care!" she cried. Her hands were all over him, pulling at his tunic, tugging at the waistband of his breeches. "C-curse your clothes!"

"Lusty little wench," Hawkwind gritted and pushed her gently back to jerk off his tunic and fling it aside. Then, before he could do anything more, Deidra had grabbed his hand and pulled him across the tent to his bed. Shoving him backward until the back of his thighs touched the edge of the mattress, she flung herself against him. With a startled laugh, he toppled over and onto the bed with her clasped in his arms.

She slid down his passion hardened body until she knelt between his legs. "Lift your feet," Deidra commanded, a seductive little smile on her face.

Intrigued and amused, Hawkwind did as ordered. His boots were soon tossed to the side. Then Deidra rose to stand between his outspread legs. "I want you naked."

"As I want you," he said, grabbing for her.

"Nay." She nimbly eluded him. "You first. Just like that first time."

He eyed Deidra, deciding he was becoming too painfully thick and swollen to play her game much longer. And his breeches were a definite hindrance to the intimacy he longed for. With a quick motion, Hawkwind unfastened the clasp of his breeches and spread them open. A dark river of hair arrowed down from his navel and tautly flat abdomen to a much thicker and darker nest of crisp, coarse curls.

"Do you wish to do the honors, or should I?"

Startled brown eyes lifted to his. "You. You do it. I wish to watch. I've never seen a man strip before. And I think I'll particularly like seeing you do it."

Hawkwind's glance turned darkly smoldering. "Will you now? And aren't you the bold and saucy wench, to admit to such a thing? I see you'll be as shameless in bed as you are in everything you do."

Deidra shrugged a slender shoulder. "And why not? I want freedom in everything. Including," she added pointedly as Hawkwind's huge erection sprang free of the restraints of his breeches as he slowly shoved the fabric down, "the right to enjoy you as much as you enjoy me."

Yet, for all the boldness of her speech, at the sight of him Deidra's eyes widened. She swallowed hard. A fierce male pride swelled in Hawkwind. "Is everything to your satisfaction?"

"Wh-what?" Deidra stammered, distracted at last from her incredulous staring.

Casually, Hawkwind gestured to himself. "Do you like what you see?"

"A-aye," she said, struggling to regain her composure.

She shot him a heated look. "You appear . . . adequate . . . for the task."

"Adequate?" Hawkwind threw back his head and gave a shout of laughter. "I'm more than adequate, I can assure you, lass." He grabbed for her and pulled her down atop his hard-muscled body. He grinned as she stiffened at the intimate contact with him. "What say you now? Am I just 'adequate'?"

"You seem quite magnificent at closer inspection," Deidra admitted with mock gravity. "But what exactly can it *do?*"

He grasped her about her waist and rolled her over onto the bed. Bearing most of his weight on his arms, Hawkwind smiled down at her. "What can it do, you ask? Most anything you ask of it. But first," he muttered, his voice going hoarse, "you need a bit more gentling."

Before she could utter another teasing remark, Hawkwind once more covered her mouth with his, thrusting his tongue to meet and tangle with hers in a primitive imitation of the more intimate dance to come. His hand snaked down her cloth-covered body until it found bare flesh.

Clenching the tunic in one fist, Hawkwind jerked it up Deidra's body until the cloth was bunched above her breasts. Then, he released it and slid his eager fingers about a firm young breast. With thumb and forefinger, he grasped a soft nipple and stroked it to a hardened arousal.

Deidra gasped and writhed beneath him. Hawkwind's dark head lowered, his long hair cascading down to shield his face. His lips closed on an already turgid nipple. With quick little nips interspersed with flicks of his tongue, he drew the sensitive bit of flesh once more to a taut, crimson peak.

Long, slender fingers slipped through his hair, then clenched, digging into his scalp. "H-Hawkwind!"

Fighting to ignore her excited little arches and thrusts, he turned his attention to her other breast. Deidra's breaths came ragged now, her chest seesawing erratically. A fine sheen of moisture broke out on her body. She flushed becomingly.

Damn, but he was so hard he thought he'd explode, shame himself by spewing his seed right there on the bed! He nuzzled her breasts, burying his face in the soft, damp, woman-fragrant valley of flesh. He needed her badly, needed to bury himself in her tight, wet, fire-hot depths. But he also wanted it to be good for her. 'Twas all he could give her—at least for now.

He just . . . didn't know . . . if he could . . . be gentle.

Gazing up at him, Deidra saw the passion and arousal darken Hawkwind's features, strain them. She imagined she must look as fevered, as mad with desire. Her hands moved to grasp his massive shoulders, slick with sweat, then slide down the bulge of taut pectoral muscles. She could feel his big body atop hers, trembling with his efforts to hold himself back, awaiting . . . what?

Her permission? Her readiness?

Though permission she'd gladly give, Deidra knew as well her body, untried, unused as 'twas, would never be adequately ready for his. Not this time, no matter how much she wanted him. There was naught he could do to prevent the pain of their first coupling, no matter if he waited half the night. He was just too big. And too in need to go easy with her.

Her hand snaked down to him, grasped his manhood and drew him to the soft, most secret part of her. "Come, lover," she whispered achingly. "Come and fill me with your hard, delicious flesh. I want you. That is all that matters."

"N-nay, Deidra," Hawkwind groaned. His anguish and barely leashed control was a heated, palpable thing. Muscles bulged, sinews strained as he fought to hold himself back. "I want the same pleasure for you. I don't want—"

Then there was naught else he could say. Deidra slid beneath him, wrapped her legs about his hips, and thrust him into her. The words died in Hawkwind's throat. There was naught, save the sleek, exquisitely tight feel of her sheath closing around him, and his instinctive, most primitive of responses. On a shuddering intake of breath the last of Hawkwind's control shredded, exploding in a dazzling burst of light.

With a guttural sound, he thrust into Deidra again and again, piercing her maidenhead with one deep, sure, savage plunge. She cried out, stiffened for a brief instant, then relaxed beneath him. But he was past caring. All Hawkwind knew was the slick, snug warmth of Deidra's body—and the rising tension spiraling higher and higher. He clasped her tightly to him, losing himself, surrendering to the pleasure, the passion, the need.

The pain passed quickly for Deidra. A wild excitement built within. A fire flared to life between her legs, growing to a roaring conflagration demanding surcease. She whimpered her confusion, her need, her helplessness to do anything to ease it.

Her breasts trembled, rising and falling in quick little panting breaths. She arched against him, the slap of their sweat-slick flesh an erotic, exciting sound that only drove her onward. She glanced down, caught a glimpse of his rock-hard shaft, glistening and red, thrusting in and out of her plump, wet woman's flesh.

Then everything went black. Deidra's eyes clenched shut. The thick, rhythmic tremors began, arising from deep within her secret core to spread outward in delicious, shattering, ecstatic vibrations. With a strangled cry, she flung back her head, arched against him, and sobbed out her release. Sobbed yet, through it all, heard Hawkwind's cry, felt him go suddenly rigid, then shake with uncontrollable spasms.

His breath caught, the sound strangled, half moan, half sob of its own. Then, with a tremulous sigh, Hawkwind, brave and powerful warrior that he was, collapsed atop

Deidra. He moaned, pulled her to him and cradled his head upon her breast.

She snuggled close, clasped her arms about him, smiling in secret satisfaction. A part of her freedom and power, Deidra realized in a sudden swell of insight, had always lain with him. Lain in the arms of a man sated and vulnerable, so much like a young boy now, taking a solace from her woman's body he dared not seek or hoped to find anywhere else.

Aye, Deidra thought as a warm drowsiness engulfed her. 'Twas a wondrous power indeed. And, for now, 'twas more than enough.

Chapter 13

The first faint fingers of sunrise streaked the horizon as Deidra woke from a deep, satisfying sleep. She stirred, mumbled drowsily, and rolled over onto her side. Her hand touched something warm and solid, smooth-skinned but rippled below the surface by a hard bulge of muscle.

Her eyes opened. For a brief, disoriented moment, Deidra stared in disbelief. Beside her, on the huge bed, lay Hawkwind. A most disconcertingly naked Hawkwind.

He sprawled in sleepless abandon on his belly, the comforter thrown aside, one arm beneath his head, the other encircling the pillow he no longer lay upon. Deidra's gaze narrowed appreciatively, taking in the wide-shouldered, powerfully muscled back, narrow waist and hips, and enticing flare of his tautly rounded buttocks. His legs, iron thewed and hair roughened, tapered to well-shaped feet in sinuous, attractively masculine curves.

Despite the scars tracking his body and the puckered, maimed flesh of his right shoulder, Hawkwind seemed the most handsome and sensually appealing man Deidra had ever seen. Even now, after several heated bouts of lovemaking that had left her sated but exquisitely sore, she found the sight of him made her want him again. Would the sweet ache and swell of desire ever abate? she wondered.

Somehow, Deidra doubted it ever would for a man as

magnificently virile and skilled a lover as Hawkwind. She well understood now the reason for the hateful looks Bella sent her whenever their paths crossed. She'd find it difficult to give Hawkwind up to another woman, too.

The thought pricked at her newly awakened feminine awareness. Would Hawkwind tire of her like he had Bella? Would another pretty face and figure someday lure him away? Deidra found even the remotest consideration of such a possibility deeply disturbing.

He seemed to care for her, found her special—indeed had said as much last night—and their couplings had been intensely satisfying for the both of them. She pleased him, moved him in ways few other women had before her. That much was apparent even to her inexperienced eyes, if his words hadn't already assured her of the same thing.

But did he love her, *could* he love her? Deidra hoped so. She knew he possessed the heart capable of such a deep emotion, but his past had scarred not only his body but his soul. Without knowing the source and depth of his psychic injuries, she had no way of discerning how to heal them, or if she were even the right woman to do so.

The future stretched out before Deidra, uncertain, unsettled. So much had changed in but the span of one night. To become a mercenary warrior, to be free of all feminine constraints, though still of great import, was no longer enough. She had willingly bound herself to a man of many secrets and now had no idea what to do next.

Her eyes lifted to the long expanse of grayish brown hemp cloth stretching overhead. A wistful sigh escaped her. Ah, if only she were more experienced, more worldly! She might then know what she must do to win Hawkwind's heart, and everything else she'd ever dreamed of.

"What saddens you so?" a deep voice rumbled beside her.

Deidra jerked her gaze back to Hawkwind. He lay there,

unmoving, but his head was turned to her and his dark green eyes were open. She swallowed hard.

"N-naught," she stammered as she struggled for some plausible answer to his question. "I was but thinking I will miss this war camp. I have learned so much, made some good friends, and," she said, smiling down at him, "come to know you."

He grinned wolfishly and rolled over onto his back. "And long and well, too, I might add." His hand captured hers. "We must depart soon, but I'd wager there's time for one more coupling."

Warmth flushed Deidra as his appreciative gaze took in the decidedly exposed length of her body. A corresponding desire for him flared deep within her, stirring a fire so intense it momentarily took her breath away.

He lay there, his firm, sensually molded lips curved in a smile, his long, dark hair deliciously tousled, his big, muscular body already growing rigid with his renewed lust. Her fascinated gaze dipped to the thick swell of his manhood, jutting from its dark nest of hair to hover over his flat belly and rippling abdomen.

Deidra smiled in turn. Aye, he did indeed fascinate and stir her. And she most definitely wanted him, but . . .

With a rueful sigh, she shook her head. "As much as I also wish to couple again with you, I fear I cannot ride today if you take me even one more time. 'Twill be uncomfortable enough as 'tis."

Concern furrowed his brow and flared in his eyes. Hawkwind pulled her to him and tenderly stroked the wild mass of auburn curls from her face. "Truly, lass? Was I such a brute last night I've harmed you in some way?"

"Nay." Deidra laughed. "Or at least no more than any man would who had so eagerly taken a maiden. You only made me sore. 'Twill ease soon enough, but only," she added with an impish grin, "if you grant me a day or two to heal."

"Aye, lass," Hawkwind growled. "That I can, and will. I

beg forgiveness for my selfish demands. 'Twon't happen again, I swear it!"

"And why not?" Deidra demanded in mock outrage and poked him in the chest. "Are you so soon tired of me?"

He quickly captured her hand and pulled it down to clasp around his still turgid shaft. "Does that feel like a man so soon tired of you?"

She lightly ran her fingers up his swollen length. At her touch, Hawkwind shuddered. Deidra smiled. "Nay, I suppose not. But what shall we do about it then? It seems a pity to waste such a magnificent effort."

As if considering her question, Hawkwind cocked his head, then shot her a pointedly suggestive glance. "A magnificent effort, you say? Then why don't you just keep on doing what you're doing? I'm certain something will come of it." He grinned wickedly. "Sooner or later."

In less than another two hours, his bed dismantled and packed along with his locked money chests and tent, Hawkwind stood ready to depart. Deidra, however, was still without a mount. She glanced up at him after he'd settled onto his big bay war-horse.

"My comments earlier weren't misconstrued, were they?" she asked. "I didn't mean to imply I'd prefer walking to riding this day."

He flung an errant, breeze-borne lock of hair out of his eyes. "Indeed? Would you mayhap prefer to ride up here with me?"

The offer had its appeal, Deidra thought for a fleeting moment, but somehow she imagined such an act would also irrevocably alter his army's view of her as a budding warrior. And, though her relationship to Hawkwind had changed in the course of but one night, she was still determined to be more than just his lover.

Deidra shook her head. "Nay, if you don't mind, I'd much prefer to ride alongside you than before you. I've worked too hard to be considered a soldier to toss it aside so easily now." She looked around. "Is there not an extra horse to be found? I require nothing special, just a strong back and four legs—"

As she spoke, something white and black flashed in her peripheral vision. Deidra turned just in time to see Belfry, eyes white and nostrils flaring, half-rear against the grip of Bruno's hands upon his reins. With a joyful cry, she ran to where the soldier stood. "Give him to me!" she cried.

Bruno shot her a startled glance, then swung to Hawkwind. His leader nodded. The soldier lost no time in shoving the reins into Deidra's waiting hands and stepping hurriedly back. "Have at 'him, lass. That horse is crazed!"

Deidra grinned. Maintaining a tight hold on the skittish horse's reins, she moved slowly forward. "Easy, lad," she crooned, her voice low, soothing. "Easy now. 'Tis only me. Only me . . ."

Belfry's ears pricked forward. He eyed her closely, his sides heaving, but this time he remained on the ground. Ever so carefully, Deidra moved up, speaking quietly until her outstretched hand touched his neck. The horse started, snorted in surprise, then calmed.

His head lowered to sniff her shoulder then, as if finally recognizing her, he gave Deidra a playful shove. She chuckled and patted him on the shoulder. "Well, old friend," she murmured, "I never thought to see you again."

"Bardrick recognized him several days ago, when Maud brought him outside for some sunshine and fresh air," Hawkwind offered, easing his war-horse over as close as he dared let the two high-strung animals get to each other. "Your horse had apparently been captured that night along with you and, when all attempts to trade him to the locals failed because of his . . . ah . . . irascible nature, he was brought back to camp. Someone, now with a broken leg for his efforts, seemed to think this crazy beast might be trained to pull supply wagons."

Deidra slung her arm over Belfry's neck and turned to Hawkwind. "He's a bit unpredictable at times, but has a heart of gold." She gave him a quick hug. "And he's totally devoted to me."

"Is he now?" Hawkwind's mouth twisted wryly. "So Bardrick tried to tell me, but I wouldn't have believed it until now." He eyed the horse with a slightly jaundiced look. "Are you sure you'll be safe on him?"

"Quite safe," she assured him. "Belfry would carry me to hell and back if I asked him."

"Belfry, is he?" Hawkwind gave a disparaging snort. "And does he have bats in his belfry then? He appears crazy enough for them."

Deidra shrugged. "Mayhap to some, but he suits me just fine." She flung his reins over his head and, in one lithe move, mounted. Settling herself in the saddle, she grinned over at Hawkwind. "Thank you. You can't begin to imagine what this means to me."

He reined in his war-horse and shook his head. "Nay, mayhap I can't. All I know is you seem to have a propensity for acquiring the strangest collection of misfit animals. First that cursed falcon, and now this horse."

Just then Mystic squawked and rattled around in his box securely tied to the side of Hawkwind's personal supply wagon. Hawkwind shot Deidra one last, long-suffering glance, then wheeled his horse about. With a shouted command and motion of his upraised arm, he signaled the journey to the next battle campaign to begin.

Though the day started out clear and sunny, by midday thunderclouds loomed on the horizon, building to towering heights. By sunset, lightning flashed from cloud to cloud and thunder rumbled in the distance. The air turned heavy and still. A sense of the impending storm grew with each passing hour.

Heralded by a chill surge of winds, the storm struck just after dark fall. The army, well versed in such vagaries of the weather, had prepared. The horses were securely staked out and hobbled in the shelter of a thick stand of trees. The supply wagons had been covered and battened down with the sturdy, waterproof tents. And, when all preparations were complete, the men took to the numerous spots beneath the wagons, pulled up their thick woolen cloaks, and settled down to wait out the storm.

One of Hawkwind's two personal supply wagons also served as his sleeping quarters. Though space was cramped, there was still room for a bed among the rolled up carpets and money chests. It was there he finally joined Deidra, after one last tour of the camp to assure himself the sentries were stationed appropriately and all animals, wagons, and men were secure.

The heavens had opened in a torrential deluge shortly before he arrived back at the wagon. Hawkwind climbed in, soaked to the skin. After lowering the hemp cloth flap and tying it in place to shut out the blowing sheets of rain, he shed his cloak and sat on one of the chests to strip off his boots, breeches, and tunic.

Then he turned, naked and shivering in the cool night air, to find Deidra at his side. She quickly wrapped him in a soft, thick, toweling cloth. As he stood there, she rubbed him dry, from the top of his sodden hair to his toes.

At her thoughtful ministrations, a tender gratitude flared within him. Finally, he stayed her hands.

She glanced up, a slender brow arched in query.

"I've better ways in mind to get warm." Hawkwind gestured to the little bed. "Your body next to mine will do wonders to drive away the night's chill, as well as take my mind off my aches and pains."

At the mention of his old battle injuries, Deidra nodded. "Aye, lying close to you, mayhap I can ward off the worst of your torment."

He grinned, took the drying cloth from her, and let it drop to the floor. "I'm indeed a fortunate man. How many can claim to have their own, personal little witch?"

A shadow crossed her eyes. "You know, and it doesn't bother you?"

Hawkwind shrugged. " 'Twould take a blind man not to see what you've done for me. Your skills are wondrous indeed—and deeply appreciated. Besides, I finally asked Maud. She confessed she'd been teaching you."

Anxious brown eyes searched those of deepest green. "And you're not repulsed by my powers? You don't wish to turn from me?"

"Do you intend ever to use your skills to do harm?"

"Ah, nay, Hawkwind," Deidra breathed with fervent conviction. "Never!"

"Then I have no qualms. I've never feared magic. 'Tis the wielder who bears the power and responsibility for its use, good or bad." He paused. "She said you have special talents, talents that have potential for great things."

"Who?"

"Maud."

"Oh." To hide her embarrassment, Deidra sat down on the edge of the bed and began to remove her boots. "I'm not certain how far I wish to go with those 'special talents.' They frighten me at times."

He crawled around her and slipped beneath the furs. "Yet there must have been some reason you were gifted with them. They were meant to serve a purpose." He studied her for a long moment. "Mayhap your magic could be used in my behalf. I may well have need of it in the future."

"I don't know." Her voice was muffled momentarily as she slipped her tunic over her head. "Mayhap they could, but these powers have the potential for great harm as well as good." Deidra turned to him. "And, however well-intentioned I may be in their use, there is always the possibility I might lose control of them . . . do harm."

She turned to her breeches, when a large hand pulled her back. "Aye, 'tis true," Hawkwind agreed, his eyes gleaming with a fierce burning light. "And you are wise to go carefully in this. But I think you cannot deny where your destiny calls, either."

The memory of Maud's words, spoken on a similar topic,

were stirred anew. Deidra smiled. "Aye, you're right, of course." On a sudden impulse, she leaned over and gave Hawkwind a fierce hug.

He smiled, his expression puzzled. "What was that for? A prelude to a coupling, mayhap?"

At the wistfully hopeful note in his voice, Deidra laughed. "You're most certainly a hot-blooded stallion, aren't you? But the hug was purely out of gratitude for your kindness and acceptance of me. You could have been different. You could have found my powers repulsive and turned away."

"As Bardrick did from Maud?" he gently offered.

Inexplicably, tears filled her eyes. "Aye. And I don't think I'd have the courage to go on if you ever looked upon me that way!"

"Ah, lass," Hawkwind crooned as the tears suddenly spilled down her cheeks. "You'd have to do far worse than that before I'd ever turn from you. Far, far worse."

With a strangled sob, Deidra came to him then, seeking haven within the strong comfort of his arms. Joy filled her, even as she wept her fears and insecurities away.

As the rain thrummed overhead on the sturdy cloth roof of the wagon, Hawkwind held her, praying she would know the same trust and acceptance of him—when the time finally came to tell her all.

The rain continued for the next two days, turning the land into a quagmire. Hawkwind's agreement with Lord Firston entailed a set arrival date and, though he had begun the journey two days early, Hawkwind decided to slog on in the attempt to make as much forward progress as possible. Finally, by midday of the second day, he deemed further travel an impossibility.

The army settled down to await the end of the rain, well aware the need for increased speed to make up the lost time would necessitate the remainder of the journey being made without rest. Hawkwind, along with Renard and

Alena, studied the maps, plotting out and discussing various changes in the route to shorten the distance left to travel. As they did, a dangerous alternative surfaced.

"A crossing over the Sabarcane River," Renard observed glumly as he leaned against the curved interior wagon supports, "would be the quickest and straightest route to Firston's army."

"Aye," Hawkwind agreed from his spot on the bed beside Deidra, "and also a difficult river to ford when high, which it most certainly will be after over two days of heavy rain. All attempts to span a bridge across its wide expanse have failed. Which isn't surprising, considering one has rarely remained intact for more than two or three years, thanks to the frequent flash floods."

Renard straightened. "Well, wooden, flatbed ferries, pulled back and forth by oxen on each side, will serve. 'Twill be slow, getting the entire army and wagons across, but 'twill also buy us back the lost time."

Hawkwind shot a quick glance at Alena, who sat on a chest at the end of the bed. "And your opinion?" he demanded. "You've been singularly quiet this night."

The blond woman sighed and shook her head. "The choices are few, whichever way we go. But we dare not hold up Firston's march. His element of surprise will be lost if we tarry. That will only result in greater loss of life."

"Then the choice seems obvious to me." Hawkwind stood. "Send an advance party to make the arrangements with the ferrymen. If we set out at dawn, we should reach the Sabarcane by midday. One way or another, I want the army on the other side of the river by nightfall."

Alena nodded and rose. "Aye. 'Twill be done as you command. If all goes well, we can still reach Firston in time." She worked her way through the crowded little wagon until she stood before Renard. "Care to accompany me?" she asked.

Renard grinned. "Think Hawkwind and Deidra need some time alone, do you?"

"Something like that," was the warrior woman's sardonic reply.

As the wagon emptied of his two war captains, Hawkwind chuckled and turned to Deidra. "It gets increasingly difficult to hide our relationship, does it not?"

Deidra shrugged from her cramped little corner of the bed. "Your extreme possessiveness might be partially to blame for that. Not to mention your unusual eagerness of late to turn in each night."

He grinned and made a grab for her. With a giggle, she scooted out of his reach. Poised on the edge of the bed, Hawkwind eyed her like some panther about to strike. "Well, I've yet to hear complaints about your terrorized screams of protest," he softly growled, "or mention of you ever straying too far out of my sight."

Before she could react or recover herself, he lunged for Deidra, grasped her about the waist, and pulled her over. "Not only have you healed my old battle wounds, but I vow you've stirred me to exert myself in bed like I've never done before. Do you mayhap wield your witch's powers in ways I've yet to suspect?"

She laughed and came to him, her arms entwining about his neck. "Nay," she murmured contentedly. "I've done naught but attempt to ease your pain. And it seems I've succeeded well." Deidra lifted her head to glance up at him. "It has been raining for three days now, and I've seen naught of your former discomfort return."

"Discomfort?" Hawkwind gave a harsh laugh. " 'Twas torture of the cruelest kind! But you are correct in saying 'tis gone. You *have* cured me." He bent to kiss her tenderly on the tip of her pert little nose. "How can I ever thank you?"

A mischievous look sparkled in her eyes. "Oh, I can think of a myriad of ways, if you can be coerced to 'exert' yourself this night."

Hawkwind's mouth quirked in amusement. "Truly, you're one of the most insatiable little wenches I've ever known."

"Are you complaining?"

At the seductive shimmer of long, dark lashes and the alluring press of her soft, young body against his, Hawkwind felt his sex fill and harden. Once again, a rush of hot, savage desire flooded him. By the Mother, but she plied her feminine wiles better than any woman he'd ever known! She was far too quick a study for her—and his— own good. But, be that as it might, he wasn't fool enough to turn away what was so joyously and passionately given.

Tomorrow promised to be a danger fraught undertaking. But tonight, alone in the cozy confines of a rain battered wagon, was theirs. He only hoped there'd be many, many more.

"Nay, lass," Hawkwind replied, his voice husky with a mix of heartfelt emotion and desire. "I've no complaints with you. Far, far from it."

The river was high, the current swift and powerful. Its depths, churned to a murky, dark gray by the pouring rain and runoff from the land, looked sinister, foreboding. Hawkwind stood on the riverbank, weighing the possibilities and options.

"The ferryman says he's forded worse than this," Renard offered beside him. "With the rain continuing to fall, 'twill not improve at any rate."

"Aye," Hawkwind muttered. " 'Twon't get any better." He turned to his captain. "Let's get on with it, then. The day passes as we wait."

Renard nodded and strode off. In but the span of fifteen minutes' time, the ferry was loaded with the first of the wagons and had begun its journey across the river. From the security of the far bank, Hawkwind watched the rough trip with an anxious eye.

"Damn it all," he cursed, as one especially violent wave rocked the ferry. "We'll never get everyone across by dark at this rate!"

"You can only do the best you can," Deidra said. She

gripped his arm in a comforting gesture. "Lord Firston's deadline or no, the safety of your army comes first."

"Aye," Hawkwind breathed, his gaze never leaving the ferry until it finally docked on the opposite side of the river. "My army does indeed come first. But I am loathe to fail in the fulfillment of a promise. I have little else of honor left me, but I cherish my word above all."

"Lord Firston will understand."

He shot her a cynical glance. "Will he now? Don't be so certain of that, lass. He is a nobleman. In his eyes, I am lower than the swill the hogs eat. Nay," he emphasized the word with a vehement shake of his head, "I succeed by remaining strong, invulnerable, faultless. In doing that, I give my enemies no chink through which to wound me."

"I cannot believe they would turn on you just because—"

"They'd not only turn on me, lass," Hawkwind furiously interrupted her, "they'd tear me limb from limb. Me *and* my men."

At the grim certainty in his voice, Deidra shivered. Had it always been this way—men leaping for other men's throats at the first sign of blood? Had they always been so cruel, so brutal, so heartless?

The vision of that winter day, of a young Hawkwind being viciously attacked by the band of soldiers, filled her mind. He spoke from bitter experience, Deidra knew without having to ask. He survived only by being stronger and craftier and more cynical than his opponents. Yet, in the end, what would living that way do to him? Would he not someday become as cruel and treacherous as all the rest?

"Not everyone is as soul-rotted as you seem to think all your employers are," she softly protested. "There are still good, honorable men left. My father—"

At the mention of the man, next to King William, he hated above all, something in Hawkwind snapped. "Don't speak to me of Rothgarn! Father of yours though he be, he is the king's toady. He has accepted lands not his; he has cozied up to William whenever it suited him. He's no better than the rest!"

Deidra stared up at him, speechless. Never had she seen Hawkwind quite so furious or so vehement. Whatever her father had done, it had seriously affected Hawkwind. But to call her father the king's toady!

"You are wrong about my father," she said, stepping away from him. "And I'd thank you not to speak ill of him again in my presence. Whatever he may have done to you, I cannot believe it was meant with any malice against you."

"Believe what you will, Deidra," Hawkwind growled, his gaze moving once more to the ferry as it began its return trip across the river. "I was wrong to bring up the subject at any rate. What I feel for your father has no effect on our relationship. I resolved that problem a goodly time ago."

"Did you now?" In spite of herself, she felt the anger rise within her. "And is this all yet another example of secrets you choose not to share with me? Is my father part of it, too?"

"Enough, Deidra!" he rasped in warning. "I already said I erred in mentioning it. Let it be!"

"Fine," she gritted. "Have it your way. You always do at any rate!" Grabbing hold of Belfry's reins, she began to tug him over to the ferry dock.

"Where do you think you're going?" he shouted after her.

"I'm on the next ferry across this river!" she yelled back. "One way or another, I'm placing as much distance between us as possible. I don't know what happened between you and my father, but 'tisn't something I care to be caught in the middle of. Not now, not ever!"

"Fine! Get across the river then," Hawkwind roared. "I've got better things to do than fight with you this day!"

Twenty minutes later, he had ample opportunity to regret his words.

Chapter 14

The rough water rocked the little ferry, slamming into it, then cresting over the bow in huge, foaming torrents of water. A curse welling in his throat, Hawkwind watched the futile attempts to keep his supply wagon from shifting as the wooden barge heaved to and fro. His hands clenched at his sides in impotent frustration as he saw Deidra fight to keep her fear crazed horse in control. Sweat beaded his brow as men, one by one, were carried off by the surging water.

Then, the stout rope cables towing the ferry across the river snapped, and there was nothing else anyone could do. The barge sailed helplessly downstream, buffeted mercilessly, twirling and whirling in the wild current. Hawkwind grabbed hold of the reins of his horse from the soldier who held him and swung up onto his back. "Bring ropes," he shouted to his men. "We'll need them to rescue Deidra and the others."

As he urged the animal along the riverbank downstream to follow the barge, Hawkwind saw Deidra stagger to the box bound to the side of his wagon. She ripped the covering loose and pulled out the peregrine falcon. With a great heave, she tossed the bird into the air.

Mystic soared above the water, circled over Deidra, then headed for the bank where he stood. For a fleeting moment, Hawkwind followed the bird's flight until he saw it safely alight in a tree. Then his gaze swung back to Deidra.

Her face taut and white, she fought to assist his men in freeing the cross ropes that enclosed the ferry. Hawkwind's heart pounded in his chest, his fear for her an acrid, tangible thing. The wagon team was next freed and the horses forced off the barge. Then, Deidra stumbled back to Belfry.

Fighting the bucking, rearing horse, she calmed him for a moment and led him to the open side of the ferry. She mounted him then, with a stinging swat to his haunches, forced him into the water. For a heart stopping moment they disappeared in the river, then resurfaced. Out of the corner of his eye, Hawkwind noted the rest of the men abandoning the barge as well.

At that moment his supply wagon finally toppled over, then slid across the deck until the weight of the conveyance broke through the ropes. It disappeared into the river, then bobbed up to be carried downstream and out of sight.

As white water broke over them the piebald sank beneath the surface, then he fought his way back up. Deidra was nowhere to be seen. Hawkwind's stomach did a crazed flip-flop. By the Mother, where was she?

Deidra bobbed to the surface an instant later and grasped again for her horse's mane. Laboriously, she inched her way up his body until her arms encircled the animal's neck. Belfry's ears flicked back as if listening to her. It seemed to soothe him, for he settled down and began a determined stroke toward Hawkwind and the shore.

Renard was the first to reach him with a coil of stout rope as Hawkwind continued to follow Deidra and her horse downstream. He shot his captain a grateful glance, then leaned over to grab the rope from him. Urging his horse along the bank in an effort to outrun the current carrying Deidra downstream, he quickly formed a loop at one end of the line. Then, when he was sufficiently far enough below them, Hawkwind twirled the rope over his head and flung it out as Deidra and her horse swept by.

It sailed high into the air and out across the river. For a heart stopping instant, Hawkwind thought he'd missed them. Then, blessedly, Belfry tossed his head and the noose settled about his neck.

"Quick!" Hawkwind cried to Renard. "Tie the end around that tree!" He tossed the end of the rope to him and motioned toward the nearest sturdy oak growing but five feet away.

Renard flung himself off his horse and swiftly did as instructed, just in time to withstand the fierce tug on the other end as the rope went taut. He looped and knotted it, then ran back to Hawkwind's side. "Pull," his chief roared. "We've got to get them out before Deidra loses her grip!"

The current was fierce. Several soldiers not engaged in the attempts to rescue the other men in the river rode up to join Hawkwind and Renard. Muscles bulged, sinews strained, and progress at times seemed infinitesimal. Yet, inexorably, the piebald and his human burden drew closer and closer to shore.

Deidra felt herself weakening. Her hands slipped from about Belfry's neck. She slid down the horse, grasping wildly at anything. Her fingers snagged in his mane.

Her desperate glance swung to the shore. To Hawkwind, his features a mask of tortured anguish. Their eyes met for a fleeting instant. A look of the most intense emotion, of acute fear admixed with a helpless, loving, longing arced between them.

Then, another surge of white water crashed over Deidra. Her grip broke again. She grabbed at the saddle, seemed, for a moment to find a hold, but the leather was too slick.

With a frightened, frustrated cry, Deidra slipped away.

"Nay!" Hawkwind roared and flung himself into the river. Powerful strokes carried him to her but before he could reach her, Deidra was gone, dragged beneath the water. He dove down, frantically groped about in the blinding, foaming swirl of water—and found her. His lungs screaming for air, Hawkwind pulled Deidra back to the surface.

He flipped her around, slid his arm beneath her breasts, and turned back to shore. The going was arduous. He fought to make his way against the powerful current that was equally intent on dragging them downstream.

His heart thundered. His lungs felt as if they would burst. His muscles screamed from the pain of exertion, but still Hawkwind struggled on.

He saw them drag Belfry from the water, hurriedly remove the rope, then reloop it and toss it to him. With a superhuman effort to keep his head above water, Hawkwind flung an arm into the air. The rope caught it, tightened, and tugged.

Choking, gasping, he jerked Deidra to him in a death grip, struggling to keep both their heads above water as they were slowly pulled to shore. Then there were strong hands reaching out to them, dragging them from the water. All the while, Hawkwind refused to relinquish Deidra as he half stumbled and was half carried up the bank.

He collapsed there, taking Deidra down with him. "The men?" he gasped. "Were all rescued?"

"All but one," Renard grimly replied. "Your wagon wasn't so fortunate. It broke up downstream and everything either sank or was carried over the falls."

"Falls, eh?" Hawkwind managed a weak grin. "I'd forgotten about them in all the excitement."

"They were just around the next bend. If we hadn't reached you with the rope, we'd have lost more than your money chests."

A shadow of pained realization flashed in Hawkwind's eyes. "The money. By the Mother, our money is gone!"

Deidra stirred in his arms. "I-I'm so sorry, Hawkwind. We tried, but there was naught we could do . . ."

He turned to her and brushed a wet tendril of hair from her face. "Hush, lass. 'Twasn't your fault. 'Twas mine, trying to force a foolhardy river crossing. I pushed too hard and am fortunate that only one life was lost."

"But all your money!" Deidra wailed. "What will you do now?"

"What I've done before. Begin anew. What other choice is there?"

She gazed up at him, her eyes filled with tears. "I don't want you and your army to suffer. Without coin you will starve in these lands. Mayhap 'tis best if you do ransom me back to my father."

He pressed a finger firmly to her lips. "Nay, no more of that. Especially not now where the men can overhear. They know naught of the ransom and 'twill remain that way."

"Aye." Renard stooped to take Deidra from Hawkwind and pull her to her feet. "Speak no more of such things. We've work to do and another route to embark on if we're ever to reach Firston. 'Tis already too late to make his deadline, but the sooner we get there, the better."

Hawkwind rose. "Aye, and we'd best make it a quick trip. What food we carry is nearly all we'll have until we arrive there." His gaze narrowed as he watched Deidra move off toward the trees. "And where do you think you're going?"

"To retrieve Mystic," she shot over her shoulder, waving toward the tall oak back upstream where she could just make out the bird, perched on a sturdy limb.

"Wait."

She turned, her brow arching in inquiry.

"Here." Hawkwind tossed her his thick leather gauntlet. "'Tisn't as strong as a falconer's glove, but 'twill protect you a sight better from the bird's claws than will your tunic sleeve."

Deidra caught the glove and grinned her thanks. Then, turning, she strode away.

Hawkwind sighed and shook his head.

"She's a rare one, the lass is," Renard observed from beside him.

"Aye," his chief agreed, "but I fear her impulsive nature will get the better of her someday if she isn't careful."

" 'Tis fortunate she has a man like you to govern her."

"Govern her?" Hawkwind gave a disparaging laugh. "I can barely *restrain* her, much less govern her! She's a greater challenge than managing an entire army ever was."

"But you're man enough for it," Renard softly countered.

A determined light flared in Hawkwind's eyes. "Aye. I'm man enough."

The rain stopped that evening, but the roads took two more days to dry. Thanks to the thick mud that slowed the wagons progress, the journey required three full days. They finally joined with Lord Firston's army at dawn, after marching all night. Food supplies ran out the second day and only the sparse game in the forests kept Hawkwind's army even meagerly fed.

Though a small contingent of his soldiers wanted to loot some of the villages they passed, Hawkwind was adamantly against it. Never before had he allowed them to rape and pillage the lands they traveled through and he refused to do so now. What little remained of his personal wealth in the supply wagon not destroyed in the river, he sold to purchase additional flour for bread and ale for his men. His army, however, wasn't in the best of moods by the time they arrived two days late to their next battle campaign.

"Will they follow you into battle?" Lord Firston demanded as he looked down from his luxurious tent situated on a hill above the small valley Hawkwind's army had filed into. "They look none too happy, and a more ragtag bunch of soldiers I've yet to see." He turned a disdainful nose to Hawkwind and his two war captains, then paused to sip from his golden goblet of wine. "At this point, I begin to wonder if you're even worth the money I paid you in advance."

Renard muttered a few choice words under his breath before Hawkwind silenced him. "The journey was arduous, thanks to the heavy rains," the warrior chief growled. "We lost most of the money we'd have used to buy food and the men are hungry, dirty, and tired. Give us a few days with rest and food and they'll be back to fighting mettle."

"Food?" Lord Firston gave a disparaging laugh. "That was never part of the bargain. You agreed to pay for it out of your advance and, once the battle was won, I'd pay you the rest. Plus," he sniffed, "permit you to loot the castle for additional booty. A quite generous concession, in my opinion."

"We need the rest of the money now," Hawkwind growled, close to his breaking point at having to deal with Firston's arrogance, not to mention forced to all but beg for more money to feed his army. How swiftly one's fortune could change due to a simple quirk of nature!

"For what?" the nobleman demanded. "I see naught you've yet done for me. And there's no time for rest. We must be at Castle Trifals at dawn tomorrow. We've yet a good day's journey. Your tardy arrival lost you your days of rest."

Hawkwind exchanged a look with Renard and Alena. Renard shrugged. " 'Tis your decision, Chief."

Alena nodded her agreement.

Options roiled through Hawkwind's mind. One part of him wanted to turn and walk away from Firston and the pact he'd made with him. Another part wanted to send his army against the lesser force and rout them, then help themselves to the food and booty. But yet another part, the more sensible, honorable side, knew he'd given his word, accepted money, and owed the man, however despicable and haughty, the service already paid for. His reputation and that of his army's rested in the unswerving fulfillment of his contracts.

"Fine," he muttered. "We'll march in two hours' time— after we've had a meal. A meal," he added pointedly, "you will provide out of your stores, as well as the rest of the meals until the battle is over."

"How will this extra food be paid for?"

"From the remainder of the money, where else?"

Hawkwind snapped. "Take it or leave it. An army can't march or fight without food!"

Firston eyed him with a narrowed gaze, then nodded. "So be it. But we march in two hours whether your men are ready or not. Agreed?"

"Agreed." Hawkwind motioned to Renard and Alena. "Come on, we've got an army to feed!"

"Nay. Absolutely not!" Hawkwind whirled around in the supply wagon and nearly lost his balance in the cramped space. He stretched out an arm to steady himself against the interior support posts, then vehemently shook his head. "You aren't ready and will *not* go to battle with us on the morrow!"

"That's not true," Deidra argued from the bed, her chin lifted in stubborn defiance. "You just don't want your 'woman' going into battle, that's all! And if you think just because you've bedded me it gives you permission to—"

"I need no permission from you or anyone else in this camp!" Hawkwind growled, keeping his voice low with the greatest of efforts. "I am chief. My word is final."

Glaring down at her, her auburn hair a glorious mane about her shoulders, clothed in one of his voluminous tunics that revealed the enticing swell of her breasts, she was the picture of delectable womanhood. Hawkwind didn't want to fight with Deidra, he wanted to pull that curve smothering tunic over her head and make love to her.

"Well, chief or no, you're being unfair," Deidra retorted doggedly. "Your army is exhausted and even with tonight's rest won't be fully recovered by the morrow. You'll need every able-bodied warrior you can muster."

"Aye, and I'll need every able body paying attention to the task at hand, not watching out for you. Me, included."

He sat down on the bed and reached out for her. With a angry shrug of her shoulder and scoot of her hips, Deidra moved away from him. Hawkwind sighed and let his hand rest where she'd just been. "Lass, listen to me. 'Tisn't just my feelings of concern and possession. 'Tis my ability to concentrate in battle. I need all my wits about me if the army is to be successful. Lives are at stake if I err in my battle strategy. If you were down there in the thick of things, I'd be watching for you, not the overall fighting. Men could die because of that."

"Then mayhap you shouldn't count me more important than any of your other soldiers," she sniffed. "I didn't come to you originally to be your mistress. I came to be one of your warriors."

"But things have changed, Deidra," he softly countered. "You know that as well as I. Can't you give up this foolish dream of being a warrior, and instead find happiness in just being with me?"

She bit her lip in thought, hesitated, then shook her head. "I *do* find happiness with you, but 'tisn't enough. I want more than just being your woman, as wonderful as that is. Would you find fulfillment in just being my man?"

" 'Tisn't the same." Hawkwind frowned. "A man is responsible for making a life for himself and his woman. For his children, as well, if he chooses to sire a family. By necessity he must go out into the world, make his way and a living. But you"—he reached over to grasp Deidra by the shoulder, anchoring her in the corner of the wagon where she couldn't move away from him—"were never meant for a warrior's life. I knew that from the first moment I saw you, and told you as much as well."

"You haven't changed a bit, have you?" she cried. She leaned back as far from him as she could get, a frustrated pain twisting in her chest. "I was a fool to have imagined you would. I was a fool in thinking you could ever be the man for me!"

Hawkwind sighed, rolling his eyes back in exasperation. "Deidra, we are both sore weary and not thinking clearly. No good will be served if we continue this discussion tonight." He released her and scooted over to the edge of the bed, where he proceeded to pull off his boots. "Let's go to bed. We can talk more in the morning."

"Will your mind be any more open then? Will you reconsider letting me go to battle with you and the army?"

He shot her a narrow-eyed look. "And send you to a certain death? I think not."

"Fine." Deidra grabbed up a pillow and fur throw and crawled off the foot of the bed. She pulled on her breeches and boots.

"What do you think you're doing?" he growled, one boot still dangling from his hand.

She paused at the other end of the wagon. "Going outside. I couldn't sleep a moment beside you tonight!"

With that, Deidra lifted the hemp cloth flap and climbed out, letting the flap fall back in place with a sharp snap. As she stalked away from the wagon, fighting back tears of impotent rage and a deep, soul-searing anguish, she heard Hawkwind throw something against the inside of the wagon, then savagely curse, "Bloody hell!"

It didn't matter, Deidra told herself over and over as she strode across camp, not knowing or caring where she was heading. All she wanted was to get as far away from Hawkwind and his boorish, controlling, *male*-dominating ways as she could. All she wanted was to escape from the sense of betrayal, of her utter stupidity in trusting, hoping he'd be different. And, to make plans as to how she'd still get what she desired on the morrow.

Immersed in her chaotic thoughts, Deidra would most likely not have stopped until she'd reached the nearest town if Alena hadn't climbed out of her bed beneath the trees and gone after her. "Where do you think you're going at this hour?" the blond woman demanded as she jerked her to a halt.

"I-I don't know," Deidra quavered. "I just want to get as far away as I can from that despicable, pigheaded—"

"Ah, I see," Alena interrupted her with a chuckle. "You and the chief have had a fight."

Incensed by the warrior woman's amusement, Deidra wrenched her arm from her grasp. "Aye, and don't be so smug and condescending about it. He denied me what I've worked so hard for since the first day I joined his army. And I won't have it! I'm not his or any man's chattel!"

"Nay, you're not, Deidra," Alena tried to soothe her. She took her by the arm again and began to tug her in the direction of where her own bedding lay. "Come, you can sleep by me this night. Come and talk to me. Mayhap I can help."

Deidra blinked back the tears and obediently followed. "I thank you for your kindness, Alena, but naught can move Hawkwind when he sets his mind to something. You know that as well as I."

Alena led her over to the shelter of the tree, then glanced wryly at the fur and pillow Deidra carried. "Is that all you brought? Have you naught to lay on the ground to protect against the dampness?"

"Nay. I was so angry with Hawkwind, I grabbed the first things I saw and left the wagon."

"Well, let's see what we can do with my bedding." Alena squatted and began to unfold the waterproof ground cloth until it was big enough to accommodate two. She gestured to it. "Lie down there and cover yourself with your fur. 'Tisn't much, especially after the soft bed you've shared of late with the chief, but better than naught."

"'Tis the resting place of a woman free to choose her own fate," Deidra huffed as she lowered herself to the simple bed. "I far prefer it to that of a man who has never cared for me save for the pleasure my body could give him." She stuffed her pillow behind her against the tree trunk and pulled her fur coverlet up. "I hate him, Alena! He is so cruel and unfair."

Her companion sat down beside her. "Hawkwind? A cruel, unfair man? Ruthless and calculating, mayhap, but I've never known him to be cruel or unfair. What did he do to cause you to think that?"

"H-he refuses to let me fight in t-tomorrow's battle!" she choked. "After all my hard work, my progress, he deems it as naught. He never meant to let me be a warrior, did he?"

"He never *wanted* you to be a warrior," Alena calmly corrected. "He hoped you'd become discouraged and meant to see that you did eventually. Be that as it may, 'tis too soon for you to go into battle at any rate. You're not ready, Deidra."

"I am so," she wailed. "The last time we trained, you said I was improving rapidly. I've progressed to the use of a real sword. And I was beginning to give you a good workout. How many men in camp can do that?"

"Not many," Alena admitted. "But you still lack the stamina and battle experience—two potentially lethal shortcomings—not to mention the lack of a killer's instinct."

"Well, how am I ever to gain battle experience unless I fight in battle? Answer me that, Alena!" Despite Deidra's best efforts, the tears began to fall. Frustrated sobs soon wracked her body.

The other woman sighed and patted her on the shoulder. "He overprotects you, that much I'll admit. But 'tis only because he cares for you."

"Oh, aye, I-I see quite clearly h-how much he cares f-for me." Deidra hiccuped, fighting to contain her weeping. "So much he wishes to take away what I cherish most—my freedom to do what I wish."

Alena took Deidra's chin in her hand and turned her face to hers. "Listen to me, you proud, stubborn little firebrand. You have made Hawkwind happier than any woman he's ever known. I should know. I've been his friend since that first day Bardrick brought him to us, maimed and half-dead from his injuries. I've seen his pain, his wariness, the way he distances himself from almost everyone—women included. Yet with you, he has opened up so quickly that I fear for him, for his heart."

"I've done naught to hurt him," Deidra staunchly defended herself. She jerked her face aside, swiping the tracks of moisture away. "*He* is the one who has hurt me!"

"By refusing to allow you to go to what would most likely be your suicide?" Alena gave a mocking laugh. "Little fool, he cares so much for you he doesn't want to risk losing you! Mayhap that means denying you your precious freedom, but I, for one, would assist him in that, if that is what he wants."

"You'd help him deny me what you have and cherish dearly?"

"We have become friends in the past weeks, Deidra," Alena replied with a solemn emphasis, "but Hawkwind is family. I'll do anything for him, even ride to a certain death if he ordered me to. And if he wishes to have you for himself, I'll help him in that, too."

Brown eyes, wide with shock, stared back at her. "Are you in love with him, then, Alena? Have I inadvertently come between you and Hawkwind?"

The blond woman smiled wistfully. "Once, I'd have imagined so, but we are as close as brother and sister now. He sees me as naught more and never will. You took naught from me when Hawkwind fell in love with you."

Deidra's mouth dropped in stunned incredulity. "F-fell in love with me? Are you daft? He has never said such a thing to me, or, I'd wager, to you or anyone else, for that matter."

"Nay, he hasn't. I doubt Hawkwind has even realized it himself, much less admitted it. But I can see it, nonetheless."

"Well, it matters naught." Deidra turned away and, lying down, bunched her pillow beneath her head and pulled her fur over her shoulders. "I don't want a man who won't give my needs an equal value to his."

"Then 'tis your loss," Alena murmured and settled down beside her. "There is not a finer man to be found."

Her only reply was an indignant sniff.

Sometime later, Alena woke to soft footsteps drawing near. She reached for her dagger, then halted when she saw who it was. Hawkwind stood there, searching for Deidra. When he recognized who Alena's sleeping companion was, the tension visibly eased from his tautly strung body. With a slight nod to Alena, he turned and silently headed back to his wagon.

Overall, the first skirmish was going quite well, Hawkwind thought from his hillside vantage of the battlefield. The right flank was having considerable difficulty holding back the largest onslaught of mounted knights, but the rest of his army was doing admirably. In a short time, the main body of his force would finish off the foot soldiers, then turn their efforts to aiding the right flank. If all went as expected, they'd win today's battle in an amazingly short time.

He glanced up at the sun blazing overhead. 'Twas but two hours past midday. Hawkwind uttered a small prayer of thanks. His concerns that his men would lack the stamina to sustain an extended fight had come to naught. The battle would soon be over and his men still fresh. 'Twas the least fate could do for them, after the misfortunes of the past several days. Now, if only the fight to claim Castle Trifals for Lord Firston was short and sweet, he could mayhap recoup—

Something snagged the corner of his vision. He swung his gaze back to the right flank. Men fought in a melee of hacking swords, colorful flags, and milling horses. What had he seen that had caught his eye?

A face, white as snow. Eyes, wide, brown, and terror stricken. Then a flash of fiery-colored hair as the helmet covering it was knocked askew. Fear knifed through him.

Deidra!

He drew his sword and shouted to Renard. "Come! Now! Deidra's down there!"

As his big war-horse thundered down the hill to the thickest, most vicious part of the battle, Hawkwind's shock turned to a raw, seething fury. Damn her! He'd told her, nay, ordered her not to disobey him in this, and the little fool had gone and done it anyway! Now she was in the midst of it, and in serious danger of losing her life.

He'd beat her, turn her over his knee and blister her bottom when he got her to safety, Hawkwind vowed, his emotions roiling wildly, nearly incoherently within him. Then he'd take her into his arms and kiss her, and beg her never to leave him again. If only . . . if only he could get to her in time . . . .

Then, there was no time for further thought. With a fierce battle cry, Hawkwind raised his sword and plowed into the fray.

His shout pierced the fog of noise and rising panic surrounding Deidra. She barely had the strength to fight on. Her sword arm was all but numb. Her helmet had been knocked off and her shield was the only thing between her and certain death. True, she had managed successfully to fend off many attackers up to now, wounding them sufficiently to send them charging off the battlefield but, in the process, she had also belatedly realized something about herself.

She loathed taking a life.

What a fool she'd been to think 'twould be easy. That the battle lust would clear her mind of the cruel realities of war. That being a brave, proficient warrior would be enough.

Hawkwind, Bardrick, Alena. All of them had seen that failing in her and still she'd refused to listen. For them, war was a necessity of life, fighting, killing the only way to survive. But for her . . . For her, 'twasn't justification and would never be. She would always need more, something deeper, truer—more honorable.

The noise, the deafening clang of steel upon steel, the scent of blood and sweat and fear. The agonized screams, the jarring thud of horses slamming into each other, the looks of hatred and determined intent. Intent that would ultimately result in another's death. And, because she found it so hard to kill, ultimately in her death as well.

She wasn't afraid to die, but she wanted to die honorably, not as some floundering, hopeless fool who had ventured out where she had no right to be. She wanted to see Hawkwind one last time . . . tell him she loved him . . . and that he'd been right.

Then came his battle cry. She saw him, far away, hacking his way toward her like some man possessed. Wild hope flooded Deidra. Hawkwind. He'd come for her. He'd save her.

Deidra tried to fight on, knowing she must keep her shield up, must parry the sword thrusts aimed at her. The sweat beaded and trickled down her brow and into her eyes, blinding her. The dust, churned up from the hooves of the horses milling around, choked her. And still she fought on, the sight of Hawkwind, powerful and magnificent, strengthening her.

Then, as if suddenly realizing who was now in their midst and the certain victory that would be theirs if they cut him down, the enemy knights turned on Hawkwind. Immediately, he was surrounded on all sides and found himself fighting for his life.

"Nay!" Deidra cried, unwilling to take the chance for escape Hawkwind's attackers had afforded her in turning all their efforts against him. Horror filled her. All concern for her personal safety, all hesitation at taking a life, fled.

She spurred her horse forward, attacking the nearest knight. She must help Hawkwind. He needed her.

Yet, even as she did, Deidra knew she'd never reach him in time. The numbers between them and against him were too great.

Two knights came up behind Hawkwind as he fought off three others attacking from the front. In a moment frozen in time, Deidra saw their maces swing over their heads, then sail down toward Hawkwind. Felt them imbed in his helmet, pierce the metal, and lodge in the back of his skull as if 'twere her own.

"*Nay!*" Deidra screamed as Hawkwind lurched forward then jerked backward from the impact. His shield lowered momentarily. 'Twas all his opponents needed. As one, three swords plunged into Hawkwind's chest. He arched back, his mouth opening in soundless agony.

Something shattered, exploded in Deidra then. Fire leaped from her, arcing out in billowing tongues of flame. In one huge conflagration of light and sound, it engulfed her and the knights—and the mortally wounded Hawkwind.

Chapter 15

Screams, like none Deidra had ever heard before, filled the air. Heat consumed her. She could barely breathe. And the light . . . 'twas blinding.

Terror filled her. Her powers. She had finally lost control of them. Yet it no longer mattered. Naught mattered but that Hawkwind was dying and still they hacked at him. Hacked and stabbed and hurt him.

Anger welled, dispelling the mists of her fear with a red-hot blast of emotion. Curse them all! If they didn't move away from Hawkwind of their own accord, she'd *make* them move!

A force, even more powerful than the flame aura, burgeoned within her. It hurt. It tore at her, rending her apart. Yet still Deidra forced her mount through the milling throng of terrified, rearing horses and befuddled, shouting knights, shoving them aside as she went.

At her touch they fell, shrieking in agony, convulsing, then dying. All around her was death, destruction, and the excruciating pain of her own personal agony, but Deidra didn't care. All she saw was Hawkwind.

At last, the flame aura shielding her, her auburn hair billowing wildly in the air like tongues of fire, she reached him. He lay there on the ground, blood streaming from a multitude of horrible wounds, gasping his life out. Deidra swung down from her horse and ran to him.

"H-Hawkwind," she sobbed, gathering his limp, bloody body to hers. "Ah, by the Holy Ones, what have I done? What have I done?"

His eyes flickered open. "You w-wouldn't listen to me . . . would you, lass? I told you . . . this might happen. I warned you . . ."

He shuddered in her arms. His eyes slid shut. She could feel the life ebbing from him, his heart stop. Nausea, terror flooded her. "Nay!" she screamed. "I love you. I *won't* let you die!"

With all the strength left within her, Deidra willed her powers to heal him. Willed, fought, and was finally rewarded by the feeble resumption of his heartbeat. The sickening spurts of crimson slowed to an ooze, but Deidra knew that was all she could do.

The fire aura and killing rage that had brought her to his side had drained her of everything. She was naught herself but an open, gaping, psychic wound. She had naught else to give. Even to Hawkwind, the man she loved.

Around her, the sounds of renewed battle pierced the thick fog of her anguish. She heard shouts of *"Fire Queen"* and *"Witch"* hurled at her. She didn't care. Naught mattered but that Hawkwind was dying, and 'twas all because of her. Her and her selfish, stupid dreams. Dreams that had helped no one—not even, in the end, her.

Gradually, the battle seemed to fade. She forced herself to look up, glance around. The enemy force was nowhere near them anymore. Hawkwind's army, at the fall of their chief, had rallied around, driving back the attackers. Then Alena and several soldiers were beside them, stooping down to take Hawkwind's limp body from Deidra and lift him up to a man on a huge war-horse.

'Twas Bruno, Deidra realized dimly, staggering to her feet. Bruno would take care of Hawkwind.

A firm hand settled on her arm. She turned, dazed,

sticky with Hawkwind's blood upon her hands and clothes —and slammed into Alena.

Cold, furious eyes glared back at her. "Stupid, proud little fool!" the blond woman snarled. "If he dies, I swear . . ." She inhaled a shuddering breath and gestured to Deidra's horse with her sword. "Mount up. We need to get out of here."

Sick to the marrow of her bones, Deidra did as ordered. There was naught to say, and certainly no defense she could make in her behalf. She followed Alena and the soldiers protectively surrounding Hawkwind from the battle that was purposely being drawn away from them. They were soon back behind the lines and riding into camp.

Maud and Bardrick awaited their party. Her old bodyguard spared her one shocked, puzzled look before limping over to assist Maud and the others in helping Hawkwind down and into Maud's hospital tent. Deidra stood there, alone, awash in a shocked misery of her own, not knowing what else to do.

Somehow, she doubted anyone wanted her in the hospital tent right now. She didn't feel worthy of being there at any rate. Though she loved Hawkwind with all her heart, the realization had come too late to have heeded his words over the demands of her pride and need for independence. And now, because of that, the people at his side were the truer friends and deserved to be with him. Her shoulders slumped in dejection, she walked over to the small wooden bench standing outside the hospital tent and took a seat.

The sounds of activity, of tense, hushed voices, reached her ears. Deidra heard the order given for cautery and winced. Maud intended to staunch Hawkwind's wounds with a fire hot iron. She prayed he remained unconscious long enough to—

"D-Deidra!" Hawkwind suddenly moaned, his voice, carrying across the tent, surprisingly strong for what he'd so recently endured. "W-where is she? Is she all right?"

Maud's voice, indistinct but low and soothing, attempted

to hush him. Hawkwind refused to be silenced. "Where *is* she? B-bring her to me!"

There was a murmur of voices, then the sound of footsteps drawing near. Her heart in her throat, Deidra rose and turned. Alena stepped outside, a thunderous expression on her face. "He wants you. Why, I don't know, after what you caused, but he wants you."

At the thought of facing Hawkwind and the angry, accusing looks of the others in the tent, all courage fled her. "Nay." Deidra shook her head and backed away. "I can't . . . I won't . . ."

The warrior woman grabbed her. "Do you think I give a fig for what you want?" she demanded furiously. "All I care is that Hawkwind lies in there, mortally wounded, and he wants *you!*" With a painful twist of her hand, she wheeled Deidra around. "One way or another, you're going to see him!"

With a surprising strength, she wrenched free of Alena's viselike grip. "Fine. I'll go in. I'll see him. But keep your hands off me. I'll not be dragged before Hawkwind like some wretched piece of vermin."

"Vermin? You don't deserve even to be his whore!"

Tears glinted in Alena's eyes and, in a rush of anguished realization, Deidra saw the full extent of her foolhardy, thoughtless act. She had imagined the battle between only her and Hawkwind, with the consequences impacting only on them. She had been wrong. Because of her, an entire army's welfare now hung in the balance.

"I won't ask for his forgiveness, Alena, if that's what you're so afraid of," Deidra said, her voice low and strained. "I don't deserve it. But I will go to him and offer whatever comfort he wishes. I won't have him dying, crying out for me. 'Tisn't enough, but all I have left to give him."

With that, Deidra turned on her heel and strode over to the tent. She lifted the flap and walked in, struck immediately by the sudden dimness and sense of hushed expectancy. They, too, think he will soon die, she thought with a sudden, stabbing pain. Several pairs of eyes lifted to hers. For an instant, Deidra wanted to turn and run. Then, with a superhuman effort, she squared her shoulders and walked over to Hawkwind's bedside.

They'd pulled his cot over to one corner and fashioned a makeshift partition by slinging a length of cloth over a rope tied to two interior tent posts. As Deidra passed the other wounded soldiers lying in neat, orderly rows inside the large tent, she felt their eyes follow her, eyes that were angry, confused, and accusatory. She had failed each and every one of them, but Hawkwind most of all.

He lay there, his padded undertunic and mail stripped away, his chest swathed in crimson-stained bandages. His skin was pallid, his beard clotted with blood from multiple facial wounds. His body glistened with a fine sheen of sweat. His breathing came shallow and fast.

He looked on death's doorstep.

With a strangled sob, Deidra sank to her knees beside him and took his big hand in hers. She stroked his fingers, caressing the hair-roughened flesh and long, strong bones that lay beneath it, memorizing the feel and look of him. Tears fell unchecked, but Deidra said nothing.

Hawkwind stirred, groaned, and opened his eyes. For a moment, his glance was glazed, unfocused, and then his eyes narrowed. "D-Deidra?" he whispered. "I'd thought . . . I'd imagined . . . but you *did* survive."

"Aye, Hawkwind," she whispered back. "Thanks to you."

He managed a wan smile. "I-I'm not so certain the same . . . will be said for me." He squeezed her hand when she made a move to discount his words. "It matters naught, lass. Arguing won't change . . . what must be." His mouth quirked. "And you argue . . . far too much as 'tis."

Her head drooped like a flower dying on its stem. "Aye, that I do. I'm sorry to have been such a problem to you."

"Your heart means well, even if you don't always use your head." He stroked the side of her face, then lifted his gaze as if searching for someone. "Alena?"

She stepped forward from her spot directly behind Deidra. "Aye, Chief?"

"I don't want Deidra . . . punished." At her look of protest, he shot her a warning glance. "I mean it, Alena. I want her . . . safely escorted back . . . to her father. Give me your word on it."

Alena hesitated, then heaved a great sigh and nodded. "You have it. You know I'd never disobey you." Her glance cut to Deidra. "Not like some others, whom you erred gravely in trusting."

Hawkwind's gaze turned to Deidra who still knelt there, eyes downcast. "But I tried, nonetheless. D-didn't I, lass?"

At his words, the sobs, so precariously held in check, burst forth, wracking her body. Maud hurried over and quickly disengaged Hawkwind's hand from Deidra's. "Enough talk. 'Tis past time we see to yer wounds." She pulled Deidra to her feet and gave her a gentle shove. "Go, ye're in no condition to be of any help in here just now. Go outside and allow me to see to his healing."

"N-nay!" Hawkwind reached out to Deidra. "Let her stay. I-I need her to help me get through this." His glance met hers, his anguish-darkened eyes softly entreating. "You've helped me . . . bear pain before. Stay with me now."

She shot Maud a questioning glance. After a moment's hesitation, the healer woman nodded. "Just stay out of my way, whatever ye do."

Deidra immediately kneeled again at Hawkwind's side and took his hand back in hers. "I'll do whatever you ask. Just tell me what 'tis."

He arched a dark brow, his mouth quirking wryly. "Indeed? A pity . . . I had to go to such extremes . . . to finally win your obedience." He winced as Maud gently peeled his bandages away and his grip on Deidra's hands tightened.

When he made an attempt to look down at himself, Deidra cupped the side of his face in her hand and moved his head away. "Don't," she murmured with a firm insistence. "Look at me. 'Tis better that way."

He relented then and turned back to her, the look he sent her tearing Deidra's heart asunder. He hadn't had a chance to see the extent of his wounds, she knew. She'd stopped him before he had. He didn't need to know the magnitude and number of sword thrusts he'd suffered. 'Twas sickening enough just having to see them herself.

Love, and a soul-deep tenderness, swelled within her. He was so good, so brave, so wonderful even at a time such as this. Her gaze swept his face, memorizing each and every beloved feature for the future—a future that wouldn't include Hawkwind. Even if he lived, he'd be so crippled by these newest of wounds he'd never forgive her—if he ever truly forgave her for her flagrant disobedience of him.

She wondered now what had been so important, why she'd felt compelled to force the issue of her warrior's right to fight in his army. She could have waited, been a bit more patient. But that had never been her way; she had always seized life by the throat and taken what she wanted.

And there was more, Deidra realized. She had battled not only for the respect of Hawkwind's army, but for his respect as well. For all their growing closeness and affection, she had always doubted the depth of his commitment and his trust in her.

Had she thought finally to prove her worthiness by forcing his acceptance of her as a warrior? That if he could be brought to see her in the same light he viewed Alena, whom 'twas more than evident he trusted implicitly, he'd finally trust her as well?

A deep sorrow welled in Deidra. She had tried to force what 'twas impossible to force. She had tried to control, to gain power over a situation 'twas impossible to manipulate. Though always before she had succeeded in whatever she'd sought to accomplish, this time 'twasn't possible. This time she had gone too far in attempting to win the love and respect of a man by outward acts and demands rather than by just allowing it to happen if 'twas fated to be.

Mayhap, no matter what she had done, Hawkwind wasn't capable of a mature relationship with a woman or at least not with a woman he viewed as his own. Alena was his compatriot, not his lover. There was potentially a world of difference in that kind of relationship.

It didn't matter anymore. One way or another, she had ruined it all. Hawkwind would either die or turn from her forever now. And she had no one to blame but herself.

The hiss of hot metal caught her attention, drawing Deidra back from her morose musings. She glanced up to find Maud approaching with the red-hot cautery iron. Fear swelled within but, for Hawkwind's sake, Deidra masked it as best she could.

"Hold on now," she whispered to him, stroking his face with a tender, anxious motion. " 'Twill be over in a moment."

His eyes widened and he inhaled a shuddering breath, then willed his bow-strung taut body to relax. As the iron neared the first of his wounds and he felt its heat, he closed his eyes and waited.

The cautery sizzled and popped as it made contact with Hawkwind's ravaged body. He went rigid, his eyes clenched, and he arched backward in soundless agony. For a fleeting moment his hand tightened painfully about her fingers then, as if remembering himself, he willed his grip to relax.

The scent of burning flesh filled Deidra's nostrils. She thought she'd vomit. Only the greatest of efforts controlled her urge to retch. Frantically, she inhaled a few quick, deep breaths.

The cautery moved then. Once more the hiss of hot iron meeting moist, open wound cut through the air. Hawkwind gasped, ground his teeth and released Deidra's hand to grab the edges of the cot. "B-bloody h-hell!" he groaned.

Even before Maud pulled the cautery back, he began to writhe in agony.

"Make him still!" she commanded, her own voice strident with the tension. "Grab his shoulders and hold him down!"

Throwing aside the spent iron, Maud motioned for a fresh one. Bardrick immediately handed it to her. She turned, pausing but an instant to meet Deidra's gaze. "Hold him down as if yer life depended on it. I don't want him moving and we need to get this over with."

"A-aye," Deidra agreed unsteadily. Leaning over Hawkwind, she shoved down on his shoulders with all her might. "Hold," she crooned to him. "Hold for just a bit longer. " 'Twill soon be over. I promise it!"

The fresh iron, glowing bright red, was pressed to yet another of his countless wounds. "Uhhh!" Hawkwind grunted and threw himself up against Deidra with such force she was almost thrown off balance. Then he went slack and slumped onto the cot, blessedly unconscious at last.

Five minutes later, Maud was done. Deidra leaned back, dripping wet, her body quivering from the stress. She glanced over at Maud. There was little sympathy in the healer's eyes.

"Go, rest yerself," she ordered tautly. "Hawkwind will sleep for a time now. He won't know ye're gone."

"Nay." Deidra shook her head. "I want to stay with him." She struggled for the right words to express the emotions roiling within her. "I-I *need* to."

"*Ye* need?" Maud gave a harsh laugh. "And what of Hawkwind? What about his needs?"

Deidra stared up at her, stunned. "I . . . He said he wanted me . . . here."

"Well, I don't just now," Maud snapped. "I've still hours of work left to finish sewing up his other wounds. If he wakens in the meantime, I'll send for ye. But right now, *I* don't need—or want—ye here."

At Maud's words, something snapped in Deidra. "And I

don't care what you, or any of the rest of you, want! I may well be the only one here with the power to save Hawkwind's life and I won't let your animosity against me, however justified it may be, keep me from doing that!"

Maud motioned toward Hawkwind. "Then go ahead and heal him. What's keeping ye?"

What indeed? Deidra thought in surprise. True, her powers had been severely drained in rescuing Hawkwind from his attackers, but surely—

As she began to gather the magic about her, a sharp, searing pain lanced through her, lodging in the center of her chest. Deidra gasped and wrapped her arms about herself. Whatever was the matter?

She took Hawkwind's hand in hers, struggling to ignore the pain that throbbed like a pulse within her. She closed her eyes, cleared her mind, and strove to visualize only him. The pain subsided. Deidra inhaled a steadying breath and tried again.

Agony, excruciating, mind-numbing, surged in to grip her in the throes of a pulsating torment. Her mouth opened, she tried to scream, and her body arched in convulsive spasms.

Then there were hands on her, pulling her back, away from Hawkwind. There were voices, calling to her through the black mist swirling about her. Then, the darkness cleared.

Deidra found herself on the ground, Maud, Bardrick, and Alena staring down at her. She blinked to clear her vision, then tried to shove herself to a sitting position. The effort proved too much. Her stomach churned; she felt dizzy, weak, and confused.

"What h-happened?" Deidra whispered, her lips thick and awkward around the words.

Maud knelt beside her. "I'd say 'twas something wrong with yer powers. Ye either harmed yerself when ye summoned yer fire powers, or yer inner being is fighting further use of them. Either way, ye'll not do anything this night for Hawkwind without harm to yerself."

"I don't care!" Fueled by anger at her failure, Deidra shrugged off the hands holding her and levered to one elbow. "I don't care if I harm myself. If Hawkwind dies, I don't care what happens to me!"

"Well, I do," the healer countered firmly. "I've got wounded men here and more soon to come. I don't need someone burdening me with extra work because she's too overwrought to think straight right now. Ye must conserve yer strength and allow yerself to heal. Later, we may need ye worse than now, and I want ye ready." She bent down and grasped Deidra by the shoulders. "Do ye understand me, child? Will ye, for once in yer life, listen and pay heed before 'tis too late?"

Deidra's eyes locked with Maud's. Shame flooded her. Maud was right. 'Twas past time she began listening . . . and learning. The tension ebbed from her body.

"Aye," she whispered. "I understand."

"Then here, take this and drink it, then hie yerself back to Hawkwind's tent." Maud held out a small flagon of an amber-tinted fluid.

Deidra eyed it suspiciously. "What is it?"

"A sleeping potion." She unstopped the flagon and offered it to Deidra. "Drink it down, all of it. Now."

There was no refusing her, Deidra realized, noting the look of firm resolve in the healer's eyes. She did as requested.

"Good." Maud rocked back on her heels and motioned over Bardrick. "Come, ye old wolfhound. Carry yer young mistress back to Hawkwind's tent. There's naught else she can do here.

"And I," she pointedly added, her glance snagging on the wounded soldiers being carried in, "most certainly have work to do."

* * *

'Twas a sign, Deidra decided as she rose the next morning, curiously refreshed after Maud's sleeping potion, and hurriedly bathed, dressed, and braided her hair before heading over to see how Hawkwind was doing. Her horrible dream last night had been a sign of the inherent evil in her powers, and a warning not ever to use them again. Though she'd hardly realized what was happening around her yesterday, she now knew she had killed, viciously and without thought or remorse, in the act of rescuing Hawkwind.

Her body's severe response to the attempted use of her powers later, when she had tried to heal Hawkwind, was also a sign she should never dare use them again. She had misused her magic before she'd even learned truly to understand and control it. Whatever good that was left in her was crying out to cease before 'twas too late. Cease before it killed her or she totally lost control.

But what of Hawkwind? What would happen to him if she didn't attempt her healing of him again? Were Maud's powers sufficient to save him?

For Hawkwind—and only Hawkwind—Deidra was still willing to risk it. Her life would mean naught if he died. But she feared her powers now, didn't know if she could even control them anymore. And she didn't want to cause yet more harm.

Mayhap Maud had some answers, Deidra decided as she made her way across camp to the hospital tent. The hostile looks and mutterings, the furtive warding signs she caught out of the corner of her eye as she passed the men preparing for another day's battle, filled her with shame. They feared and hated her now. Men who just a few days before had treated her with friendship and growing respect, now loathed her.

Not that she blamed them. 'Twas she who had destroyed it all. 'Twas she who was responsible for the attack on their chief. Still, 'twas hard to continue on, striding past all those men, enduring their animosity. Deidra lowered her head to block out the looks sent her way and forged on.

In the process, she nearly slammed into Renard. Strong hands grasped her arms to steady her as she stumbled backward. Calm gray eyes locked with hers as, with a gasp, she glanced up.

Surprisingly, instead of the revulsion and anger she expected, there was only a concerned sympathy gleaming in Renard's eyes. "How are you, lass?" he asked, releasing her as soon as she caught her balance.

Deidra flushed. She didn't deserve any kindness, especially not from one of Hawkwind's closest friends. She managed a small shrug. "As well as can be expected. I-I was going to see how Hawkwind fared. Maud never sent for me last night and I slept longer than intended."

"The stress of the past day exhausted you, I'd imagine. I just came from Hawkwind." An anxious light flared in his eyes, then was quickly extinguished. "He hasn't regained consciousness. I don't know whether to find that a good sign or bad."

She knew he was asking for any glimmer of hope, but Deidra had none to give. "I truly don't know, Renard."

"Will you help him with your healing powers?"

Her eyes widened in surprise. "You would want me to, after what I did? You would trust me not to cause greater harm?"

He smiled. "Though you thoughtlessly caused the chief's injuries, you then saved him. And I know you would never wish him harm."

Tears, maddeningly frequent of late, filled Deidra's eyes. "Nay, never that, Renard. Never."

"Then go to him, and let none keep you from him. If any should stop you, tell them you are under my orders, as acting chief, until Hawkwind recovers."

"Alena won't like that." Deidra swiped away the tears trickling down her cheeks. "I fear she now hates me."

"I've already spoken with her. She's very angry with you, but give her time. In the meanwhile, she, too, has her orders and will obey." He grinned down at her. "Like all good soldiers should do, eh, lass?"

Once more the warmth stole into Deidra's face. "Aye, Renard. Like all good soldiers should."

He made a move to walk on, when she stayed him for a moment more. "The battle. You desperately need the money Lord Firston will pay. What will you do without Hawkwind?"

Renard's expression went hard. "It took a lot of convincing, by both Alena and myself, that the men would follow us in Hawkwind's stead, but Firston finally agreed. We continue the battle today."

"*Will* the men follow you?"

His mouth quirked slightly. "Aye, they will, or at least as long as Hawkwind lives. After that, who knows? A lot will depend on how today goes. If we're successful, aye. If not . . . ?"

He let the rest remain unspoken, but Deidra well knew what the results might be if they lost today's battle. The army might dissolve, chaos would ensue, and the men desert. She shuddered to think of the death, destruction, and pillage that would result if an army the size of Hawkwind's went on a rampage. 'Twas frightening to imagine the power and potential for destruction one man held in his hands, and what could happen if he ever lost it.

A fierce resolve filled her. She lifted her chin and met the war captain's gaze. "Hawkwind will live, if there's anything I can do about it. *Anything.*"

He clasped her on the shoulder. "I knew you wouldn't fail us when the times grew hard. 'Tis why Hawkwind cares so much for you. You're a very special woman."

Deidra smiled sadly. "Yet still not special enough for a man like Hawkwind, Renard." With that, she stepped back and turned, unable to bear another moment of his kindness, or the reminder that Hawkwind had once cared for her. Though Renard meant well in trying to ease her guilt and encourage her, Deidra knew better. She wasn't special at all and didn't deserve Hawkwind's affection. But that was hardly the point anymore. All that mattered, for *all* their sakes, was saving him.

The hospital tent was full but, from a quick survey of the various occupants, Deidra could see that most would recover from their wounds. That heartened her. At least yesterday's battle hadn't resulted in terrible losses for their side.

She found Maud at Hawkwind's bedside, dozing. Deidra moved to the other side of the cot and quietly knelt, not wishing to waken the healer. She took up Hawkwind's hand and gazed down at him.

With a start, she noted his beard and mustache were gone, his face clean-shaven so Maud could more easily tend to his facial wounds. He looked different, yet just as pleasing, despite the presence of multiple cuts Maud had so deftly sewn. She'd never realized how really broad and strong his jawline was, nor noted before the slight prominence of his chin. It only made him appear, Deidra decided, even more determined and masculinely arrogant.

And she definitely liked the liberation of his mouth from its former fringe of hair. His upper lip was long, somewhat thin, but complemented nicely with his full lower lip. Aye, Deidra thought to herself, Hawkwind had very firm, sensual, kissable lips.

An impulse, to kiss him once more, filled her. 'Twas mayhap unfair to take something she no longer had any right to, but suddenly, Deidra didn't care. Just once more, she craved the taste of his mouth beneath hers, the scent of him, the feel of his warm breath as it caressed her cheek.

With a quick, furtive glance to assure her Maud was still sleeping, Deidra leaned down and brushed her lips against Hawkwind's. Memories of his mouth, hot, sweet, and savagely passionate, slanting over hers, rose in her mind's eye. She remembered his hands, pulling her to him, stroking and squeezing her. His body, so big, hard muscled—and aroused.

She choked back a sob and leaned away. How would she ever live with the memories of what had and could have been? Angrily, she wiped away the single tear coursing down her face.

"He doesn't wake." Maud's calm voice pierced the painful jumble of Deidra's thoughts. "I worry for him. And for ye."

Deidra glanced up. The healer gazed back at her, the tension and anger of yesterday gone. All that remained was a tender concern and sympathetic look. Just like Renard.

Illogically, anger filled her. Deidra's lips tightened. "Save your concern for where it belongs. With Hawkwind. I am unharmed and whole; he isn't."

"Are ye indeed?" Maud asked softly with an arch of a slender brow. "I saw much yesterday, especially when ye attempted his healing. Ye're as injured as he, only yer wounds are of the spirit . . . and of yer magic."

She had guessed as much, Deidra grudgingly admitted to herself. "I care not for what happened to me. Do I have any magic left to heal Hawkwind? If I could just do that, naught else would matter."

"Even if, in the using, ye might injure yerself further, mayhap fatally?"

Deidra's lips quivered momentarily, then she clamped them together. "Aye, even then." Her glance dipped to Hawkwind. "Does he need me, Maud? Or can you heal him?"

"I have done all within my power. He lives, but that's all I can do."

Nut brown eyes, glistening with emotion, lifted back to hers. "Then tell me what I must do."

"His wounds begin already to fester." Maud gestured to each area of Hawkwind's body as she spoke. "One sword thrust pierced his lung. The others have hopelessly damaged his chest muscles. And the blows to the back of his head appear to have shattered the base of his skull."

Deidra's eyes slid shut in horror. How was she ever to

heal so many horrible injuries? She forced open her eyes.
"I'm so afraid. So afraid I'll fail."

"But ye'll accomplish naught at all if ye don't try."

"Aye." Deidra forced a wan smile. "True enough." She
reached out to Hawkwind, then hesitated. "Will you help
me if I falter? Promise to tell him I loved him with all my
heart, if . . . if I don't survive?"

Maud nodded. "Aye, I'll do it all."

Closing her eyes once more, Deidra gathered all the
powers she possessed, stoically ignoring the flash of pain.
Then, reaching out, she touched Hawkwind, tracing a
light, sinuous path down his face and chest with a single
finger. The warmth flared within her, the pain grew, but
Deidra fought past the discomfort, concentrating only on
the heat, the healing . . . the magic.

Then, with a searing jolt, the magic left her, spiraling
down her arms, through her fingers, and out into
Hawkwind. He jerked, arched up in bed, fierce spasms
wracking his body. Joined as one by the terrible force,
Deidra threw back her head, her mouth opening in silent
anguish. On and on the fearsome powers surged through
her and into Hawkwind, yet still she hung on, fighting past
the pain, the fire, the terror of it all.

Bit by bit, she saw him heal. His muscles mended, his
lung resealed, his wounds closed, his skull bones realigned
and knit. Yet still Deidra forged on, determined to give him
back everything her thoughtless act had wrought—his
strength, his vigor, his life.

A deep pit loomed before her. She felt herself falling,
fading. Felt her life force ebb, but didn't care.

Hawkwind. Naught mattered but Hawkwind. . . .

Chapter 16

Hands were upon Deidra, wrenching her away, calling her back. Voices, muted, distant, were shouting at her. Something struck her, then again and again.

Deidra moaned, her hand moving to her stinging cheek. "D-don't," she moaned again. Her eyes flickered open.

Hawkwind and Maud knelt over her. Deidra blinked, not believing what she saw. *Hawkwind? Alive and well?*

She lifted a hand to his face, stroked it tentatively. 'Twas him, warm, breathing, and whole. Deidra's gaze swung to Maud's. "It-it worked, didn't it? I-I healed him."

Maud's soft gray eyes glittered with tears. "Aye, child, that ye did. But ye almost killed yerself in the process."

Deidra shuddered, recalling the deep pit, the sensation of falling, the endless blackness. "Mayhap. But it matters not." She shot Hawkwind a searching glance. "You're quite recovered?"

"Better than before. You seem to get more and more proficient with each healing." He grinned. "Mayhap, next time, you can carve a few years off my life. I've a sudden need to be as virile as when I was eighteen."

She stared up at him with uncomprehending eyes. "I don't think I understand . . ." Her voice faded. Then, as the meaning of his words struck her, she flushed. "But surely you're not talking about us. After what I did, caused . . ." Deidra turned away. "Nay, 'tisn't possible."

Hawkwind leaned down and pulled her up into his arms. His body, so warm and alive, pressed against her. His heart, beneath the bare, battle-scarred chest still swathed in bandages, thudded rhythmically, reassuringly against her ear.

Deidra's hands snaked up to entwine about his strong, thick neck. He was but being kind, attempting to spare her so soon after the terrible stress of his healing. But, be that as it may, she'd take what little was left her, even if 'twas just the comfort of being held close to him.

"What isn't possible, lass?" Hawkwind crooned, his voice rumbling deep and rich against her ear. "That you'll never forgive me for refusing to let you go to battle, or that I won't forgive you for disobeying me?"

"For what I did to you, of course," Deidra replied tautly. "You nearly died and I almost destroyed your army because of it. Not to mention turning Alena and all your men against me." She swallowed hard. "They fear me now, for what I did in rescuing you. They think 'twas evil."

"And was it, lass?" he asked as he stroked her hair.

"I-I don't know. Nor," she added with a firm conviction, "do I ever want to. I'll *never* use the fire powers again! Never!"

The force of her resolve and the emotions of the past day were suddenly too much. Wracking tremors began to shake her. For all her efforts to contain it, Deidra couldn't. In but a few moments, she was a shaking, teeth-chattering bundle of tightly strung muscles.

Hawkwind glanced over at Maud, an anxious look in his eyes.

"She'll be fine," the healer soothed. "Put her to bed and cover her warmly, then set someone near to watch her. 'Tis just the horror of the past day catching up with her."

He nodded and rose, carrying Deidra with him in his

arms. "My thanks to you, Maud, for what you've done for the both of us."

"Get on with ye," she urged, making a shooing motion with her hands. "I did naught. 'Twas all Deidra's doing. Now go, take care of her as I told ye to."

Hawkwind turned and strode across the tent, pausing only for a few moments to assure his wounded men he was indeed well and would return to visit them later. As he departed the tent, Deidra still shivering in his arms, he was greeted by a huge, joyous shout of welcome. He blinked in the bright morning sun, grinned, then headed out across camp to his tent.

There were wondering looks, some frowns of puzzlement, and a few wary glances at Deidra's presence in his arms, but Hawkwind chose not to react to them. The sooner he demonstrated all was well once again between him and Deidra, the sooner the camp would settle down and accept her once more. He was not prepared, however, for the fury in Alena's eyes as she came racing across from where she was preparing to mount up to join Renard in going to battle.

"I knew she'd cozen up the first chance she had," the warrior woman cried, "but I didn't think she'd throw herself at you just as soon as you left your sickbed! The conniving, selfish little—"

"Enough, Alena," Hawkwind commanded, his voice pitched low, but tight with warning. "This is not the time nor place for such a discussion. Deidra is ill and I must get her to bed. We can talk later." His glance took in her battle garb. "Do you ride out with Firston this morn?"

"Aye," she replied, shooting Deidra one last, scathing glance before turning her full attention to her leader. "He agreed to allow Renard and me to lead the army today."

"Very reluctantly, I'd wager."

Alena's mouth tipped up in a small grin. "*Very* reluctantly."

"Good, then tell him I've nearly recovered but have decided to leave the battle in your and Renard's most competent hands today. On the morrow, if complete victory isn't already ours, I'll rejoin you."

She arched a slender brow. "I thank you for the vote of confidence, Chief, but do you think that's wise? Firston will be livid when he hears of your recovery and refusal to lead the battle."

Hawkwind shrugged. "Most likely, but I wish to teach him a lesson he won't soon forget. No man insults my two war captains or impugns their competence. Nor," he added, "my judgment in choosing them to lead in my stead."

Alena nodded. "As you wish." She turned and began to stride away.

"Alena?"

"Aye?" She halted and glanced over her shoulder.

"Nor should you doubt again my judgment in choosing whatever woman I want. Is that understood?"

The blond warrior's eyes narrowed momentarily as she shot Deidra a seething glance. Then she nodded her acquiescence. "Aye, Hawkwind. 'Tis understood."

"She'll never forgive me, never again be my friend," Deidra murmured mournfully the next day. Though she felt immeasurably better, Hawkwind had insisted she remain in bed another twenty-four hours. And Deidra, determined to turn over a new leaf to prove to him she could obey, stayed where he bid. Luckily, between Maud and Bardrick's frequent visits, she found the day passed reasonably fast.

"Don't sell Alena short," Bardrick said from his chair drawn up beside Deidra's bed. "She loves Hawkwind like a sister and feels rather protective of him. She'll come to accept ye again in time. For Hawkwind's sake, if not for yer own."

He looked nearly recovered from his horrible head injury. Save for a slight sag to the right corner of his mouth and residual weakness to his right side, 'twas impossible to tell how close he'd come to death. Deidra knew, however, even if she'd wished ever to use her powers again, Bardrick would never accept her offer of healing. He'd already refused Maud's: There was no reason to think he'd now want hers.

"But that's no acceptance," Deidra protested, reluctantly returning to the subject at hand. "I want acknowledgment for myself, not as leavings of another's favor." She sighed. "But I've learned well enough of late that respect and acceptance can't be forced. I suppose I'll just have to live with that—and the loss of Alena's regard."

"Mayhap. Why don't ye just wait and see? Now that Renard and Alena have routed Firston's enemies and our assignment here is soon finished, things will quickly calm and people regain their perspective."

"Aye, mayhap." She brightened as another thought assailed her. "How goes it with you and Maud these days?"

Bardrick's eyes narrowed. "As always," he warily responded. "Why do ye ask?"

"Oh, for no special reason," Deidra replied with an airy little wave of her hand. "She's a very attractive woman and you're not getting any younger. I thought—"

"Well, ye thought wrong," he cut her off. "There is naught between Maud and I, and never will be again!"

"And I say you protest far too strongly for a man who claims disinterest," she countered, fixing him with a stern gaze. "You're breaking her heart, Bardrick, and all because of some silly superstitions."

"They're *not* superstitions!"

"Nonetheless, your beliefs haven't turned you from me and my powers are far greater than Maud's. I'd wager you even knew of my mother. Did you, Bardrick?"

He scowled. "Aye, I knew of her. I saw what her magic did to her, too. Why do you think I worked so hard to keep yer mind off such things all these years? 'Twas part of the reason I taught ye the swordplay and told ye all those tales. I meant to distract ye from yer powers and hope they'd never materialize."

"But you couldn't. No one could. One way or another I was meant to discover them."

"And look where they got ye," Bardrick said. "Ye're now feared and reviled, not only by Alena but by the army. Is that what ye wanted, lass?"

"Nay, I never wanted that," Deidra admitted with a small sigh, "and, though I will never regret using my powers to save Hawkwind, the knowledge I carry the potential for such evil sickens me. Because of what happened, I may never use my magic again."

"Yet ye want me to take Maud back, accept the same potential in her that ye carry."

"Hawkwind has forgiven me and he seems not to fear my powers. I don't know what will become of our relationship, but 'twas never the fault of my magic. And Maud is a seasoned sorceress, not as I, who am untrained and erratic. Can't you reconsider, give your relationship another chance?"

"Nay." Bardrick firmly shook his head. "Leave it be, lass. We're friends. I find comfort in that."

Inexpressible sadness filled Deidra. "Ah, Bardrick," she cried, "why won't you allow yourself to be happy? What are you so afraid of?"

"And aren't you the fine one to be haranguing Bardrick about personal fears," a new voice suddenly intruded.

Deidra glanced up, her gaze slamming into Alena's. "Oh, I didn't hear you enter." She flushed. " 'Twould have been polite to have announced your arrival. We were engaged in a private conversation."

The warrior woman shrugged. "Mayhap. Would you like me to leave?"

"Nay." Bardrick hurriedly climbed to his feet. "I was just leaving." He motioned to his chair. "Please, have my seat."

"Bardrick," Deidra shouted after him as he made his rapid retreat across the tent, "this subject isn't closed. We'll talk later . . ." Her voice faded as he disappeared beneath the tent flap.

"I'd say 'twas," Alena observed in wry amusement, turning back to Deidra. "Or at least if he has aught to say about it."

Tamping down an urge to rail at Alena for her untimely and inconsiderate arrival, Deidra forced a tight smile. "He doesn't know his own mind. Like all men, he's as stubborn as a jackass."

"And you aren't?"

Stopped short by the blunt query, Deidra paused. Anger surged through her. "Why are you here, Alena? Come to insult and berate me further?"

Alena cocked a slender brow. "If you need it, aye. 'Tis past time you learn to quit meddling where you've no right to be."

Deidra eyed her. "He is my friend. I care about his happiness. And Maud's as well."

"Aye," Alena agreed. " 'Tis a sad thing, how the two of them can't seem to work out their differences. But 'tis *their* affair, not yours. How would you have liked it if everyone kept meddling between you and Hawkwind?"

"There's naught to meddle with," Deidra snapped, immediately on the defensive. " 'Tis over between us."

"Is it now? I'd have thought differently."

"Well, you've been known to be wrong!"

Alena grinned. "Aye, but at least I've the courage to recognize it. What about you?"

Deidra scowled. "What's your point? I've already said I was sorry for what happened. How long must I grovel before you'll be satisfied?"

"A novel consideration, you groveling and all," the blond woman replied. "But that's another day. I came to offer my apology."

Shock jolted through Deidra. She shoved herself farther up in bed. Then, her eyes narrowed in suspicion. "Hawkwind put you up to this, didn't he?"

Alena shook her head. "Nay. Aside from telling me not to doubt his judgment in choosing whichever woman he wanted, he made no other demands. This was my decision and mine alone."

Deidra's lips tightened. "Well, you needn't apologize. I deserved what you said, and more."

"Why *did* you go against Hawkwind?"

"I wanted to be accepted as you were. 'Tis just that simple."

"Hawkwind will never look upon you as he does me. And," Alena added with a rueful smile, "he'll never look upon me as he does you. If you had the choice, which would you choose?"

"Both."

Alena rolled her eyes. "You're being unrealistic and greedy again."

"Fine." Deidra sighed in exasperation. "I'd take his love, just as long as it came with his regard. Love without it isn't worth much."

"And you don't think you have his regard?" Alena's brow crinkled in disbelief. "After what you put him through in the past month—the battle aside—do you think his treatment of you is solely due to his lust for you?"

"I-I don't know." Deidra's head lowered. "And I'm afraid to hope for . . ." She lifted a stricken face to Alena. "What am I to do? I-I love him."

Alena's mouth softened. "I know. I don't know what to tell you to do about it, though. I've never had a man love me." She managed a small smile. "My experience, because of that lack, is sadly deficient."

"You?" Deidra's response was as startled as her expression. "Why, you're beautiful! I can't believe no man—"

"Since Hawkwind, I never encouraged anyone, nor do I wish to. I'm a warrior. I've no time for other things. Besides, love softens not only the heart, but the brain."

"Aye, that it does," Deidra agreed glumly. "I'm not so certain I like it, either. My plans never allowed for a man in them. In fact, a large part of them included ways to avoid any possible attachments to men."

"I never thought much about it, one way or another, either," Alena said, finally pulling up Bardrick's chair and sitting down. "But then, I didn't grow up with a doll in my hands. From my earliest years, I played with a wooden sword and shield."

Deidra's eyes brightened with sudden interest. "When did you first come to camp? It sounds like you were well prepared from the start."

Long-ago memories darkened Alena's eyes. "When the famine first struck the land my father, whose heart was already broken by the death of my mother in the bearing of me, soon gave up his attempts to farm his small patch of land. I was but three when we set out to join the first of many mercenary armies. To ease my acceptance, my father dressed me as a lad and I grew up thinking I was one for many years. Of course," she added, her mouth twisting mockingly, "I was soon disabused of that when my body began to blossom. But still I didn't care, until the winter Hawkwind arrived."

"How old were you then?" Deidra asked.

"Sixteen, and in the full bloom of my maidenhood." She shot Deidra a self-conscious grin. "I fell immediately and madly in love with Hawkwind."

" 'Twould be an easy enough thing," Deidra murmured. "Especially when one was sixteen. Or seventeen, for that matter."

"He never saw me as anything but a little brother, and then sister when I finally revealed my secret to him. From thence on, he took me under his wing, insisting I live as a woman. And, when others in camp demanded I relinquish my warrior's status, he stood up and defended me. He, alone of all, fought for my right to live as I chose. Because of him, I became the warrior—and his war captain—I am today."

"I must admit to a certain envy at your success."

"And I, for yours," Alena countered. "But both of us must accept our destinies, however differently they might deviate from our original plans. Until we do, we cannot learn to profit from our own unique talents. And, in the doing, achieve the happiness we are meant to find."

"Aye, I suppose so." Deidra sighed. "I know I almost destroyed my chances. Not only with Hawkwind, but with all of you." She smiled over at Alena. "I'd like to try again, though, if you'd let me. 'Twas truly painful to lose your friendship."

The blond warrior woman blushed. "I've never been much for friendships with other women. But I feel a strange bonding with you." She stood. "We'll start anew and see what comes of it."

"Alena?" Deidra called after her as she turned and began to stride across the tent.

Alena halted. "Aye?" she tossed over her shoulder.

"Does that mean we can resume our battle practice?"

"What does Hawkwind say to that?"

"Oh, I haven't brought up the subject as yet," Deidra blithely replied. "But I'm sure he can be made to see my way of it."

"Indeed?" Alena chuckled.

"Indeed," Deidra firmly countered.

"What are you about?" Deidra asked suspiciously the next day as she viewed the wicker basket in Hawkwind's one hand, and his other, outstretched to her.

"Our business with Firston is over, our contract completed and paid in full. I felt a need to celebrate and thought you'd like a short ride to the meadow to try out Mystic," he calmly replied. "The falcon is well recovered and needs some flying to rebuild its strength."

"Aye, that would be fine, but what's in the basket?" She shifted her position in her chair in an attempt to peer into the basket.

"I had a small repast prepared for us for the midday meal. 'Twill be past time to eat after we're done with Mystic." Hawkwind grinned. "Of course, if you've no appetite, I'm certain I can make short work of the roast quail, cheese, fresh baked bread, and apple tarts," he said, lifting the basket's lid to peek inside.

Deidra rose and strode over. "Aye, I'm sure you could. Have you packed a blanket as well, so we can lounge on the sweet meadow grass together afterward?"

"If I have, would that be such a terrible thing?"

The heated look glinting in his eyes told Deidra his own opinion of the answer. The realization stirred a small surge of joyous anticipation within her breast. Though she didn't quite believe 'twas true, she couldn't help but hope Hawkwind did indeed want her again.

"Nay, 'twouldn't be terrible at all," she answered him. "In fact, it sounds like a delightful way to spend a few hours. Flying my bird, eating a fine meal, and basking in the sun."

"Am I, mayhap, included in that most pleasant of plans?" Hawkwind grumbled, a small frown wrinkling his brow. "Or would you prefer for me to stand a short distance away, holding the horses so as not to intrude on your private enjoyment?"

Deidra grinned. "I would be honored to have you beside me the entire time, if you so desire. I just didn't wish to presume—"

He grabbed her hand and pulled her forward. "Well, you always were a presumptuous little wench, but I find I've come to like that in a woman. Shall we be on our way?"

She laughed as she allowed him to tug her along. "Was there ever any doubt?"

"A bit there." He chuckled. "You did have me going for a minute or two." He released her hand and lifted the tent flap, motioning for her to walk ahead. "One would think I'd have learned all your tricks by now."

"Not by a long shot, m'lord." Deidra giggled. "I'm a very creative woman."

"Aye, so you are." Hawkwind strode over to where their two horses were tethered and tied the basket onto his saddle. Once Deidra was mounted on Belfry, he handed her a thick leather glove, then quickly retrieved Mystic from the perch placed outside his tent and handed him up to her.

The peregrine nimbly took his position on her left, gauntleted hand, settled himself with a brief flutter of mottled, black-and-white feathered wings, then stilled. Hawkwind grinned. "He's found his new master, I'd say."

Deidra smiled. "Do you think so? I only hope I can handle him properly. I flew several hawks at Rothgarn, but never learned much about their training."

"I know a bit about falconry," Hawkwind offered, tamping down on his sudden surge of uneasiness that admission stirred. "I think I can aid your training of the bird, if it even requires much training."

The past be damned, he angrily thought as he mounted his war-horse, and that included his former aversion to the birds of prey. He'd not let anything mar the beauty of this day or what he hoped to accomplish. He had barely escaped with his life and found, strangely enough, he now valued it more than ever before. 'Twas time to put the past, or at least some of it, behind him.

The realization filled him with a curious sense of release. He had allowed too much of what had happened to him to burden his heart and soul, and keep him hard and bitter. Now, he found he no longer wanted to feel that way or at least not when he was with Deidra.

They rode out to a brilliant day, kissed by sunshine and warm, gentle breezes. Though the grass was still green and lush from the frequent rains, the trees were beginning to turn. Leaves, in hues from golden yellow to flame-bright reds, shimmered and danced as the errant wind played among the branches. The sky above was a deep, pure cerulean blue, feathered by wisps of snow-white clouds.

Deidra inhaled deeply of the crisp, sweet air and grinned over at Hawkwind. " 'Tis so beautiful, isn't it? So wonderful to be alive."

"Aye," he admitted gravely. "I find that especially true, after having barely survived my last battle. Strange, but the possible loss of my life never bothered me before, nor enhanced the life around me."

"Indeed?" As they rode along, Deidra shot him a considering look. "You've lived all these years, not caring if you lived or died? That seems passing sad to me."

"I survived, Deidra." His teeth flashed in a lazy grin. "But meeting and getting to know you has definitely made my life a lot more challenging and interesting."

She blushed, heartened by his words. "I hope some of the 'getting to know me' has been worthwhile and pleasant as well. I'd not like to think all I've caused you is anger and pain."

"Oh, 'tis very pleasurable at times." He chuckled. "And I'd like to experience that pleasure again, if you're willing."

As he spoke the words she caught the hungry light in his eyes, and something akin to a briefly unmasked vulnerability as well. He's no more certain of me and my feelings for him, Deidra realized, then I am of his. Yet dared she reveal her own feelings and risk his rejection? Well, Deidra resolved, someone must make the first move and, after all the problems she'd caused him, 'twas only fair she be that person.

She smiled tentatively. "I would things be between us as they were before I . . . I disobeyed you. I would things be even more, as well. I-I love you, Hawkwind."

Somehow, the words, so feared for the imagined bonds they'd entwine about her heart and life, were freeing instead. She had offered him the gift of her love. She had told him the simple, honest truth. 'Twas up to him now to accept or reject it, as he must accept or reject the person she was. But, no matter what he did, she had shared the secrets of her heart. Whatever the outcome, Hawkwind deserved to know he was loved.

His green eyes darkened in fleeting pain and some equally fleeting, but far more tender, emotion. "I thank you for the honor, and compliment, lass. I'd hardly say I was the sort of man for one such as you, though."

"Because you're a mercenary soldier?"

"Aye, but even more so, because of the kind of man I've become." He sighed and turned his gaze to the land ahead. "I have scars no one can see. I have wounds that refuse to heal. And I have naught of any worth to give you. You'd do far better to find someone else to love."

"Wounds can heal if you let them, Hawkwind. And every soul bears its scars." Deidra reined in Belfry. At her action, he was forced to do the same.

"Deidra," he began when he saw the thunderous look build on her face. "I didn't mean to—"

"Will you even make the decision as to whom I choose to love?" she demanded hotly. "Curse you, Hawkwind, but you're the most pigheaded—"

"Deidra," he warned, his voice dropping to an ominous rumble. "Don't start—"

"I'll start and finish this, once and for all!" she snapped. "Spurn my love if you wish. 'Tis your right to do so. But never, ever, disparage my choice of whom to love, or tell me to find another. Ohh!" she cried out her anger and frustration, turning her face away. "Why can't you just once afford me the same respect you do Alena? I must be mad to love a man like you!"

"I'm afraid to let myself love you."

Deidra whirled around, her eyes wide in disbelief. "What did you say?"

"I'm afraid to love you," he softly reiterated. His hands clenched about his horse's reins. "You don't know me, Deidra. Nor know what formed me into the man I am today. But I greatly fear, if you did, you'd no longer love me."

"So you avoid the possibility of being hurt by pushing me away from you. By not even giving us a chance."

"Something like that." His mouth twisted in a bleak smile. "Not so brave and wonderful now, am I?"

"Tell me then, Hawkwind," Deidra urged. "Tell me and have it done with. But don't keep putting barriers up between us in preparation for what might never happen."

At her sweet entreaty, at the undisguised love and yearning shining in her eyes, Hawkwind's resolve faltered. Why not reveal all, and see where it led? He could never feel totally safe with her until he did. But what if she turned from him then? What would he have left? Not only would he lose Deidra, but the advantage he'd finally gained in the potential to force Rothgarn to give him back his lands. Though the consideration of losing Deidra seemed suddenly far worse than the potential loss of his lands, Hawkwind didn't want to risk losing either if he could.

"Nay." He firmly shook his head. "I'll tell you naught save this one thing, and 'twill have to suffice. I have lost something of great value to me and mean to get it back. Nearly everything I do is done with that goal in mind." He shot her a pleading glance. "Will you accept that, trust I have good reasons for the rest of my reticence, and still not turn from me? How deep does your love really run? Enough to accept the secrets I must still bear alone, and still want me?"

Deidra's eyes narrowed. She silently studied him. Hawkwind knew a sharp, twisting pain in the center of his chest. Had he finally placed one too many conditions on her? Had he finally driven her away?

He couldn't bear the thought of losing Deidra—not without sharing the final, heart-wrenching truth he, heretofore, had dared not reveal. Hawkwind inhaled a ragged breath and looked away. "For what it may be worth, after all I've refused to share with you, I will tell you this." He swung his gaze back to her. "I love you, Deidra."

"Indeed?" she asked, her voice taut. "You have a strange way of showing it. You tell me little of what happened to you, you offer no hope for us or any commitment, and then think an 'I love you' will suffice? Well, I say your words are without substance!"

·She made a move to turn Belfry around back to camp when Hawkwind halted her with a firm grip on her horse's reins. "Would you agree to be my wife? Is that the commitment you seek?"

Tear-filled eyes, glittering with a pained disbelief, met his. "You can't mean that. And I curse you for playing such cruel games with me!"

Hawkwind's mouth curled in a self-mocking grin. "As unlikely as such a proposal is coming from me, I do indeed mean it. Is that hope enough for you? 'Tis all I can offer at present. The rest you'll have to accept and trust me for, until a later time. Will you wed me, Deidra, knowing how such a joining as ours will anger your father and mayhap condemn you to a life of hardship and danger?"

"My father will disown me."

"Aye, 'tis a possibility. Is that of more import to you than me?"

"You place me in an untenable position," she accused, indecision clouding her eyes.

"Then what do you want from me?" he asked, unable to tamp down the sharp twinge of pain her quite evident hesitation stirred. "I have offered all I can. There is naught more."

"I am the heiress to Rothgarn and its lands!"

"And how has that changed anything?" he prodded ruthlessly, determined to bring things to a head. One way or another, he'd have her decision today. "You gave no thought of that when you ran away from your home. Why should it suddenly have any value now?"

She closed her eyes and threw back her head. "Because you have forced me to look at my life with more care for others and the future, curse you! And I realize now I've been selfish and thoughtless not only in my treatment of you, but of my father and filial responsibilities as well."

"Then you wish to go home, return to your father?"

And leave you? Deidra thought with a piercing anguish. The answer to his question flooded her in one sharp, clear rush. "Nay." She adamantly shook her head. "I wish to stay with you for as long as you'll have me. I'll deal with my father and those responsibilities when the time comes, but I don't want ever to leave you."

Hawkwind sidled his horse next to hers and, leaning over, took her chin in the callused clasp of his big hand. "Look at me, lass," he commanded when she still averted her gaze.

Reluctantly, Deidra did as he asked. Hawkwind paused for a moment more, steeling himself for the question—and its answer—still hanging between them. "And what of my offer to wed you?" he whispered. "Is it aye or nay?"

Her eyes went huge, her soft, full mouth atremble. "What else *could* it be?" she whispered in reply. " 'Tis aye, of course, Hawkwind. 'Tis aye."

Chapter 17

Mystic leaped from Deidra's gauntleted fist, jetting skyward to quickly gain altitude and soar effortlessly overhead. Then, in a rapid whir of wing beats, the falcon circled above Deidra and held his position in the air. 'Twas called "waiting on" Hawkwind had told her, a peregrine falcon's special talent for hovering overhead in anticipation of quarry being flushed out from beneath it. And Mystic, to both their surprise, had been particularly adept at that ability.

She urged Belfry through the tall grass, hoping to flush out a quail. The meadow, this day, seemed bereft of wild fowl, however. Not like yesterday, Deidra mused in fond remembrance, when she and Hawkwind had hunted the bird for the first time. The day he had asked her to become his wife . . .

A soft, happy smile curved her lips. He'd have been with her today as well, she mused, if a messenger hadn't arrived shortly before they were to ride out, bearing a missive that a nobleman traveled, even then, to meet with Hawkwind. So, rather than skip even one day of training and Mystic's new program to rebuild his strength, Deidra had gone out on her own.

'Twas just over the hill from camp and Hawkwind had sent Bruno and Hubert to watch her from afar, so Deidra had felt quite safe. Or, rather, Hawkwind had felt safe in allowing her to do so. *She'd* never had any qualms one way or another.

A pigeon flew suddenly from one of the trees, startled by Deidra's approach. It fluttered down, low to the ground, then began a slow ascent. From high overhead, Mystic's keen eyes caught sight of the pigeon. He dipped in a lightning swift dive.

With bated breath, Deidra watched as the peregrine neared, caught the hapless pigeon in its talons, hesitated an instant as the bird struggled wildly, then settled down with it to the ground. Wrapping its wings protectively about its victim, the falcon finished the kill.

As she dismounted and walked quietly over, Deidra extracted a slice of raw quail from the large leather pouch hanging at her side. Gripping the meat in her gloved left hand, she squatted near Mystic and whistled softly twice. The peregrine shot her a disgruntled look, then obediently released his prey and climbed onto her lowered hand.

"Good bird," Deidra crooned as the falcon tore into the proffered piece of meat. She quickly captured the dead pigeon and slipped it into her pouch.

Glancing up at the sun blazing nearly overhead, Deidra decided there was still enough time to make it to camp and have the pigeon cooked for Hawkwind's lunch. Rising, she strode to where Belfry waited. Ten minutes later, she was back in camp.

Deidra deposited Mystic on his perch outside Hawkwind's tent, placing the hunting pouch nearby but well out of the falcon's reach, then led Belfry over to the grove of trees where the other horses were tethered. As Deidra unsaddled, then watered him in the cool, leafy shade of a huge oak, a small party of men rode into camp.

Her casual glance, shot over her shoulder at them, was quickly followed by a sharper, more startled one as she recognized the man who led the others. D'Mondeville! In an instinctive move, she stepped farther back into the protection of the shade and watched as he drew up and dismounted outside Hawkwind's tent.

Heart hammering in her chest, Deidra saw Hawkwind come out, offer D'Mondeville his hand, the two men talk for a few minutes, then reenter the tent. Apprehension, and a rising sense of dread, snaked within her. What business did D'Mondeville have with Hawkwind? And, even more importantly, why would Hawkwind welcome such a man into his camp?

She swiftly tied Belfry to the tether line with the other horses and hurried back to Hawkwind's tent, taking care to avoid catching the notice of the men who accompanied D'Mondeville. The odds were slim any had ever seen her, much less would recognize her dressed as she was in drab homespun tunic, breeches, and her tall boots, but Deidra didn't dare risk taking a chance. No matter what D'Mondeville's reason for being here, she'd not compound the problem by revealing her presence.

One way or another, though, she meant to slip inside and hear what the man had to say. Whatever D'Mondeville was up to, 'twas sure to be dishonest and self-serving. And the only way to advise Hawkwind afterward would be first to learn what his evil visitor wanted.

"The time has come for me to require your services," D'Mondeville began without preliminary after they'd reentered Hawkwind's tent. "In two days' time, I wish for you to break camp and march on Rothgarn Castle."

At mention of Rothgarn, Hawkwind stiffened. To cover his growing presentiment and buy himself an opportunity to find some way out of his predicament, he motioned to the brass table whereon sat a flagon of ale and two cups. "What, no requests first for some of my fine ale before you launch into business?" he asked, striding over to the table.

"Aye, pour me a cup," his visitor growled. "But time is short and we've a siege to lay. I've a need to pay Rothgarn back for his arrogance."

The rich, dark ale flowed from the flagon into first one, then the other cup. Hawkwind watched it with an almost mesmerized fascination as his mind raced for a way out of this suddenly untenable and most heartrending of situations.

D'Mondeville . . . back . . . Demanding he lay siege to Rothgarn Castle.

Deidra.

Pain lanced through Hawkwind, leaving an aching, gaping void that naught seemed to be able to fill. Not logic, not emotion, not even a plausible plan. Hawkwind picked up the cups and strode back to D'Mondeville.

He handed him one cup and lifted the other to his lips. For once, the strong, full-bodied liquor failed to please him. It tasted flat, bitter—as bitter as gall. How was he going to extricate himself this time?

"Why the sudden rush?" he asked, finally lowering the cup from his mouth. "A month ago you claimed we were only to be at the ready and might not even be needed. Now you want us on the march in two days' time. I'd like to know why."

D'Mondeville smiled thinly. "Since when does an employer's reasons decide whether you sell your services or not?"

Hawkwind frowned. "Since now. Why the rush?"

Cold black eyes studied him for a long moment, then D'Mondeville shrugged. "Because my former, far more peaceful plans have come to naught. I am a man of short patience and my patience is at an end." He cocked a challenging brow. "I did pay you a sizable retainer, did I not? Now, you're free of further obligation to Lord Firston. I see no reason for your less than prompt response to my request."

"Well, I do!" Hawkwind snapped. He downed the contents of his cup and set it aside. His hands, lowering to rest upon his trim hips, fisted. "I've decided not to accept your tasking."

"Indeed?" D'Mondeville's smile tautened. "And what gives you the right to back off from our agreement? You seemed none too reluctant to accept my money when we last talked."

"Things have changed."

"*What* things?"

Anger flared in Hawkwind and he mastered it only with the greatest of efforts. He knew he was in the wrong in this. He had agreed, given his word, accepted advance payment. A man of honor, a man whose army survived and thrived on that honor, wouldn't go back on the deal.

But a man of honor wouldn't lay siege to the castle of the woman he loved and intended on wedding, either. A man of honor wouldn't try to destroy her father . . . however justifiably he might deserve it.

"I would pay you back the advance money," Hawkwind said, hating the shame of his offer even as he spoke. " 'Twill take a time, though, as we've suffered severe monetary losses, but I give you my word—"

"Your word?" D'Mondeville gave a mocking laugh. "And what use is that to me? You've already reneged on one agreement. What would lead me to believe you won't back away from repaying the rest of my money, once I am gone?"

Hawkwind shoved a hand through his hair, his fingers rough with rising exasperation. As much as he despised the man, D'Mondeville had a point. Why would anyone again accept his word after what he'd just said? "In every case but this," Hawkwind forced himself to reply, "my word is my bond. This is but a rare exception."

"How so? What makes this time so special?"

"Personal reasons I've no desire to reveal to you or any man!" Hawkwind snarled. "Take it or leave it, D'Mondeville!"

"*Take it or leave it?*" the other man repeated in disbelief. "And do you speak for your army, as well?"

"My army will do as I bid."

· "Even when the tale of your failure to meet our agreement gets out? Even when no other lord will hire them, for fear you'll do the same to them?" D'Mondeville smiled grimly. "You have little money left. I knew that even before I came here. 'Twon't last long in feeding an army the size of yours. What will you do when it's gone? What will become of your army then?"

His words were like a knife, gutting Hawkwind's insides, but instead of blood, rage poured out. Rage and a seething, burgeoning frustration. D'Mondeville spoke true. They desperately needed another military assignment to supplement their now meager coffers. He could keep the men satisfied with promise of payment from the next battle as long as he kept them well fed in the meanwhile, but if no one chose to hire them . . .

Like an animal caught in the jaws of a trap, Hawkwind felt his options, one by one, ensnared and rendered useless. Would it come down to a choice then, between Deidra and the welfare of his army? By the Mother, he hoped not. He *prayed* not!

"Nonetheless," he quietly said, determined not to let D'Mondeville see how close to home he'd struck, "I'll take my chances with other potential employers. In the meanwhile, as doubtful as you might find my promise to repay you, 'twill be done. But," Hawkwind continued, locking gazes with the other nobleman, "as far as Rothgarn goes, find another lackey."

The low, indistinct rumble of male voices became louder and clearer as Deidra slipped under the tent beside Hawkwind's bed. Pausing to note that the two men stood across the shelter's huge expanse, their backs turned, she hurriedly scooted beneath the bed and comforter that fell almost to the floor.

A grim satisfaction filled her. 'Twas the perfect spot to spy on their conversation and, though the admission of doing such a thing to Hawkwind filled her with guilt, she firmly pushed it aside. In the end, she'd find some way to convince him her action was meant to help. She crawled as close to the foot of the bed as she dared, and settled down to listen.

"You seem as good a lackey as any," D'Mondeville was saying. "A lackey I mean to have, or destroy, if you persist in this stubborn, futile resistance."

Hawkwind's hands clenched at his sides. So now, on top of it all, he must tolerate this soft, spoiled, seedy nobleman threatening him. He thought not! " 'Twill take more than the likes of you to destroy me! Now," he said, taking the cup from D'Mondeville's hand, "our meeting is done. Leave while you can still safely do so."

"And if I did, who would protect you from King William's wrath when the truth of your real identity reaches him? Eh, Lord Nicholas of Todmorden, traitor to the late king and murderer of your own brothers?"

Shock jolted through Hawkwind, then a chilling blast of fear. How had D'Mondeville discovered his closely guarded secret? Who had told him? And why now, when he was so near to regaining what was rightfully his?

He'd been a fool to imagine he'd ever be able to clear his name, much less keep his true identity hidden long enough even to attempt to do so, once he'd regained his lands. It didn't really matter who had betrayed him. If D'Mondeville knew, so must others. The man wouldn't have revealed this information—and in such dangerous circumstances—without making certain the secret wouldn't die with him.

"You want your lands back," D'Mondeville forged ruthlessly on as if sensing a sudden breach in his opponent's defenses. "I'll give them to you in return for the defeat of Rothgarn. I care not for Todmorden lands. I wish only for Rothgarn. 'Tis a generous offer, is it not? And worth far more than the other twenty thousand gold crowns I still owe you." He smiled. "Think long and hard, my proud and stubborn young lord. You have everything to gain and much to lose if you refuse me."

Deidra heard Hawkwind pause, inhale a long, unsteady breath. Breathlessly, she awaited his reply. Thoughts, realizations, painful emotions bombarded her over and over, until everything swam in a crazed tumult in her head.

Hawkwind, the evil, murderous, treacherous Lord of Todmorden? Hawkwind, hired henchman of Basil D'Mondeville, the man who wished to destroy her father and take Rothgarn Castle? Hawkwind, the man who had claimed he loved her and wished to wed?

She should have known 'twas all too good to be true, that Hawkwind couldn't possibly be as wonderful as she'd imagined him to be. It all fell into place now. Hawkwind's words yesterday, admitting he'd lost something of great value and meant to get it back no matter the cost. His surprising and sudden desire to wed her, so as to secure his eventual acquisition of not only his lands but hers as well. His reluctance to share his past—a past so horrible 'twould surely have turned her from him. His virulent rage when he'd spoken of her father, that day at the Sabarcane River . . .

If Basil hadn't arrived today, the end result would have still been the same. Hawkwind had meant to use and manipulate her all along. He was indeed like all the rest.

Deidra's fists clenched at her sides and she bit her lip to keep from moaning out her anguish. Had she never, ever, known the real man? Had she truly been that big a fool?

It didn't seem possible. She recalled the tender look in his eyes when he'd told her he loved her, his unabashed passion when they made love, his deep concern for his army, his unyielding principles . . .

None were the actions of a coldly calculating, evil man. A man who felt naught for her and only wished to use her. But if he'd truly done those terrible things and planned all along to manipulate her to regain his lands, 'twould explain his reluctance to tell her of himself. Ah, but 'twas too much to fathom at such a—

"And how will I know if you intend to keep *your* word,

when all of this is done?" Hawkwind softly intruded into her anguished thoughts. "You could well use me and my army to take Rothgarn, then still turn me in to the king. What guarantee do *I* have of your sincerity?"

"What would you like? That I sign over your lands to you now in payment for your services?"

"That would be a fine way to begin," Hawkwind growled. "But what about my true identity? How will you convince me you won't betray it?"

"The word of one nobleman to another?" D'Mondeville offered mockingly.

Hawkwind snorted in disgust. "Try again. I long ago ceased to trust any of the nobility. 'Twas what got me in my unfortunate predicament as 'twas."

"Then what?" the blond man demanded. "What else can I offer?"

"Rothgarn's daughter. I want her as wife."

For a long moment, D'Mondeville just stared at Hawkwind. Then he gave an unsteady laugh. "And if I gave you her, 'twould assure your rights to Rothgarn and its lands. You'd have it all."

"But I don't *want* it all," Hawkwind calmly reiterated. "I want only my own lands back and a guarantee you'll not betray me. The Rothgarn heiress will serve as that guarantee. I'll not lay claim to her lands unless you turn on me."

D'Mondeville scratched his chin in consideration. "It seems we both are constrained to trust the other in this. But I like it. You have what you want and power over me in the form of the Rothgarn heiress, and I have power over you in the knowledge of your true identity." He grinned wolfishly. "I like it. You'll be a most valuable ally, as I will to you. Men with shared secrets usually are."

Hawkwind quirked a skeptical brow. "Indeed? Then we have a bargain, do we?"

"Aye," D'Mondeville lied smoothly, well aware he had no intention of honoring his part of the deal. Hawkwind would die before all was finished between them. He had no intention of giving up anything to the warrior chief—not Todmorden lands nor the lovely Deidra, if she could ever be found. He'd take great pleasure in destroying the former Lord of Todmorden as well. As would William, who needed no living witnesses to his treachery.

He made a motion to a small writing table where parchment and quill were set. "Shall I scribe our agreement, then both of us sign it?"

Hawkwind nodded. " 'Twill do for a start. And one thing more, D'Mondeville."

The other man turned. "Aye?"

"I want Rothgarn alive and delivered to me. We have unfinished business."

"Want to properly 'thank' him for taking your lands those many years ago, do you?"

"Exactly," came Hawkwind's harsh reply.

Deidra was waiting for him when he returned several minutes later after seeing D'Mondeville off. Hawkwind stopped dead in his tracks when he saw her, sitting in one of the chairs near his bed. He frowned; his gaze narrowed, then he strode over to stand before her.

"How long have you been here?" he demanded.

She shot him a smoldering look. "Long enough to hear all about your schemes with Basil D'Mondeville."

"Indeed?" Hawkwind flung himself into the chair opposite her. "Then why are you still here?"

"I thought you might like the opportunity to explain yourself." She arched a slender brow. "You do have some plausible explanation for this bargain you made, don't you?"

He eyed her warily. "I'd have thought my position was quite clear. D'Mondeville didn't give me many options."

"So you plan to go along with him, destroy my father and be rewarded with your lands and me as the prize?" Deidra gave a disparaging laugh. "Think again, before you go up against a man as treacherous as Basil D'Mondeville.

'Tis the work of a fool, if you do. A fool who'll be lucky to escape with his life."

"I'm no fool," Hawkwind muttered darkly. "But, for the time being, 'tis better if I appear so to D'Mondeville. And to you, if you choose to believe that of me."

"What else would you have me believe?" Deidra leaped to her feet, her fists clenched at her sides. "You offer no other explanations, continue to plot treachery, then have the gall to expect me to accept all this because you ask me to?"

"I ask naught of you. I but hope your love and trust is sufficient to allow me the opportunity—"

"Nay, 'tisn't an issue of my love and trust," Deidra cut him off. " 'Tis and always has been one of your love and trust in me. And I grow tired of it, Hawkwind. Tell me all, now, while you still have opportunity to do so. Tell me now, before 'tis finally too late."

"What would you have me tell you?" Slowly, he rose to his feet to tower over her. "Do you want me to deny the tales, to assure you I didn't plot against the old king, that I didn't kill my brothers? Well, I shouldn't have to do that, Deidra. You should know me, trust me enough to know the truth of that. And know, as well, that I wouldn't willingly go against Rothgarn, at least not now you've come into my life."

"Oh, aye," she hotly retorted. " 'Twould be stupid to agree to fight against Rothgarn now, when you can have it all by wedding me. Isn't that so?"

"Aye," he admitted, averting his gaze. " 'Twould serve both our purposes, would it not? If only D'Mondeville had been a few weeks later in his demands, 'twould have been a moot point. But now . . ." His voice faded.

"But now?" Deidra prodded. "What will you do now?"

"See it through."

"You could kill D'Mondeville instead," she offered, desperation slowly wending through her. " 'Twould solve everything."

"You mean murder him, don't you?" Hawkwind lifted his head, his eyes glittering dangerously. " 'Twould indeed solve everything for you, wouldn't it? But not for me. Taking D'Mondeville's life would not only be dishonorable, 'twould ruin my reputation and army. Every nobleman in the realm would turn on me. They'd be forced to, for I could never be trusted again. Nay," he growled, "my plan is the best of all options. D'Mondeville may think he'll betray me in the end, but he's dealing with the wrong man. I'm used to treachery in others; indeed, I expect it. 'Tis difficult to take me unawares."

"So, you intend to attack my father, do you?" Deidra demanded. "And how far will your ruse go? To the taking of Rothgarn?"

"Mayhap. It all depends on D'Mondeville. I must bide my time until he reveals a chink in his armor. Then I'll be on him so fast he'll have no chance to defend himself."

"In the meanwhile, I must content myself with trusting you. Is that it, Hawkwind?"

He grasped her by the arms and pulled her to him. "Aye," he softly replied, his voice low and rich and deep. "Is that such a hard thing to do? In the end 'twill be worth it. I swear."

"Nay!" With a fierce motion, Deidra twisted free of his hold. "This time, you ask too much. 'Twas hard enough when you asked me to trust, to believe in you though you'd tell me little, but then 'twas only between the two of us. Now . . . now it involves others—my father, my people, Rothgarn. I need more now, far, far more, than you seem willing to give." She took a step back. "And 'tisn't enough. Not nearly enough!"

"Your devotion to Rothgarn comes late," Hawkwind snarled, a frustrated anger twisting his features. " 'Twasn't so strong in the past. I could have sworn you first came to me to escape your responsibilities to home and hearth. Your sudden change of heart now is most puzzling."

"Mayhap 'tis," Deidra admitted slowly, "but some things

are but buried, awaiting the right stimulus to bring them to life. I've learned much since I came to you of life, of loyalty and honor, of myself. And I find I've been wrong about many things."

"Indeed?" Hawkwind drawled. "Pray, enlighten me to some of those wondrous revelations."

"Aye, that I will," she cried, stung by his bitter sarcasm. "You speak much of honor, but yours is of a shallow, unstable kind, shifting with every turn of fate to suit your needs. True honor lies in facing one's responsibilities no matter how difficult or unpalatable, of making a commitment and summoning the courage to see that commitment through, of being faithful to one's upbringing and ideals. Not," she added, her voice momentarily breaking, "in following a dream or cause grounded in false motives and ever-changing morals."

"My honor has stood me well for a long time now," Hawkwind snarled. "I'll make no excuses for what I've done or will do."

Her gaze lifted to his, tear bright but resolute. "Nor will I, for what I have found of my own honor. An honor," Deidra whispered, "that now seems in direct opposition to yours."

Pain flashed in Hawkwind's eyes, then was mastered and muted. "What do you propose to do then?"

"Go back to Rothgarn," she said simply. "My destiny no longer runs with yours, mayhap never did though I once imagined . . ."

"And you're a fool if you think I can let you go now. 'Tis enough I must deal with D'Mondeville. I'll not have you in the middle of this as well."

He made a move to grab her by the arm, but for once Deidra was quicker. She leaped aside and, withdrawing her dagger, crouched in a fighting stance.

Hawkwind eyed her, his mouth curling wryly. "Has it come to this then, that you now feel compelled to defend yourself against me?"

"You have driven me to it!" Deidra cried. "You've only yourself to blame."

His grin faded. "Aye, mayhap I have, but I intend to heal what's come between us, too." He took a step toward her. "Drop the dagger, lass. You know such a puny weapon is no match against me."

She froze, the utter futility of her act of defiance striking her with a frightening clarity. Hawkwind was right. No man-made weapon in her hands had any hope of prevailing against him. But there were other kinds of weapons, known by many and mastered by few, that could overcome even as potent and skilled a warrior as Hawkwind was.

With a small, reluctant sigh, Deidra's dagger fell to the carpet. And, as Hawkwind advanced, triumph gleaming in his jade green eyes, she lifted her hands and wove a spell of slumberous enchantment about him.

Deidra hurried across camp, not knowing where she was going, just that she must run, get away. Hawkwind and Basil D'Mondeville in league. Two of a kind—ambitious, ruthless, hard-hearted men who'd stop at nothing to gain what they wanted. Ah, why hadn't she seen the similarities before?

Guilt surged briefly through her at the memory of the spell she'd cast upon Hawkwind. Never had she imagined using her powers against him. But then, never before had she envisioned him as an enemy, either.

An enemy. The consideration sent an agonizing spasm twisting through her. Was that all that was left them then? Two lovers torn apart by the call of differing codes of honor and ties to differing ways of life?

With a fierce mental effort, Deidra shrugged the poignant questions aside. There was work to be done, and soon, before Hawkwind's sleeping spell wore off and he awakened. She must slip away and return to Rothgarn, hopefully in time to warn her father of what was to come. If there was any way to thwart Rothgarn's takeover, she must give it to her father. She owed him and her people at least that.

Her steps slowed as she neared the horses, fearing to spook them and draw unnecessary attention to herself. 'Twouldn't be wise to be stopped now and taken back to Hawkwind. But 'twasn't wise to ride out alone and un-armed, either. Naught would be served if she were set upon by bandits and captured.

Bardrick. She needed Bardrick. But would the old warrior go with her? Had his loyalties shifted once more to Hawkwind, now that he was back in his leader's camp? Or did he still honor his primary commitment to her?

Deidra halted, considering how to approach Bardrick. Her request of him would have to be couched carefully so as not to give away her true motives. Somehow, she sensed he'd be so outraged by what she'd tell him of Hawkwind he'd drag her to his chief and demand an explanation. An explanation, Deidra knew, fearing Hawkwind's temper when he finally woke, that could be as unpleasant for him as for her.

Bardrick was a good, loyal, trusting man, but he hadn't been with Hawkwind for over five years. A lot could have happened to change a man in that time. Nay, she'd not risk Bardrick in telling him the truth, no matter how it pained her to lie.

She found him outside Maud's hospital tent, sharpening his sword. Deidra waited for a few minutes at the edge of the tent, watching the smooth glide of sharp-edged rock over the keen edges of the blade. The metal gleamed in the afternoon sun, sending glinting shards of light arcing in the air. Gazing over at Bardrick, Deidra's heart did a small flip-flop beneath her breast.

He looked so happy, so content, so back in his element sitting there, engaged in his warrior's task. An impulse to walk away, to leave him where he truly wished to be, filled her. But she knew 'twould easily be the end of her plans if she did.

"Bardrick?" Deidra stepped forward into his line of vision.

He lifted his shaggy, grizzled head of hair. As he recognized her voice, his craggy features broke into a smile. "Ah, lass, what brings ye to visit on such a fine day?"

"Can we move elsewhere to speak?" she forced herself to begin. "I've a need to talk privately with you."

"Indeed?" He squinted up at her, his brow knitting in puzzlement. "And what can be so private ye cannot speak it here?"

"Please, Bardrick," Deidra cried. "Just trust me in this."

He shook his head and laid down his sharpening stone, then resheathed his sword in the scabbard strapped to his hips. "As ye wish, lass. Move on," he ordered with a curt motion of his hand. "Lead me to yer 'private' place."

She didn't speak until they were safely out of earshot, near the spot where the horses were tethered. "I want to go home," she began without preliminary. "Back to Rothgarn. Will you take me?"

"What?" Bardrick stared down at her, dumbfounded. "Ye now wish to leave Hawkwind and return home? Truly, ye are the most confusing, headstrong—"

"Please, Bardrick," Deidra pleaded. " 'Tis over between Hawkwind and me. I-I made a mistake in ever coming here. 'Tisn't where I belong and I finally know it. Take me back home. *Please.*"

Indecision warred in his eyes. Deidra waited with bated breath, fearing the outcome of his mental battle. The seconds ticked by and the tension grew. Finally, Bardrick spoke.

"Hawkwind won't be happy if I take ye from him. He loves ye, lass. And I thought ye loved him. Why would ye now want to hurt him?"

"I-I thought I loved him," Deidra replied, grasping at any plausible explanation for her sudden change of heart. "But I realize now 'twas but an infatuation. 'Tisn't kind nor fair to lead him on any further. My place is back at Rothgarn."

"And ye think slipping away without farewell or explanation is the kind and fair thing to do?" He eyed her intently. "Are ye sure about that?"

"There isn't any way to spare him pain, but my leaving this way will make the break between us quick and sure. Once I'm gone, 'twill be easier for him to forget me. To get on with his life."

" 'Tisn't right, what ye do," Bardrick muttered. "Hawkwind has never had a fair chance at happiness." He glanced up at her. "I'd begun to hope he'd find it with ye, lass."

Tears stung Deidra's eyes, but she blinked them back. Strange, she mused sadly, but she'd begun to hope for the same thing. Yet Hawkwind had never been the man she'd imagined him to be. Never . . .

"I am not the woman for him, Bardrick. I can't be what he wants, what he needs." She paused, inhaled a steadying breath, then forged on. "Now, I ask you once more. Will you come with me? One way or another, I intend to leave."

He sighed in defeat. "Ah, lass, ye put me at such odds. But ye are still my mistress. Because my taking ye back may wound Hawkwind's feelings but not harm him, I will do what ye ask."

"Thank you, old friend," Deidra breathed out her relief. Once more guilt flooded her. Bardrick's assessment that her departure wouldn't harm Hawkwind was far from accurate, knowing the information she carried back to Rothgarn might harm him indeed. Harm him not only in his plans to join D'Mondeville in attacking Rothgarn, but in the revelation of who he truly was.

She wasn't so certain she'd ever use that bit of information against him, though. For all the beautiful times they'd shared and the wondrous awakening of her womanhood she'd found in his arms, Deidra would keep his shameful past a secret. No good would be served in revealing it at any rate. More people than Hawkwind had been involved in the treachery those eight years past. Indeed, the guilt might reach all the way to the late king's son, now ruler of

the land, if some of the more sordid rumors were true.
'Twould serve no purpose—or justice—to punish Hawkwind as the scapegoat while others went free.

She forced her painful thoughts back to a more practical
course and locked gazes with Bardrick. "I'll need a weapon.
Can you find me one while I saddle the horses?"

"Aye, and gather us some victuals and bedding for the
journey ahead, too." Bardrick paused. "Is there anyone ye
wish to say yer farewells to in the meanwhile?"

Deidra hesitated. Alena was too fiercely loyal to
Hawkwind to risk telling her. But Maud would understand
and accept her decision. She smiled sadly. "I'll go and say
my farewells to Maud. 'Twon't take but a few moments."

He frowned. "And what will ye tell her of me?"

"What would you like me to tell her?"

For a long moment, Bardrick hesitated. Vulnerability,
longing, indecision flickered in his eyes. Then his gaze
shuttered. "Tell her farewell. That's all. Just farewell."

"Where is she? Does no one know where Deidra has gone?"
Hawkwind demanded tautly hours later, as the day eased
into twilight. His head throbbed, his eyes were gritty, and
his stomach churned sickeningly. Curse Deidra and her
foul spells!

Alena and Renard exchanged glances. "She was with
you, last we saw of her this morning," Alena finally replied.
"Where did you see her last?"

He bit back a furious reply, remembering quite well
where he'd seen her last. But 'twas too soon to share that
final, most painful of meetings with anyone. "It matters
not," Hawkwind snapped. "I've not seen her for a time
now."

He slammed his fist down on the arm of his chair and,
for his efforts, was rewarded with a fresh surge of nauseating dizziness. "Damn it all! She can't have just disappeared
into thin air!"

"May I intrude?" came a soft voice from the vicinity of the tent flap.

All eyes swung to where the last fading rays of the setting sun now pierced the tent's dimly lit interior. Maud stood there, her expression solemn.

"Aye, come on in and join the general confusion," Hawkwind growled, motioning her forward. "Some problem in the hospital tent, is it? Are the men now complaining about the food or the enforced bed rest?"

"Nay," Maud replied as she halted before him. "My patients aren't the problem. 'Tis Deidra."

"Deidra?" Hawkwind leaned forward in relief. "Have you found her then? Was she in your tent all along?"

The healer shook her head. "Nay. She left five hours ago with Bardrick."

"Left?" A thunderous expression formed in Hawkwind's eyes. "Where?"

"Deidra has gone back to Rothgarn. She doesn't wish to be with us anymore."

Hawkwind rose and stepped forward to grab Maud by the shoulders. "Why didn't you immediately come and tell me? I could have stopped her, made her see . . ."

"'Twouldn't have mattered," the healer replied, full knowledge of Deidra's reasons gleaming in her eyes. "Ye know that as well as I."

"Bloody hell!" Hawkwind cursed and released Maud with an angry, frustrated motion. "I care not for catering to her whims. I want her back. And I ask you again," he added savagely, "why you let her go? Your first loyalty is to me, not her. Why did you betray me, Maud?"

"Deidra is like her mother," the healer said. "To keep her where she had no heart to be would lead to her eventual death. If ye want Deidra, go after her. Win her back, if ye can. But somehow, I think 'twill not be as easy as ye imagine. When it comes to Deidra," Maud added darkly, "ye have made some grievous errors."

"Have I now?" Hawkwind snarled. He glanced wildly

around, struggling to come to terms with the harsh truth of Maud's words, words that seared a hole clear through to his heart. And, no matter where he looked, all he saw was concern and barely veiled sympathy. Sympathy . . . from his friends.

And betrayal from the one woman he'd dared let down his guard for, dared allow himself to want, to need, to love. Aye, betrayal, Hawkwind thought furiously. Deidra's love had been too weak, too cowardly to withstand the test of events that had cast him in a most unfair and unfavorable light. She had chosen, instead, to turn against him, to misunderstand, to believe the lies.

When it had finally come to what really mattered, Deidra had not been there for him.

"Out, all of you!" he roared. "There's naught we can do with night drawing on. Bardrick is too clever to allow us easily to find their trail. And it doesn't matter anyway. In three days' time, we'll be at Rothgarn. I'll have her back," Hawkwind muttered half to himself as he fought to contain the searing, seething pain twisting through him, "one way or another."

Chapter 18

Hawkwind watched from his command post as the catapults flung huge rocks at the thick stone walls of Rothgarn Castle. Men strained, muscles bulged, as they winched back the rocks held on beams, then released them to sail into and over the walls. Nearby, similar machines, adapted to propel heavy, arrow-tipped bolts, were also set and fired. At the north end of the castle, tall. wooden towers had been rolled over stone filled bridges spanning the width of the moat, up to the fortress itself. From them, men battled to gain control of the walls.

A grim satisfaction filled Hawkwind. It always did when he viewed the results of a well-planned and orchestrated siege. The castle was surrounded, no escape was possible, and 'twas but a matter of time until Rothgarn fell. One way or another.

If his army's overt frontal attack and underground efforts to undermine the stability of the castle's walls didn't work, starvation and disease eventually would. But this time the dogged patience Hawkwind was famed for was in short supply. He didn't want to wait months for Rothgarn to fall. He wanted Deidra now.

And he didn't care if she came gladly or not. She had betrayed him, discarded his love as easily as one would toss aside an old, worn glove. She'd soon learn no one did that to him.

No one.

The capture of her castle and imprisonment of her father would be only the first of her punishments. He'd never wed her now, but he'd continue to take his fill of her lush body until he was finally sated. And, when he wasn't using her for his own pleasure, he'd keep her locked in Todmorden's tower. He'd take away the one thing she valued above all —her freedom.

Yet, even when he set aside the perverse pleasure his tortured imaginings of Deidra gave him, the cruel irony of his situation gnawed at Hawkwind still. For the past eight years he'd dreamed of and single-mindedly worked toward the goal of regaining Todmorden, avenging himself on Rothgarn and, through him, the king—the man who symbolized all he'd lost. But now, when he was so close to finally achieving his goals, the impending victory loomed bitterly empty and strangely meaningless.

An impotent rage swelled in Hawkwind. Deidra, curse her conniving, faithless little soul, was responsible for that. She had shown him what had been lacking in his life, filled him with a newfound happiness and plans for something richer, deeper—then taken it all away.

Yet thanks to some cruel vagaries of fate, when 'twas all over she would still remain entwined in his life and heart. And the downfall of Rothgarn Castle would only set into motion their own, mutual destruction. In his ultimate victory would also lie the seeds of his defeat. His pain and anger at what she'd done, and how he'd punish her for it, would eventually destroy the both of them.

The crunch of booted feet upon the gravel strewn ground jerked Hawkwind from his brutal musings. He glanced up, saw 'twas Renard, and cleared his mind of everything but the battle in progress. "How goes the work of the sappers?" he immediately demanded when his war captain drew to a halt before him.

Renard grimaced. "Well enough. They dug a bit too close to the base of the moat and sprung a leak that flooded the tunnel. 'Twas necessary to back off and tunnel in a different direction."

"And hopefully a mite deeper as well," Hawkwind added dryly. "Keep a closer eye on them, will you, Renard? I want this siege over in record time, whatever the cost."

His friend arched a dark brow. "Even at the cost of extra lives? If that's the case, I'd say your need for revenge against Deidra borders on obsession."

Hawkwind's eyes narrowed. "And I say you overstep yourself in presuming to—"

"You made me war captain not only to carry out your orders, but to advise you as well," Renard quickly cut him off. "If you now find my counsel not to your liking, mayhap you should find a replacement. Of course," he added, "I'd start looking for one for Alena as well. She's none too happy with this situation, either."

"So, we've been at battle not even a week and already there's mutiny in the ranks."

"The men are quite content with how well the siege goes," Renard cooly replied, uncowed by the aura of barely contained anger emanating from Hawkwind. " 'Tis those of us who know the truth of this agreement with D'Mondeville who are concerned. The man is a treacherous snake and will turn on you at first chance. If 'twasn't for what Deidra did to you—"

"Bloody hell!" As soon as the words left his mouth, Hawkwind caught himself and dragged in a few deep, calming breaths. "You don't know it all, Renard," he began again. " 'Tisn't just Deidra. You know I agreed to fight for D'Mondeville even before she first came to camp. That second meeting but reconfirmed the agreement. Besides," he added, a dark look clouding his brow, "I had no choice. We owed him money, needed a lot more, and risked never finding another employer if we backed away from our commitment. Not to mention the fact D'Mondeville now knows my true identity and threatened to reveal it."

Renard's mouth twisted and he slowly shook his head. "Indeed? A fine time for that to surface." A sudden thought struck him. "Yet, 'tis still the rift between you and Deidra that pains you most. It also clouds your mind to the siege and what must be done about D'Mondeville. Those are potentially fatal shortcomings."

"And how do you suggest I remedy those 'shortcomings'?" Hawkwind demanded irritably.

"Talk with her. Delve deeper into her reasons for turning from you. And be a bit more willing to compromise some of your own stubbornly held beliefs." Renard lay a hand on Hawkwind's arm. "She's a fine lass, for all her proud, headstrong ways. And just the woman for you."

Hawkwind shrugged off Renard's hand with a disbelieving look. Though his war captain's words had stirred him to reconsider Deidra's motives for leaving him, the inescapable fact was she didn't trust him to do the right thing. That upon hearing who he truly was, she'd immediately believed he was capable of the treachery and atrocities surrounding the old king's death. Those doubts, still dwelling within her heart, bound the extent of her love, limiting it to a small, miserly offering.

Then there was the additional anguish of knowing she considered him capable of such foul, depraved acts.

She had never truly known him for the man he was, nor cared ever to discover that man. In the end, that was all that mattered. 'Twas the one and only shortcoming he couldn't tolerate. Her love was worth naught if 'twas incapable of spanning the doubts and reaching past the outward contradictions to the true faith in another that love should bring.

His expression hardened. "It matters naught, Renard. Whatever Deidra's motives in leaving, they speak most eloquently of the shallowness of her love. 'Tis over between us. 'Tis now war."

His captain eyed him for a long moment, then sighed. "And I say you are wrong in this, Hawkwind. Love must also be willing to forgive, to span the doubts and see to the true person within."

"My point exactly."

"It applies to your love for Deidra as well as to hers for you."

"Well, 'tis a moot point, wouldn't you say?" his leader challenged through gritted teeth. "There's naught I can do to span the chasm separating us. In case the fact has escaped you, there's a mighty, stone-walled castle keeping us apart. A castle," he bitterly added, "as strong as the heart-deep walls now lying between us."

The night air was cool, wafting gently, soothingly across Deidra's face. From her vantage on the castle battlements she peered down on the clutter of broken and burned towers, of boulders tilting precariously against the walls and piled in the moat, of the carefully built and protected wooden siege weapons now lying far out of range of their archers. 'Twas so peaceful now, where a few hours ago the horrendous sounds of strife had filled the air. Sounds that would resume at dawn, when Hawkwind again called his men to battle.

Hawkwind.

Even the thought of his name filled Deidra with an aching, tormented anguish. Never, if she lived the full span of her years, would she ever understand or accept his betrayal of her. Whether he believed Rothgarn meant aught to her or not, the fact he'd so easily go to war against her home cut to the quick. To raise sword against Rothgarn was the same as raising sword against her. Surely he knew that.

And surely he knew he served King William's purposes in attempting to destroy her father. D'Mondeville's alliance with the king was common knowledge now. In her absence things had come to a head, with D'Mondeville accusing her father of spiriting her away to avoid fulfilling his agreement to give his daughter to him as promised. When her father had instead informed him she had fled on her own, the younger nobleman had given him the final ultimatum. Find Deidra and return her within two weeks' time or suffer his wrath—and the wrath of the king.

After that, it had been a simple thing for the Lord of Rothgarn to do some discreet sniffing around regarding the true loyalties of Basil D'Mondeville. His worst fears confirmed, her father finally made his fateful decision to throw his considerable influence and wealth behind the rebel lords—a decision that had apparently brought D'Mondeville back to Hawkwind's camp.

But no matter the scheming nobleman's ongoing dedication to King William's cause, there was no excuse for Hawkwind's decision to cast his lot with D'Mondeville. Especially knowing now he was raised to the same life and expectations as she. But then, nobleman that he truly was, Hawkwind must have always been as bereft of heart and honor as D'Mondeville. What other reason was there to betray the old king and kill his own brothers?

Yet, though the facts of what had transpired those eight years ago seemed indisputable, the motives were still a mystery. And some part of her, though Hawkwind had refused to deny it when they'd last talked, still doubted he was capable of such acts. Hawkwind, she mused, or should she now instead call him who he truly was—the Lord Nicholas of Todmorden—had never seemed the kind of man to deal in treachery and murder. But if she could just bring herself to think of him as that other man, mayhap 'twould hasten her acceptance of him as the person he had really always been.

'Twould be easier and far less painful if she could.

Soft footfalls intruded on Deidra's bitter, tumultuous thoughts. She turned to find Bardrick climbing the stairs. With a tiny sigh, Deidra resumed her view of the scene before her, her gaze lifting past the destruction lying below, past the now deserted little town of half-timbered, wattle and daub houses surrounding a market square and sturdy stone church, to the eerily flickering campfires in the distance dotting the inky blackness.

Ever since their return home and her revelation that Hawkwind and D'Mondeville were on their way to attack Rothgarn, Deidra's old bodyguard had refused to speak with her and avoided her as if she bore some vile, contagious disease. She knew he saw her secretive departure from the mercenary camp now not only as a betrayal of his former commander, but as a lack of trust in him as well.

In a sense, she *had* doubted him and the extent of his loyalty to her. But there had been no other choice. Suddenly, there seemed *no* choices left in life, save the choice of duty over that of the heart.

She stood there, all breath suspended, as Bardrick halted beside her. She shot him a quick, furtive glance, then looked away. His face was riveted out on the night sprawling like some potently dangerous, sleeping dragon, far beyond them.

The tension grew in Deidra. The need to speak, to try to explain why she had done what she did, filled her. She might never have the chance again to speak with Hawkwind, but she wanted to with someone who'd been close to him. 'Twas a strange desire, she well knew, but in the doing she hoped someday he'd know and finally understand.

"I am sorry to have lied, to have put you in the position of having to make a choice between Hawkwind and me," she finally began when Bardrick remained stoically and she guessed stubbornly silent. " 'Twasn't fair to use you so, but I was desperate. I had to get home and warn my father. In the end, that had to be where my first loyalties lay."

"Hawkwind won't see it so," Bardrick's deep voice rumbled from out of the darkness. "He'd have thought a woman who made vows of love to him and agreed to be his wife owed the first loyalty to him."

"Is that what you think as well?" Deidra awaited his answer with heart hammering in her chest. After all this time, all they'd been through, all they meant to each other, she didn't think she could bear it if Bardrick, too, turned from her. "Do you condemn me as I'd imagine he has done?"

"Nay, lass," her old bodyguard replied on a soft, soughing sigh. "I don't condemn ye. But I don't understand, either. He loved ye. He'd have done anything for ye. And he isn't and never has been the kind of man who'd betray yer trust."

"Then why did he do this to me, Bardrick? Why did he join with Basil D'Mondeville? And why," she added on a broken sob, "did he hide the truth of who he really was from me?"

Bardrick turned to her then. His hands grasped her by the upper arms, his touch gentle, comforting. "What are ye saying, lass? Who do ye think he truly is?"

She searched his face in the dim, torch-lit night. "Don't you know? He's the Lord Nicholas of Todmorden. The man who plotted to kill the old king and, when his foul scheme succeeded and he was forced to flee for his life, returned to murder his own brothers who had turned against him." He stared down at her, the minutes ticking by until Deidra thought she'd scream out from the frustration of awaiting his response.

"And do ye truly believe Hawkwind would ever be capable of such a heinous act?" Bardrick finally asked. "After knowing him, sharing his bed, his heart, do ye still think those tales about him are true?"

Deidra lowered her head. "I-I don't know . . ." She inhaled a shuddering breath and forced herself to face the truth. "He refused to deny it and, after what I heard him agree to that day he met with D'Mondeville, I can't help but think him capable of that and more. He bartered my home and lands away to keep his name secret, then demanded me as security that D'Mondeville could never use that information against him.

"And not because he loved me, but only to use me, Bardrick," she whispered hoarsely. "I was never more than a pawn in Hawkwind's hands. An object to be manipulated to further his own means. I now believe that's why he asked me to become his wife. Even if D'Mondeville hadn't returned and demanded what he did, Hawkwind still would have had what he wanted by taking me to wife. His lands *and* Rothgarn."

"Lass, ye can't be certain—"

"Can't I? 'Tis the reason he decided against ransoming me." A bitter little smile twisted her mouth. "And I, romantic fool that I was, imagined instead 'twas because he loved me and didn't wish to send me away. That even the generous ransom my father was sure to have paid wasn't worth the price of losing the woman he loved."

"And I say again. Ye can't be certain such ignoble thoughts were in his mind, lass. And, whether 'twas or not, I truly believe he loved ye. Would it have been so terrible a thing to have wed him, even knowing what he stood to gain in the process? Any man would have done the same whether he loved ye or not."

"Would he? Then I want no one. Not now. Not ever."

"Hawkwind had made that same decision years ago . . . after the terrible things that had happened to him," Bardrick said, a sad, reminiscent tone creeping into his voice. "After that winter's day when his own two brothers conspired with William to murder the old king while he was visiting Todmorden. 'Twas all so carefully planned to make it appear 'twas Hawkwind's intent, when 'twas the act of an ambitious, treacherous princeling and brothers who coveted Hawkwind's right, as firstborn and heir, to their ancestral lands."

"What?" Deidra stepped close, her glance riveting on her old bodyguard's face. "What are you saying?"

"Hawkwind was as innocent of the plot to kill the old king as any man could be. 'Twas why he was set upon when out hawking and nearly murdered before I and some of my men came upon him. We were the ones who drove away his attackers, carried his mangled and bleeding body—the body still bearing the horrible scars of that day—back to camp to save his life. We, simple soldiers of lowly birth, cared for him and nursed him back to health when his own, highborn kind only wished to see him dead to further their cruel, greedy plans."

The memory of her strange winter vision and of Hawkwind's mutilated body, of his agonizing attacks of pain whenever it rained until she finally cured him, filled Deidra with a surprisingly strong surety that Bardrick spoke true. "So, that's why Hawkwind is so bitter against the nobility," she murmured, her gaze dropping. "I'd thought 'twas just the usual common man's jealousy for his betters, but 'twas of a much deeper nature."

She glanced back up at Bardrick. "What of his brothers? 'Twas said the Lord Nicholas returned to Todmorden several months later, secretly confronted them and when they refused to return rule of his lands or help vindicate him, he killed them both. Is none of that true, either?"

"What do ye think, lass?" Bardrick quietly challenged. "If ye think Hawkwind capable of plotting against the old king, then he's equally capable of murdering his brothers who went against him in it, is he not? Ye should know the inner man better than I. Ye shared his heart, his love."

"Did I, Bardrick?" A haunted expression gleamed in Deidra's eyes. "I wonder how much of himself Hawkwind ever really shared. Mayhap that's why his actions in this whole sordid mess are so hard to fathom. I doubt I ever truly knew him." She smiled sadly. "Sharing a man's bed is no guarantee of sharing his heart."

"And I think ye should stop analyzing everything and follow the stirrings of yer own heart." Bardrick stepped back and, turning, leaned on the battlement wall. "I was the one with him in the long days and nights of his healing, when he writhed on his bed of pain, delirious, confused, heartbroken at what they'd done to him. I was there in the long days and nights when he fought to sort through it all, to rebuild his mangled body and mind. And I was with him when he returned to Todmorden six months later, through secret passages known only to his kin, and sought out his two brothers."

"You were there?" Deidra asked in breathless anticipation. "You saw what actually happened?"

"Aye, after a time," he replied, his voice gone suddenly flat, dead. "At first Hawkwind bade me wait in the secret tunnel leading to the family library so he could speak in private with his brothers and convince them to put their past problems behind them and join together against the newly crowned King William. They, however, young, hot-headed fools that they were, not only refused, they set upon Hawkwind with murderous intent."

"What did Hawkwind do?"

"He wouldn't fight to harm them, only to protect himself. I think they'd have finally killed him if I hadn't heard the sounds of battle and disobeyed Hawkwind's order by rushing in."

An anguished look twisted the old man's face. "In my anger, I quickly cut down the older of the two brothers. The younger one escaped, when Hawkwind bade me cease my attack upon him. He ran out of the room and fled down the hall. I hurried after him, intending on bringing him back to take with us for further questioning, but he was too swift. Just as I was ready to return to Hawkwind, a terrible cry reached my ears. I ran in the direction of the sound and found the young man lying there in a pool of blood, his throat slit."

"Someone else killed him?"

Bardrick swung to her. "Aye. Someone within the castle."

"But why? How?"

"I'd wager 'twas someone set to spy on Hawkwind's brothers and make certain they didn't betray the new king. The man most likely had come upon us when Hawkwind was speaking to them and, as he eavesdropped outside in the hall, realized the danger to William. Then, when

Hawkwind's brother escaped, the man followed him and finished him off before we could learn more. We learned enough, though," Bardrick muttered darkly. "We knew who had killed the old King and why. We just had no proof, no witnesses."

"So you're saying 'twas *William*, intent on gaining the throne for himself?" Deidra frowned. "My father had begun to suspect as much himself."

"And 'tis past time, too," her bodyguard agreed. "His all too eager fealty paid to William at his coronation didn't help things at all. Not to mention," he added, "his all too eager acceptance of Hawkwind's lands as reward."

"Father didn't know who to believe in those days, and when the Lord of Todmorden returned to kill his own brothers . . ." Deidra inhaled an exasperated breath. "He made a mistake, was misled, but so were many others. And when I tell him the real truth of Hawkwind's identity, and what happened—"

"Nay, lass!" Bardrick wheeled about and, in two quick strides, reached her. Taking her by the arm, he pulled her to him, his voice lowering. "If ye care even a whit for Hawkwind and what happens to him, don't give away his secret. D'Mondeville will be dealt with. I know Hawkwind well enough to know that. But if ye tell yer father . . ."

"Father will understand," she whispered back. "He'll help Hawkwind. Then Hawkwind won't have to fight for D'Mondeville anymore! Then . . . then he can join with us and—"

"Hush, lass," Bardrick murmured, pressing a gentle finger to her lips. "Better first ye speak with Hawkwind himself, than make plans that could well mean his death."

"But how can that happen?" Deidra pulled back slightly. "We are at siege. Besides, if I went to Hawkwind now, he'd most likely take me again for ransom. I cannot jeopardize my father and Rothgarn—"

"Hawkwind would give his word for an honorable truce,

where both parties could meet and depart in peace. I'd not sanction any other plan."

"You'd go to him, see if he'd meet with me?"

"Aye."

A wild hope fluttered to life beneath Deidra's breast. Then fear rushed in to quench the feeble desire. How could she face Hawkwind after running from him? What could she say to convince him this time, to change his mind and commitment to Basil D'Mondeville? And, worst of all, what if, when he looked upon her, the love was gone?

It wouldn't matter. She couldn't *let* it matter. Her own needs were secondary to the welfare of her people, her father, her home. In the end, that had to be the reason for meeting again with Hawkwind. She must harden herself to that task, to the stirrings of her heart, to even Hawkwind's difficult and most unfortunate plight. Her first duty must lie with her people and their welfare. As Hawkwind's had always lain with the welfare of his army.

If, in the meeting, other things between them were resolved as well, so much the better. Deidra hoped, prayed 'twould be so, but so much depended on Hawkwind now. One way or another, though, she had to save Rothgarn.

"Go to him, then," Deidra ordered, resolutely squaring her shoulders. "Arrange a meeting between us on neutral ground." Her glance caught sight of the tall spire of the town church, its lead-sheeted roof glinting dully in the moonlight. "Aye, arrange a meeting in the chapel. 'Tis safe enough." She smiled grimly. "I know a secret way for us to get there."

"I don't like this," Hawkwind growled as he stood with Renard in the shadowy refuge of the church two days later. "It could be a trap."

"Bardrick would never be party to such a foul act and well you know it," his war captain soothed. "Though I must admit to some curiosity and surprise that Deidra wishes to speak with you. Mayhap she wishes to beg your forgiveness and ask to be yours once more."

"Aye," Hawkwind muttered dryly. "And I'll believe that when the mythical dragons of Cadvallan Island pay us a visit. Nay, I know her well enough not to waste my time hoping for a lover's reconciliation. The wench is too proud and stubborn ever to admit wrong doing. And I'm too angry at her to accept her apology at any rate."

"Then why the meeting tonight?" Renard asked. "If you've no hope of working things out between you . . ."

"I want to see what she has to say," his leader snapped. "A good strategist is wise to learn all he can about the enemy."

"And when did I suddenly become your enemy, Hawkwind?" came a low, soft voice from the darkness beyond the altar.

With a start, Hawkwind wheeled around, his hand going to his sword. Try as he might, however, his acute vision couldn't pierce the heavy veil of shadow shrouding the now empty, unused altar.

A chill breeze, rife with dank, fetid odors, wafted by, then was gone. Hawkwind's nostrils twitched. A secret tunnel, unused for years. Motioning for Renard to stay behind, he forced himself to step forward, crossing the thick, stone-tiled floor, drawing ever near to Deidra.

Anticipation dried his mouth and quickened his pulse. His hand, clenched about his sword hilt, dampened. A fine sweat broke out on his brow.

He knew 'twas a normal response to going to battle, but he hadn't envisioned this meeting with Deidra as a battle. Or at least not until he'd heard her speak. But her voice plucked at some well-buried memories, stirring emotions he'd thought he'd discarded. And the impulse, potent and nearly overwhelming, to take her into his arms and kiss her until she went limp with desire, flooded him with a devastating force.

But this wasn't the Deidra he'd once known, Hawkwind

realized with breath-grabbing shock as she finally stepped from the shadows and into an errant beam of moonlight. Her long, thick, wavy hair was pulled up into an intricate coil atop her head. Golden earrings, set with some precious stones that winked brightly with each movement of her head, dangled from her ears. And her slender body, from long, slim neck to the tips of her toes, was covered with a cloak of some intricately woven cloth interspersed with glittering bits of gold and silver threads.

She was regal, cold, the consummate noblewoman, gazing down at him from the short flight of steps leading from the altar. Distant, brittle—her manner instinctively evoked similar feelings in him. With an inward summoning of his own emotional barriers, Hawkwind climbed the steps before her, forcing Deidra finally to back up or risk him slamming into her.

Still he forged on, drawing ever near, until Deidra was pressed against the huge altar. At the contact of unyielding stone at her back, her control snapped. "Enough, Hawkwind! Stop your pointless games. I didn't come here to be intimidated or physically threatened."

He arched a dark brow, eyed her a long moment, then took a step back. "Nay, I suppose you didn't, though I must admit to a strong urge to do both—over my knee to begin the official ceremonies."

"There'll be no hands laid on me tonight." She slipped around the altar until she faced him across its smooth marble top. Her hands splayed out and she leaned forward. "I came here for one thing—and one thing only."

"And that was?"

"I want you to take your army and depart." Deidra forced her gaze to lock with Hawkwind's. "I want you to leave Rothgarn. Without you and your army, D'Mondeville hasn't a chance of taking the castle."

Hawkwind's mouth twisted. "I made an agreement, gave my word, and accepted payment. Didn't I make that clear the last time we spoke? I can't go back on it."

"I have jewels. My own and my mother's." She flipped back her cloak and untied two bags hanging from her belt. In a quick movement, Deidra heaved first one, then another large leather bag onto the altar to lie between them. As they slammed down on the marble top, they tinkled and clanked seductively. "I'd wager they'll cover the first half of your payment *and* the rest still owed you, with a handsome profit to spare."

His features hardened into a mask of cynical incredulity. "So, you think to buy me off, do you? Well, I've never accepted charity in my life, and won't begin now. And I won't shame myself by going against my word, either. Especially not for you or your greedy, grasping father!"

"My father isn't greedy or grasping," Deidra shot back, stung by his insulting refusal of her offer and the hard-edged anger that slammed the door shut on the possibility of any more tender considerations. "He made a mistake following William all those years ago," she forced herself to continue, "but he has realized his error and now sides with the rebel lords. Why do you think Basil D'Mondeville—the king's *true* toady—is now at our gates?"

"I don't know," Hawkwind mockingly responded. "Why don't you tell me?"

She glared at him for a long moment, then clamped down on a stinging retort. "Because William wishes to make an example of my father and teach his rebel lords a lesson. You're being used to make the point mercenaries will be called in against anyone who dares dissent in the future."

"I won't be used to further William's goals!" Hawkwind hotly responded. "I work for no man but myself!"

"Well, even once is too much, to my view of things!" She shot him a smirking glance. "You don't like it much when the boot is on the other foot, do you?"

"What are you talking about?" he snarled and leaned halfway across the altar toward her.

"What do you think I'm talking about?" Deidra met his

aggressive move with one of her own, locking gazes only inches apart. Though she dreaded pressing her next point in so ruthless a manner, she had to know the truth once and for all. "Why, your heartless, calculated wooing of me so as to win Rothgarn for your own, of course. You never loved me nor wanted me for wife save for the castle I'd ultimately bring you. Did you?"

At the flicker of hesitation and guilt Deidra saw in Hawkwind's eyes, pain lanced through her. Curse him! She'd been right all along. He *had* meant to use her. So be it, she thought. 'Twas over between them. All her efforts now focused on saving Rothgarn. "Well, my brave warrior," she taunted, relentlessly forging on, "I don't hear you denying it, so it must be true."

He averted his gaze to some spot past the wooden pews that lined the right side of the chapel. "What does it matter now? I'll admit that was part of my motive and I wasn't particularly proud of it, but 'twasn't all of it." Hawkwind inhaled a ragged breath and swung back to face her. "And what of your behavior, my fine, honorable lady? I'd say your trust in me was sadly lacking, the man you claimed to love and agreed to wed. I'd say there was enough deceit on both sides to deter you from so easily tossing out the accusations."

"What was I to think, hearing you agree to fight for D'Mondeville in revenge on my father, with me as the prize?" she cried. "Not to mention after learning who you really were!"

Hawkwind's big body went taut. "Back to that again, are we? I told you there was naught I could do but go along with D'Mondeville for the time being. I had my army to consider—"

Deidra leaned back. "Aye, your army and your honor and your lands. They would have always come between us, wouldn't they?"

He shook his head and heaved a deep sigh, as if the admission had been rung from some place he rarely visited, much less faced. "Nay, but it seemed the only solution at the time."

"And now?" she prodded, excitement at possibly finding some way out of this tragic situation filling her. "What of now? Would you go to my father, tell him all, and offer to join with him and the other lords against William?"

"Hardly." Hawkwind gave a low, mocking laugh. "Do I look that big a fool? Join with a man who changes loyalties as easily as the wind changes directions? Or place my life and that of my army's in the hands of men who, in their own ways, are as grasping and treacherous as William?"

"You can't know that without trying!" Deidra protested. "They need you. They wouldn't turn you away."

"Oh, aye," he gritted, shoving a hand raggedly through his hair. "They'd use me all right. Who wouldn't want my army on their side? But I don't delude myself for a moment that afterward, when the threat was gone, they wouldn't band together and turn on me. A mercenary army, led by a man who owes no one allegiance, will always be a potent danger. One the rebel lords don't need any more than William will, once *he* has won.

"Nay," Hawkwind rasped, fiercely shaking his head, "I washed my hands of the lot of them those eight years ago. I don't want to get involved in this foolish, futile struggle. Naught will change for anyone, no matter who's in power."

Deidra's hands fisted on the altar before her. "You can't live your whole life straddling the middle. Sooner or later, you must make a commitment or your life will never amount to aught."

He leaned forward and grasped her by the wrists, anchoring her to him. A savage, scorching fury blazed from his eyes. "Like you did with me, mayhap? I committed to you, gave you everything I had to give—some of which I'd never shared with anyone before—and where did it get me?"

His grip tightened painfully. Deidra was suddenly, overwhelmingly, assailed with a sense of his unremitting rage, gut wrenching frustration, and anguished, confused love. The realization of his love startled her. She struggled to fathom it, to capture that most fleeting of emotions but it eluded her. Dizziness swallowed Deidra. She felt light-headed.

And still Hawkwind pressed on, grinding her down to a quivering mass of apprehension and tumultuous emotions simply by the overpowering strength of his masculine presence and relentless force of his nature.

"Answer me that, Deidra, *if* you dare," he drawled silkily, his utter disdain glittering in his eyes.

"D-don't blame this on me." She fought past the sudden sense of the room whirling about her and, with a fierce shake of her head, met his gaze. " 'Twasn't I who agreed to side with Basil D'Mondeville against Rothgarn. 'Twasn't I who trusted so little that the truth about a certain Lord of Todmorden's betrayal by his own brothers and King William wasn't shared. And 'twasn't I who cold-bloodedly decided to use a woman, to lie to and manipulate her solely for his own purposes." She wrenched her hands free of his hold with a painful twist. "So speak to me not of *your* reluctance to trust or commit to anyone!"

"Who told you?" he quietly asked. "And what do you know of the 'truth' about me?"

"Bardrick. He was finally forced to do what you should have done." Unaccountably, tears flooded Deidra's eyes. "That hurt, Hawkwind, and deeply so. But it doesn't matter anymore. Only Rothgarn matters."

" 'Twill be all right in the end," he muttered, touched by the shimmer of tears that had sprung to her eyes as no show of anger could ever have done. "I'll have you, my lands, and your father will be safe as well. No matter William's or D'Mondeville's plans, your father will be safe, as will you, in Todmorden."

She gave a bitter laugh. "And what makes you think that is any consolation to us? If you take Rothgarn and its lands and give it to D'Mondeville, 'twill break my father's heart.

And you're a fool to think D'Mondeville will so easily give me over to you. He's my betrothed, the man I ran away from Rothgarn to escape." A haunted, anguished look flared in Deidra's eyes. "Yet, in the end," she asked, half to herself, "what did my escape accomplish? All I did was run from one man to another man bent on using me."

Even in the dimness of the church, Deidra could see the dark flush slowly suffuse Hawkwind's face. " 'Twasn't meant to turn out that way," he whispered. "That much I swear."

"And what worth is your word to me?" Deidra bit out the question, refusing to forgive or trust him again. 'Twas hopeless. She could see that so clearly now.

Hawkwind had done naught but argue and defend himself, attacking instead her own reasons for what she'd done at every turn. Not once had he apologized, offered to change what he'd wrought, or said he still loved her. He'd offered naught and, in his arrogance, still expected her to understand, to forgive, to take him back.

Deidra sighed and shook her head. "You have always claimed your honor was the most important thing in your life. Well, I see no man of honor standing here tonight. I see instead a hard, ruthless beast who'll trod over everyone and everything to get what he wants." She inhaled a tremulous, sob-choked breath. "I can't fathom why I ever thought you anything else!"

Her words struck deep, piercing Hawkwind's heart, sending pulsing bursts of agony coursing through his body. His honor. By the Mother, that was all he had left in this miserable travesty of a life! 'Twas why he was still bound to D'Mondeville, as much as he loathed and mistrusted the man. 'Twas why he fought so to maintain his mercenary's reputation. Not for himself, but for his honor—and his army.

Why couldn't Deidra see that? Didn't she know, didn't she care the decision had been hard enough to make to begin with and only increased in torment with each passing day?

But how *could* she understand? She'd never been forced to claw through each minute of each day in a battle just to survive, nor endured the excruciating torment of a body fighting to heal itself of horrible wounds. She had never experienced long months of painful rehabilitation, nor struggled to learn to walk again, move arms, ride a horse, and bear weapons. And she had most certainly never lived through the endless nights of despair, of unanswered questions and grinding self-doubts, and the haunting, seductive temptation to put an end to it all.

Nay, she'd never known any of it, yet still, in that haughty way of the nobility, felt quite capable of judging him. That realization shattered the last hope Hawkwind had of reconciling with her. "And I say you're incapable of thinking of, much less understanding, anyone else," he answered her with scathing sarcasm. " 'Tis an unfortunate trait of your kind and why I turned my back on that life long ago."

He stepped away from the altar. "I don't care what becomes of Rothgarn, nor the rebel lords, nor William. You can all fight it out amongst yourselves. And, when all the fighting is over, I'll still be here, my army intact, my conscience clear. I'll still have everything I had to begin with and more, for I'll also have you. Remember that, Deidra. I'll have you, if I have to take your castle down stone by stone."

"Will you now?" she taunted, her slender body going rigid with her wrath and frustration. "Then you make yet another grievous error, one you may well regret the rest of your days."

His mouth curled in a sneer. "Indeed? And what is that?"

"You think you're the only one of honor, but I say you're mistaken. I, too, live for honor and that honor will *never* permit you to have me again. Before I let that happen, I will kill myself!" Deidra heard the thread of hysteria rise in her voice, but no longer cared. "I will *not* be used ever again, by anyone. Not by you, not by D'Mondeville, not by my father. But above all, *not by you.*"

Uncertainty and surprise flickered briefly in Hawkwind's eyes. Then he gave an unsteady laugh. "If you think I believe that for one moment, you understand less about me than you thought. I know people. I know you. You're a survivor, Deidra. You'll find some way to turn all of this to your advantage."

"Will I now?" she asked hoarsely. "Then try me, push this to its furthest limits, and see how well you ever truly knew me!"

With that, she snatched up her bags of jewels. Turning on her heel in a shimmering swirl of long cloak and haughty, anguished disdain, Deidra disappeared back into the shadows from whence she came.

Chapter 19

The siege dragged on. Days of rocks shattering against walls, of smoke-filled air, of shouts of battle, and cries of the wounded and dying. Nights of bleak despair, when Deidra tossed and turned on her plump, feather-tick mattress, the air thick and heavy about her, reliving the day's horror in her mind.

And, when she'd finally fall into an exhausted, fitful slumber, she'd dream of Hawkwind. Hawkwind, heartbreakingly handsome of countenance and powerful of body. Hawkwind, holding her in his arms, his lips slanting savagely, passionately over hers, whispering words of desire, of love. And then, always, something would startle Deidra awake—to deep, dark, silent night, alone in her bed, the horror of reality engulfing her.

She'd weep each time, until there was naught left to give, then dry her face and rise, knowing she'd rest no more that night. Knowing there was naught else she could do for either herself or Hawkwind. He was as solid, as implacable as the walls of Rothgarn Castle. And, like those walls, his decision to separate from her was just as final. 'Twas over, she told herself again and again. She must put the past, no matter how much she preferred it to the present, behind her.

The weeks passed; the siege worsened. They ran low on

food and their meager supplies had to be strictly rationed. Then, thanks to the past years of drought, the castle well began to run dry. With the additional stress of needing water to put out the frequent fires set by the attackers and supplying it to the hundreds of villagers who had taken refuge in Rothgarn for over two months, the most feared danger of long sieges became a reality. If some break-through didn't occur soon, Hawkwind would force them to surrender, or die of thirst.

Deidra assumed the onerous task of measuring out the daily water rations. The work wasn't much, when she longed to be on the parapets with her father, but she knew her efforts at the well took at least one concern from his already overburdened shoulders. Yet, that morning, as she ladled out the meager ration of water to the castle soldiers in the outer bailey, Deidra's worried glance sought her father again and again.

He stalked the battlements, shouting orders at John Betson, his captain of the guard, who, working beside him, then relayed the commands to his subcaptains. Deidra was thankful for the solid ability of the man even as she tamped down yet another shudder of distaste for him as a person.

Betson was supremely competent in castle defense and its daily management, but he was also the coldest, most hard-hearted being she had ever met. He ruled the fortress guard with a brutal, unrelenting hand, meting out harsh punishments with little provocation. True, the soldiers obeyed instantly thanks to Betson's tight rein, but they were also fearful and sullen in their response.

Strange, Deidra mused, she'd never noted it before, but ever since her return from Hawkwind's camp, so many things now stood out in her mind. For all his cruel manipulations of her, Hawkwind was a superb leader who treated his men strictly but fairly. And 'twas more than evident, she thought with no small amount of bitterness, he cared for them and put their welfare above his own. She had experienced that truth most painfully in her relationship with Hawkwind. *Most* painfully . . .

With a fierce shake of her head, Deidra recalled her attention to the task at hand. With each ladle of water she doled out to the men lined up before her, she managed a smile of encouragement and word of thanks. 'Twasn't much to give them, when one considered the hardships they suffered, but 'twas all she had. 'Twas surprising yet true how pain and deprivation could finally strip away all the trappings of rank and privilege, laying bare the true nobility of the soul. A nobility not limited to those of finer bloodlines and social standing.

Deidra smiled as young Thomas, the sheepherder who had been commandeered into assisting the castle smithy, stepped up before her. His face was grimy with soot and sweat, but his toothy grin and rapt expression heartened her. She spared a few extra words with him before she gave him his ration of water, then laughingly waved him on.

As she glanced back up with another ladle of water, Deidra's gaze slammed into the sternly frowning one of John Betson. In spite of herself, her hackles rose. She arched a challenging brow. "Is there aught amiss, Captain Betson?"

He stepped close so none could overhear, his mouth twisted sourly. "Aye, mistress. I'd ask ye not to talk so with my men. They are already slow and slovenly as 'tis, without ye telling them what a fine job they're doing."

"Indeed? I hadn't noticed any problem with your men of late. I'd say, instead, they are holding up admirably, considering the situation." Deidra bit back the impulse to tell him what she thought of *his* leadership abilities, and contented herself with the more bland reply. 'Twouldn't do to antagonize the man at a time like this, not when they needed every able-bodied soldier they could get. But she'd be damned if she'd let the arrogant, thick-skulled man lecture her on the treatment of soldiers, either. She'd never let

Hawkwind push her around and John Betson was definitely no Hawkwind.

"Ye wouldn't notice, mistress," the man blundered on, so caught up in his mission he failed to perceive the frosty reception he was receiving. "But, though I hate to be so bold as to say it, ye nonetheless undermine my discipline with yer cheery smile and words."

"I've certainly no intent to do that, Captain Betson," Deidra replied, smiling her sweetest. "But I learned a bit about the leading of men when I was with the warrior chief, Hawkwind, and found no lessening of morale because of an occasional word or two of thanks. On the contrary, it only helped strengthen the men's courage and commitment."

Betson shot a quick glance about him to assure himself he wouldn't be overheard, then turned back to Deidra. "Begging yer pardon, mistress, but I'd hardly say yer experience in that slimy scoundrel's camp gave ye a fair representation of a good leader—or of a man, for that matter. He is naught but a cruel, ruthless, money-hungry killer." The captain smiled grimly. "But thank the Holy Ones he won't be a problem to us much longer. Whether he takes Rothgarn or not, his days are numbered. There are many who wish his death."

His glance narrowed, turned sly and speculative. "We'll have him sooner or later. Then ye'll have yer revenge against him, and the insults he paid ye while ye were held captive in his camp. Yer people don't take kindly to a man who dared lay hands on a fine lady such as yerself."

Deidra clamped down on an automatic response to defend Hawkwind. Strange that even after all he'd done, and still tried to do to her, she couldn't bear to hear him reviled. Especially by a man not worthy to wipe his boots.

Despite Betson's sordid implications to the contrary, Hawkwind had never forced himself on her, had never taken what wasn't freely offered. She had no one but herself to blame for that. But her father, when she'd first returned home, had made her swear not to reveal the real reasons for her flight to Hawkwind's army, nor the fact she'd lain with him. She had yet to tell him she now carried his child, but after almost two months with no woman's courses, and the mild bouts of nausea she now endured each morning, Deidra knew. For all her father's well-intentioned efforts to protect her reputation, the truth would be known by all soon enough.

Not that Deidra cared. Hawkwind's child was the only thing of value that would come out of the whole, tragic mess, a mess she realized had become even more complex with the admission of her pregnancy. She couldn't kill herself now, no matter what Hawkwind did. Or at least not until the babe was born.

But she *could* spare her father for a time longer. He had enough to bear. Later, if some miracle didn't occur to save them, 'twouldn't matter anyway.

"He left me untouched," Deidra blatantly lied to Betson, her father's peace of mind more important than the sin she'd just committed. "And, though I will take into consideration your words and attempt to temper my response to the men, I won't begrudge them the simple kindnesses. I'll leave that," she pointedly added, "to you."

John Betson blinked in surprise, then, as his slower wit finally grasped the barb hidden beneath the sweet words and beguiling smile, he scowled. "As ye wish, mistress. But I think ye'll rue yer actions before this siege is out. Mark my words."

"Aye, mark them I will," Deidra replied, then waved him on with the ladle. "In the meanwhile, if you don't mind, I've still a long line of soldiers waiting their turn."

"Aye, mistress," he growled and, shooting her a final, furious look, strode away.

Deidra watched him walk across the courtyard and back to the steps leading to the parapets, an unaccountable feeling of unease snaking through her. There was just something about the man, something that boded ill. But whether that ill was soon to befall or much later, she had no further time to dwell on it. There were men who waited for her and their daily ration of water.

"Nay, absolutely not!" the Lord of Rothgarn vehemently refused. "You're daft even to think such a thing, much less ask it!" He wheeled around from his wide, iron-grilled bedchamber window and faced his daughter. "I won't talk with nor consider making an offer to join forces with that treacherous mercenary. He can't be trusted. Besides, with William behind this, I can never hope to pay Hawkwind enough to bribe him over to our side at any rate."

"But you don't understand, Father," Deidra protested. She rose from the huge oaken chair and walked over to her father. For a long moment she stared up at him, struggling to decide if she should tell him the full truth about Hawkwind or not. Mayhap if he knew the tale of Nicholas of Todmorden's own betrayal by their present king, he'd listen to her plan with more enthusiasm.

Hawkwind had naught to lose by her father knowing about him. If the two men chose not to join forces, her father's inevitable defeat would end any threat to Hawkwind. And if they did choose to ally against D'Mondeville, there was hope the Lord of Rothgarn could eventually use his considerable influence to clear Hawkwind's name. Aye, Deidra thought resolutely. 'Twas past time to reveal Hawkwind's secret.

"And what, pray tell, Daughter," her father silkily inquired, "don't I understand? 'Tis a fool's plan you propose. There's naught more to be said about it."

"Nay, there *is* more." She laid a hand on his arm. "Hawkwind is the Lord Nicholas of Todmorden. And he is innocent of the charges he masterminded the plot to kill the old king."

The Lord of Rothgarn eyed his daughter for an incredulous moment, then threw back his head and laughed. "And who told you that? That lying, treacherous mercenary?" He shook his head and gently took her chin in his hand. "Ah, lass, you've been misguided by one of the finest schemers in the realm. If this Hawkwind is truly who he says he is, 'twould explain much. I've always wondered why William allowed that mercenary army to roam free, without controls or sanctions, wreaking havoc on both sides. Now, 'tis all apparent."

"What, Father?" Deidra's smooth brow furrowed in puzzlement. "What's apparent?"

"Why, can't you see it, lass? William owed Hawkwind a boon for helping him gain the throne. Though he couldn't outwardly support the murderer of his father, he could allow him to succeed in disguise. 'Tis why William never went after his army. Why Hawkwind's army has become the most successful and feared force in the realm. And why William has managed so quickly and easily to solidify his standing. With Hawkwind out there continually stirring up unrest, no one had time to unify against the king."

"Nay, Father," Deidra protested, wresting her chin from her father's grip to shake her head. " 'Tisn't so. Hawkwind hates William. He was tricked by D'Mondeville into going against you."

"Then why doesn't he now turn from D'Mondeville?" he demanded, fixing her with a piercing stare. "A man can make a mistake. I did for many years in following William. But even I know now I was wrong and have admitted it. Nay, not just admitted it, am trying to rectify it at great cost to myself. 'Tis why I'm currently in this sorry position. But what has your precious Hawkwind done?" He gave a disparaging snort. "Naught, Daughter. He has done naught. And do you know why? Because he is William's man, no matter how he protests to the contrary. *He is William's man!*"

Frustration flooded her. By the saints, but she was surrounded by fatally proud and stubborn men! Men who'd rather ride to their destruction than consider that mayhap they were wrong. And God forbid either should ever admit to such a possibility!

Her lips clamped shut as anger surged in to drive the rising sense of helplessness away. Her fists clenched at her sides. "You and Hawkwind really should reconsider becoming allies," Deidra bit out the words. "You both have a lot more in common than just me."

The Lord of Rothgarn arched a graying brow. "Indeed? And how so, Daughter?"

"You're both the most pigheaded, arrogant, and prideful men I've ever had the displeasure of knowing. And both of you would vastly prefer going down in defeat than dare admit you might be wrong. Which is exactly what will happen, no matter who wins this siege!"

"And who will you side with in the end, Daughter?" her father demanded, anger beginning to thread his voice as well. "Your father and home—or your treacherous, mercenary lover?"

"You have my answer to that already," Deidra cried. "I am here, aren't I?"

"Then why not prove it? Prove it by destroying the greatest threat to us of all."

Confusion gripped Deidra. "What are you talking about?"

"Your fire powers. Surely they've had sufficient time to rejuvenate. Use them again, this time for me. Use them as your mother never had the courage to do. Use them to save Rothgarn."

"How?" Deidra whispered, even as the horrible premonition of his answer filled her, sending a clammy chill prickling down her spine. "How do you want me to do that?"

Her father shrugged. "How else, Daughter? As bloodthirsty as it may seem, use your powers to kill Hawkwind and rout his army. D'Mondeville hasn't a chance without him."

An image—or was it a vision?—swept through Deidra's mind. Of an army, a fiery swath of devastation cut through it, hundreds milling about in panicked chaos, the rest in wild retreat. Then her vision narrowed, swooping down to the body of a man lying there on the field of battle, his face and form scorched, unrecognizable, dead. Yet still Deidra knew him and knew what had killed him. Her powers, used once to heal Hawkwind and save his life, had now destroyed him.

With a small, anguished cry, Deidra cast the vision aside. Never, she vowed. Never again. She shook her head to clear her mind, then looked up at her father. "Nay. I won't do it. Not for you, not for anyone. You don't know what you're asking of me."

"I ask a lot, that I well know," her father quietly replied, noting her pallid features. He took her by the arm and led her back to her chair. "Sit, Daughter. I did not mean to alarm you so. I'd never ask more than I thought you were capable of giving. But when you told me of your special talents, this time I wanted to accept them and not turn you from me because of them, like I did with your mother. And I thought, mayhap, this time they could be used to Rothgarn's advantage."

He sighed and glanced away, a distant look darkening his features. " 'Tis a terrible thing, powers such as yours. They demand much, yet you can never escape them. They change you whether you wish them to or not. And they change those close to you as well, some for the good, others for the bad." He looked back at her, a haunted, anguished light gleaming in his eyes. "I'd not wish to have them harm what lies between us. I-I couldn't bear it if I lost you as well."

Deidra leaped from her chair and threw her arms about her father's neck, burying her face in the comforting haven of his chest. "You'll never lose me. Never! Just don't ask me to use my powers," she begged, her voice breaking. " 'Tis too much to bear. Too much . . ."

"Hush, Daughter," her father soothed, stroking her shining, fiery mass of hair. "I won't ask it. I swear. Somehow we'll find a way through it all without them. But heed me and heed me well. Your powers, as fearsome as they might be, must be faced sooner or later. 'Tis your destiny, as 'twas your mother's. You cannot walk that tightrope between avoidance and acceptance for too long. No one can."

Deidra poked the thick tapestry needle through the fabric, pulling a crimson strand of yarn down, then up again, in a mindless, methodical effort to drive away the thoughts yammering, incessantly, tauntingly, in her mind. 'Twas woman's work of the most tedious kind, this effort to commemorate some special event of Rothgarn's history in thread. Work she had always avoided whenever possible in the past, save for the minimal mandatory instruction required of all noblewomen.

But today, as the stench of burning timber filled the air, and the sickening sounds of boulders slamming into the wall and shouting men reverberated throughout the castle, Deidra struggled desperately to distance herself from reality. The reality of the battle raging outside, certain to end soon in their defeat as their water stores dwindled to nothing. The reality of the irreparable rift between her and Hawkwind, that neither he nor her father would consider breaching. And the reality of her powers—powers that now absolutely terrified her, yet held the potential for Rothgarn's salvation.

The price to use them in such a way was too great. She'd rather die than call upon them again. If used wrongly, they would kill her one way or another—whether it be of the body or the spirit. She didn't know why or how she knew that, but she did.

The yarn moved back and forth effortlessly in a crimson trail that blurred her gaze. Deidra blinked back the sheen of tears that had suddenly filled her eyes, staring down at the hand that held the needle. It felt lifeless, no longer a part of her. Like the heart beating within her breast—a cold, thudding mass of flesh pulsing on but feeling naught.

She wondered why it continued to function. There was naught to live for, not anymore.

Her gaze lifted and sought the sky through the tall window of the oriel room, a small wooden chamber projecting out over a stone built ground floor room. 'Twas situated just off the Great Hall and Deidra liked to slip away to it when she wearied of the lack of privacy of castle life. Besides the tapestry frame and stool, the room contained a fine padded bench beneath the window, four chairs set before the small, circular hearth faced with bright blue-and-white tiles wherein burned a fire to ease the unseasonably cool late October air, and several wooden chests holding the thread, fabric, and needles for the castle sewing.

As she sat there, gazing out at the brilliant sunset, a maid servant entered with a flaming taper and proceeded to light the wax candles impaled on the vertical spikes of the wall-mounted iron candlesticks. Deidra shot her a quick glance of gratitude, then averted her gaze back out the window. 'Twould be time for the supper meal soon, she thought, then bedtime.

She wondered how many days they had left before they were forced to surrender Rothgarn or die of thirst. A week at the most, Deidra reckoned, maybe sooner if John Betson failed to keep his men in hand. The soldiers were becoming increasingly unhappy with the rapidly diminishing water rations. Deidra knew 'twas only a matter of time before even Betson's harsh discipline was insufficient to control them.

Not that she could blame the men. No one could survive long without water. Surrender, however, wasn't a subject she could get her father to consider, much less discuss. The Lord of Rothgarn refused just as adamantly to name terms for Basil D'Mondeville as he had refused to heed her suggestions of joining forces with Hawkwind.

Deidra sighed and shook her head. They were all trapped by their destinies and pride, and no one seemed willing to make the first overtures to get any of them out of this untenable, self-destructive course of events.

With a small sigh, Deidra laid down her sewing, rose and walked over to the window. Her glance alighted on the wrought iron grillwork protecting the precious glazed glass. She fingered the ornate curlicues, tracing the twists and flourishes.

What, indeed, she mused, would it take to placate Basil D'Mondeville and save Rothgarn? She knew he still wanted her and the riches wedding the heir of Rothgarn would bring, but he also served the king's purposes in the destruction of her father. Even if she went to him now and offered herself, he could well afford to wait and still have it all.

Notwithstanding, there was also his promise to Hawkwind to give her to him. Though she suspected Basil had no intention of turning her over to Hawkwind, she wondered how he planned ultimately to betray the mercenary leader. And betray him he would, sooner or later. Of that, Deidra was certain. Basil D'Mondeville would betray them all before he was done.

But betrayal could cut both ways. If D'Mondeville wished to play that game, so could she. She had naught left to lose—and he had everything. All she needed was a plan to take D'Mondeville alone, before Hawkwind had a chance to interfere. But how? How?

The secret passage to the chapel, Deidra thought with a sudden surge of inspiration. She would take the tunnel to the chapel, slip through the town and make her way to D'Mondeville's tent. There, she'd offer herself to him in exchange for sparing her castle and her father. If he'd order Hawkwind's army to leave, she'd agree to wed him.

And if he refused, she'd kill him.

Though Hawkwind's honor seemed too exalted for him to consider such a thing, hers wasn't. Not anymore. Not when it came to Rothgarn's salvation.

She'd kill him in the usual manner, though, with a dagger surreptitiously hidden in her boot, not with her fire powers. No matter what her father had said last night, when he'd asked her to use her magic, she just couldn't. There were other ways to save Rothgarn and she meant to do just that. Even if it required her life.

Fortified by that resolve, Deidra left the oriel room. There were clothes to obtain, a tunic, pair of breeches and boots, a dark cloak and a dagger. Then tonight, after the supper meal, when all were snug in their beds, she would once more depart Rothgarn. Her mission, this time, was far less lofty, far less a glorious adventure rife with excitement and challenge, but a mission, nonetheless. One she did for others, rather than for herself like she had two months ago when she'd set out to find the famous mercenary leader named Hawkwind.

Hawkwind, Deidra thought with a dull, aching pain. Resolutely squaring her shoulders, she shoved open the door and slipped out.

From the shadows, the dark-eyed captain of the guard watched her. Then, as she passed, he surreptitiously set out to follow.

The night was black, as black as the depths of hell, the moon shrouded behind dense clouds, the stars absent. It was still—too still—as if the earth and all its inhabitants waited in tense anticipation for what would happen next.

Deidra couldn't help a small shiver as she ran along the deserted streets of town, staying close to the buildings, taking care to use stealth. Though there seemed not a living soul about, she couldn't risk coming upon some soldiers unaware. She might never make it to D'Mondeville if she did.

She knew his tent and where it lay in the war camp. From the castle parapets, she'd seen his banner of boar and ax flapping from it plainly enough in the past month. And this eve, after she'd finally made her decision to go to D'Mondeville, Deidra had fixed his tent's position and plotted the route to it in her mind as she gazed down once more on the war camp.

Nay, there was no question as to how to find D'Mondeville, once she infiltrated the enemy army. The only question was whether she could slip through without detection, or anyone barring her way. She knew the majority of D'Mondeville's force was massed on the east side of the camp, near their leader's tent, and that the wisest course was to make her way there. Then, if she were captured, at least his men would take her to D'Mondeville. But if Hawkwind's soldiers found her first . . .

Everything would be ruined if she were taken to Hawkwind. He was too proud, too honorable, too cursedly pigheaded, to turn against his employer. Only Basil D'Mondeville had the power to end the siege. Only he had reason to do so as well. Nay, Deidra resolved. She *must* reach him. There was no other recourse.

Would he take her, though, once he knew she came to him bearing another man's child? There was no good served in telling him the truth, Deidra decided. Not that he deserved it at any rate. And later, 'twould be too late for him to do aught about it. Somehow, she sensed he'd not particularly care one way or another. All she was to him was a potential possession who could increase his power and wealth.

Fleetingly she worried about her babe. What would become of it after 'twas born? More than anything, she wished to rear it. 'Twould be the only happiness she might ever have in this sad, sorry mess that had become her life. But if 'twas necessary to send her babe away to save it, she'd do whatever it took. There was naught she could do to change what must be done tonight, though. She'd have to deal with the issue of her babe later.

As Deidra ran along a sense of unease, of approaching danger, wafted over her. She shook it aside, needing all her concentration focused on stealth, speed, and vigilance. Yet, again and again, it returned, until Deidra finally recognized it for what 'twas.

Someone was pursuing her.

She halted, flung herself against the half-timbered wall of a house, and listened. Her heart hammered in her breast, sending blood rushing and pulsing through her head. She inhaled several slow, deep breaths and willed herself to relax. Gradually the rhythmic sounds in her ears eased. She heard the soft footfalls.

They were a man's, one trained in silent approach, drawing ever near. They rose from the direction she had come, though Deidra couldn't be certain if their owner had followed her out of Rothgarn or had been about in the town as she'd passed. It didn't matter. The man was after her.

She considered hiding in the hope he'd pass her by, but couldn't be certain she wouldn't come upon him again once she left her hiding place. And time was of the essence in reaching D'Mondeville. The sappers had reached the north tower. Tomorrow might be too late.

There was naught to do but run on and pray he'd not catch up with her. Squaring her shoulders, Deidra stepped out and once more made her way through the streets, her pace careful but as rapid as she dared allow it and still not give herself away. As she ran, she lifted a silent entreaty to any saint who might care to hear her, beseeching him to help her, to get her safely to Basil D'Mondeville. For the sake of her people, her father, for Rothgarn . . .

The sounds of pursuit faded. Relief surged through Deidra. She'd outrun him. She'd make it yet.

Then, as she rounded a corner, a huge form loomed from the darkness. Before she could dodge to the side in an attempt to evade him, the man's arms reached out, grabbed her, and pulled her to him. A cloth, reeking of some strong, choking scent, was forced over her mouth.

Deidra struggled wildly, kicking, twisting, fighting with all her strength. The deep breaths she took to fuel her efforts only hastened the drugging effects of the fumes she inhaled. She grew dizzy, light-headed. The night grew yet blacker. Then she was falling, tumbling into a deep, light-scattered void.

A voice pierced the terrifying chaos but briefly, rough with triumph, gloating, the last sounds Deidra heard before unconsciousness claimed her. "I have ye at last, ye haughty miss," John Betson said. "And ye'll make a fine package to barter my way once more into the enemy's favor. A fine package indeed."

The soft, mournful hoot of an owl pierced the darkness. Hawkwind's hand halted halfway to his mouth, the cup of ale sloshing gently over the sides. The sound unnerved him, as if 'twere an ill omen, warning him of some danger to come. But of what, and from whom?

He shook his head, his mouth twisting in a wry grimace. By the Mother, but he was becoming superstitious of late, and uncharacteristically skittish. There *was* danger all around him, but he knew from whence all of it came. From Rothgarn, from D'Mondeville, from King William and every other noble of the realm. From enemy soldiers, from every stranger, and from those yet closer, like a certain flame-haired witch.

Aye, life was full of danger, but no more so because of some owl hooting nearby in the trees. With that thought to bolster him, Hawkwind downed the contents of his cup and poured himself yet another, then swallowed it as quickly as the first. The ale sent a fine warmth coursing down his throat and into his chest on rippling fingers of fire. He set the empty cup down and wiped his mouth with the back of his hand.

A strong wind whistled through the camp, sending tents to flapping and dust to blowing. Hawkwind frowned. Was an unexpected storm gusting in? He hoped not. They'd been blessed this past month with dry weather and didn't need the hindrance of rain and mud now. Not when they were so close to victory.

Tomorrow they'd reach the north tower with their tunnels. Tomorrow, they'd drive the pigs underground, kill them, stack wood around the carcasses, and set them all afire. The lard would keep the fires hot, burning a long while, until the earth and masonry above collapsed into the hole beneath it. The tower would fall, the outer walls of Rothgarn would be breached and victory assured with the taking of the castle well in the outer bailey.

'Twould be but a matter of days after that before the garrison in the inner ward surrendered. No one could long fight, nor even live, without water. Aye, no one, Hawkwind smiled grimly. Deidra would finally be his.

He knew she wouldn't keep her vow to kill herself rather than fall into his hands. He *had* to believe that. Any other consideration filled him with horror. She'd just been angry, that night in the chapel, wanted to wound him as he had known he'd wounded her. But she wouldn't kill herself.

Would she?

With an angry growl, Hawkwind shoved the question aside. He didn't need those doubts, those fears, nibbling away at his concentration and confidence. Not now, when he was so close to being finished with this odious, exquisitely painful assignment. All he wanted was to be done with it, to take his money, win back Deidra, and walk away. He didn't care what became of Rothgarn or his castle. He didn't care if William punished his former ally. They deserved each other.

All he cared about was getting away from them all—and having Deidra back. He knew now he could never punish her as he'd intended in his earlier fits of rage. He loved her still. All he needed was time to win her heart again. He knew she'd forgive and love him again as well. She had to. He was so empty, so incomplete, so unhappy without her.

The guard rapped his sword on the door of his tent, requesting entrance. "What?" Hawkwind snarled, irritated at being interrupted in his tender, hopeful thoughts. "What is it?"

Bruno stuck in his head. "The healer Maud wishes to speak with ye? Shall I admit her?"

Hawkwind sighed. "Aye, let her in." He turned to the flagon of ale and poured himself yet another cup. Somehow, he knew Maud's visit didn't bode well. He'd need the meager solace of his favorite drink as fortification against her.

The tent flap snapped open in the gusting wind. Hawkwind turned, cup in hand, to face Maud. Without preliminary, she strode over to stand before him. She noted his cup of ale with a jaundiced eye.

"Deidra is in danger," she stated flatly.

Hawkwind nearly choked on the swallow of ale he'd just taken. "Wh-what?" he gasped, then sputtered as some of the rich brew trickled down his windpipe. "What d-did you s-say?"

"Deidra is in danger. D'Mondeville has her."

He paused to calm his choking coughs. "And how do you know this?" he finally demanded.

"A man from Rothgarn brought me the information. He said," the healer paused, "to tell you D'Mondeville has your leman."

At the slur against Deidra, Hawkwind's jaw went taut with rage. "Why didn't he come to me instead?" His eyes narrowed. "Sounds like some sort of a trap, to my way of thinking."

"Aye," Maud agreed. "The man's purpose in seeking me out is indeed suspicious. I don't know who he is, but I didn't like him. His eyes were too black, too cold . . ." She shivered. "There was just something about him. But he spoke true. Deidra is indeed in D'Mondeville's clutches."

"How do you know that?" Hawkwind asked, scowling. "And why is she there? There was no reason for her to leave the castle and go to him. She hates the man as much as she hates me."

"No reason ye might comprehend, at any rate, but she is desperate. And a desperate woman will risk much for what she loves," Maud softly replied. "As to how I know where she is, 'twas a simple enough thing to summon Deidra's image and whereabouts with the proper herbs and incantations." She cocked her head, studying him intently. "What will ye do about it? Will ye leave her to D'Mondeville? Ye'll never get her back if ye do."

"Maybe I don't want her back, if she went to him of her own accord," he muttered.

"Are ye interested in even knowing why she went to him?"

He shot her a flushed, angry look. "Aye, you know I am, though 'twill most likely be the death of me. Don't play games, Maud, not at a time like this. Just help me."

"My magic can take ye there, but once ye're in his tent, the rest is up to ye."

"I don't like it, Maud." Hawkwind ran a hand raggedly through his hair. "I've qualms enough about D'Mondeville as 'tis, without Deidra now in the middle of things."

"And hasn't she always been there in the middle of things since that first day ye met her?" The healer smiled. "Ye've just to decide where ye stand, once and for all."

"Aye, so it seems," Hawkwind glumly agreed. "Mayhap I *have* been running for far too long. Running away rather than toward what really matters in life."

He set down his cup, strapped on his sword, and motioned her onward, a grim foreboding filling him. He knew now what the owl's hooting omen had foreshadowed. Knew it, as well, for the terrible danger 'twas. Tonight, whether he wished it or not, he must finally make a choice between the woman he still loved and what was fast becoming a nebulous, empty, and all but pointless issue of honor.

Chapter 20

Deidra woke slowly to a brightly lit tent, to the sounds of two men talking, nay, arguing loudly. She shook her head from side to side, trying to block out the jarring noise, and clamped her eyes shut against the blinding light. Her head throbbed, her mouth tasted foul . . . vaguely reminiscent of the strong chemicals she realized now had been used to drug her into unconsciousness.

Her eyes snapped open, as the immediate awareness of her danger assailed her. Where was she? Where had Betson brought her? She well knew his motive—the slime-ridden, conniving traitor! He meant to curry favor with the soon-to-be victors of the siege. But had he brought her to Basil D'Mondeville or Hawkwind?

Deidra attempted to shove herself up and found her hands tied behind her back. Carefully she moved her legs, discovered they were unbound, the dagger still in place inside her right boot. At least that part of her plan was intact, she thought in silent gratitude. She lifted her head, blinked to clear the sudden surge of dizziness, and found Betson in heated argument with Basil D'Mondeville.

Relief filled her. At least she'd arrived where she'd intended to go. Now, if she could just get rid of Betson . . .

". . . and I tell you I don't care who Hawkwind is," D'Mondeville was calmly explaining to an irate John Betson. "It serves my purposes for the present to ignore the fact of his past treachery."

"The man is a danger to the Crown!" Rothgarn's captain of the guard protested. "What will King William say when he discovers ye've hidden the truth of the Lord of Todmorden's existence from him these past months?"

"Are you threatening to go to William, then?" D'Mondeville demanded, his voice tightening with anger and a barely veiled threat. "Didn't I pay you enough to buy that treacherous tongue of yours?"

Betson was astute enough to catch the danger to him. He lifted his hands, palms forward, and took a step back. "Aye, m'lord. Ye paid me quite handsomely, as I knew ye would. My first loyalty is to ye now, not William. I'm not a stupid man. I know when to keep my mouth shut. 'Tis why I survived after the plot to depose the old king succeeded. 'Tis why I kept the secret of Lord Nicholas's new identity for all these years. I but intended to point out that as long as Lord Nicholas lives, there is danger to William."

"Aye, that I well know," Basil agreed carefully. "And the Lord of Todmorden will soon be disposed of, just as soon as Rothgarn falls. Be assured of that. It must just be done very carefully, or his army will slaughter us all."

Betson grinned broadly. "Oh, I've already seen to that, m'lord. I've arranged for him to come here to 'rescue' his woman, with the full knowledge of others in his camp that he does so. 'Tis a simple enough thing for ye to claim he attacked ye in a fit of rage when ye refused to turn the Rothgarn heiress over to him, and ye killed him in self-defense. His army will have no recourse but to accept that, knowing he did come to ye of his own free will. As will the king, once he knows of Lord Nicholas's false identity."

For a moment, an unleashed fury flared in D'Mondeville's eyes, than was tamped down. "You seem to have it all quite nicely planned." He studied the man before him with a speculative gaze. "You also seem eager to see Hawkwind dead as quickly as possible. Why is that?"

Betson smiled and shrugged. "Why else? I led the force that day to seek Lord Nicholas out and kill him, as well as spied on him when he returned later to confront his brothers. He'll remember me till the last breath he draws. As long as he lives, I remain in the gravest peril. Lord Nicholas must die if I'm ever to live in peace."

D'Mondeville's mouth twisted. "Indeed. I see your point." He motioned toward the opening of his tent. "Summon my guards, will you, then go, find some spot out of sight until I need you again. I must make preparations for Hawkwind's arrival. I'd wager he journeys here even now."

"Aye, I'd wager the same." The man gave D'Mondeville a brief nod, then strode across the tent to do as requested. In but the course of a few minutes, orders were given to have soldiers at the ready throughout camp, with several stationed just outside the tent as well. Then, the preparations made for Hawkwind's arrival, D'Mondeville turned to Deidra.

He gave a small start when he realized she was awake. His glance met hers and he smirked. "How much did you hear?"

"Enough to know you've just lowered yourself yet deeper into the cesspool of deceit and treachery," Deidra rasped, levering herself to one elbow. "John Betson's a foul traitor. He'll be no more loyal to you than he was to Hawkwind all those years ago, or my father now. The man will sell his soul to the highest bidder, whoever that may be."

D'Mondeville made a small moue of unconcern. "I know his kind well. But he serves my purposes for the time being. When he doesn't"—he shrugged negligently—"he'll be taken care of. Whether William realizes it yet or not, the man is a danger to him."

"As a witness to his treachery?"

"Aye. As your precious Hawkwind is as well."

"He's not my 'precious Hawkwind'!" Deidra hotly protested, not wishing to give Basil D'Mondeville the advantage. "I hate the man. He's as foul a traitor as Betson!"

"Why? Because he went to battle against your father?" D'Mondeville shook his head pityingly. "You're singularly unsympathetic to your lover's plight. He had no choice, being the man fate has made him. Unfortunately for him, 'twill also be his downfall."

"He's not my lover!"

"Indeed?" D'Mondeville skeptically arched a blond brow. "Well, no matter. Whether used goods or not, your value is the same to me." He strode over and squatted beside her. "How did Betson come to bring you to me? He claimed he kidnapped you, but I find that difficult to believe, knowing your fiery temperament and headstrong ways."

Deidra squarely met his inquiring gaze. "I was already on my way to meet with you when Betson took me unawares and drugged me asleep. I'd hardly call that kidnapping."

D'Mondeville smiled. "Nay, neither would I. But, more importantly, why would you now come willingly to me? 'Tis a bit late, considering we're but days from taking Rothgarn."

"Mayhap, but I still felt it worth the risk." Deidra swallowed hard, then forged on. This was the moment she'd been planning for. If only her hands were free. She glanced down at herself. "This seems a poor way for us to talk, me on the ground, bound, and you squatting over me. Could we not speak in a more comfortable position?"

He grasped her by the arms and pulled her to her feet. "Aye, I suppose that could be accommodated. But I won't free you. You're a bit too unpredictable, and considering we'll soon have another visitor . . ."

"I came to offer myself to you, to wed you if you'll still have me," Deidra snapped. "I'd hardly call that the act of someone wishing to betray you!"

"And why should I accept your offer? I'll soon have you and your castle one way or another."

"Aye." She forced herself to remain calm despite the infuriatingly triumphant sneer curling D'Mondeville's lips. "But a willing, loyal bride who swears to support you will sit much better with my people. And ease your rule of Rothgarn and its lands considerably."

"Granted," he replied, eyeing her with a speculative gleam. "What are the terms of this 'willingness and loyalty'?"

"Spare my father's life, keep Hawkwind's secret and let him live, and go gently with Rothgarn. That's all I ask."

"And naught for yourself?" D'Mondeville looked genuinely surprised. "I find that hard to believe. You ran from me before. What is there to keep you with me this time, once I assent to your requests."

"My oath. My honor."

He chuckled. "Words, m'lady, given to a man who places little value upon them not only in himself, but in others."

"Mayhap, but they still mean something to me," Deidra proudly proclaimed. "I *will* abide by them. I can live my life no other way."

"Then you're as big a fool as your mercenary lover." D'Mondeville paused to stroke his chin thoughtfully. "But the appearance of a willing wife does have its value. I will accept your offer on one condition."

Deidra's mouth went dry. "And that is?"

"I've no intention of allowing you to slip away at a later date, shaming me as your mother did your father. You must agree to always appear the loving, obedient wife when we are in public together. And," he added with a hard glitter in his eyes, "willingly submit to confinement in your quarters under heavy guard the rest. You will come and go only at my desire, and will not complain to any because of it."

Her freedom, Deidra thought. He asked for what she valued most. He asked she bend her will to him in all things, surrender her independence to him. He asked for her life's blood.

'Twould eventually be her death. Yet what could she do but acquiesce? There was no way to kill him now. There was naught to do but give him what he demanded. And hope that something, someday, would set her free. She must never lose hope.

"What of Hawkwind?" Deidra forced herself to ask. "Will you let him go, with his secret still safe?"

"If he allows it. But if he fights me in this, I'll have no recourse but to have him killed. He'll be too great a threat otherwise."

"Will you let me first talk with him, attempt to convince him to accept your terms?"

"Aye." D'Mondeville gave a harsh laugh. "For what good 'twill do. Do you seriously think he'll accept them?"

Deidra blinked back a sudden swell of tears. Hawkwind's sense of pride and honor was fierce. There was only one possible way to save him—convince him she hated him and truly wished to be with Basil D'Mondeville. And that realization gave her the first flicker of hope.

"There is a way," she began, carefully choosing her words. "If I convince him I want to be with you, he might accept your terms. But I must appear to be here willingly. You'll have to free my hands."

He scowled. "Do you plan some treachery if I do, m'lady? Like a dagger hidden somewhere on your person?"

Deidra's mind whirled. If she kept the dagger from him, she risked losing it all. The trap was too well laid for Hawkwind and her puny dagger would mean naught against well-armed soldiers. She must show D'Mondeville good faith or all would be lost.

"I came armed, if that's what you're asking," Deidra admitted. "I'd have been a fool to attempt to reach you without some weapon at my disposal."

"And where is this weapon hidden?" he asked silkily.

"In my right boot."

"And where else?"

"Nowhere else. I swear it."

He moved close, a strange, heated look in his eyes. "How can I be certain your boot's the only hiding place? Mayhap I should examine you myself?"

Deidra swallowed back a surge of nausea. "If you wish. But I swear I speak true."

"Indeed?" D'Mondeville squatted, reached inside her right boot and found the dagger. Slowly he brought it up to her face. "A wicked little weapon, is it not? I wonder if you'd planned to use it on me? Did you, m'lady? Hmmm?"

His breath, hot, reeking of old ale, wafted over her as he leaned close, pressing the dagger against her cheek. Deidra choked back the bile that rose in her throat. "If you'd refused to bargain with me, aye."

"But I did bargain, didn't I? And you've agreed to my terms, haven't you?" He slid the dagger around her back, poising its tip against her bonds. "Haven't you, m'lady?"

"A-aye."

"And you swear to allow me to examine the rest of your body as I see fit for additional weapons?" he prodded, his voice gone husky and rough. "Even if I must strip you naked to do so?"

She clenched shut her eyes, dreading the liberties she'd give him with her reply. Dreading his filthy hands on her body, his leering gaze raking over her. But what did it really matter if he took her now, or later? She'd vowed to give herself to him. If this would seal their bargain and assure him of her sincerity, then so be it. There'd be naught left of her pride when he was done with her at any rate.

She nodded, awash in a sea of shame and misery. "Aye. Do what you must to prove my honest intent to you."

The dagger sliced through her bonds. Deidra's hands fell free. She paused for a moment to massage the circulation back into them, then let them drop back to her sides. Squaring her shoulders, Deidra glanced up at him. "I am ready."

He smiled thinly and slid the dagger beneath the fine leather belt cinching his narrow waist. " 'Tis past time that you were, my haughty little witch." His arm ensnared her waist and he jerked her hard up against him. "You've always been mine, you know. And I don't care if another has already had you. In the end, you'll be mine and mine alone."

With that, D'Mondeville tore open the front of Deidra's tunic with one powerful wrench of his hand, fully exposing her breasts. He slid his fingers inside the torn fabric, sweeping her body for any hidden weapons. Then, apparently satisfied there were none, his groping hand returned to her breasts.

"You are exquisite, you know," he breathed. "I'll take great pleasure in bedding you this night, once I've dealt with Hawkwind and sent him on his way." He cocked an inquiring brow. "You *will* lay with me, won't you? Let me finally take what was always mine to have?"

"A-aye." Deidra choked out the word on a gasp as D'Mondeville captured a firm, plump breast and squeezed it painfully. "I am yours to do with as you like. I keep my bargains."

"And so do I." He chuckled, taking her nipple between his fingers and compressing it as cruelly as he had her breast. "When the bargain suits me. And you suit me quite nicely. Quite nicely indeed."

His other hand snaked up her back, grasped her hair and jerked her head back. His mouth descended, ground down on Deidra's lips, taking her in a hot, brutal kiss. His tongue probed wetly for entrance and she opened to him on a strangled sob, knowing to refuse would only anger him to harsher means.

He thrust into her then, slobbering, frantic, as if he couldn't quite contain his excitement, grinding his hardened groin against her as he did. Deidra willed herself to submit, even as her mind fled to a safer, less sickening plane. Ah, she thought, if only she hadn't known the true extent of a loving, passionate union with a man both gentle but savagely skilled. Then, she'd have no knowledge of what could be. Then, mayhap D'Mondeville's rough handling wouldn't have seemed so disgusting, so shameful, so heartbreaking.

But there was no forgetting what had been and how inadequate and sordid the experience would be with the man she'd now promised herself to. And no turning back, either.

"Let her go, D'Mondeville," a deep voice, familiar and taut with rage, suddenly intruded. "Now, before I cut your vile heart out where you stand!"

With a startled cry, Basil D'Mondeville released Deidra and swung around, dragging her along with a firm grip on her arm. Hawkwind stood there, but a few feet away, Maud beside him. Deidra saw Hawkwind's gaze dip briefly to her exposed breasts, his mouth tighten, then glance back up to lock with D'Mondeville's in an ice rimmed stare.

"H-how did you get in here?" the blond man stammered. "There were guards. No one could have gotten past . . ." His voice faded as he eyed Maud. " 'Twas witchcraft, wasn't it? You used your witch to get in here."

"And if I did, what of it?" Hawkwind demanded. "You apparently were waiting for me. Who told you we were coming? Eh, D'Mondeville?"

"Does it really matter?" the man inquired smoothly, regaining the shreds of his composure at last.

"Aye. We are partners in this. I'd like to know my betrayer."

"As you wish," D'Mondeville replied. He indicated Maud. "Send your witch woman to fetch my guard. I'll have the man brought before us." He smiled slyly. "I think you'll find his identity of great interest."

Hawkwind motioned to Maud. "Call in his guard."

Long minutes ticked by in ponderous silence as they awaited the return of the guard. A few quick, whispered instructions from D'Mondeville and the man departed. Finally, John Betson was reluctantly led in, accompanied by four guards.

His glance skittered off Hawkwind's stunned gaze, then he shot D'Mondeville a furious look. "There was no need to reveal my presence to him. He will only—"

With an enraged cry, Hawkwind sprang for Betson. He

had his hands about his throat before anyone could react. Pandemonium reigned for the next several minutes, as the four guards, quickly joined by six more who rushed into the tent at D'Mondeville's command, fought to wrestle Hawkwind off the other man. Finally, a gasping, choking John Betson lay on the floor, a wildly struggling Hawkwind standing above him, captured in the grip of six winded guards.

"Get up off the floor," D'Mondeville ordered Betson with a disdainful flourish. "You're safe enough from him now."

The man climbed to his feet, shot Hawkwind a savage look, all the while clutching his now bruised and reddened throat. "No one is safe while he lives," he finally gasped. "Not I, nor you, nor King William. Kill him now, while you still have the chance!"

"I'll take your counsel to mind," D'Mondeville replied, "but for the present I have an interest in discovering the reason for Hawkwind's most untimely visit." He turned to where Hawkwind stood, his fierce struggles finally contained. D'Mondeville motioned to the sword hanging at his enemy's side. "Disarm him," he ordered a guard who stood nearby. "We don't need Hawkwind in close reach of his weapons."

Once his opponent was divested of his sword, scabbard, and dagger, D'Mondeville leveled a mildly amused gaze on him. "And why *are* you here this eve? If you planned on rescuing the Lady Deidra, your efforts are wasted. She came to me of her own accord."

Hawkwind's piercing green eyes riveted on Deidra. "Is that true? Did you come to him freely?"

Momentarily she quailed before the fierceness of his gaze, then forced herself to nod. "Aye, something had to be done to end this before 'twas too late. *You* certainly weren't willing to do aught."

"Little fool!" Hawkwind snarled. "And you think D'Mondeville is? You forget who hired whom to take Rothgarn!"

"He has already agreed to my terms."

His eyes narrowed. "And they are?"

Here it comes now, Deidra thought. "Basil will spare my father's life, be merciful to Rothgarn when he takes the castle, and," she paused to inhale a deep, steadying breath, "he will keep your secret and allow you to leave here in peace."

"How kind. How merciful," Hawkwind bit out. "And what did you give in return?"

The query was clipped and harsh, but still Deidra heard the undertone of rising apprehension. "I agreed to become Basil's wife, as 'twas meant to be from the beginning. 'Tis a fair bargain for sparing Rothgarn and you, wouldn't you say?"

"Nay, I wouldn't," Hawkwind rasped. "I don't need you sacrificing yourself on my account. 'Twill be a cold day in hell before I ever need you taking care of me!"

"Well, then do so!" Deidra cried, stung by his edge of bitter sarcasm. "Take care of yourself. Just do it as far away from me as possible. After all this is over, I never want to see or hear from you again!"

"Indeed," he ground out. " 'Twould suit me well, too, but you—and D'Mondeville—forget one thing."

"And that is?"

"I still have an agreement to fulfill."

" 'Twon't be necessary," Basil D'Mondeville calmly intruded. "Rothgarn will soon fall. You and your army have fulfilled your part of the agreement. I will pay you the rest in the return of your lands of Todmorden. But Deidra stays with me."

"And I say, nay." Hawkwind squarely met the other man's gaze. "I will have what we agreed upon, *and* you will leave without taking Rothgarn. I have come to a decision, however late, that I don't like your and William's plan to make an example of the Lord of Rothgarn. 'Tis over, D'Mondeville, the siege, your treachery, and all your plans."

The blond man smiled thinly. "You hardly seem in any position to threaten me." He gestured to the guards who stood nearby. "Bind him. Now!"

Before Hawkwind could break free, the additional guards were upon him. He fought them with all the force of a man gone wild, yet the overwhelming numbers were too great. They forced him to the ground in order to tie him, then wrenched him back to his knees when they were done.

"Good, good." D'Mondeville chuckled, viewing the scene of his enemy bound and kneeling before him with the utmost satisfaction. "I find the sight of your submission most gratifying. Mayhap, since you're now in the proper position for it, you'd like to beg for your life?"

"Bloody hell!" Hawkwind spat. "I'll never beg you for aught!" He flung back the hair that had cascaded into his face in his battle with the guards and glared up at his captor. "I suggest you free me immediately. My army won't take kindly to your treatment of me."

"They'll have little choice, once you're dead."

"My murder won't be tolerated. They'll wipe you and your small force out."

"But 'twon't be my fault," D'Mondeville replied, a look of injured innocence on his face. "The man, John Betson, will be the one to so foully kill you. 'Twas a trap, you know, his message to your witch woman, and you never even reached my camp. When the story gets out of how he feared your recognition of him as one of the men involved in the plot to murder the old king and knew he must eliminate you as the last one who could implicate him, there'll be naught else anyone can do. Sadly, the truth of your own innocence will have come too late."

"And what of Maud?" Hawkwind demanded tautly. "She, too, is a witness to your treachery."

"She must die as well." D'Mondeville shook his head in pity. "Surely you must realize that?"

"Nay!" Deidra made a move for her dagger, still sheathed

in D'Mondeville's belt. With a lithe motion, the blond man jerked her away, then twisted her hands behind her.

"You swore Hawkwind could go free if I agreed to wed you," she cried. "And I won't let you kill him, nor Maud, either!"

"And since when are you dictating the rules of this game?" He pulled Deidra to him, wrapping his arms about her snugly to imprison her against the hard wall of his body. "Be content with the fact I'm still willing to spare your father and Rothgarn. You knew as well as I Hawkwind might not acquiesce to our terms."

"Let me talk with him! You said I could." She struggled wildly in his grasp. "I can make him see. I know I can!"

"You had your chance. 'Twon't matter at any rate. He's far too proud and stubborn to bend to your or anyone's will."

"He'll listen to me." Deidra twisted around to peer pleadingly up at him. "Give me one more chance. I beg you!"

"Beg me?" D'Mondeville arched a brow in sudden speculation. "You'd beg for him? You'd get down on your knees before me and grovel for that mercenary's life?" He shoved her away from him. "Then do it. Show me how badly you want to save him. Beg me for it."

Deidra stood there, shocked, embarrassed, and totally speechless. Go down on her knees before Basil D'Mondeville? Debase herself before him and all his men? By the saints, the shame, the unfairness of it all! "You play some game with me," she forced herself to say. "You won't spare him even if I did kneel before you."

"But you won't know that for certain unless you do it, will you?" D'Mondeville motioned to a guard who stood nearby. "Withdraw your sword and place it against Hawkwind's neck. You others, hold him still."

As Deidra watched in horror, a big, burly, florid-faced soldier unsheathed his sword, the metal rasping sickeningly in the sudden stillness. Then he strode over and laid the long edge of the weapon across Hawkwind's neck. Bent down by the power of six men holding his body and one, his head, there was naught Hawkwind could do.

"Well, m'lady?" D'Mondeville prodded. "I'm waiting."

"Don't do it, Deidra!" Hawkwind cried suddenly, his voice taut and anguished. " 'Twon't save my life. Don't debase yourself for me!"

She stared down at him, at the powerful body so cruelly restrained, struck speechless by his heroic but futile attempt to spare her pride. The realization he had risked all to come for her, and that he had finally made the choice, however tardy, to stand beside her and her father, filled Deidra with a curious, soaring joy. At long last, Hawkwind had found the courage to trust, to commit, to love.

From whence the surety came she didn't know, but Deidra was filled with the strongest sense of his love for her—a love that hadn't died even in this past month of pain and betrayal. A love that had finally grown to fruition in his willingness to give his life for her and the cause she held dear. Rothgarn, her home.

Deidra sank to her knees. "Spare him, Basil," she pleaded, looking up at the blond man with the cruelly glittering eyes. "Let Hawkwind and Maud go and I'll do anything you ask. I swear it."

"Nay, Deidra!" Hawkwind roared, writhing and twisting in the guards' clasp. "Don't do it. Not for me!"

She turned to throw him a glance over her shoulder. "Then whom else should I do it for, if not for you? I love you. I couldn't live if I didn't try everything possible to save you. Everything . . . even if it means surrendering my pride." Deidra dragged in a shuddering breath. "A-aye, even my pride."

He lifted his head then, as far up as the sword's pressure against the back of his neck would allow. "And I love you, lass. And surrender *my* heart, my complete and utter trust to you."

A look of ineffable, aching, soul-deep affection lanced between them. Deidra smiled through the tears that sprang to her eyes and coursed down her face. Hawkwind's mouth twitched in wry, loving response. Then D'Mondeville's hand was in her hair, tugging her roughly, painfully, to her feet.

"Enough!" he snarled. "You plead so prettily, but 'tis all for naught. Hawkwind is far too dangerous an enemy to be allowed to roam free to fight another day." He signaled to the guard holding the sword. "Kill him. Run your sword through his back so 'twill look as if he was foully murdered."

"N-nay!" Deidra screamed. She clawed frantically at the hand ensnaring her hair, holding her a helpless prisoner. "Nay, Basil! I beg you, don't do it!"

"Kill him. Now!" D'Mondeville commanded. "Kill him!"

And, as the sword rose high overhead, time suddenly slowed. Deidra saw it all. The triumphant look, the eager anticipation in D'Mondeville's eyes. The hushed, expectant expressions of the guards. Hawkwind, forced down, his big, powerful body straining with his efforts to free himself, but to no avail. And Maud, whose glance met and locked with hers and spoke in words without sound.

"I demand the fulfillment of my promise," the healer said. "The one ye gave me that day of yer warrior's potion."

"What? What is it?" Deidra cried frantically.

"Go to Hawkwind. Fight for him," Maud said. "Use your powers once more, for good, for the man ye love. That is all I ask. That, and the final acceptance of yer true destiny."

The blood drained from Deidra's face. The room spun wildly about her. "N-nay," she stammered, the sudden surge of fear forcing the breath from her body. "I-I cannot. I *dare* not."

"'Tisn't evil I ask of ye, child." The healer gestured toward Hawkwind, held to the ground, the sword poised above him. "I gave ye my word that day, and I give it now. Will ye let him die then, because ye're too afraid to face yer magic?"

Deidra gazed down at the man who now depended on

her for his very life. His long brown hair hung in his eyes, shielding his strong, handsome face. She recalled how surprisingly soft and silky his hair had been, those times she had run her fingers through it, stroked it tenderly back from his eyes. And his big body, trembling now with his futile efforts to break free of the guards. She remembered the feel of his smooth, muscle-hardened skin, of the potent power of his manly form, yet how careful he had always been with her, even in the throes of their most wildly passionate lovemaking. Even then, he had never forgotten . . .

A bittersweet realization filled her. He was a good, honorable man. A man who, despite all the terrible things that had been done to him, still found the courage to fight on, to face his own demons and personal fears and still be willing to change for the better. Indeed, in turning against D'Mondeville and for Rothgarn, Hawkwind had taken the second step in his healing. The first had been in daring to love her—and give her his trust.

Her father's words, spoken but a few weeks ago, filtered back into Deidra's mind. *Your powers . . . must be faced sooner or later. . . . You cannot walk that tightrope between avoidance and acceptance for too long. No one can . . .*

As painful as they'd been to hear, he spoke true. She had voiced the same thoughts to Hawkwind that night they'd secretly met in the chapel, when she'd urged, nay, taunted him for his reluctance to choose a side or make a commitment. He, too, had had legitimate reasons for his fears, but she'd spared him no sympathy or consideration.

Her words had been true when spoken that night. Words, Deidra now realized with a piercing clarity, that applied to her as well. As terrified as she was of her powers, they *were* her destiny. She couldn't avoid them or their presence within her the rest of her life. Like her mother, she must face them and find some way to incorporate her magic into the essence that was uniquely her.

And she must use them to fight for what mattered most in life.

Though her battle was of a different kind, Deidra realized in a rush of insight so clear, so poignant it took her breath away, she could do no less. Not, and still be worthy of a man like Hawkwind.

With a shuddering sigh, Deidra loosed the bonds she'd woven about her powers, bonds she'd never thought to free again. Her spirit swelled, grew within her. Then, like her falcon as it leaped into the air to gain the heavens, she felt her spirit soar. With a fierce joy, Deidra's glance lifted from the man she loved to lock with Maud's.

"So be it, then," she whispered. " 'Tis past time to face what is mine. Face it and bind it to me—or let it die as I die."

"Aye, child." The healer smiled, a look of tender, loving encouragement gleaming in her soft gray eyes. " 'Tis past time. For ye and for Hawkwind."

Deidra turned then, back to the scene of struggling men and upraised sword, the lamplight glinting dully off its lethally sharp blade. And, as she did, she felt the fire grow, flame hot and bright, within her.

Chapter 21

The room took on an eerie red glow. A wind rose from within the tent, billowing around Deidra, lifting her hair about her in fiery tongues of flame. A guard glanced up, startled by the sudden surge of air, and gave a strangled cry.

As one, D'Mondeville and the men holding Hawkwind followed the guard's terror-stricken gaze. Deidra smiled grimly, exultantly back at them, the power, the magic, swelling within her. "Let Hawkwind go. Now!"

For a tension laden instant Basil D'Mondeville stared down at her, stunned speechless, as if seeing her for the first time. "You," he forced the words past a constricted throat. "You've the same foul powers as your mother. Witch. Sorceress. Devil's whore!"

"Aye, Basil," Deidra silkily agreed. "Still wish to wed me now, do you?"

He released her, shuddering in revulsion. "N-nay! Never!" He hesitated a moment more, then swung to the guard who stood ready to execute Hawkwind. "Kill him. Now, before the witch interferes!"

The huge blade held in the man's two hands lifted high, then plunged downward. Deidra whirled around, fire shooting from her hands straight toward the man fool enough to dare attempt Hawkwind's murder. The flame crackled through the air, struck the guard, then exploded in a burst of fire and light.

The man screamed in agony, flung backward by the force of Deidra's power. He fell, the sword still clenched in his hands, striking the ground hard, then lay there, unmoving. Deidra's gaze swung to the other guards. "Release him, I say, or suffer the same fate."

In a frantic scramble the men leaped off Hawkwind, scooted away, then hurriedly climbed to their feet. Wide-eyed and trembling, they shot D'Mondeville anxious, questioning glances. He said naught, only stood there, glaring furiously at Deidra.

" 'Twill do you no good," he snarled. "I'll find some way yet to thwart you. And William won't be denied. You've only begun to taste his anger."

"I care not for your or William's threats," Deidra said, helping Hawkwind to his feet. Then, with a tiny, searing blast of fire from one finger, she cut through his bonds.

He shot her a wry glance as he pulled the singed ropes from his wrists. "You seem to be gaining a bit of control over your powers. Amazing what the proper motivation will do for gaining some mastery, wouldn't you say?"

She arched a slender brow. "And you think you're that motivation, do you?"

"One would presume so, if what you said was true."

"And that was?"

"That you love me."

A warm flush crept up Deidra's neck and face. "Aye, I suppose I did say that." Unwilling to discuss that particular topic further, she gestured to D'Mondeville. "What shall we do with him? We're in danger the longer we tarry here."

"Still wish to wed him?"

She shot him an enraged look. "Of course not! You were the one who forced me into such an untenable position in the first place."

A look of pained regret passed across Hawkwind's face, then was gone. "Well, 'tis best we talk of that later. In the meanwhile, you spoke true. We're in the middle of D'Mondeville's camp and surrounded by his men. 'Twould be wise to get back to mine posthaste."

"And what of our host?" Deidra prodded, noting, as her glance swung around to the blond man, that Maud had disappeared. She paused, thinking that most strange, then forced her attention back to the matter at hand. "Mayhap he'd serve well as a hostage to get us safely out of here?"

Hawkwind grinned and took a step toward D'Mondeville. "A wise plan."

" 'Twon't happen!" D'Mondeville snarled. He leaped back, withdrew his sword, and widened his stance. "Come and get me, mercenary, if you dare!"

An impatient anger filled Deidra and she lifted her hand toward him. Her wrist was immediately clasped by strong brown fingers.

"Nay," Hawkwind said. "He is mine . . . one way or another." With that, he slipped back to where the guard who had taken his weapons stood. He quickly divested the man of them and rearmed himself. "Care for a fight, D'Mondeville, man-to-man?" he asked, as he finally slid the dagger beneath his belt.

Faced with a potentially fatal sword battle against a man who was an experienced warrior, D'Mondeville hesitated. With his men standing there, quite evidently cowed by the witch, he knew he'd face Hawkwind alone. There had to be some way to thwart them both. He was not a man without guile, nor slow to seize any opportunity presented him. But first, he must lull them into a false sense of victory.

The sword dropped from his hand. "You know the outcome of any battle between us. I may as well fight you weaponless, for all the good 'twould do me."

"A wise decision." Hawkwind sheathed his sword, then motioned him over. Grasping him by the arm, he pulled the blond man close. "This is the plan, D'Mondeville, and I expect you to follow it implicitly." Hawkwind withdrew his dagger from his belt and pressed it to the other man's side, out of sight between their bodies. "We'll attempt to stroll across camp in a leisurely manner, as if we were merely surveying our troops. If you make one untoward move or say the wrong thing, I'll finish you off. And be assured," he added with a menacing growl, "I can easily kill you before any of your men can reach you."

To add emphasis to his words, Hawkwind pressed the dagger tip until it pricked D'Mondeville in the ribs. The man gave a jerk.

"I get your point," he whispered. D'Mondeville glanced over at his guards. "Stay here and don't leave or call out to anyone. Is that understood?"

The men nodded, eyeing him uncertainly.

"Come on then," Hawkwind muttered, shoving him forward. "And, Deidra, stay close. Betson is probably still in the camp and if he sees us, all will be lost."

She smiled grimly. "Indeed? Then D'Mondeville's army mayhap needs a taste of my powers."

He grinned. "Mayhap, but I'd prefer to save those as a last resort." He gestured toward the tent entrance with his dagger. "Open the flap, if you will. I'd prefer to keep both hands occupied with D'Mondeville."

With a few quick strides, Deidra reached the tent flap and lifted it high, then stepped aside to allow Hawkwind and D'Mondeville to pass. She shot one last, quelling look at the guards still standing inside, then slipped through and out.

Small groups of soldiers stood about, talking, laughing, but the aura of almost palpable tension arcing between all of them was evident. They were still on guard for any sign of unusual activity or call from their leader. Deidra knew 'twould take only the smallest incident to alert them and set them on the attack. She inhaled a steadying breath and strode on, keeping as close to Hawkwind and his hostage as she dared.

The night bore down on her, ripe with the scent of unwashed bodies, smoldering campfires, horse sweat, and refuse carelessly discarded. It turned her stomach to see the filth and disorder permitted in D'Mondeville's camp, after knowing the strict adherence to sanitation and orderliness of Hawkwind's army. 'Twas fortunate disease hadn't spread through the entire force like wildfire.

Her glance swung surreptitiously to and fro as they marched through camp. There were a few, narrow-eyed looks as they passed, but none challenged them. Up ahead, Deidra could see the campfires of Hawkwind's army flickering brightly. A few minutes more, she thought, and they'd be safely—

With a snarl that was more animal than human, a form leaped from the darkness of a nearby tent. Before Deidra could react, a man grabbed her and wrenched her to him. A dagger pricked Deidra's throat. She froze, knowing there was naught else she could do.

Hawkwind wheeled about, dragging D'Mondeville with him. Fury flashed in his eyes, but he maintained his hold on his hostage, the dagger pressed to his side. "Let her go, Betson," he rasped. "'Tis a stalemate, and you know it."

"Is it now?" John Betson demanded harshly. "I think not. I have something of great value to ye, and I value D'Mondeville's life little. 'Tis over for ye, unless ye wish to see yer whore die." To emphasize his point, Betson angled the razor sharp blade of his dagger against Deidra's throat and sliced a shallow line down the side of it.

A thin river of blood welled against the ivory skin, then trickled down her exposed neck and upper chest. Hawkwind's fury exploded within him and only the look of anger and sudden resolve in Deidra's eyes halted him from leaping once again for Betson. She'd kill herself for sure if she tried to interfere between them—and he knew she would.

Hawkwind shot her a fierce visual command not to try anything, even as he realized what he must do. 'Twas her life at stake. Betson would surely kill her. 'Twas more than evident from the grim, determined intent gleaming in his eyes.

The man knew his fate was sealed if his old enemy was allowed to live. 'Twas his life or Hawkwind's. But would Betson indeed spare Deidra if he released D'Mondeville?

There was no choice, Hawkwind thought with a sudden swell of frustration. He had to surrender. He couldn't risk her.

He cast one last, longing glance to his own camp. If only they'd had a few minutes more, they'd have been within shouting distance.

Hawkwind let the dagger fall and stepped back from D'Mondeville. "Let her go, Betson. You have me. 'Tis enough."

The man gave a shrill, triumphant laugh. "Is it now? And I say 'twon't be enough until I see you dead, Todmorden!" He shoved Deidra to one of the many soldiers who hurried up, finally alerted that all was not as it had originally seemed. He made a move toward Hawkwind, dagger poised to strike, when D'Mondeville's panic-stricken cry halted him.

"Don't!" he screamed, even as he saw the fire aura engulf Deidra once more. "Don't let her go—"

Betson turned, his mouth agape, to see the flames shoot from her hands, arc toward him, then encompass him in a seething ball of heat. He screeched in terror, dropped his dagger, and clawed at his face and hair.

"Don't, Deidra!" Hawkwind shouted over the sudden roar of flame and wind. "Don't kill him! He's my only hope to prove my innocence."

She started, blinked in confusion, then recognition flared. Her hands lifted, stirring the fire aura to enlarge and surround both Hawkwind and Betson. With a fierce cry, D'Mondeville's soldiers attacked. Attacked and were driven back by the intense heat and crackling flames. Again and again they tried, and were driven back.

Then Hawkwind stepped away from them, out of the

protective aura, and advanced on D'Mondeville. The man paled, staggered backward, before noting his opponent was unarmed. He withdrew his sword, a broad smile of triumph on his face. "Die then, fool. You should have stayed where you'd be safe, under your whore's protection. Or mayhap," he added with a sneer, "you'd like to run back to her now, while you still have the chance?"

"She'll stay out of it, won't you, Deidra?" Hawkwind said, tossing the terse query to her over his shoulder.

"Let me at least arm you," she protested. " 'Tisn't a fair fight—"

" 'Tis more than fair," Hawkwind cut her off. "The day has yet to dawn I can't handle a man like D'Mondeville, armed or unarmed. Stay out of this, I'm telling you!"

She backed away then, drawing her fire aura tightly around her and Betson, stung by Hawkwind's harsh demand though she knew his pride could bear no less. Even as she did, she noted a tumult behind her and turned. Hawkwind's camp was alive with activity, men arming themselves and moving toward them. She could make out Renard and Alena at the force's head and behind them Maud and Bardrick.

Maud, Deidra realized, had left to summon Hawkwind's army. If only they could reach them in time. If D'Mondeville fell to Hawkwind, D'Mondeville's army would be on him in an instant, cutting him down before she could stir her powers to intervene. Powers she felt already beginning to wane.

Though Deidra had finally grasped the delicate nuances of controlling and containing her fire powers, they were not a limitless source of magic. Mayhap in time, with further training, she could increase their duration and intensity, but not this night. She was nearly at the end of her strength. If only she could hold on until Hawkwind's army arrived. 'Twas only her fearsome fire aura now that kept D'Mondeville's army at bay and Hawkwind alive.

D'Mondeville lunged suddenly, his sword thrusting

toward Hawkwind. If Hawkwind hadn't been swifter, the weapon would have skewered him through the chest. But he had read the intent in the other man's eyes an instant before he struck, and lunged aside. D'Mondeville, however, was an agile man for all his seemingly indolent way of life and possessed some prowess with the sword.

He spun on his heel and slashed with a surprising back-handed skill, leaving a gash across Hawkwind's upper arm. Hawkwind staggered backward, nearly lost his balance, then righted himself. Once again D'Mondeville thrust.

This time, however, his opponent was ready. As the sword pierced empty air, Hawkwind ducked low and tack-led him. With a cry of rage, D'Mondeville plummeted to the ground, Hawkwind atop him. Both grappled wildly for the sword, rolling and twisting about in the dirt.

Deidra felt her powers fade, the heat subside. She heard a cry, as if from a distance, of an army nearing, then the clash of weapons as one force turned and met that of an-other. The air grew thick, heavy, but she couldn't discern if 'twas the press of bodies fighting around her or her strength draining.

Her knees buckled. Bright lights whirled before her eyes. Her gaze turned once more to the scene of Hawkwind and D'Mondeville battling on the ground, a battle swiftly turn-ing to Hawkwind's favor.

D'Mondeville make a desperate move with his sword. Hawkwind dodged then grabbed for the hilt. They slammed together as both fought for possession of the weapon. Powerful bodies strained and twisted, breaths coming ragged and rasping.

Then, in a swift, sly movement, D'Mondeville released one hand to grope at his side. Something flashed in the torchlight—a dagger—gripped in his fist. A dagger that plunged downward, straight toward Hawkwind's heart.

Deidra opened her mouth to scream warning, but no sound emerged. A thick, gray mist swirled about her, smothering her cry, shutting out everything. She felt herself falling, saw a void open up beneath her feet. And then there was blackness and deep, heavy silence.

"Deidra? Deidra, child? Wake up."

From a distance, Deidra heard Maud's soft, soothing voice. She moaned, clawing her way up from the darkness. Something cool, wet, was pressed to her face. Her hand groped for it and found a damp cloth. It felt good.

Deidra moaned again, her lids flickering briefly upward, then closing once more. 'Twas enough, however, to reveal a glimpse of Maud bending over her, and Bardrick close behind. Both wore strained, worried expressions.

But she was fine, she thought in a muddled daze. She was alive. The terrible killing potential of her powers had been vanquished. They would never be a threat to her again. Maud and Bardrick must be upset over something else. But why—and over what?

Hawkwind.

The scene of D'Mondeville's dagger, slicing downward toward Hawkwind's chest, flashed through her mind. Hawkwind. Had D'Mondeville killed Hawkwind?

The sudden surge of terror sent a quickened rush of blood through her veins. It cleared the lingering cobwebs in her mind. With a fierce movement, Deidra levered to one elbow, blinked furiously, and locked gazes with Maud.

"H-Hawkwind. Is he all right?"

The healer smiled. "Mayhap ye should see for yerself." She shot a glance over her shoulder at Bardrick. "Help her, will ye, ye old wolfhound? Deidra wants to see Hawk-wind."

"Does she now?" He moved around to Deidra's side and gathered her up into his arms. "Well, lass, I suppose that could be seen to."

With a surge of whipcord lean muscles, Bardrick rose. Deidra grabbed for his neck and entwined her hands about it, searching for some hint of an answer to her question. He stared back, his dark eyes kind but devoid of any information. She didn't know what to make of it and was suddenly afraid to ask more.

His long strides carried her out of Maud's hospital tent and across camp—a camp she recognized to be Hawkwind's. Relief flooded Deidra. At least the battle must have gone in Hawkwind's army's favor. At least they were safe.

But what of Hawkwind? Even the contemplation of his demise was too much to deal with. If he were dead, she didn't know what she'd do, how she'd go on. He had told her he loved her, trusted her, and would help Rothgarn. To lose him now would tear her heart out. Now, when he'd finally opened himself to her and to the hope for a new and better life.

Bardrick halted at Hawkwind's tent. She could make out the hawk standard fluttering in the late morning breeze. 'Twas good to see it again, so close, so much like old times. Deidra glanced around. The camp was alive with activity, men striding about, swords being sharpened, horses readied. She frowned. What was amiss? If D'Mondeville was defeated, who were they preparing to go to battle against?

She shot a glance over her shoulder. Rothgarn still stood, the gate closed, the parapets massed with soldiers. Surely the two sides weren't still at war? But if Hawkwind were dead, no one would know of his intent to join with her father. Naught may have changed.

"Bardrick, what is going on?" Deidra forced herself to ask. "Where is the army—?"

"Hush, lass," he cut her off as he drew up before Hawkwind's tent. "One thing at a time." He flung back the flap and stepped inside.

For a moment, Deidra couldn't see well in the sudden dimness after the brightness of outside. Then her vision cleared. Across the tent stood two men. One was Renard, the other . . .

Deidra's heart leaped in her chest. "H-Hawkwind?"

At the sound of his name, Hawkwind turned. For a long, searing moment, his glance met and locked with Deidra's.

Then he smiled, a beautiful, open, almost boyish expression that filled her with a wild surge of joy. He was alive!

She released her hold on Bardrick's neck and squirmed in his clasp. "Put me down. Please. Now."

He shot her a doubtful look, then carefully lowered her to her feet. A brief flare of dizziness, a few deep breaths to steady herself, and Deidra was running across the tent to Hawkwind.

Arms wide and with a grin as big as the heartfelt look in his eyes, he awaited her. She flung herself at him, her hands sliding up his big body to entwine about his neck. And there Deidra stood for long, emotion-laden seconds, clasping him to her as if she doubted the reality of what her body and eyes told her was true.

She inhaled his bracing scent of musky male tinged with the heady tang of campfires. She pressed close to his warmth, reveling in the feel of strong muscles and masculine bulk. Against her ear thudded the slow, reassuring beat of his heart. Deidra had never known such joy, nor soul-deep peace. All within the protective, possessive clasp of his arms.

In that moment of exultation and relief, she knew she could never be whole without this man. Knew that her life would always lack a certain completeness and fulfillment if she didn't spend it with Hawkwind. But knew, as well, 'twas very possible they might never be able to spend it together.

Her destiny had always lain in her magic and the use of it for the good of all. Not in running from her responsibilities to seek out a mercenary's life—a life she had never truly been suited for.

Though she'd gladly share her life with Hawkwind no matter where it called them, she wasn't so certain 'twas what he desired. He had always wanted to possess her, to make her his, but all Deidra's attempts at winning some semblance of freedom and accomplishment as her own person had been blocked by his well-meant but most definitely masculine sense of superiority.

She knew he loved her; she just had no reason to believe his outlook on her woman's role had changed. And she had to be more to him than just his lover. Her powers could not be squandered, no matter how much she loved him.

Deidra inhaled a fortifying breath and pressed back. Though she'd meant the action to put some distance between them, Hawkwind refused to release her. Deidra had to content herself with leaning against the iron clasp of his arms.

She managed a wan little smile. "You're safe. I was so afraid . . ." Soft lips pressed together in an effort to still the sudden tremor in her voice. "I saw D'Mondeville lift his dagger to stab you. I-I think I tried to warn you, but then 'twas too late and I fainted."

"He didn't succeed." Hawkwind's voice turned hard at the memory of the battle. "I killed him."

"Oh." Her eyes lowered.

He captured her chin in the callused grip of his palm and gently lifted her gaze back to his. "Is that sorrow I hear for him? Do you suddenly regret the loss of your betrothed?"

Beneath the husky timbre of his voice, Deidra thought she heard a tinge of jealousy and uncertainty. Though she shouldn't let it, the realization gladdened her, this rare glimpse into his more vulnerable self. A vulnerability he now endured because of her.

She smiled sadly. "Nay. I'll never regret the loss of Basil D'Mondeville as my betrothed. But I do mourn the loss of life, even a life as cruel and self-serving as was his."

His thumb stroked the line of her jaw. Amusement tugged at the corner of his firm, sensual mouth. "Those are definitely not the sentiments of a warrior, lass. But then, I always knew you weren't the stuff of sword and battle, for *all* your swordswoman's skills," he added quickly as he noted the flash of anger that sprang to her eyes. "You have other talents, however, some of which I don't care ever to share with anyone else."

"Aye, that I do," Deidra admitted, thinking of those he hinted at and others. 'Twas the others that solidified her resolve. She glanced over at Renard. As if reading her unspoken request, he nodded and silently exited the tent.

Deidra watched him go, then turned back to Hawkwind, suddenly loathe to confront him with the painful decision she'd made. A change of subject was definitely on the agenda, at least for a time more. "And John Betson? What happened to him? I overheard him admitting to D'Mondeville he knew of your secret identity for years, and that he was the one who spied on you when you later returned to Todmorden to confront your brothers. I suspect he may also have been the man who killed your brother."

"Aye, I guessed at his involvement as soon as I again saw him." A bleak, despairing look settled over Hawkwind's features. "But that realization has come too late to aid me. Betson disappeared in the fighting. And with him went my last hope of a witness to corroborate my story and innocence."

"We'll find some other way," Deidra murmured, an angry frustration filling her. "Somehow, someway, we'll clear your name." She paused, as another thought struck her. "How goes it with D'Mondeville's forces? I saw your men girding themselves as if for battle."

"D'Mondeville's men quickly surrendered, once their leader was dead. They've lost their will to fight and pose no further threat to us. 'Tis your father's forces we prepare to go against."

Confusion darkened her eyes. "But you said you would join him against William. Have you so quickly regretted that decision?"

Hawkwind's mouth twisted in exasperation. "How little faith you have in me. I meant what I said, as I always do. But my attempts so far to convince your father have fallen on deaf ears. He refuses to accept my offer of alliance." He arched a dark brow, an accusatory light gleaming in his eyes. "Seems someone has told him of my less than savory past."

A warm flush stole into Deidra's cheeks. "Oh, aye, that. I was desperate to do something after my attempt to convince you that night in the chapel failed. I thought if I could win my father over, and he made the first overtures to you, you might yet be swayed to our side. So I told him of your true identity and what had really happened."

"And he obviously was unimpressed."

"Aye," Deidra said. "He was as singularly pigheaded and proud as you. 'Twas both of your stubborn refusals to bend or trust that drove me to D'Mondeville. I was that desperate."

Hawkwind sighed. "I am sorry for that, lass. I *was* pigheaded and proud. But I was also right about others refusing to believe my tale or accept me. Wasn't I?"

"We could go to my father, you and I," she offered, a sudden surge of hope swelling in her breast. "Once he knew the truth of what happened last night, I know he'd reconsider. And he'd never turn you over to William now that . . ." Her voice faded, recalling her father's accusations that Hawkwind had always been in league with the traitorous king. Nay, her father would think there was no point in giving Hawkwind back to his ally. But he'd also not trust Hawkwind for that same reason.

Frustration filled her. Was there no way out of this morass of doubts and suspicions that so unfairly judged and condemned Hawkwind again and again? Despite all his efforts to the contrary, would he carry the mark of traitor with him to his dying day?

Her frustrated compassion for him hardened into a fierce resolve, as a plan, albeit painful, took form in her mind. No matter what it took, or how long, she would fight to clear his name and someday she *would* succeed. She owed him that much, for all he had given her.

"Aye, lass?" Hawkwind prodded, reading the reality in

her eyes before she'd even admitted it to herself. "And why wouldn't your father turn me over to William? Mayhap because he suspects 'twould be a wasted effort? Because he knows William wouldn't harm a man who aided in his climb to the throne?"

She met his knowing gaze with a determined one of her own. "It doesn't matter. In time I'll find a way to convince him otherwise."

He frowned. "You speak as if you intend to return to Rothgarn."

The sudden look of pained wariness that flared in his eyes was more than she could bear. Deidra pushed back, breaking at last the firm hold of his arms. She took a few steps away, needing the distance to fortify herself. Then, squaring her shoulders, she met his gaze.

"Aye. I can best aid your cause, and that of the other rebel lords, by returning to my father."

"And what of us?" he demanded hoarsely. "Where does that leave us?"

"You said yourself I've never been cut out for a mercenary's life."

"Mayhap not as a warrior, but I think you could adapt nicely to being my wife." In a quick movement, Hawkwind grasped Deidra by the arm and pulled her back to him. His other arm snaked around her, imprisoning her against the hard length of his body. "Or is that no longer sufficient for you?"

Pain snared Hawkwind's heart in an iron clasp, squeezing tightly with each suddenly constricted breath he took. By the Mother, why now, when he had bared his soul to her, when he had opened himself to her in the most vulnerable of ways, did she do this to him? He loved her, needed her, and the thought of losing her was enough to make him roar out his agonized frustration.

But the fragile shreds of his once well-guarded and cherished pride remained. And that pride would never permit him to grovel or beg. Not even for Deidra. He had offered her everything of value he possessed—his love, his commitment, his trust. Though he might yet someday regain Todmorden and his rightful inheritance, Hawkwind finally saw them for the fleeting, superficial trappings they were. If Deidra couldn't accept him as he now was, stripped of lands and standing, all but an outlaw with the truth of his past rapidly becoming common knowledge, then he had naught more to offer or bargain with.

"Well, Deidra?" he prodded ruthlessly, determined to have it finally settled between them no matter the anguish it caused. "What is it to be for us?"

His deep pain and rising despair washed over her in a smothering flood of emotion. More than anything she'd ever wanted, Deidra wanted to comfort him, to pull his head to her breast and soothe that wary, hurting look from his eyes. 'Twas so unfair. No matter how hard he tried, vindication seemed always to elude him. Vindication . . . and the chance for happiness.

He deserved better. He was a fine, brave, honorable man. He deserved more from everyone than he had ever received. Everyone . . . including her.

In a breath-grabbing rush, Deidra finally realized where the fulfillment of her life and powers truly lay. There was naught more she could do for Hawkwind than stand by him and offer the final gift she had always been so afraid to give. Therein had always laid her real worth as a woman, a person—and of her powers. With Hawkwind, for his happiness . . .

"What is it to be?" she whispered, her fists clenched at her sides in an effort to contain her urge to touch him. "I will go with you, wherever that may lead. I will be your woman, your wife, for the rest of our days, even if your destiny calls you back to a mercenary's life, or worse."

At her words, the bleak, tormented look in Hawkwind's eyes faded. A wondering expression filled them. "You would do that? Renounce Rothgarn, your freedom to do whatever you wished, and follow me?"

"Aye."

He stared down at her for a long moment, then dragged in a shuddering breath. "You risk much in your offer."

" 'Tis worth the risk." Deidra smiled. "I love you."

"And I love you," he choked out the words, pulling her head to lie upon the broad, strong expanse of his chest. With an infinitely tender touch, he stroked her fiery, tumbled mass of hair. " 'Tis enough, is it not, to brave the uncertainties of a cruel and unfeeling world together?"

"Aye, my love," she breathed, her voice muffled by the tears that clogged it. " 'Tis the only hope for any of us." A sudden thought struck her and she lifted her head to gaze up at him. The look gleaming in his eyes nearly took her breath away.

"There is more," Deidra hesitantly began. "Something you should know before you make your final decision to commit to me."

"And that is?" he softly prodded, a beautiful smile upon his lips. "As if there were aught that could turn me from you."

"Children."

His brow furrowed in puzzlement. "Children? What has that to do with us?"

"How do you feel about children?" She rushed on before she lost her nerve. "About becoming a father?"

Hawkwind's confused expression deepened as his gaze swept over her. Then, realization dawned. "Why do you ask, lass? Are you—"

"With child?" Deidra quickly finished for him. "Aye, Hawkwind, I am. I carry our babe."

"Do you now?" For the longest moment he studied her, his face an inscrutable mask. "And how do *you* feel about it? A babe would tie you to a woman's role, constrain your freedom even worse than I could ever hope to."

"I would have borne our babe no matter what you decided. And our daughter would have soon run as free as her mother, at any rate. It could be no other way for women of our sort."

"Women of your sort, eh?" Hawkwind's mouth curled in amusement. "And who's to say you wouldn't bear a son?"

She laughed, her voice gay and tinkling with a woman's deep, abiding joy. "Who, indeed?" she replied, shooting him a knowing look. "But, one way or another, will you want it?"

His mouth widened into a huge grin. "Aye, one way or another, I would. If the mother comes in the bargain."

"Oh, she does, you can be sure," Deidra said with an impish little smile and patted her still flat belly. "At least for the next eight or so months."

"And after that?"

"After that, we'll just have to see. But be forewarned. I'm a very loyal sort of person."

"As am I, my beauteous little witch," Hawkwind growled, swinging her up into his arms. "In fact I can be quite pig-headed, I've been told, when I want my way."

"Indeed?" Deidra murmured from the solid, comforting haven of his chest.

"Indeed," Hawkwind growled, "and I intend on proving it to you most thoroughly and intimately."

With that final word on the subject, he carried Deidra to his bed. Yet even as Hawkwind lowered himself to lie beside her, a voice called from just outside the entrance to his tent. 'Twas Renard.

Groaning in frustration, Hawkwind rolled off the bed and rose to his feet. "Enter," he snarled.

Renard stuck in his head. "Do I have your lady's leave to reenter?"

"*Her* leave?" His leader scowled. "And since when—"

"She's the one who wished me gone the first time," his captain interrupted with a roguish grin.

"Fine," Hawkwind muttered. He shot Deidra a glance over his shoulder. "He has your leave, doesn't he, lass?"

"Aye," she smilingly replied from the bed. "But only for a

few minutes. We have important business of our own to attend to."

Renard stepped inside. " 'Twon't take even that long. First, a messenger has just arrived from Rothgarn Castle. Seems the Lord of Rothgarn has reconsidered your offer and now desires a truce." He grinned. "*And* the opportunity to speak with you."

Deidra shot Hawkwind a joyous look. "My father. Mayhap he has changed his mind and—"

"Aye, mayhap," Hawkwind smilingly silenced her. He glanced up at Renard. "Send word we accept his offer of truce and will meet with him in an hour's time." He paused expectantly. "Was there more?"

"Aye," his captain replied. "A man Maud has identified as one John Betson was caught skulking from camp last night. We now hold him in custody. She said you'd want to know."

A slow grin spread across Hawkwind's face as the full implications of Renard's message struck him. "Indeed, I definitely wanted to know. Thank Maud for me, and keep Betson under *very* close guard. He holds the key to my future."

His captain nodded. "Aye, 'twill be done as you command." He hesitated. "Is there aught else I can do for you?"

"Nay."

"Then my time is up," he shot Deidra an inquiring glance, "isn't it?"

"Aye," she purred throatily from the bed. "Thank you, Renard."

He graced her with a gallant bow, then turned on his heel and departed.

Hawkwind frowned in puzzlement. "What was that all about?"

"Naught, my love." She patted the spot beside her. "You were about to prove something to me, were you not? Before we took John Betson with us to see my father?"

"Aye," he replied, striding back to join her, a wondering

expression on his handsome face. A few feet from the bed, Hawkwind suddenly halted, threw back his head and gave a huge shout of joy. Then he flung himself on Deidra and proceeded to most thoroughly and intimately make good his threat.

Epilogue

" 'Tis past time we were going," Alena said, casting an imploring glance over at her fellow war captain. "Isn't that so, Renard?"

Renard jerked his attention from the tiny babe Deidra cradled in her arms and back to Alena. "What? Uh, aye, so 'tis." He managed a crooked smile of apology to the man who had led them through many a successful battle campaign, a man, who, despite the disparity in standing that had only widened with the reinstatement of his good name and titular lands, he had always looked upon as friend. " 'Tis early yet, but you know Alena. Always one for a full day's travel."

"Aye." Hawkwind chuckled. "Well do I know Alena." His expression sobered. "Are you two certain this is what you want? There is much to be said for a safe, stable life. And much work still to be done before the land will ever return to its former bounty. You are both still needed—and wanted—here."

Renard managed a lopsided grin. "Aye, I know, but 'tisn't the sort of life either I or Alena crave. You have Todmorden back, a wife and child to care for, and a castle and lands to challenge you. You were always meant for this sort of life, were raised to it. Alena and I were raised for another."

Hawkwind nodded his understanding. "So, whose cause will you fight for next?"

"Naught as ambitious as yours have always been. With half the army willing to stay behind and form your new garrison, 'twill take time to rebuild our size and strength." Renard shrugged. "The Abbot of Langshire Abbey has a small dispute going with some knight who owns the surrounding farmlands. He hopes our presence will 'encourage' the man to listen to reason."

"A fitting calling for you, Renard," Deidra teased, tenderly smoothing the red curls from her daughter's forehead and glancing up at him. "Have a care, though, or the abbot will soon have you talked into taking holy orders and settling down at the abbey."

Alena gave a small, disparaging snort. "And risk a full-fledged mutiny by all the local maidens? I hardly think so. For all his advanced years, Renard is still as hot-blooded as a youth. He'll not waste his considerable talents in monkish pursuits."

"Advanced years!" her compatriot cried in mock outrage. "For all my gray hairs, I'm but twelve years older than you. Nearly the same age difference as between Hawkwin—er, I mean Lord Nicholas—and the Lady Deidra. But you are correct in saying I'm still hot-blooded enough to keep many a lass content and wanting more. And far too independent ever to tie myself to a religious life."

"Or a woman," Alena added with a sly grin.

"Aye," he agreed, "unless of course *you* change your mind. I vowed long ago not to lose my heart to any woman who couldn't hold her own against me in battle."

Alena flushed crimson. "Stop it," she muttered. "We're partners and that's the extent of it."

Renard clutched at his chest and groaned melodramatically. "Ah, sweet, gentle lass, once again you've taken my fragile heart and stomped it into a bloody pulp on the ground. How much do you think a man can take?"

She shot him a disgusted look and turned to Hawkwind.

Her expression sobered. "I'll miss you, Chief, but am happy for you, nonetheless. Renard spoke true. You were always meant for this life, and I'm glad you've finally won back what was rightfully yours. I wish you much happiness with Deidra."

"And I wish you much happiness, lass," Hawkwind säid, stroking her cheek in tender farewell. "You are special to me. If ever you need me, send word and I will come."

Alena smiled. "Aye, that I will. Of that you can be certain." She turned to Deidra and knelt beside her. "The babe is a precious treasure, is she not?" she whispered. "Hawkwind's daughter." Her glance lifted to Deidra's. "You have been a blessing for Hawkwind, though I must admit there were times . . ."

Both women laughed at the memory of the days long past and the conflicts that initially kept them apart. "I thank you for your friendship," Deidra finally said. "It has been a precious treasure to me, then, and in these past months of your aid in the restoration of Todmorden for Hawkwind. Will you promise to come back from time to time and visit us?"

Alena nodded and gave Deidra's hand a farewell squeeze. "Aye, that I will." Then, she rose and turned to Renard. "Are you finally ready to depart, my hot-blooded friend?"

"Aye, lass. But a moment more to say my own farewells." He strode over to stand before Hawkwind and extend his hand. The two men clasped, arm to arm, in a fierce warrior's handshake. Then, wordlessly, they released each other and stepped apart.

Renard glanced down at Deidra. "Farewell, m'lady."

She smiled up at him, a tender affection gleaming in her eyes. "Fare *you* well, my brave friend. And come back to see us soon."

"Aye." He motioned to Alena. "Well, wench, what's keeping you? The morn burns on while you linger here."

A warning light glinted in her eyes. "Call me wench

once more, you old goat, and I'll lay you out here for the rest of the day recovering from a most thorough trouncing."

Renard laughed and waved her on. "A fine way to begin our new partnership, I'd say," he groused good-naturedly as he followed Alena across the stone balcony and down the steps leading from the lord and lady's sleeping chambers. "I can see keeping you in line will be as great a task for me as 'twas for Hawkwind . . ."

From their vantage point high over the inner bailey, Hawkwind and Deidra watched Alena and Renard stride toward where their army awaited, holding their horses. The two mounted, paused for one final wave back, then signaled their horses forward. In a thunder of hooves and cloud of dust, the troop of mercenary warriors rode out of Todmorden Castle.

Hawkwind followed their progress until they finally disappeared from view. Then, with a sigh, he turned back to Deidra. She studied him with a small frown of concern.

He smiled and, walking over, squatted beside her. "You wonder if my heart doesn't ride out with them, don't you?" he asked gently.

She shot him a startled glance. "Has but a year of marriage already gained you the ability to read my mind? And I thought *I* was the one with the magical powers, not you!"

A low chuckle rumbled from within the depths of Hawkwind's big chest. "When two people love as deeply and intensely as we do, lass, the bonding surpasses ordinary insights. And, who knows?" he added with a wry grin. "Mayhap some of your magic *is* rubbing off on me?"

Footsteps sounded on the steps leading up to their balcony. Deidra glanced around Hawkwind to see Bardrick drawing near, Mystic perched on his gauntleted fist. At the renewed memory of her old bodyguard's final and irrevocable decision to turn from Maud those many months ago, a bittersweet pain pierced her heart. He had chosen to take a different path than that of Hawkwind, chosen not to confront his fears and vanquish them. And, because of that, he would live the rest of his days without the woman she knew he still, and would always, love.

Different paths, different decisions, and a price paid by both men in the doing. With one final pang of sadness for Bardrick and Maud, Deidra recalled her thoughts to the present. She gestured toward the approaching old man. "Your new falconer seems anxious to be out hunting this morn."

"Does he now? He shows a decided talent for the birds. As fine a one as an old falconer I once knew." For an instant memories of another day, now so long ago, and people long dead, flashed across Hawkwind's mind. Strange, he mused, how life could come full circle, that from the bitter ashes of tragedy a great happiness could finally be reborn.

" 'Tis your courage and indomitable will that made it so," Deidra softly answered him.

He shot her a startled glance. "And are you, too, able to read minds?"

She smiled mysteriously. "My magic is still evolving. Who knows where it might lead in time?" Deidra arched a slender brow. "Does that disturb you?"

"Nay." Hawkwind rose in one lithe, powerful motion. "I ask only one thing."

"And that is?"

"Keep your witch's spells away from me. I'm my own man and intend to stay that way. Use your powers to help the land and people."

A freshened breeze gusted suddenly around them, billowing her fiery hair about her in a torrent of flame. "I wouldn't have it any other way," Deidra whispered huskily. "The only powers I'll ever use on you are the ones all women possess . . . and ply to hold the men they love. You have my word on it."

The wind whipped Hawkwind's own long brown hair

about him as he smiled down at her and their tiny, sleeping daughter, his face wreathed in beauty and love. "Ply as you will, sweet lady. You will always be the queen of my heart, magic or no. My very own Fire Queen. My very own love."

Dear Reader:

I hope you enjoyed the tale of Deidra and Hawkwind. They were both such compelling characters who virtually wrote their own story. If only all books could be so much fun to write! My next fantasy romance comes out in either the spring or summer of 1995. I haven't quite decided who the hero and heroine will be as yet (ah, for so many choices and other books to write in the meanwhile!), but I'm leaning toward a story involving Alena and Renard. And then, for those of you who may have also recently read my first fantasy romance, *Demon Prince*, there's the Lord Dane Haversin, who definitely needs a new love. What do *you* think?

If you'd like a list of my previously published romances and an autographed, excerpted flyer of my next upcoming book, write me at P.O. Box 62365, Colorado Springs, CO 80962. Please include a self-addressed, stamped envelope. In the meanwhile, happy reading!

Kathleen Morgan

Kathleen Morgan

With *FIRE QUEEN*, Kathleen Morgan, award-winning author of both historical and futuristic romance, ventures into yet another romantic realm, this time set in a land of knights and ladies, magic and superstition. Stories of heroes (and heroines) who embark on mythical quests to accomplish brave and glorious things have always held a special place in Kathleen's heart. She is thrilled at last to be able to share those same kinds of stories with her readers.

Kathleen lives in Colorado with her husband of fourteen years, two children and various and assorted pets. A former Army nurse with a master's degree in counseling, she now stays home to write full time.

Heading for a new life in California across
the untracked mountains of the West,
beautiful Anna Jensen is kidnapped by a
brazen and savagely handsome Indian who
calls himself "Bear." The half-breed son of a
wealthy rancher, he is a dangerous man with
a dangerous mission. Though he and Anna
are born enemies, they find that together
they will awaken a reckless desire that can
never be denied…

SECRETS OF A
MIDNIGHT MOON
Jane Bonander

IN THE BESTSELLING TRADITION OF
BRENDA JOYCE

SECRETS OF A MIDNIGHT MOON
Jane Bonander
_____ 92622-7 $4.99 U.S./$5.99 Can.

The historical romances of
JEANNE WILLIAMS
from St. Martin's Paperbacks

Award-winning author of *Creole Fires*

"Kat Martin has a winner. *Gypsy Lord* is a page-turner from beginning to end!"

—Johanna Lindsey